Advance Praise for

A DIFFERENT DARKNESS

'Worthy of being mentioned alongside his horror contemporaries like Joe Hill, Stephen Graham Jones, and Paul Tremblay, Musolino is a writer whose stories are a dark journey through the shadowy Italian countryside, the depths of human despair, and the heights of imagination.'

—*Library Journal* (starred review)

'Luigi Musolino enters the territories of superstition and folklore knowing that fairy tales are always terrible and legends hide unspeakable truths. Small towns, supermarkets, apartments, schools, or farms: when horror touches reality, it becomes the only thing that exists. These stories have a distinctly European feel: there's a sense of old but not quite forgotten rituals, a touch of Pan and the deities that still linger behind the haunted fields and forests.'

—Mariana Enríquez, author of *Things We Lost in the Fire*

'The pleasure of these stories lies in the writing itself, in Musolino's deft ability to find horror where we least expect. He embraces strangeness, and does so through an agile narrative style that keeps us on our toes . . . Musolino has a strong and original voice, and uses it to get to some uniquely dark places. Rather than blood or gore, he's ultimately interested in what's truly terrifying: the vertiginous darkness that threatens to open up and swallow us.'

—Brian Evenson, author of *Song for the Unraveling of the World*

'Musolino will catch you in the meshes of his nightmarish landscapes and paranoid scenarios, his engrossing stories and powerful endings. He's the real thing.'

—Michael Cisco, author of *The Divinity Student*

'An experience worthy of David Cronenberg, a sick and monstrous universe where authors like Barker and Ligotti would feel right at home.'

—Nicola Lombardi, author of *The Gypsy Spiders*

A Different Darkness

and other abominations

by

LUIGI MUSOLINO

Edited and translated from the Italian by James D. Jenkins

Introduction by Brian Evenson

VALANCOURT BOOKS

A Different Darkness and other Abominations by Luigi Musolino
First edition 2022

Copyright © 2022 by Luigi Musolino
Introduction copyright © 2022 by Brian Evenson
Translations and compilation copyright © 2022 by Valancourt Books, LLC

All rights reserved. In accordance with the U.S. Copyright Act of 1976,
the copying, scanning, uploading, and/or electronic sharing of any part
of this book without the permission of the publisher constitutes unlawful
piracy and theft of the author's intellectual property. If you would like to
use material from the book (other than for review purposes), prior written
permission must be obtained by contacting the publisher.

Valancourt Books and the Valancourt Books logo are registered trademarks
of Valancourt Books, LLC. All rights reserved.

Published by Valancourt Books, Richmond, Virginia
http://www.valancourtbooks.com

ISBN 978-1-954321-73-1 (trade hardcover)
ISBN 978-1-954321-74-8 (trade paperback)
Also available as an electronic book.

Cover by Vince Haig
Set in Bembo Book MT

Contents

Introduction

A year and a half ago, judging anthologies for the World Fantasy Award, I stumbled onto the first volume of Valancourt's *Book of World Horror Stories*. It was a strong, interesting collection, filled not only with great recent stories that suggested intriguing things were happening in Horror around the globe, but above all filled with stories by writers I had – despite being a translator and an avid reader of non-American fiction – never heard of before. Among these was a story by Luigi Musolino (b. 1982), 'Uironda', about a truck driver who, without realizing it, steps outside of the world into a 'place that doesn't exist but is there. Or rather, it exists, but not on this plane.' In exiting the known world, he steps inadvertently deeply and disconcertingly into a truth that he's carefully hidden from himself, but in a way that renders that truth strange, nightmarish, and surreal.

The eleven stories in *A Different Darkness*, the first collection of Musolino's to be published in English, are just as compelling, disturbing, and surprising as 'Uironda'. Many of them are set in Piedmont, where Musolino hails from. Several of them take place in Orlasco, 'a rosary of houses and potato fields beading toward the Alps, twenty miles from Turin' or in the larger but still strange town Orlasco borders, Idrasca. In these imagined and hapless towns, extremely bad things happen. One story, for instance, 'Black Hills of Torment', reads like an update of Jerome Bixby's 'It's a Good Life', if that story's protagonist, a god-like boy who has absolute control over the town in which he lives, had gone missing, leaving his ghost or malevolent essence or even his death in charge.

What makes these stories successful is that Musolino not only embraces the horror genre: he makes it his own. His horrors are decidedly Italian. Not only Italian: many of these stories could only take place at the foot of the Alps. Some have an affinity to certain of Algernon Blackwood's stories set in mountain environs ('The Glamour of the Snow', for instance, or 'The Wendigo'), but with a more contemporary feel and less mystical wonder. As one character suggests, 'The countryside is magical. And terrible. That's all you need to know.'

Whether it's really all you *need* to know or not, that's all you *get* to know. Musolino is expert at making us feel the void yawning below us, waiting to swallow both us and his characters up – the characters often literally so. Strange things happen, and when people try to discover why they're happening, they fail. 'There must be an explanation,' a dazed parent mutters in another story as the town's children act stranger and stranger, and another parent whispers back in response, 'Yes, there must be an explanation, we have to understand.' But there are no answers to be found in this story. When, in a later story, a husband insists, again, that something awful they are experiencing must have an explanation, his wife, already well on her way to slipping out of the world, responds, 'There's not always an explanation for everything.' Even at those moments when things seemingly go back to normal, the weight of not knowing, of not understanding what has happened to you, not comprehending what you've been through, remains. Or rather, as yet another Musolino story suggests, 'Maybe some things only stop being enigmas when we accept them for what they are: different, incomprehensible planes of reality, of which we can perceive only vague and blurry contours.'

Musolino has a commitment to unearthing the basal strangeness of the world, even as he understands that if you manage to expose this strangeness to the light you risk it opening its baleful eye and fixing you in its gaze. A character can suddenly develop 'an error in her anatomical structure', and even if Musolino's narrator is very deft at describing exactly what this error consists of, he cannot formulate a rational logic for why it occurred. Or a man can go on a run through a town that is familiar to him ('Lactic Acid') and then make the mistake of taking a shortcut and, as a result, stumbling into an adjacent version of reality, a slightly off version of the world he thought he knew and from which, once entered, there might be no escape. In Musolino's hands a tongue-in-cheek mythical creature from local legend might take on darker and more deadly overtones, become a kind of locus for madness. Or a long extinct creature will rise again with a local folk festival as a kind of undead demon or god. Whether presenting a haunted septic tank, a perverse reworking of the Pied Piper tale, or offering a contortionist with a will to make himself so compact that he no longer exists, the pleasure of these stories lies in the writing itself, in Musolino's deft ability to find horror where we least expect. He embraces strangeness, and does so through an agile narrative style that keeps us on our toes. A Musolino story can be linear, but more often it is 'a mule track full of curves, hair-pin bends, and wrong turns'.

You know those houses that you can buy in small Italian towns for a nominal fee as long as you promise to fix them up? They're probably so affordable because a Musolino story has already occurred in them. Or will start to occur the moment your remodeling begins. Musolino has a strong and original voice and uses it to get to some uniquely dark places. Rather than blood or gore, he's ultimately interested in what's truly terrifying: the vertiginous darkness that threatens to open up and swallow us. A darkness that calls to us, calls to us, until we can't help but answer and stumble toward it.

BRIAN EVENSON

BRIAN EVENSON is the author of a dozen books of fiction, most recently the collection *The Glassy Burning Floor of Hell* (2021). His previous book, *Song for the Unraveling of the World* (2019), won the Shirley Jackson Award and the World Fantasy Award and was a finalist for the *Los Angeles Times'* Ray Bradbury Prize. He is the recipient of three O. Henry Prizes, an NEA fellowship, and a Guggenheim Award. His work has been translated into more than a dozen languages. He lives in Los Angeles and teaches in the Critical Studies Program at CalArts.

Translator's Note

The pieces collected in this book were chosen jointly by me and Luigi to represent the best of his work over his career, which thus far spans about ten years. Four tales included here – 'Les Abominations des Altitudes', 'The Carnival of the Stag Man', 'Queen of the Sewers', and 'The Strait' – first appeared in Italian in the author's two-volume collection *Oscure Regioni* [*Dark Regions*] (2015-16); those volumes included a total of twenty stories, one from each of Italy's regions, each inspired by local folklore from that region. Three stories – 'Uironda', 'Lactic Acid', and 'Black Hills of Torment' – originally appeared in his collection *Uironda* in 2018. The novella *Pupils* was published as a standalone volume in Italy in 2021, and the remaining tales – 'The Last Box', 'Like Dogs', and 'A Different Darkness' – are drawn from his newest (2022) Italian collection.

'Uironda' first appeared in *The Valancourt Book of World Horror Stories, vol. 1* in 2020, though I have revised that translation slightly for this volume.

James D. Jenkins
Richmond, Virginia
June 2022

JAMES D. JENKINS is the co-founder of Valancourt Books. He holds an M.A. in Romance Languages and Literatures from the University of Chicago, and his other translations include many of the stories in the acclaimed two volumes of *The Valancourt Book of World Horror Stories* as well as André Bjerke's novel *The Lake of the Dead*, translated from the Norwegian.

Lactic Acid

It was five-thirty in the afternoon.

Friday afternoon.

Sergio Bandini walked into his apartment and dropped his laptop bag on the couch, whistling a random tune.

Made it through another week. Tired, but everything's going great. Turning thirty-two tomorrow. And a good meal tonight, he thought, pulling his phone out of the back pocket of his jeans.

He scrolled through his contacts, still whistling the same tune through half-closed lips, and called Chiara. His girlfriend's voice answered after the third ring.

'Hey there. Home already?'

'Hi, yeah, just got here. How about you? Still at the office?' replied Sergio, walking over to the window and casting a glance at Via Martiri della Libertà and the outline of Orlasco's bell tower and the evening that was starting to take over the town's cerulean ceiling.

'Yes, still here for a while. Listen, let's just meet at your parents' house, okay? I'll go straight there when I leave work, I won't stop by home first. I have so much to do that I'll be here till at least seven, and I've got your present here with me to give you tonight . . .'

'Okay, sure thing, we'll meet at my parents' place,' he cut her off, laughing. Sometimes Chiara had a tendency to ramble. 'Listen, I'm going to go for a run. Just a quick one, five, six kilometers. Then I won't feel so guilty about pigging out.'

She responded with a loud laugh. 'Come on, it's your birthday tomorrow. It's okay to cheat now and then.'

'I know, but I really feel like a quick jog. You know, it helps me to unwind, to relax.'

'Yeah, I know, it's like a drug, etc., etc.,' Chiara mocked him, and he replied by doing his impression of her, the way only lovers can.

'Okay, baby, I'm off now or I'll be late. I'll run, shower, and we'll meet at my parents' a little after seven, all right?'

'Go on, Sergio, I'll see you later. And let's hope your mother made tiramisu.'

'Right. Bye.'

'Sergio?'

'Yeah?'

'I love you.'

'M-me too,' he replied, more hesitantly than he meant to. Chiara rarely said those three simple words. She had caught him off guard, like always. And it made him feel damned good every time.

He heard the *click* of the call being disconnected. He dropped his phone on the couch by the computer, tried to remember what tune he had just been whistling, and peered out the living room window.

Mid-October, but the days were still warm. He could just wear shorts and a hoodie. The dark and the cold wouldn't chase away the warmth and sunlight before seven. He had plenty of time for a quick run.

He got dressed, slipping on a pair of shorts, a T-shirt, and a faded Miami Dolphins hoodie. MP3 player, smart watch to keep track of his distance and average speed. He was ready. He jumped into his sneakers and dashed into the bathroom to brush his teeth. He always did that before a run. A kind of ritual.

He had started running a couple of years earlier, after noticing he could no longer make it up the stairs without coughing and shortness of breath. And he only lived on the second floor.

An overly sedentary lifestyle, a desk job, an inborn inclination for the sin of gluttony, for having one too many at times, and for generally being lazy, all of that had made him pack on quite a few kilos.

Never been the athletic type, he thought with a smile, fastening the watch strap around his wrist.

His first outing as a DIY athlete had been a disaster.

A pair of extremely thin-soled shoes, a baggy jumpsuit, and off he'd gone into Orlasco's countryside. Kilometers of unpaved roads running like gashes through the cornfields, mule tracks covered in grass and dust, paths leading to brooks and irrigation canals, practically shrines for all the couples in and around Orlasco looking for a romantic spot. He had been living in that sleepy village for two years but had never ventured outside the residential area. It was a whole other world.

After about a kilometer at a fairly slow pace he had felt a stitch in his right side but had kept on running, thinking *It'll pass.* After another five hundred meters the sting in his ribs had become a throbbing pain in the center of his chest. He had stopped, bathed in sweat.

He had walked home with his hands on his hips, his head tilted back, his mouth open wide and gasping for air. When he had recovered a little he cursed himself for giving up so easily, for giving in to the pain, and had returned home, head bowed, crestfallen.

When he'd told Chiara about his first experience with exercising, in a tone halfway between comical and dramatic, she had laughed until she cried.

He didn't give up. He kept at it, asking friends for advice, reading tips online, and buying himself proper gear – decent shoes, some breathable T-shirts, shorts (pants for winter evenings), a smart watch. He ran at least three days a week after work, and gradually he had found that consistency was the only way to improve his times and his physical condition.

A little at a time, I've just got to take it slow, he told himself, and eventually he had developed a taste for it.

Then, one fateful day, after about two months of training,

he had managed to cover ten kilometers in under an hour. It was silly, but he had gotten so emotional that he almost cried, as if he had reached some kind of milestone.

He had never stopped since. He had lost ten kilos, he felt fit, in shape at last, and now he was training for his first half marathon. Twenty-one kilometers of suffering and sweat and swearing, but it was too soon to think about that. He still had two more months of training to go.

Sergio grabbed his keys from the coffee table and walked downstairs, putting on his headphones as he went. Lingering for a moment on the doorstep of the building, he cast an admiring glance at the sky. On the horizon the Alps showed off all their majesty, casting sharp shadows on the surrounding countryside. Beyond Monte Viso, some vaporous, ragged, grayish clouds were starting to appear. The sun highlighted their contours, brushing them with beautiful hues.

Walking slowly, Sergio reached his personal starting point – a paved country road which after a few hundred meters turned into a winding dirt path – and spent a few minutes stretching.

He glanced at the bell tower soaring above his head, its red bricks corroded by moss and pigeon droppings.

He started the timer on his smart watch, hopped in place a couple of times, then began to run. A flock of herons accompanied him for the first hundred meters.

He had been running for about ten minutes and had barely covered one and a half kilometers. Way below his usual pace.

He realized he wasn't in form today. Stiff legs, shortness of breath, aching in his shins and calves. It happened sometimes. It was perhaps one of the things he liked most about running, its unpredictability. He might leave home feeling like a twenty-something athlete and run like shit, or he might feel like crap and beat his best time ever. It depended on a number of factors. Nutrition, sleep, stress. Not that he worried that much about it. He was a dabbler, an amateur; he liked running but didn't see the need to deprive himself of the pleasure of a hearty dinner, a drinking binge, a few cigarettes.

He sped up a little, glancing distractedly at the rows of poplars marching alongside him. Tangles of leaves and branches casting weary shadows over the red clay soil of the fields. In the distance he made out the dark shapes of some farmsteads, old residences belonging to those few residents of Orlasco who still practiced farming.

The MP3 player served up an old Rage Against the Machine track whose name he didn't remember. The kind of song that energized you. Sweat was starting to run down his forehead and his chest, gluing his sweatshirt to his nipples and back. A capricious gust of wind rustled through the cornfields and surged towards the road, smacking against his clammy face. He slowed down.

His route was always the same. An almost perfect circle that started at the bell tower and ended up near the dam of an old irrigation canal a few hundred meters from home. He turned right, and out of the corner of his eye he glimpsed the massive outline of the bell tower, which had been behind him until then. His first few times out, when he was still unfamiliar with the labyrinth of narrow lanes cutting through the countryside, it had been a very helpful reference point.

He looked at his watch. Three kilometers in seventeen minutes, twelve seconds. In a little less than twenty minutes he would be back home under a jet of steaming-hot water.

Come on. Move your ass. What are you, a wuss? A real man should be able to do a kilometer in under five minutes thirty, he spurred himself on, angrily. He always did that, a macho, slightly silly way of pushing himself to do better, not to give up. It usually worked.

Not that night.

He had almost reached the turn that would lead to the finish line when he noticed a narrow path that cut across a huge, uncultivated meadow, possibly fallow land some farmer was using as a pasture for his sheep. He had seen it before, sure, but he had never paid any attention to it. It ran parallel to his pre-established route, the usual road, which glimmered a hundred meters farther on, its sandy dust sparkling in the sun that was now skimming over the mountain tops. Surely this path also went towards the last leg of his route, the final stretch of dirt road leading to the little dam.

Not knowing why, Sergio made a sudden swerve and took it, panting. He was tired, maybe he hoped it would get him home quicker, a shortcut, a *scursa,* as he sometimes liked to say in his dialect.

His MP3 player was playing Pink Floyd's 'Run Like Hell'.

He thought about Chiara, about his parents waiting for him to get there so they could celebrate his birthday, and the image of his mother sprang to his mind, setting the table, her makeup on, her hair pulled back behind the nape of her neck; pretty, a little sad.

He wiped his forehead with the back of his hand and racked up another three hundred meters, pumping his legs like pistons. The lane was only slightly wider than a tractor and was dotted with potholes and piles of gravel. There was a strip of green running through its center, where a hodgepodge of grass, noxious weeds, and withered snapdragons grew. Sergio knew it couldn't go on for more than five or six hundred meters before opening out onto the main road.

Sergio spat a whitish glob into the grass as he looked at the anorexic trees lining the road. Beeches. The further he went the denser they got, their autumn-stripped branches reaching towards him like imploring, emaciated arms. He was forced to move from one side of the road to the other a couple of times to avoid running into them. He sped up. The smart watch showed an average pace of five minutes twenty per kilometer. Good.

He took his eyes off the display and glanced to the right. In the distance, a thick cluster of oaks, their dark green foliage bent by a strong wind. They looked like huge balls of coagulated, rancid cotton candy. They swayed above the corrugated roof of an old farmhouse, its shingles twisted by age and inclement weather. The farmhouse gave off an unpleasant aura, not sinister, but rather a sense of abandonment and desolation that seemed to exude from the image itself, from the angle of the light, from the shadows cast by the columns of the barn.

He pondered. *I've never noticed those trees before. Or that building, for that matter.*

He picked up the pace, stretching his legs in longer strides. The autumn breeze, pleasant until a few minutes ago, was turning into a crisp, almost cold wind. The clouds had now climbed over the Alps, like an army of ashen, elusive warriors, hiding the sharp tooth of Monte Viso and the sun, whose rays nonetheless still managed to light up the plains.

He couldn't be more than a kilometer or so away from the finish line, he was heading towards the final sprint.

A sticky patina of sweat covered his back and sides, flowing in little streams towards his navel.

'Speed up, come on,' he hissed between his teeth, trying to keep his breathing under control.

The beeches grew denser, more curved, forming a natural tunnel that was dark and humid; only for a few meters, then they thinned out, letting the last rays of daylight filter through. For a moment the sudden transition from shade to light blinded him and he had to squint to see his footing.

Further on, where the trees gave way to withered cornstalks, Sergio was able to make out the end of the dirt road as well as the street running parallel to it.

Here we are, the home stretch.

He reached it, then turned right and suddenly realized something was out of place. At first he couldn't tell what was bothering him. Then he realized.

He had run that last stretch dozens and dozens of times, and the bell tower had always been visible from there.

Not now.

He could make out the shabby farmhouse and the oaks that he had found slightly unsettling, the glimpse of landscape he had never seen before; logically, the belfry had to be more or less on the hypothetical line between himself and the house, only set back a little.

But the tower wasn't there. From where he was standing he should have been able to see it, and yet it wasn't there. As if the ground had chewed it up, swallowed it, digested it.

'Fuck,' he cursed himself and went on running in place, spinning around in search of the tower, or any reference point.

He noticed a garden fence ahead of him, yes, he knew that fence, there were usually a couple of growling furballs carrying on behind it. The dogs weren't there, but it was the right direction, no doubt about it. Wasn't it? Was he sure?

Going a different way was a dumbshit move, he thought, and for a moment he thought about retracing his steps, taking the beech-lined path in reverse and returning along the road he had taken dozens of times, just to be sure, to be safe. But that would mean extending his run by at least two or three more kilometers, and his birthday dinner would be starting in an hour.

He kept on running, more slowly, passing a little wooden bridge over a creek – another confirmation, he had crossed that creek before – and, his heart skipping a beat, he caught a glimpse of the bell tower's roof to his right. He breathed a sigh of relief and rushed homewards, spurred on by adrenaline and the thought of a lavish meal, unable to admit to himself that the tower seemed shifted to the right, too far to the right compared to its usual position.

The sky was a slab of bluish marble, the clouds running fast and compact, the closed ranks of an exterminating army.

The dirt track turned to the right and Sergio Bandini slackened his pace, spitting in the dust. He took off his headphones, turned off the MP3 player and slid it in his pocket.

The road should have made a wide turn to the left. Instead,

it continued in the opposite direction, downhill, and then dissolved in a meadow dominated by the sparse foliage of a poplar
grove. The bell tower was behind him again.

'Damn!' he cursed aloud, and the word seemed to echo
through the countryside in discordant tones.

The road ended there, in the shade of the poplars. Sergio
slowed his pace until he stopped, doubled over, his hands on his
thighs and panting.

His apartment was in the opposite direction, towards the
bell tower. He kicked himself for being stupid, convinced now
that he had to turn back. He had no other choice.

He turned on his heels and resumed jogging at a slow pace.
Three, four hundred meters at most, and he would come to
the bridge, and then right after that he would be back to the
supposed shortcut flanked by beech trees, the path that had led
him to a dead end.

When his watch display told him he had run back a whole
kilometer and he still hadn't encountered a creek or pathway,
Sergio started to get worried.

It was as if some spiteful god had torn a section of road from
somewhere and forcibly stuck it onto his route, like one of
those old puzzles made up of a few interchangeable pieces that
form a coherent picture no matter in which order you put them
together.

He wanted to get back home. It was already six-thirty, the
afternoon was giving way to the evening. His shadow, barely
visible, stretched on the ground like a scrawny and very tall
mannequin.

It was getting dark.

And silence reigned absolute.

Even the wind seemed to have lost its voice. An incessant
wind that stirred the grass and stroked the clouds, which were
growing thicker, darker, more menacing.

A croaking raven, a chirping cicada, the distant rumble of a
tractor would have been a comfort. He heard nothing but his

own increasingly labored breathing and the blood pounding in his temples with the roar of a gushing river.

He stopped again, trying to glimpse a familiar tree, a farm-house, a farmer stooping in the fields whom he could ask for directions.

But now the road stretched out in front of him all the way to the horizon. It seemed to have no end. No crossroads. No turns. Only that strip of dust and gravel and empty fields and wisps of misty fog slowly rising from the ground. He squinted, turned in a complete circle, and when he saw the bell tower he put his hand over his mouth.

It was impossible. It was too far away. A barely discernible black stump silhouetted against the sky, a lopsided rocket out of a Jules Verne novel. How far off was it? Seven, eight kilo-meters? It didn't make any sense.

Sergio looked at his watch. He had run almost eleven kilo-meters.

No. It didn't add up. It was as if time and space had decided to follow their own very personal path.

A pain in his chest.

'Good God,' he mumbled, and he realized his lips were coated in sticky, whitish drool. It reminded him of those fat, slimy snails that swarmed onto sidewalks after an autumn rain-storm. He closed his eyes and took two deep breaths.

They were waiting for him. Chiara, Mom, Dad. To cele-brate his birthday. He had to be there by seven-thirty. He wasn't going to make it, not unless he found the right path fast.

A series of comforting images suddenly burst into his mind. His father opening a bottle of wine, yes, a full-bodied Barbera, the ruby reflections forming bright, symmetrical images in the crystal goblet. He could almost taste its strong flavor, the alco-holic warmth in his mouth, soothing.

He saw his mother at the stove, checking the roast, the oven lit, lasagna foaming with bubbles of melted cheese. Chiara laughing, a graceful, sibylline laugh, pleasant smells spreading through the family home. Then there was Lady, his parents' puppy, rolling over with her paws in the air so you would scratch her belly, and the lasagna, that lasagna . . .

He swallowed a couple of times, his mouth watering. His stomach rumbled loudly, almost angrily.

Then a drop on his nose. Freezing. The vision vanished, hurtling him back to reality. It was starting to rain and Sergio felt like an idiot; his mother had been right all along when she told him to bring his phone with him, because you never know. But he always told her no, how was he supposed to run with a phone in his pocket?

Dumbass . . .

He opened his eyes again and hugged himself tightly. The wind had gotten stronger, blowing on his sweat-soaked hoodie, on his bare, wet legs. Black clouds chased each other across the sky, ghosts of mist and rain tossed by currents that now seemed to be coming straight from the sneering mountain peaks.

Within a minute the drizzle turned into a persistent rain. Somehow the cold helped him to shake it off.

You're panicking. Idiot. You got lost. Only a few kilometers from where you live, to boot. That's all. Nothing that can't be fixed. Go home.

He inhaled the humid air in long, deep, painful breaths, then, shaking his head, he burst into laughter.

The solution was there, right in front of his eyes. He was lost? All right, but who said he had to follow the road? He would cut across the fields, head straight for the bell tower. He'd get muddy, sure, and his feet would get wet from sinking into the slimy clay soil the area was covered in, but in no more than twenty minutes he would be back in downtown Orlasco.

He would call his parents, telling them about his little mishap, and that night they would laugh about it around the table, a little drunk, all of them together, happy. He could almost hear his father's wry jokes.

He had to hurry, though. He could still see the bell tower,

but he knew it wouldn't be too long before the structure was swallowed by darkness.

He had to hurry.

While it was still light.

He had been walking for about ten minutes, keeping his eyes fixed on the belfry and maintaining a brisk pace, when the sticky, uncultivated soil began to be dotted with fruit trees. Bare apple trees, kiwi vines, a small cluster of peach trees. He wondered what the owner's logic was in planting these particular plants. The rain drummed against the few remaining leaves, producing a deafening music.

He wove his way through the trees, careful not to run into the branches. Every now and then he turned towards the road in the hope of seeing a car, a tractor, a farmer on a bicycle.

At the edge of the orchard he thought he heard the sputter of an engine, so he whirled around, walking backwards, his eyes fixed on the horizon. He tripped over a root, swinging his arms and taking a clumsy step to keep his balance, and wound up sinking ankle-deep into a muddy puddle. He thought for a moment that he had landed in quicksand, then he jumped out of the mud swearing and shaking his legs to get the filth off his shoes. His feet were frozen, soaked. His socks stuck to his toes like a second skin.

'Shit!'

He realized he had mistaken the prolonged rumbling of thunder for the sound of a vehicle. Lightning paraded across the sky, a procession of violet, electric skeletons. Once again he forced himself to keep calm. He started to make his way forward again, zigzagging through the trunks.

Having passed the motley orchard, Sergio found himself facing a creek. A winding, greenish canal, four or five meters below him. Its banks were steep, but the water, littered with plastic bags, tires, and cans, was shallow and slow-moving. The rain formed concentric circles on the canal, shapes that resembled ghostly eyes in the sickly light of the setting sun. He looked to the right, to the left, hoping to spot a bridge. Nothing. His vision was limited, blurred by the wall of rain and his anxiety.

To hell with it. He'd wade across. He was already soaking wet anyway, and the creek couldn't be more than five meters across.

Sergio made sure the bell tower was still straight ahead of him – yes, it was there, a shadow among the shadows – then he started to climb down, dragging his feet. It was steeper and more slippery than he had thought. He helped himself down by grabbing on to some tufts of grass. Tough grass with roots running deep into the ground, grass that left imprints on the palms of his hands, its tenacity making him feel safer.

Halfway through his descent, somewhere far away, a dog howled. It was the first sound he had heard in at least twenty minutes – besides the rain and his own breathing – but he would have rather wandered the rest of the way home in the rumble of the squall than hear that sound.

A dog whining . . . maybe. But it could also be the cry of a boy fallen down a well, the scream of a farmer with his legs trapped in some piece of farm machinery, the distress call of a prostitute being beaten up by a group of junkies, the . . .

'What's gotten into you? What are you doing?' he murmured, trembling like a leaf, still making his way towards the creek. Thoughts like those were unlike him, it was as if they belonged to somebody else, but he didn't have time to worry about it. He slipped, covering the last stretch of the slope in the blink of an eye, sliding down on his buttocks. The grass and crumbly soil rendered the fall harmless, and he found himself in front of the creek, sitting on a tiny beach of sand and gravel.

He got up, brushing off his shorts with his hands, a gesture whose futility made him smile, and began the 'crossing'. Trying to jump on some gray rocks that winked at him from the waterway, he made it to the middle of the creek, where he rested for a few seconds on a small stone slab. But now it had gotten too dark to see all the rocks clearly, and when he started going again he only made it a couple of leaps before plunging into the creek with both feet.

The water was like crushed ice. His toes started to go numb. He rushed to the other shore, sloshing through algae and litter. The opposite bank hid the bell tower from his view.

He was seized with panic, certain that once he was on the other side he would never see it again.

Lost.

There.

In the mud.

In the nothingness.

In the dark. The poisonous dark. Rotten with damp. Numb.

He climbed up the slope, his fingers clawing at the boggy earth, and felt the fingernail on his right index finger scrape against a rock and break. The pain came lightning fast, shooting up his whole hand.

He clenched his teeth, tried to ignore it.

He plodded on again, panting, groaning. He would tumble down, then start over again, clambering like he was running on a spiteful treadmill set to a forty-five degree incline and filthy with slime and vegetation. He had almost made it to the top for the fourth time when a clod of dirt crumbled beneath his feet. He plummeted to the bottom like a doll, landing with a crash. He didn't even have time to scream.

His right hip rammed into a black and white rock jutting out from the ground like a broken tooth, and a crack, like the sound of a branch breaking, echoed through the countryside. All the air was knocked out of Sergio's lungs in a single, powerful exhalation.

He tried to scream but couldn't.

'God, God, God, God,' he wheezed, writhing on the ground.

He was hurt. Badly. He couldn't breathe. He pressed his fingers to his aching hip and flames of pain exploded through his body, sketching lights and shapes behind his retinas.

Years earlier Sergio had cracked a rib in a minor car accident.

Judging from the pain and difficulty breathing, he was almost certain he had done it again.

Come on. Get up. You have to reach the bell tower before it gets dark.

He groped at the surrounding soil blindly, found a fairly long branch and used it as a crutch, planting it in the soft soil. He tried to imagine what Chiara would say if she saw him in this condition, lost and desperate like a child who has gotten separated from his parents in a supermarket.

He resumed the ascent.

Slowly.

Methodically.

Helping himself with the improvised crutch.

Every step a lash, a stab in his side. Every breath the sound of a broken bellows, an ungainly and inconclusive hissing. He knew now there wasn't going to be any birthday party that night. No wine, no lasagna, no warmth.

If I make it home I'll be spending the night at the hospital, no doubt about it. As soon as he formulated that thought, he was assailed by an unbearable wave of nausea. *What's that supposed to mean, 'if I make it home'? Of course I will. I'm. Here. In Orlasco. Jesus Christ.*

He kept going, trying to stem the pain, and finally reached the top of the embankment. His eyes moved frantically, his pupils dilated to make out the bell tower.

The rain had calmed. The streetlights in the center of Orlasco were on. Distant phosphorescences swayed in mid-air, a pale radiance against which the outline of the tower stood out.

He was getting closer.

'Yes. Yes, goddamnit!' he rejoiced, only to regret it an instant later when a flash of pain went up his spine. All he had to do was keep going. To march stubbornly towards the church, towards the glimmer of the town.

He pressed the LIGHT button on his watch, and the display lit up.

He had been walking and running for seventeen kilometers

now. Almost a half marathon. He burst out laughing, an eerie, unhealthy laughter.

It was seven-thirty.

It had gotten dark. Plunged into the gloom, he could see nothing but the electric glow of the distant streetlights. A lighthouse in the night, a North Star in an ocean of bewilderment.

The dog let out that same ominous howl again. This time it sounded closer.

Resolutely Sergio walked on.

Blindly. Across the fields. It had started pouring again. Sometimes he tripped over a root or a clump of grass and had to summon all his strength not to tumble, steadying himself with the stick. His hip tormented him. He coughed a couple of times, and he didn't like the sound produced by his lungs at all.

Maybe a rib snapped and punctured one of my internal organs. Maybe I'm dying.

He noticed a salty taste at the back of his throat and couldn't tell whether it was phlegm or blood. Fear was starting to press against the dam of hope, making cracks in it.

I can't have gotten lost like this. It isn't real. It's a nightmare. One of those awful nightmares that never end, never stop. The kind that leave you tired and depressed all the next day.

He was thirsty. Drenched and hungry, he could no longer feel his extremities. With dismay he heard his upper and lower teeth chatter against each other, like castanets played by a girl with tarantism.

Thirst. He thought of wine. A Prosecco, maybe.

Hunger. Lasagna in the oven, French fries, breaded mushrooms, tiramisu, piles of ladyfingers drowned in mascarpone.

Cold. His mother drying his hair with a blow dryer when he was a child and wrapping him in a towel warmed on the radiator.

Exhaustion. Chiara cuddling up with him in bed, naked.

He kept going, head down, worn out, letting those images lull him, glancing every so often at the bell tower.

He ended up running straight into a thorn bush without seeing it. It was huge, dense, dark. It seemed to be alive. The thorns clawed at his hoodie, his shorts, the skin of his hands, and Sergio drew back abruptly. His lightweight shorts got snagged on the tangle of vegetal spines, and the crotch split open. Mechanically he slipped out of them and threw them on the ground. He looked up.

The bell tower was there. It couldn't be more than a couple of kilometers off, three at most. Spurred by that vision, Sergio hit the bramble bush with his stick, cursing, trying to open a passage through the branches, like a poacher making his way through the jungle with a machete.

An impenetrable barrier.

His strength was failing him.

His shoulders hurt like he was carrying a backpack full of lead, his calves trembled uncontrollably. Lactic acid. *Bête noire* of all athletes, it was beginning to invade his muscles, his tissues, his flesh. He pictured that toxic liquid produced by his own organism, flowing through his body like an infection, a white, viscous serum squirting into his cells, from his legs all the way up, up to his brain, to wrap it in a snowy and paralyzing sponge.

But is lactic acid really white? he wondered, and that meaningless question seemed to revive him.

He had to get around the thorn bushes. There was no way he could go through them, no, he would get stuck in the middle and they would find his skeleton months later, a skeleton dressed in underwear and a Miami Dolphins sweatshirt. No, he had to bypass them, avoid them.

But when he turned to the right and then to the left to find another way he realized that the bush wasn't a bush.

It was a wall.

A bulwark of thorns blocked his way, a wall running as far

as his eyes – by now used to the darkness – could see. Spiky, cyclopean ramparts of a nonexistent castle.

Something had gone wrong, he couldn't deny it anymore. That night something had gone terribly wrong and he was too exhausted to put it right. Maybe he *couldn't* put it right, maybe it wasn't up to him.

The rain seemed to stop all of a sudden, like somebody had switched off a colossal faucet in the sky. The clouds parted and a pus-yellow moon tore through the haze, bestowing a little light.

Sergio, in his underwear, dropped the stick and collapsed to a sitting position in the mud. He started to cry. He felt ashamed, only for a moment, then he let himself go. He didn't care anymore, he was exhausted, but he didn't know what else to do. Sitting there bawling was the only thing that seemed to make sense. It was what he needed.

A silent weeping at first, which soon turned into uncontrollable sobs that shook his chest, and then into a scream: 'Help me! Somebody help me! Mom! Dad! Mom! Is anyone out there? I'm fucking lost. HELP!'

Fear had broken through the dam. He sat in the mud, whimpering like a stray dog. Finally he fell quiet and went over the last two and a half hours in his mind, trying to make sense of it but failing. Anxiety had gotten the better of him, seeping into every fiber of his being like a serum, like lactic acid.

The countryside had changed. He had changed. His entire life had suddenly been upended in a very short span of time, in a way that was somehow both ridiculous and terrible.

He looked at his watch through a wet mist of tears.

Eight o'clock. His parents had to be worried by now.

Yes. Yes! They would wait a little longer and when he didn't show up they would try his cell phone, and then, when they couldn't reach him, they would call the police.

He had to get back on a road, any road, and wait. For Christ's sake, in the worst case scenario he would wait for sunrise and look for help then. The sun would chase the shadows away, a new dawn would break over the sleepy town of Orlasco, and people would emerge from their houses to go about their lives, plow the fields, go for a run. Things would go back to behaving by the usual rules.

What's wrong with me? I can't think anymore. I just can't.

He stood up and picked up his torn, soaking-wet shorts, and tied them around his waist as best he could with their drawstrings. His penis had shrunk to a wrinkled appendage, nothing but wet, dirty skin.

Looking up, staggering like a drunk, Sergio saw the light. A yellow rectangle in the distance, suspended in mid-air. A window. The window of a farmhouse.

Bending over with tremendous effort, moaning from the pain in his side, he picked up the stick and limped in that direction. Now the moon cast a weak glow over the countryside, but it was too cold. Unnaturally cold for late October. The fingers on his right hand, numb, could hardly hold the crutch.

He walked for what felt like an eternity and reached the road. Every now and then he turned around and squinted, trying to make out the belfry. Despite the light of the moon, he couldn't see it.

He pottered along to the edge of the field, where he was met by a dirt road that had been reduced to a swampy tongue studded with puddles that reflected the pallor of a moth-eaten moon. The light from the farmhouse couldn't be more than three, four hundred meters away. The road seemed to lead there.

Thank you. Oh, Jesus, thank you.

A hundred or so very painful steps, then he made out a faint glow near a gnarled, centuries-old sycamore. As he got closer, Sergio realized it was one of those tiny country chapels housing statues of saints or the Virgin Mary.

When he reached the building, which was protected by a small fence and lit by a couple of electric lights, he stopped for a few seconds to catch his breath. His lungs continued to emit rasping sounds.

It was a little Madonna, yes, surrounded by vases filled with wilted flowers.

Sergio rested his forearms on the fence and closed his eyes. Instinctively, although he hadn't done so in years, he mumbled a prayer.

But when he opened his eyes and focused his gaze on the statue, he drew back, reeling.

The Virgin Mary was missing her hands and head. Or rather, she had a head, but not hers. Someone, maybe a kid or some sicko, had replaced it with a doll's head. A doll with no eyes or hair, its mouth gaping in an eternal plastic scream. In the darkness, it looked like a dead newborn.

The image was grotesque, a mockery.

Grinding his teeth, he started to stagger once more towards the farmhouse. He wondered what its inhabitants would think when they saw him, half naked, soaked with water and sweat, distraught.

It didn't matter. He needed medical treatment, warmth, to embrace his loved ones.

Chiara.

Dad.

Mom.

He walked the hundred meters to the fence enclosing the farmhouse and stopped in front of its entrance gate.

The light was still on, filtering through white curtains to illuminate the front yard. An old farmhouse, one of the many that dotted the Piedmont countryside. The farmers who lived in them often seemed to be decades behind the times, even though they had made loads of money from crops and live-stock. Some called them hillbillies or other derogatory names. Uncouth people, not very sociable.

But all Sergio needed was a phone, a blanket, and something to eat. He would call Chiara to let her know what had happened, tell her he was fine, then he would dial 911 and wait for the ambulance. He could still detect that metallic taste in the back of his mouth. And in his side, where he had crashed into the rock, something scraping . . . from the inside.

Unsteady steps, a dizzy feeling, the desire to just let go. He looked for a doorbell on the columns by the house's entrance but couldn't find one.

It didn't matter. He would make sure they heard him. Somehow he would get their attention.

'Hey!' he yelled, and his throat responded with an unbearable burning sensation. He swallowed a couple of times, then began shouting again: 'Help me, please! I . . . I fell, I'm hurt. I need help. Can you hear me?'

A few seconds passed, during which clouds darker than night gathered in a compact mass, devouring the moon in their hazy womb.

Now there was almost total darkness, broken only by the beams of a lamp filtering through the window. A rectangle of light promising escape, salvation, rest.

'Hey, do you hear me? Open up, please!'

An oval shadow moved behind the curtains, swaying. A head, it looked like a head, its hair disheveled, shoulders stooped, maybe an elderly man. The curtains drew back for a fraction of a second; Sergio only had time to make out the outline of a hand, a wide-open eye staring at him.

'I'm here!' he shouted between gasps. 'I'm here!'

Then he heard the sound of steps coming from inside the house and voices that for some reason sounded familiar. Whoever was inside must have seen and heard him. He was safe.

'Thank you! Thank you! Oh, thank you,' he exclaimed in a faint voice.

He clung to the little gate, waiting for the front door to open, for someone to come and help him. He hung there like an old scarecrow, his eyes half closed. Then the light in the window went out.

Total darkness, thick like honey.

Sergio stood upright and tried to detect signs of movement.

Something. He didn't see anything. Maybe the farmers who lived in the villa thought he was a prowler, a burglar, a junkie.

'Hey,' he shouted. 'Hey, I need help, I just need a phone, please . . .'

But the farmhouse had become a dead thing nestled in the gloom, motionless, frozen in an instant of eternal abandonment and neglect. Sergio fell to his knees, his chest shaking with a gurgling laughter that didn't sound at all healthy.

Hysteria got the better of him; he started to rattle the gate, babbling disjointed words, he tried to scale the fence, but the pain in his side was too strong, horrendous.

'Open up! Open up, you fucking bastards, open up!' he squawked in a shrill voice that echoed dreadfully in the dark, the cry of a dying bird. A brutal coughing fit turned his chest inside out, and he felt a sticky, salty liquid rising into his mouth. He touched his lips with his fingertips and they came away sticky. The taste of iron in his mouth left no room for doubt.

Blood.

Blood pouring from his own body, abundant, thick, out of control.

He let go of the gate and limped along the road. Then, with the last of his strength, he left the dirt track and cut through a field towards the rear of the farmhouse, where he glimpsed a bright rectangle cast on the ground. The back of the house was unfenced, and in the middle of the plaster wall was a window. Sergio went closer.

There were no curtains.

He shaded his eyes with his hands and pressed his nose to the glass. He was about to knock, then he froze.

A kitchen. Through his tears he noticed objects he had seen before. The place exuded warmth, peace.

Three people sat at a table with their backs to him, their heads bowed in a pose that conveyed an abyssal despair.

Two women and a man.

They looked like.

They were.

Chiara.

Mom.

Dad.

Lasagna in the oven.

Sergio banged on the glass frantically, but nobody turned around. No response except a wretched cry from behind him, that same cry he had heard twice before, the bestial scream he had thought was a dog's.

It was behind him.

Right there, very close.

He turned around slowly. He saw something blurry moving a few meters from the road, a ball of darkness and fury: the sound was coming from there.

The blur began to advance, calmly, as if it had all the time in the world.

And it did.

Something in Sergio's mind snapped.

He hurled a cry towards the heavens, a sort of awkward howl, hopped a couple times in place, then began to run at breakneck speed across the field, blindly, a lunatic fleeing an asylum.

Lactic acid bit into his calves; he vomited a gush of dark blood while his chest emitted a screech like a rusty door hinge.

Sergio paid no attention. He no longer felt any pain, as though he had been given a powerful analgesic, and even if he had felt it, it wouldn't have mattered.

The only thing he cared about now was running. Running, nothing else.

And he would keep on running. On and on, yes, he would keep moving his legs and sooner or later he would get home, he would find help and comfort, he was sure of it, he would make it. Meanwhile he would keep on running like the October wind, until he felt like collapsing – until he felt like dying – to lessen the rancor of the darkness that hunted him.

Les Abominations des Altitudes

The Alps. They've always loomed over me. Their shadow will swallow mine.

Although blotted out by this gray night, they're there, white, unfeeling, and as sharp as a wolf's fangs, pointed towards a sky that holds the promise of snow. And they'll still be there long after the end, to watch over the rubble of the world, conversing in their unknown language of avalanches, cracks, and landslides.

The Pennines, the Graian Alps, Mont Blanc, the Matterhorn, giants of rock and ice teeming with stories and tragedies, terrors and wonders. If they decide to summon you, to welcome you into their universe, it's impossible not to heed the call.

I grew up among the mountains of the Aosta Valley. My father was a guide and a volunteer with the mountain rescue team, a man who had been raised with solid moral values, a substitute for courage, curiosity, experience, and nimble nerves. I followed in his footsteps on dozens of climbs. He taught me to drive spikes into the rock, to avoid crevasses, to know when it's a good day to tackle a peak and when it's better to stay inside sipping Génépy.

He explained to me that it's all about having respect for the mountain. A truism, if you like, but necessary, fundamental, rudimentary. A life lived without respect for anything isn't worth much.

For almost half my life I've looked at the Alps with reverence. In return they offer me breathtaking views, adrenaline, the peace of the heights, sensations known only to those who climb to where the dividing line between earth and sky becomes fleeting, blurred.

Later, respect turned into the infinite repetition of a single moment.

My father used to talk about these peaks with an almost religious devotion. 'Up there it's like you can touch the stars. The thin air makes you light-headed, inspires thoughts that you can only get hints of down below. The mountain is frightening. The mountain hides secrets. It comes close to the divine.' He uttered these words the first time we were together at the top of Mont Blanc.

And he was right.

The mountain comes close to the divine.

But not all divinities are benevolent.

We found that out on the 10th of October, 1985, at the Ghiglione bivouac, altitude 3700 meters, exactly thirty years ago.

A mountaineer had left the Turin shelter the morning of the 9th to brave the northern face of Mont Maudit. He had said he would return by evening. Around noon, black, snarling clouds had begun prowling the ridges, devouring the sun.

The man ('Bastien Delorme, strange guy, French, didn't talk much, always had his nose stuck in a notebook', was how our guide, Dario Allegri, the shelter's manager, had described him just before we started the search) had never come back.

Froze to death, caught right in the middle of an exceptionally intense blizzard, died outside the only shelter, the Ghiglione bivouac. Yet another mountain tragedy. Maybe that's what you're thinking. Or a lack of preparation. Inadequate equipment. Bad luck.

No.

There was much more to it. The crackpot ideas of a mountaineer and researcher who was chasing his demons. A merciless, terrible end. A story of loneliness and despair.

My dad and I were the first to lay eyes on the remains of Bastien Delorme. Sitting in the snow on a rocky ledge in nothing but a T-shirt and underwear. His crystallized skin shimmered in the pink afternoon light. Hands frozen into claws, stiff against his chest. His blue face, festooned with frozen mucus and saliva, made even more frightening by the mad grimace of rigor mortis, his exposed teeth reflecting the light of the setting sun from between curled lips.

We found a sleeping bag, backpack, and equipment inside the bivouac, from which the Frenchman seemed to have emerged in the middle of the night, in great haste, to hurl himself into the storm that was ravaging Mont Maudit. He had curled up in the fresh snow; he must have died fairly quickly, and the corpse had remained there almost a day, like a macabre sentry.

We found an egg wrapped in filthy rags clenched in Delorme's marble-hard hands. Not much bigger than a hen's egg. Black. A bluish-black that seemed to dampen every other color. Just then the wind began to blow persistently, turning into a storm, forcing us to head inside the Ghiglione shelter.

There we found the Frenchman's personal dossier. The paranoid work of a life dedicated to an obsession that had tormented him for years on end.

Now, like every year, I'm back where it all started. I sit in the dark of the bivouac, waiting for something to happen. For something to change. A uniform mantle of mist rolls over the north face of Mont Maudit, sapping hope. Gusts blow from France across the Alps; their cries echo in the hollows of the glaciers, crawl along the seracs, and shake the rock faces.

It's snowing. Hard, frozen, pitiless flakes tick against the sheet metal roof as if to mark a different temporal order.

Crashes, rumbling, the echo of an avalanche.

Behind the chaos of the elements another sound, a whistling able to worm its way to the limits of auditory perception and stay planted there, like the hum that lingers in the eardrum after a deafening noise.

Is it them?

I wait. It's all I can do.

'We found Delorme. Unfortunately there was nothing we could do, he froze to death . . . No way we can reach the shelter, it'll be dark in a few hours and it's gotten awfully windy. It's snowing. I think a major storm is on its way. We've done what we could . . . My son and I are safe. We'll spend the night here, at the Ghiglione camp. We'll come down in the morning as soon as the weather permits. Do you read me? Over.'

There was no response from my father's transceiver but a series of static discharges and the mournful wail of the wind gusts. The weather conditions made communication with the Turin shelter impossible.

'Over,' he repeated. Then he looked at me, shaking his head, and turned his attention back to the strange object we had collected from the French mountaineer's stiff grasp. He weighed it in his hand, perplexed.

'It's beautiful . . . Looks like marble, but it's light as a feather.'

He handed me the egg. The black shell was unpleasant to the touch; the surface was greasy, sticky. I lifted the object towards the battery-powered flashlight we'd hung from the ceiling.

'What do you think it is?'

'No idea.'

'It feels hollow,' I observed, shaking it. 'An empty shell. Black. What the hell is it?'

'If you're in the mood for questions . . . Well, there are a few things that don't add up here.' A shadow came over his eyes. He sank onto the wooden bench and gestured for me to light the cast-iron stove over by the cots. 'Why did Delorme leave the bivouac half naked? Look at his gear. He wasn't an amateur. He knew he wouldn't last long in those conditions. It must have been ten below out there. It's like he went out deliberately to face the storm and sat down in the snow to die. With that thing in his hand.'

I blew on the little heap of firewood and paper I had slid into the stove to feed the fire. I heard Dad unbutton his suit and hang it on a rack to dry.

I went to the bivouac's little window. All I could see was the snowflakes madly chasing each other. Delorme's body was out there; we had decided to leave it outside. The cold would preserve the corpse and tomorrow we would return to the valley with our sad burden. The memory of the idiotic grimace on that bluish face, the dead, wide open eyes staring into the darkness of the high altitudes, made me regret not being in the main lounge of the Turin shelter.

'Let's have a look through his things,' my father suggested. The Frenchman had left his sleeping bag on a cot. His backpack, boots, ropes, ice axes, and carabiners were piled up against the wall.

We sorted through the equipment, all of it expert mountaineer gear. Delorme was no novice. His Bachmann knots, tied with remarkable mastery, were further proof of this.

Dad set the backpack on the table and opened it. The flashlight made our shadows sway on the walls, making them hunchbacked, deforming them.

I took the egg, wrapped it in the rags, and put it on a mattress under some covers. I'd discovered that letting my gaze linger on it wasn't something I liked much at all.

'Clothes, a water bottle, socks, food, a gas stove . . .'

The silence that followed was interrupted by the rustling of a cellophane envelope. My father handed it to me and went on rummaging in the backpack.

'The notebook . . .' I murmured, sliding a thick folder from the envelope.

I put it on the table, and the words written on the cover in felt-tip pen in an angular handwriting made my mind start racing in the troubled night. Frosty fingers tickled my neck. *Les Abominations des Altitudes*.

I imagined Bastien clenching the egg in his hands while

hypothermia made him more and more drowsy, blind, destroying his body and his consciousness.

'The notebook, Dad. Remember? Down at the shelter, Dario told us Delorme was weird, always had a notebook in his hand. I think this is it.'

I leafed through it. A cramped, spiky handwriting, dozens of sheets of paper, photographs and drawings attached to the pages with paper clips or staples.

Drawings of the egg.

The photo of a dead mountaineer, throat slashed and legs twisted behind his back. 'Jesus!' I exclaimed.

Dad sighed and cleared the table. Then he took two logs from the pile and threw them into the stove.

'It's going to be a long night. Good thing we know French,' he said, bringing the bench closer and pointing at the notebook.

Sitting in the little cabin that guaranteed our survival, we started to read.

Bastien Delorme was born in Briançon in 1930. The son of a laborer with a passion for the mountains and a schoolteacher, the third of five brothers, he described his childhood as quiet and happy until 1939, when the incursion of German troops into Belgium and the Netherlands left little doubt about the Führer's intentions towards France.

Bastien's father, André, who had done military service in the French Alps, was called up a few months before Mussolini declared war on a France that was already on her knees. Only to wind up one of the hundreds missing after the *Bataille des Alpes*, fought in June 1940 between the Italian and French armies along the western range of the Alps.

The loss of his father had been a heavy blow for Bastien; in the summer of 1952, the war long over and anxious for new experiences, he had decided to undertake a sort of pilgrimage, visiting some of the fortifications on the Maginot line along with two rock-climbing friends, brothers Jacques and

Theodore Lemoine, and then ending the vacation with a few days of relaxation in the Aosta Valley, at a little hotel in Sauze d'Oulx.

Shortly before they reached Italian territory through the Little St. Bernard Pass, 2188 meters altitude, a thick mist had descended from the north. In his notebook Bastien dwelled at length on the nature of the mist:

I had never seen a mist so thick, so wet, so fragrant. Jacques, Theodore, and I made our way forward holding each other's hands. Visibility was reduced, and we constantly feared losing our way. Our voices seemed devoid of intonation, muffled. It was the mist. It absorbed sound. It was almost a miracle that we found the entrance to Little St. Bernard Pass.

The three of them had decided to spend the night on the other side of the pass, on Italian soil, camping on a wide plateau where the haze granted enough visibility to pitch their tent.

I walked a few meters off to empty my bladder while Jacques and Theodore fiddled with the gear. A strong wind from the west drove the mist back where it had come from. It was then that I saw the circle of stones. And found the egg.

The circle of stones to which Bastien alluded – and which he investigated in depth in the following pages – is one of the most important megalithic sites in the Aosta Valley, known as 'Little St. Bernard's Cromlech'.

Dozens of boulders arranged to form a circle eighty meters in diameter, probably a prehistoric religious site constructed by the Salassi, the first inhabitants of the Aosta Valley, a people of Celtic origins, language, and culture. Difficult to determine the structure's age or its real purpose – many of the rocks have been shifted or removed over the centuries – but a number of scholars have linked the arrangement of the stones with particular constellations and astronomical convergences.

The egg was lying in the grass, the lower part lightly pressed into the ground. I went closer. When I realized what it was, curious about its strange color and dimensions, I picked it up; it was greasy, as if smeared with lard or oil. I brought it over to Jacques and Theodore, who refused to touch it, terrified, ordering me to put it back where I'd found it.

Dad and I couldn't help but give a sidelong glance at the covers under which I had hidden the egg.

Jacques and Theodore were very religious, and they said that in some sacred texts the Black Egg was considered a bad luck omen, the Devil's egg, keeper of the Antichrist. I carried it back near the stones because night was falling and they seemed really shaken. I left the egg. But by then it was mine. By then it was mine.

These last words were written on the yellowed paper in a faint, trembling hand.

My father stood up, took the thermos from the backpack, and filled two travel mugs with coffee.

'The storm's getting even worse. It's a good thing we stopped here. It's coming down powdery, the worst kind.' He peered out the window with a squint, as if he could perceive a hidden language in the whirling of the flakes. He sipped the warm beverage, his thin torso slightly hunched over with fatigue.

I resumed reading.

That night, as the wind shook the tent, enclosed in my sleeping bag between my two friends, the dreams started. It's not easy to describe the sensations I experienced. I was awake and Jacques was snoring my ear.

A kind of plaintive whistle, like a marmot's call, crept its way into the gusts, forming a syncopated melody. I felt myself sucked upwards and I could see us. The three of us, motionless in sleep. I floated a few inches above my body and those of my companions. And then I began to ascend, rising out of the tent, as if invisible threads were pulling me towards the sky. A black sky, swollen with clouds that split apart and reformed under the attack of violet lightning.

Dragged to dizzying heights by an unknown force, up, up, ever higher; the horror and the disheartening feeling of loneliness grew with every meter of the climb. The impression of emptiness, of insignificant magniloquence and desolation conveyed by the shattered sky and the contorted peaks whizzing around me was overwhelming.

Immaculate peaks welcomed the snow, which settled on the rocks only to be immediately blown away by icy currents.

I landed on a summit and leaned over to look down: two black shapes supported on bony gray legs were climbing along a circular path; they trudged through the ice with unpredictable trajectories, then disappeared on the side that was hidden from my view. Finally they re-emerged in the night, lit up by lightning, leaving shuffling footprints in the white, and in their silhouettes pink gashes opened up that might have been mouths, oral cavities with teeth of ice encrusted with shrubbery and berries.

They wanted me. Now I clenched the black egg, perched over blue abysses, while they continued their howling and lopsided ascent.

They kept climbing. They were getting closer, and I could discern frantic movements and the hissing sound of their horns lashing the air, as if the creatures had no intention of stopping.

I was alone. In the wind. In the bitter cold. In the heights that safe-guarded horrors.

I picked up a pungent scent of licorice, mixed with another smell: the stench of the carcasses of old, sick animals that had lain down to die in the high-altitude springs.

And then I hurled myself into the void, clutching the egg. Anything at all – my rib cage crushed like a walnut, my heels and legs smashed, an anonymous burial in that light blue crevasse – anything at all to avoid their grasp. Their bite.

But, sizzling in my grip, the egg became light, an aerostatic ball of darkness, and I clung to it like a shipwrecked sailor clings to a plank in the middle of the sea; hovering in the wind, it brought me back to the tent, to safety, far from the horrid heights, from the pinnacles I had just visited and which I hoped never to see again.

I didn't wake up until morning, but the emotions and images from the dream stuck with me until we were far from the plateau, gradually loosening their hold as we faced the slopes of the Aosta Valley and put distance between ourselves and that place.

We arrived at the hotel in Sauze at dusk.

The Italians gave us a warm welcome. The owner of the inn, Carlo, had lost a brother and a cousin in the same battle that had cost me my father. We spoke of the pointlessness of that skirmish, of the wicked Fascist attack on France.

We talked for a long time, and that evening we ate delicious polenta with Carlo and his wife. We were the only guests in the place.

After dinner I went up to our small but cozy room to get some photos of my father from my backpack to show the Italians.

It was there. Wrapped in a wool undershirt, between ropes and clothes. The egg!

Here Delorme's writing was again reduced to a series of crooked lines, to the point where some passages were almost illegible. He always referred to the egg with the expression '*Cet œuf noir dégoutant*'. This disgusting black egg. Unable to get his head around how it had wound up in his backpack, he had thought it might have been a joke by the Lemoine brothers, but that couldn't be: when putting the egg back in its place he had gone off alone, and the other two had never gone near the cromlech. He was sure he had left it there, near the pass.

He had brought it to the dining room, where his two friends sat and stared at him with reproach.

The innkeeper had stood up with a start, knocking over an empty wine bottle, stammering phrases in Italian which Bastien couldn't understand, and had ordered him to leave the egg in his room. His wife had withdrawn to the kitchen, making the sign of the cross.

I came back to the ground floor confused, apologizing without knowing what for. Carlo looked at me with sad eyes and made me understand that everything was all right, pouring out generous servings of grappa for me, Jacques, and Theodore.

He said he had heard of the black eggs but had never seen one. I would have burst out laughing if I hadn't found the egg in my backpack, if I hadn't had that nightmare the night before.

'Jacques and Theodore claim they're the devil's eggs,' I explained.

He broke into laughter. 'The devil's eggs? No, they're the Dahù's eggs!'

That was the first time I ever heard of them. The Dahut, Dahù, Daru, Dairi, as they've been dubbed over the centuries in the Aosta Valley. The ones I call the Asymmetricals. Dahù is too nice a name for those things.

I paused in my reading, frowned, and gave my father a perplexed look, unable to hold back a laugh. 'Are we really talking about this? About the Dahù? A fairy tale?'

'But that egg is no fairy tale. We just pried it from a dead man's hands,' said my father, frowning in his turn from the other side of the table. A gust of wind assailed the bivouac, making the sheet metal walls shake.

I swallowed hard, dumbfounded. 'Dad, it's clear from this notebook that Delorme was out of his mind. That egg could be fake, I don't know. The only thing certain is that the Dahù don't exist. And even if by some absurd chance they did exist, I've never heard of anyone talking about them in relation to black eggs, devils, or whatever else.'

'Let's keep reading,' he urged me, suddenly serious.

We listened to the innkeeper's story with interest and curiosity. The Dahù is a creature from the folklore of the Aosta Valley, but it's found in various cultures and epochs all through the European mountain range from the Alps to the Pyrenees. It's described as a funny-looking animal similar to a chamois, with shorter legs on one side of its body, allowing it to move easily on inclines. The left-handed Dahù are the ones whose right legs are longer than the left ones. The right-handed Dahù are the opposite. Because of this bizarre physical feature they can walk around the mountain in only one direction. According to other legends, to capture one, all you have to do is surprise it from behind and yell 'Dahù!' so that the animal, curious by nature, turns around and collapses, suddenly finding itself with its shorter legs facing the valley. The Dahù reproduce by laying eggs.

That's the official *story. Innocent, silly. But Carlo had heard other stories, stories told to him by an old rock climber who had spent a couple of weeks at his hotel after the end of the war.*

That man claimed that the Dahù really existed, but they were far from the friendly herbivores whose quirky antics are recounted in children's stories. Over the course of time oral tradition had cloaked their true nature in a fairy-tale aura, to exorcize their monstrousness.

There was a very long list of expert mountaineers who had vanished into thin air in unexplainable circumstances. Others found with wounds not attributable to any known animal. And still others who returned to the valley completely insane, their eyes wild, babbling about limping spirits and black eggs brooded in cold, dark caverns.

And then there were the old petroglyphs traced on rocks scattered along the major European mountain chains; cromlechs built in honor of Bergimus, the Celtic god of heights; an inexplicable dying-off of deer on various nature reserves in the early '30s; and the disturbing suicide of an Italian man in Germany, a folklore scholar who in 1937 cut his jugular with a climbing axe before throwing himself into a ravine.

Carlo told us the old man knew these things because he was a friend of the suicide victim, Daniel Bonfatti. Bonfatti had devoted a good portion of his free time to the study of Alpine legends, and in the last few weeks of his life he had seemed worried about something. He spoke of glaciers receding to reveal sinister fossils and sleeping beasts, reawakened from millenia-long hibernation and driven by an insatiable, primal hunger.

Before his extreme final action, Bonfatti burned all his notes, the fruit of years of research.

I paged through the notebook until I found the photo I had noticed before I started reading, that horrible black-and-white Polaroid of a man mangled after a fall, his throat slashed. I turned it over and read Delorme's minuscule handwriting aloud: 'Photo of the body of Daniel Bonfatti, folklore scholar, recovered in a crevasse on the Berchtesgaden Alps two days after his disappearance. Note the wound to the throat, self-inflicted with an ice axe, found on the edge of the ravine. Bonfatti had been gathering material on the Asymmetricals for some time.'

I set the photograph down, wondering how Bastien had gotten hold of it, and tapped my temple with my index finger a couple of times. I couldn't believe what I had just read. The Dahù transformed into an aberration, a monstrous divinity worshipped in circles of stones. Suicides, mysterious deaths, psych ward nightmares.

'Let's go to bed, Dad,' I blurted out. I'd had enough. And,

though I didn't want to admit it, Delorme's story and photos had made me uneasy. But my father insisted that we finish reading.

Another nightmare, if possible even more frightening than the one he'd had on the plateau, had visited Delorme his first night at the little inn in Sauze d'Oulx.

His father André, dressed in a torn and bloodstained French Alpine uniform, spirals of snow and chunks of brain matter pouring from his cracked head, had followed him along a mountain path, riding sneeringly astride a Dahù as the dazzling reflection of the sun lashed the snow.

The next morning, accompanied by Jacques, Theodore, and Carlo, Bastien had climbed a mountain to two thousand meters altitude and, after wrapping the egg in a bundle of rags, had hurled it into a deep crevasse. But the dreams didn't stop.

They never stopped. Every night of his life Bastien Delorme was haunted by the shadow of the Asymmetricals, as he had rechristened them. The Abominations of the Altitudes.

In one of the final pages of his diary, before he climbed Mont Maudit to meet his death, this was how he described his dream journeys, in evocative and chilling French:

They're not dreams. They're the very essence of the Mountain. Its call. The cry of the crevasses, the mad dance of the glaciers, the breath of the stars on the pitiless summits. Good God, have you ever seen a starry sky above three thousand meters altitude? Swarms of galaxies, spirals of light long dead and reduced to incandescent dust that we can still see because in the immense concert of Time and Space we're nothing more than a disturbance endowed with flawed perceptions.

He returned home and a week later he found the black egg under his bed. Doubting his own sanity, he had taken a hammer and struck the egg furiously, reducing the shell to so many tiny little pieces. It was empty. Or 'full of air', as Bastien wrote. The black fragments wound up in the stove, but a few days later the egg had reappeared in a kitchen cupboard.

The nightmares grew more and more intense and terrifying. To the point where Delorme had started gulping down coffee and uppers to stay awake, night after night. Anything not to find himself drifting in those mountains, hunted by the Asymmetricals.

Asking the Lemoine brothers for help proved to be useless: terrorized at the possible consequences to themselves if they got involved, they left him on his own. Friends and relatives were convinced he was making it all up, certain that the loss of his father and the difficult wartime years had messed with his head.

Trying to destroy or get rid of the black egg had done no good. Dozens of times he had brought it to remote spots or mailed it to distant post offices. Desperate, he had even tried giving it away, hoping to rid himself of the curse – or pass it on.

But the egg always returned. *L'œuf revient toujours.* Several pages of Bastien's notes were filled with those three simple words, repeated hundreds of times.

In 1955 Delorme's mental and physical state took a downturn. Three years of troubled sleep and nervous stress had brought him to the breaking point. But he hadn't given up and had decided to launch a counterattack, gathering as much information as possible about the Dahù.

Hunting them.

An idea had taken root in his heart: there was only one way of regaining control over his life and being able to go to bed without waking up screaming in the darkness – he had to return the egg to its rightful owners.

And so for thirty years he had followed the tracks of the Asymmetricals across half of Europe, but especially in the Aosta Valley, where the myth had originated before spreading, mutating along the Alps like a virus. The Frenchman's exhausting and eremitical work, consisting of testimonials, interviews, and pilgrimages, was a crazy collage of folklore and chronicle. He had spoken in dialect with old mountainmen in remote

Aosta Valley villages; followed paths taken by hikers who had vanished into thin air in broad daylight; questioned a woman at the Le Vallette prison in Turin who was accused of having killed her four-year-old son and hidden his body, but was convinced that a 'black, crooked splotch' had carried her son off during a walk; traveled to the Jagellonica National Library in Krakow to consult an old text from the eighteenth century that mentioned the discovery of a black egg by a Polish army general in the Tatra Mountains.

Rumors. Hints. Phrases mumbled in far-flung cabins as the embers died in the hearth and outside the storms grew fatter.

A thin, very fragile thread drawn from mountain to mountain, which on October 10, 1985 had led him to Mont Maudit. Delorme's notes break off several days before his departure for the Aosta Valley. He described horrible nightmares peopled with hooded figures atop a mountain who bowed down before horned shadows. In the final dreams, suffused with an atmosphere of imminent tragedy, he had recognized the unmistakable outlines of the mountainous mass where he would meet his death, a vision that had spurred him to tackle the final climb.

A tired resignation emerged from his words, the vague awareness that he would be unable to probe and get to the bottom of the mystery that had haunted him for years. The allure and bewilderment caused by the gods who inhabit the mountain and whose characteristics are defined by the feelings they elicit in mankind.

Fear. Devotion. Allure. Wonder.

The final note read:

We're arrogant. Curious. Always have been, always will be. We stick our nose everywhere, confident that Science will always be there to answer our questions, a safe haven . . .

Extreme places. They attract us. Deserts with the lament of the sand rolling down the dunes. Immense, indomitable oceans, whole universes beneath the surface. Dizzying summits, where oxygen is scarce and only moss and lichens grow.

*They're places that draw us to them. Magnificent in their indiffer-
ence to our affairs. But they're bubbles of loneliness and despair. Where
mind and body are put to the test. Where there's fertile ground for fear to
take root, and when it sprouts it transforms into myth.*

I wish I could tell you that the mystery behind the myth has
been solved. It hasn't, but I have become part of it. We're not
always permitted to understand. Maybe some things only stop
being enigmas when we accept them for what they are: different, incomprehensible planes of reality, of which we can only
perceive vague and blurry contours.

The night of October 10, 1985, having finished reading
Les Abominations des Altitudes, my father and I slipped into our
sleeping bags and, lying on the little cots in the Ghiglione bivouac, we talked for a long time.

I remember my surprise when he hinted that in his view the
idea of there being some truth in Bastien Delorme's account
wasn't entirely out of the question. Dad had always been a
practical man, not much given to leaps of the imagination.

I think by that point he had already been infected. Like I
was. I don't know. The egg had become ours. With all that it
brought – and brings – with it.

I look at those black eggs like ineradicable infections, passing from person to person, stoking and altering the myth of
the Dahù over time. They enclose the marvelous and terrifying spirit of the mountain and the embryo of its legends. Its
deaths. They can't be given back, and the choice isn't ours.
They dictate the rules of the game, choosing an owner whose
soul they can suck, in order to feed the Asymmetricals and
their saga.

In the dead of night, when the storm's furious attacks on the
bivouac seemed to have abated, we decided to sleep. It took me
quite a while to nod off; my ears were pricked, listening to the
wind and my father's snoring.

I dreamt. A *toc-toc-toc* in the night, someone knocking at

the sheet metal door of the bivouac, light but insistent taps of knuckles. The stove had gone out and the cold seeped into my sleeping bag, making my teeth chatter like castanets. A shadow stretched across the floorboards in the semi-darkness, a shadow cast by a man.

Dad.

I got up from the cot, and I thought I could detect a vague odor of rottenness and licorice. He was standing by the window, looking out, still as a statue, his face transfixed with horror. In his rough fingers he clutched the black egg.

'Dad? What are you doing? Who's at the door?'

He started in surprise, and I thought he was going to drop dead of a heart attack. Then he brought his finger to his lips, signaling me to be quiet, and whispered: 'It's Bastien Delorme. He's calling me. He wants the egg, but now the egg is ours.' A smile of exultation curled his lips, which creased, tore, splitting his face in two, showing me for the tiniest fraction of time, and yet too long, a black, sticky mass bubbling in his body. 'The Asymmetricals have given it to us.'

'Dad, Bastien Delorme is dead!' I yelled, but then the *toc-toc-toc* became the violent hammering of a mallet, and I knew that, yes, on the other side of that door stood the Frenchman, wanting to enter, to explain to us, to speak, to take away the egg.

A cry of frustration shook the bivouac, the mountain, the Alps.

I woke up. The door of the bivouac was wide open and a confetti of snow was settling in the doorway, forming an icy doormat.

I jumped down from the mattress, bewildered, unable to draw a clear line between dream and reality.

My father wasn't on the cot.

I flung myself out into the freezing cold and called him at the top of my lungs, the syllables frayed by the gusts, and I caught the frenetic movement of two black forms staggering through the darkness, circling upward in the night in my direction. After that I remember only a pain devastating enough to lacerate spirit, flesh, tissue, consciousness.

After emerging from a pit of snowy darkness, I remember dragging myself back to the bivouac through the snow, sitting down and waiting for the night to end.

It didn't happen.

That night never ended, and I don't know if it ever will.

The egg is out there. Buried somewhere in the snow. Ownerless, but one day someone will find it and the Asymmetricals will return to frolic in the dreams and reveries of men, to satisfy their hunger and to satisfy ours.

Dad's body was never found. Just like Bastien Delorme's.

And mine.

I sit in the Ghiglione bivouac, time crystallized in that fearsome night. I don't know what happened to my father. Sometimes I fear that his spirit is trapped in the egg, and that he discovered the secrets enclosed in the black shell. I don't like that idea. But I can never know. I don't know much, and it's better that way.

I think back to Bastien Delorme sitting in the snow, and I wonder if he hurled himself out into the night, drawn by the same call that was my father's end, and mine.

No, it's not the end.

It's much worse.

The Dahù got us.

I've become a specter of the mountain, a shadow suspended in time, trapped here by laws I can't understand or control.

Nothing changes.

I don't sleep. I don't dream. In that sense I can probably count myself luckier than Delorme. I'm one of many, one of the countless ghosts atoning in this icy solitude for their curiosity, for having answered the call of the heights.

I tell my story to the wind, forever more. It's the only thing I can do. And sometimes the wind responds. It's an ancient language, of which I can only decipher certain parts. But there are nights in this eternal night when I'm certain that the merciless gusts gather up my story and carry it down to the valley, gliding through the wet streets of the villages to squeeze their way like frozen fingers through the cracks in the houses, and whisper to unwary sleepers the dark secrets of the mountains, the wondrous and tremendous deeds of the Abominations of the Altitudes.

Uironda

E rmes Lenzi couldn't take it anymore.

After fifteen years as a truck driver, after hundreds of thousands of kilometers traveled, he felt like a needle that was always running over the same vinyl record. A disc of tar, whose grooves were the highways devoured by the old Scania, the only songs the roar of the motor and the dull throb of his back pain.

Whose sad, bleary eyes were studying him from the rearview mirror? No, they couldn't be his.

When you no longer recognize your own reflection, it's time to start worrying, my friend, he mused, noticing a movement in his lower abdomen, as if someone were stirring his bowels and his conscience with a red-hot ladle.

'Fuck,' he murmured, his voice weary from an eternity of truck stop sandwiches, burnt coffee, and smog. 'Fuck these roads that are always the same. This goddamn backache. Daniela. Everything.'

From the sun visor on the passenger side his seven-year-old son Simone looked on, hugging a headless woman. The photo had been taken one sunny morning, one of those days when the sky is so blue it hurts your eyes. Ermes remembered that moment well, a piece from a period in which he had been happy and which now seemed to belong to another life, another puzzle.

In the background of the image some trees stood out, an emerald-green field, and the gentle curves of two hills.

The woman's fingernails were manicured, painted fluorescent yellow. Simone's hair was so red that it recalled a violent sunset, his cerulean blue eyes seemed to rival the sky.

Ermes had torn his wife's face off the snapshot in a fit of rage, crying and swearing. A year had already passed since she left him, taking the house, his son, and a good part of his dignity along with her.

'You're never here, Ermes. I can't raise Simone on my own. We're not a family anymore . . . I don't know what we are. I . . . don't think I love you anymore.'

Daniela's farewell could be summed up like that. A few words to tear out his heart, throw it on the ground, and dance a jig on it.

His protests hadn't done any good, his promise to reduce the hours spent in his truck, his tears, his excuses, their son who was drifting in a cloud of apathy as the days passed and the arguments grew more heated.

She wanted a divorce.

'Once a woman's made up her mind, you'd better believe it's hard to get her to change it. Always remember that,' his father, a truck driver like him, had told him once. But Ermes had never given too much weight to the old man's words, and the hope of winning Daniela back had become an obsession. Then he had discovered that she was seeing someone else, the elderly manager of a small firm in Turin.

It was like he went crazy.

In the course of a few weeks the pleas turned into telephone calls in the middle of the night, surveillance, scenes.

One evening he had intercepted the dandy who was screwing Daniela and had fractured two of his ribs and a cheekbone. If bystanders hadn't intervened, he would have kept on punching and kicking him until he killed him.

At that point the stalking and assault charges had come simultaneously, and his wife's top-notch attorney had massacred him, leaving him high and dry.

Basically he was working now so he could cover his legal

expenses and pay support to Daniela and Simone, whom he only got to see one weekend a month. He lived in the rear cabin of the truck: a bed, a fridge, a television the size of a postage stamp, and two electric burners. Like a vagabond, a gypsy.

There had been panic attacks, alcoholic blackouts, a long break from work. The situation had settled down little by little. He had stayed on his feet, but he could no longer see the point in anything.

Joyful images from the past attacked him like starving beasts, sucking the marrow from his bones and reducing him to a state of perpetual exhaustion. His existence had become a journey without a destination, a succession of streets leading nowhere. Stinking truck stops, packaged cookies, urinals, high-beam headlights, cigarettes, showers, anti-wart slip-on shoes, pitiful meals, dismal thoughts, Little Trees air freshener, rest areas. He was forty-two years old, had few friends, and the only things he managed to accumulate were debts, kilos on his waistline, and X-rays that told him: 'Well, you've spent the better part of the last twenty years with your ass on a seat, you're going to need surgery on that herniated disc sooner or later.'

He felt alone. A wanderer on life's road. So fucking desperately alone.

More and more often when he shot across an overpass he would entertain the idea of pulling over to the shoulder, getting out of the truck, and throwing himself off. A simple leap to leave all his problems, his anxiety, behind him. If it weren't for Simone, maybe ... When had he seen him last? He didn't remember. But he hadn't been well. Gaunt, dark circles under his eyes, his spirit crushed by his parents' separation.

A horn honking from somewhere brought him back to reality. The sound waned away, the cry of a dying person in a hospital ward.

Ermes struck the steering wheel with a weak, resigned fist, slipped a Camel between his lips and tried to concentrate on the road that would bring him to a warehouse located on the outskirts of Krakow for yet another delivery of Made in Italy furniture.

There were still too many hours left.

The digital tachograph, the contraption installed in the truck to monitor speed, length of stops, and kilometers traveled, informed him that in half an hour he would have to take his first break. The rules for road safety for commercial vehicles were ironclad: forty-five minutes of rest every four-and-a-half hours of driving, a maximum of nine hours a day, never more than fifty-six hours a week. He had colleagues who circumvented the system by attaching expensive devices to the tachograph, but Ermes had never yielded to the temptation. If he got caught he could kiss his driver's license goodbye for at least a couple of months.

He was somewhere on the A4, around fifty kilometers from the Verona exit. Another eleven, twelve hours of driving awaited him. He had left Turin at four with the rising sun, a fiery ball low on the horizon, casting a blinding glare on the guardrails. He weighed the idea of turning on the CB radio and talking with some fellow driver traveling the same stretch, but decided against it. The conversations were always the same. It wouldn't do him any good.

The traffic started to get more congested. Enclosed in their little metal boxes, hundreds of individuals rushed towards the usual chores, work, routine; expressionless faces behind the windshields, pale and rigid hands on the steering wheel like those of mannequins in a shopping mall.

Lenzi focused at first on the wheels of a truck identical to his that was passing him, then brought his eyes back to the road: about three hundred meters away, a small group of crows hopped around some roadkill on the shoulder, plunging their beaks into soft, yielding tissue, tearing strips of flesh with famished determination.

He eased up a little on the gas pedal, curious: there was something wrong about the upside-down shape on the ground over which the birds were going into a frenzy. It was too large to be a cat or dog, and it seemed to still be moving.

'What the hell . . . ?'

Coming up to where the crows were, Ermes stuck his head out the passenger's side to see better, and the cigarette nearly slid out of his mouth.

In the flutter of black wings, in the disorderly plunging of heads and beaks, he glimpsed a hand lying on the asphalt, a hand covered in clotted blood which might have belonged to a small woman or a child. The rest of the figure was covered by the shapes of the large birds, their feathers glistening like tar.

It was a matter of seconds.

Having passed the scene, Ermes looked in the rearview mirror: nothing but the crows, intently pecking the asphalt, then taking flight towards a dreary rest area overgrown with weeds. No corpse. No hand. He rubbed his eyes, crushed out the cigarette in the ashtray.

Yes, he needed a break and some coffee. The umpteenth stop in those glistening non-places, the umpteenth espresso, the umpteenth heartburn.

Ten minutes later he got off the highway and parked the Scania in the area reserved for trucks.

He would have given anything to get rid of his back pain, to erase the image of the crows with their idiotic eyes scampering around that helpless little hand.

Too much butter. There was always too much butter in the truck stop croissants. Even so, he couldn't stop eating them because they somehow gave him a sense of familiarity, of security. That mushy taste on the back of his tongue was always the same, it never changed.

He chugged the coffee, thanked the fat woman with the washed-out eyes who was squeezing oranges behind the counter and dragged himself to the bathroom.

He was assailed by the smell of stale urine and cleaning

products. For no particular reason, he thought of his ex-wife and his son; it took him a few seconds to remember their facial features, the way they laughed or said his name.

Yellow-painted nails, carrot-colored hair.

In front of the mirror he rinsed his face and swallowed some aspirin. His backache refused to let up, shooting out warm rays of pain just above his buttocks.

There was no one in the restroom. Letting out a long hissing fart, he headed towards the nearest toilet without looking at his own reflection.

Eat, shit, sleep, suffer, die. What a strange, repulsive contraption a human being is, he mused, surprising himself with the gloominess of his thoughts.

After cleaning the toilet seat with a large handful of toilet paper, he made himself comfortable; while he defecated, he kept his mind occupied by reading what dozens of travelers had scrawled on the restroom walls. Another certainty in his uncertain life. However far he might go in his Scania, whichever truck stop he might stop at, the restrooms always contained those written testimonials of a passage. Absences made into presences through words, scratched into the particleboard panels or traced with permanent markers.

As usual, a good ninety percent of the writings were obscene, for the most part offers or requests for sexual services accompanied by a telephone number.

Ermes stopped on

YOUNG COUPLE SEEKS HAIRY TRUCK DRIVERS
FOR MEETUPS

and

GAIA THE SLUT, CALL/FUCK

He started to laugh, a bitter, disgusted laugh. Then, as he

let his eyes run along the door of the stall, the desolate mirth caught in his throat. In the riot of obscenity and stylized male members, his attention was caught by some angular writing in fluorescent yellow that stood out from the rest.

And not only because of its color.

He read aloud:

> *There is no escape from the road*
> *of black whirlpools that swallow tar,*
> *take the junction, get to Uironda,*
> *become part of this realm!*

Uironda. It had been that name which had startled him, which had pressed a memory switch in his brain, triggering a scene he had experienced . . . how many years earlier? At least thirteen or fourteen, when he was little more than a novice at the job, a young man filled with hopes and good intentions, for whom the road hadn't yet become a bore.

Uironda. He had heard the sound of the word, and now it was in front of him, written down. Memory is a strange thing. A meaningless term linked to a stupid little story told to him by a stranger. He had heard it uttered only once, at a truck stop in the Rho Fiera area near Milan, where he had pulled off to take a short nap, and now those moments returned to the surface as if by magic, with extreme clarity.

After a siesta in the rear cabin he had climbed down from the vehicle to get a coffee and phone Daniela, who was his girlfriend at the time. He had come across three truck drivers, between forty and sixty years old, seated at the edge of a flowerbed, drinking and talking; a tattoo-covered guy with a long beard resting on his chubby belly gestured to him, holding out a can of beer fished from a cooler full of water and ice.

'Have a seat with us here where it's cool, boy,' he had invited him with a smile, showing two rows of nicotine-stained teeth. 'The highway's not going anywhere, don't worry.'

Ermes had obeyed, had introduced himself under the comradely gaze of his three colleagues, and had taken part in a discussion that was surreal to say the least.

'A pleasure, Ermes. I'm Massimo, and that's Vittorio and Roby. We were talking about weird stuff,' the tattooed man had explained, including the other two with a wave of his hand. 'When you spend a good part of your life on the road, all sorts of things happen to you, for sure.'

'Oh, yeah,' had replied Vittorio, a wiry man with the skin of an iguana and eyes overrun with capillaries. In his dilated pupils you could read his urge to speak. 'I was just telling about the time I was on the CB with a fellow trucker from Bari, Amos. Amos was his handle. We often crossed paths on the Turin-Milan stretch, and we would talk for a few minutes, as long as the signal lasted. Anyway. It's night, a shitty night, one of those where you're running behind schedule and you can't stop and you can't wait to crack open a beer and have a shower and some undisturbed sleep. Amos and I have been tuned into channel five for a few seconds, we've just greeted each other and exchanged a couple of words, but I can barely hear him. Amos sounds strange to me, his voice is tired, but most of all it's *far away*. I say to him a couple of times: "Amos, is your radio working, is your CB all right, are you already out of range? Because you sound far away." And he goes: "Vittorio, I am far away, yes. This is the last time we'll speak. I just wanted to say goodbye. Safe travels." Then the transmission jams suddenly and it's like my CB is going crazy. Static, weird sounds, I think I hear screams . . . then . . . silence.'

Vittorio had run the beer can along his sweaty brow, interrupting himself and fixing his gaze on the eyes of the others with a mysterious smile. Scratching his long beard, Massimo had invited him to go on, with the look of someone who has already heard a story dozens of times before. Roby, the other driver, the oldest and quietest, with sad eyes and only a few thinning hairs, held his head down, smoking a stinking cigar. Vittorio had resumed the story, this time looking Ermes straight in the eyes.

'So, I try to reestablish contact with Amos, but nothing. A few minutes later I catch another fellow on that frequency, we start chatting about this and that. And then at some point he goes, "Did you hear about Amos?" He knew him too. I get a chill at the base of my spine, you know, like when you have the feeling you're about to hear something you don't want to hear, and I respond, "Heard what? We talked a few minutes ago on the CB, the signal was bad. He said some odd stuff to me." My colleague is silent for a few seconds on the other end, and then he bursts out: "What the fuck are you talking about? It's impossible, Vittò. You must be mistaken. Amos died yesterday morning. He ran off the road on the Gambetti viaduct and went flying off. I thought you knew. It looks like . . . it looks like he fell asleep at the wheel. There's no way you could have talked to him." I swear, I got goosebumps, my legs started to shake and I had to pull off onto the shoulder to catch my breath. And suddenly I recalled Amos's words: "*I am far away, yes. This is the last time we'll speak. I wanted to say goodbye. Safe travels.*" And that's the strangest thing that's happened to me in thirty years of driving a truck,' Vittorio had concluded, winking at Ermes, who had listened to the tale with a mixture of fascination and disbelief.

It was then that Roby, the third trucker, had broken in. It was then that he had heard the word which now, traced in yellow lettering on the door of a stinking lavatory, was once again before his eyes: *Uironda*.

The man had begun to speak in a meek, almost childish voice. The spirals of smoke from his cigar softened his features, which were wrinkled with grooves, his fingers gnarled and twisted from gripping the wheel and maneuvering the gearshift.

'Yours is a curious story, Vittorio,' he had begun, squashing the butt of his cigar under his boot, 'but I have a better one. Well, really I don't know if it's better, but it's certainly more interesting than some run-of-the-mill highway ghost.'

Despite his feeble voice and melancholy eyes, the old man had given Ermes a feeling of wisdom and authority.

'Have you ever heard of Uironda?'

They had all just shaken their heads and fetched a second beer from the cooler, ignoring the soundtrack of horns and engines beyond the glass-and-cement outline of the truck stop.

Roby had scratched his bristly chin and opened his mouth a couple of times silently as if he couldn't find the words. 'Uironda is a highway exit that doesn't exist but is there, which takes you to a town or a city that doesn't exist but is there. Or rather, it exists, but not on this plane. Like an overlap, an interference. Uironda is a mirage. It's a story that goes around among those older than us, a kind of urban legend. A Romanian trucker told it to me when I was first starting out.'

'I don't understand,' the tattooed guy had interrupted him. 'Never heard of this Vironda.'

'*Uironda.*'

'Tell us more.'

'Well, the Romanian who told me about it wasn't very clear. According to this guy, Uironda is a place that you can reach or glimpse when you've spent too many years on the road and the continuous headlights on your retina, the repetition of certain structures and habits, has set your mind in the right way. When you've been driving for hours and the view is always the same, and the guardrails, the architecture, the road, are repeated in an identical way for kilometers, sometimes it's like you're hypnotized, have you ever noticed? And that's the moment when it's like you're in a trance, when you're driving while your mind is somewhere else, and when you're most liable to doze off. And that's the moment when the highway exit leading to Uironda can be seen: when you're at the limit, desperate and confused, when you're dead inside and the road has taken away too many hours of your sleep and too many moments of your life. You can see the exit for Uironda and in some way . . . take it. That's how it was explained to me.'

'What the hell kind of story is that?'

'It's a sort of word-of-mouth myth that goes around in our narrow circle. I've been sitting on my ass on that truck seat for forty years, and I've happened to hear that name other times too. Whispered in a truck stop bathroom, shouted by a drunken whore in a parking lot, crackled from a truck's CB radio . . .'

Ermes, who had listened to the story with extreme attention, had leaned forward. Back then he used to buy pulp sci-fi novels on his breaks and read them before bed, and Roby's story had captivated him.

'So this Uironda would be a kind of parallel reality, if I understand right? Another dimension, like you read about sometimes in science fiction books?'

'That's right, boy, something like that. Have you ever thought about the life we truckers lead? We live in a sort of alternate reality with regard to normal people. Highways, truck stops, parking lots, they're are all non-places, places people pass through and immediately forget . . . We're the ones who know them best, who live them the most. Uironda is supposed to be a kind of alternative reality in an alternate dimension. Something like that, boy, indeed.'

'And what's supposed to be in this Uironda, if I might ask, Professor Roby? And why that name?' Vittorio had mocked, concluding the question with a vulgar sneer.

'The guy who told me the story was pretty vague on that point too . . . First he said that the dead are in Uironda. Those who died on the road. Who go there to spend eternity, in a kingdom of metal and cement. Then he muttered that there's something in Uironda that none of us would ever want to see but which at the same time we would want to contemplate with all our might. The most terrible and unspeakable desires, the deepest fears, the darkest hopes, the atrocities we've committed. As for the name . . . well, I couldn't tell you. *Uironda*. It's a name like any other, for a place *like no other*.'

'And someone . . . well, does someone claim to have been

there? Have you ever met someone who says they've been to . . . Uironda?' Lenzi had asked before draining the last of his beer.

'Uironda doesn't exist, boy. It's a highway legend,' the man had cut him off, spitting a yellowish gob on the asphalt. 'And if someone claims to have been there, well . . . they're either full of shit or out of their mind.'

Ermes sat on the toilet a few moments longer, staring at the yellow writing without seeing it, the memory of the first time he had heard of Uironda unraveling in his mind, then he wiped himself, got to his feet, and took the cell phone from his jeans pocket.

He snapped a couple of photos of the poetry, read the words aloud, uncertain why he was doing it:

> *There is no escape from the road*
> *of black whirlpools that swallow tar,*
> *take the junction, get to Uironda,*
> *become part of this realm!*

Maybe to have proof.

To remember.

And maybe to spread the absurd legend of Uironda, recounting it to some fellow driver to kill boredom.

After washing his hands and rinsing his face, he headed once more to the café area. He ordered a second coffee. His eyelids felt heavy, like they were encrusted with grit. The chubby barista had disappeared, replaced by an elderly dwarf with a bristly moustache doing its best to hide an enormous harelip. The convenience store chain's cap lowered over his forehead conferred a ridiculous, clownish touch.

Ermes observed him captivated while he made the coffee, his insect-like movements, the skin of his neck a desert of wrinkles and ugly spots. His age could be anywhere from seventy to a full century.

'Here's your espresso, Signor Lenzi,' he croaked, pushing the little cup towards him with a smirk. He had too many teeth. Too many tiny teeth.

'Thanks a lot,' responded Ermes, reaching for a packet of sugar. The movement stopped in mid-air. A tightening in his lower abdomen. 'How do you know my name?'

The old man looked at him with a perplexed air, tilting his dinosaur neck a little to the side. 'Sorry, what did you say?' His harelip quivered.

'My name. You said, "Here's your espresso, Signor Lenzi". How did you know it?'

'You're mistaken,' squeaked the old man. Now his face was deadly serious, molded wax over pale skin. 'You must have heard wrong.'

Ermes tried to think of something to say, but all he did was gulp air like a fish out of water. All of a sudden he felt very tired, uneasy, *scared*. When he managed to speak, the words didn't coincide with his thoughts.

'Say, have you ever heard the story of Uironda?'

What the hell are you saying? his mind shouted. He looked around as if to make sure that no one had heard him. Only then did he realize the truck stop was empty. Not a soul. The stagnant smell of burnt toast lingered in the air, mixed with the stench of exhaust fumes.

The old barista started to laugh, the tired chuckle of a derelict. He slipped off his cap and put it on the counter, rocking his head from side to side, his skull full of dents, as though someone had taken a hammer to it.

'No. I've never heard of Uironda.' His amused expression suggested exactly the opposite. 'But let me tell you one thing . . . There are two kinds of death: sometimes the body remains, other times it vanishes along with the spirit. This usually happens in solitude, and, not seeing the end, we say that the person disappeared, or left on a long journey. Do you catch my drift, Signor Lenzi?'

Once again he showed his smile of microscopic sharp teeth, and Ermes couldn't help taking a step back.

'How do you know my name?' This time he had shouted.

The old man remained motionless beside the coffee machine, staring at him and laughing.

Ermes turned around and rushed out of the deserted truck stop. The last thing he heard before sprinting across the parking lot straight for the Scania was the crow-like voice of the barista yelling, 'The espresso is on the house, Signor Lenzi! We hope to see you again soon!'

Half an hour after resuming his drive, Ermes began to seriously doubt his own mental faculties. The more he thought about the business with the old man at the truck stop, about the little hand among the crows, about Uironda, the more he was convinced that depression and failure had once more gotten the better of his judgment.

And yet the poetry was still there, in the photo taken with his smartphone. He hadn't dreamed that.

His only desire was to return home. Rest. Spend the weekend with his son, at the sea, in the mountains, any place other than the road, the nothingness of a pointless journey. He cast a glance at the photo of Simone hugging Daniela's headless body.

He turned on the radio, but no matter how much he fiddled with the dial all he could pick up was static and a strange chanting. Radio Maria, probably. He hoped he hadn't lost his antenna, promising himself to have it checked at the next stop.

He gave up on music and put his mind on autopilot.

At 11:57 he realized that the traffic was thinning out in a strange way. It was almost lunchtime, and that stretch of bypass lined with monstrous coal-stained factories was usually so congested that you could count yourself lucky if you didn't waste more than ten minutes getting past it. Now, on the other hand, the Scania marched on without a hitch as the sky filled with clouds that were assuming a worrying yellowish tint as they advanced along the horizon.

Ermes turned his eyes towards a rickety Multipla that was passing him at a steady speed. It seemed to him that there was something out of place with its occupants: the driver's head looked squashed, featureless, dangling on a too-thin neck, while the woman in the passenger seat had her hands on the dashboard and her head bowed like she was preparing for a violent impact. In the back, nestled in a car seat, something shuddered that was more like an enormous hunk of flesh than a baby. Ermes accelerated to match the Multipla's speed, but it shot by, leaving a puff of yellowish smoke behind it; before it disappeared around a wide curve, Lenzi thought he glimpsed some bizarre shapes tapping on the vehicle's rear windshield, shiny black figures that reminded him of the jaws of a stag beetle, the exoskeleton of some exotic insect.

Could they be going to Uironda? he wondered, dumbfounded. He couldn't get that little story out of his head.

He rubbed his eyes, filled with a sensation of bewildered detachment, trying to keep his thoughts on driving, on driving and nothing else, and after having tackled another twenty kilometers with his heart beating in his chest like a bass drum, he had to accept the absurd fact that he was alone.

Alone.

There were no other vehicles on the highway. Only the old Scania with its now lusterless chromework and the tractor trailer creaking like an old rocking chair. He slowed down, looking out the windows as if he had been marooned on a desolate, alien planet.

There had to be an explanation.

You were distracted and took the wrong road, you didn't see a road work detour and you kept driving along a stretch of closed highway . . .

The cloud front, a catarrhous cascade of ochre fog, rolled in his direction, crackling with pink lightning, feeding his sense of bewilderment. The words of the old barista at the truck stop came back to him and he felt goosebumps running up his arms.

There are two kinds of death: sometimes the body remains, other times it vanishes along with the spirit. This usually happens in solitude, and, not seeing the end, we say that the person disappeared, or left on a long journey.

Nor were any vehicles to be seen in the lanes traveling in the opposite direction, beyond the dividing barrier. The landscape along the sides of the bypass seemed the result of a sloppy copy-and-paste: factories, water towers, lopsided cement high rises, all the same, gray, depressing. Ermes couldn't pick out a single recognizable building in a stretch he had driven thousands of times. On the top floor of a gloomy apartment building, behind broken windows that recalled chipped teeth, he caught sight of two figures looking out, possibly a woman and a little boy. He wondered what they were doing in that crumbling structure.

Soon it would start raining. Maybe hailing. A vague smell of iron and electricity in the air foretold it, an odor that smelled of urgency, as the storm front rushed on. Too yellow, too bulbous, too *tangible*.

Ermes Lenzi's umpteenth work trip was assuming the features of a nightmare.

He couldn't tear his eyes away from the horizon. Some frothy offshoots of cumulonimbus began to coagulate under the action of the wind, and for several moments they recalled a titanic face silhouetted in the sky, a bald head with white eyes and no nose, its mouth curved in a sardonic sneer of disapproval. An explosion of low-timbred, guttural thunder erased its features and Ermes was assailed by fear.

A primal, irrational fear, like he had never experienced before.

And you could say he'd had plenty of fear in his life. He had experienced frequent panic attacks after the breakup with Daniela. On a couple of occasions he had thought he was dying. But now it was different. As if every cell of his organism, every recess of his mind, quivered with a terror that had nothing to do with death, with annihilation.

His first idea, dictated by instinct, was to make a U-turn. Stop the Scania and drive full speed down the wrong side of the road, anything to put distance between him and those angry clouds, that deserted highway. He had to go back where he had come from, maybe get to the truck stop with its strange harelipped barista and the disturbing yellow writing in the bathroom stall.

He had to come across cars, people, someone.

He lit a cigarette with parkinsonian movements, ordering himself to think rationally.

A U-turn was out of the question. He would risk jail and lose his job for what in all likelihood would turn out to be nothing but a flight of fancy, an illogical alteration in his mind, which had been chewed up by the stress of the past months.

'Fuck!' he swore. 'Breathe. Breathe.'

He had to keep going towards the next exit, the next junction. There was no other option, and he couldn't be very far. How much time had passed since his last stop?

He directed a questioning look at the digital tachograph and was hit by a wave of nausea. It should have shown the kilometers traveled, the time elapsed since his break at the truck stop, but the digital numbers had been replaced by seven simple characters, which fluttered on the display like a crazed sign:

UIRONDA

The cigarette slid from his lips onto his lap. He brushed it away with an irritated swipe, pulling the truck over to the shoulder.

And descending from the cab so he no longer had to see that writing, his chest squeezed in a vise, Ermes Lenzi realized he had stopped the Scania about ten meters from a road sign indicating a junction. The sheet metal sign was a dark yellow color, stained with rusty streaks. The writing, in an elegant and out-of-place cursive, left no room for logic.

Next Exit – Uironda

He stood there observing the sign, his arms hanging slack at his sides. The world – which world? – was cloaked in a terrifying, unnatural silence. Lenzi knelt down on the warm asphalt, bringing his hands to his face, a tormented statue of flesh erected to challenge the road and the imminent storm.

After trying to phone his ex-wife and a couple of friends – no signal – Ermes climbed into the cab of the truck like a fat caterpillar. The pain had returned to gnaw at the base of his spine with the tenacity of a mastiff. Somehow the excruciating throbbing that tormented him brought him to a state of quiet resignation. Slumped in the seat, his hands on the wheel, he practiced the breathing exercises for panic attacks, trying to find sense in the madness that he was living.

Hadn't there been days when he had wished to be the last man on Earth? Days when the desire to disappear, to be alone, far away from problems, from anxiety, had become an obsession, a necessity?

You've got your wish. No traffic, nobody to interact with, no nothing. Just you and the road, just you and a goal, finally: Uironda.

He smiled, rummaging in his shirt pocket. There was one half-crushed Camel left in the packet. He decided to save it for a more opportune moment. Then he turned the key, shifted into first and advanced at a crawl, passing the road sign that had so greatly disturbed him.

He would drive until he reached the next exit. No, he couldn't turn back. And if that exit really led to Uironda, well ... he would take it, enter the territory of superstition, of urban legend. Deep down all he was looking for was a way to shake up his dull life, a distraction, a spark that would reignite his will to live, his curiosity. This could be his chance.

Uironda.

The storm had caught up with him. Carried on the wind,

the first raindrops beat down on the Scania's windshield. It was a dirty, yellowish rain that the windshield wipers struggled to sweep away, smearing the glass with greasy gunk. Maybe the storm was coming from Africa, loaded with sand and dirt. Ermes rolled up his window and accelerated, launching the truck into the fury of the elements.

It was like entering a tunnel full of liquid dust. The vehicle's headlights could barely cut through the rain to illuminate the center line.

The digital tachograph went completely mad, showing sequences of figures and numbers apparently devoid of meaning. Every so often, like the flash of a strobe light, the name of the mirage junction appeared on the display, the non-place that old truckers whispered about, men like Roby, the first – and last – person to pronounce 'Uironda' in his presence.

Ermes clenched his teeth and squinted his eyes, concentrating on driving, praying to get out of the storm as soon as possible. Violent gusts of wind assailed the trailer, making it swing on its suspensions. He had never driven in similar weather conditions. He was dealing with a freak storm that reduced visibility almost to zero. The wind's cries were like the howls of a dying beast, and very soon in the overwhelming yellow cloud Ermes noticed some dark shapes outlined beside the windows, in front of the windshield.

Disembodied shadows. Twisted hands stretching towards him in an attitude of supplication. He tried to ignore them. And he decided to turn on the CB radio, tuned to channel five.

'Is . . . is anyone listening? Over,' he whispered into the receiver. He hardly recognized the sound of his own voice, a gritty rasp. 'This is Ermes, is anyone there?'

The radio crackled, a hiccup of static discharge and chopped-up syllables.

'If . . . if there's somebody there, listen, I think I'm lost. There's no one on the road and I'm in the middle of this storm that came out of nowhere and . . .' Ermes swallowed saliva. He didn't like the cracking in his voice, the tears at the corners of his eyes. He was about to give in to panic, to start crying and screaming like a child terrified of a monster under the bed. He pulled himself together. 'If anyone's there, please respond. I don't know where I am. Over.'

And finally someone spoke. A friendly, familiar voice. And just because it was so familiar, it was frightening.

'*Daddy?*'

'Si-Simone?'

It was his son. The words were faint, barely audible, coming from an unfathomable distance, but without a doubt from Simone's vocal chords.

'Yes, Daddy. When are you coming home, Daddy? I miss you.'

Ermes Lenzi gave in to the irrational. He tried to calm the sobs that threatened to shake his chest. 'Simo, Daddy's coming soon, all right? Daddy's coming soon and he'll take you to the movies, okay? Daddy's coming as fast as he can.'

The realization that he was lying came over him. The terrible certainty that he would never see his child again.

'We're waiting for you, me and Mommy,' Simone crackled through the receiver, and now the voice was his *and yet not his.* Altered by a liquid gurgling, more like the sound of a flooded engine than a human voice. 'Me and Mommy are waiting for you at home. *In Uironda.* Come.'

'I'm coming. I'm on my way. Daddy's coming, Simo.'

On the other end, silence.

Ermes Lenzi put his foot down on the gas pedal, his face disfigured by a mad grin.

'*There's no escape from the road, the black whirlpools that swallow tar, take the junction, reach Uironda, become part of this realm!*' he began to murmur.

He kept going until, after an interminable while, he found himself outside the storm once more, greeted by a night without stars, black and cold like damnation.

A viaduct towards nothing, a strip of tar hurled towards a ghostly horizon. A single asphalt lane with no guardrails, suspended over the Abyss, on a dark blanket from which no light reflected. This is what Ermes' reality was reduced to. Everywhere he looked there was only impenetrable blackness. The Scania's headlights barely lit up the asphalt.

He proceeded at thirty per hour because if he made a single mistake, if he ran off the road, he was sure he would be precipitated into an eternal void of no return, like an astronaut adrift in outer space. A sci-fi movie he had seen with Daniela came to mind, a film whose title he didn't remember. There was a spaceship, a metal colossus that moved thanks to propulsion from an artificially created black hole inside it, and there were nightmares that took form to drive the passengers to madness. How did that film end? Not well. Not well. Ermes told himself that happy endings were for the weak. That in real life happy endings were nothing but an illusion.

Far off, on the right side of the road, a point of light materialized. Red. Perhaps a streetlight, or the emergence of a planet or star.

No.

As he advanced, other crimson flowers blossomed in the darkness, reminding him of a swarm of fireflies on the motionless surface of a lake.

They seemed to be the lights of a village or small town.

Ermes felt he had almost arrived. He sensed it from a dull vibration in his chest, in his bones. His back pain had disappeared. He kept his eyes fixed on the bright beads taking shape on the horizon.

Uironda?

Without thinking, he rolled down his window and was struck by a warm wind that smelled of decay. He gasped for breath. He wondered what the all-pervading darkness outside the cab would have whispered to him if that darkness could speak. Would it have told him the story of Uironda, its genesis, its why? He hoped to have an answer soon to the swarm of questions buzzing in his skull.

The road began to climb. At first gently, a false plain that made the old Scania's motor rev; then more, still more, until Ermes had the sensation of proceeding vertically.

Maybe he was.

Lost in that ditch of darkness, he wondered if concepts like direction and gravity still had any meaning. All that he could do was follow the road. Go with it, like he had always done.

The lights were still there. Clearer now, closer. Red lights that cast a scarlet glow on a river or a street.

He couldn't wait to reach his destination. He sped up.

And it was then that a noise worked its way through the awkward grumbling of the motor. It came from the rear cabin, the narrow space that had been his home for the past few months. Dull thuds, like someone was throwing punches at the dividing wall or a violent struggle was taking place. The blows ceased with a screech, a muffled wheeze, a shout.

'Don't do it! Ermes, stop, pleeeeeasehelpussssssss!'

Ermes was about to stop the truck when the headlights lit up a road sign, the first he had seen since emerging from the storm.

WELCOME TO UIRONDA

A hundred meters further on the street forked to the left. The Scania, as if impelled by an invisible force, took the junction without Ermes' having to turn the steering wheel. The wheels started to vibrate as the truck tackled a sharp bend overlooking a sea of darkness; for a moment it seemed that the vehicle had tilted forty-five degrees toward the passenger side, to the point where Ermes had to hang on to the wheel with all his strength. Finally, with a jolt, the old Scania stabilized and emerged from the curve spitting smoke in a deafening scream of pistons.

And it appeared.

Beyond the windshield.

Ermes found it before him all of a sudden.

Glistening, ruthless, dead.

Uironda.

The tires screeched on the asphalt, and the truck came to a stop a few hundred meters from the city walls.

Immense pinkish walls, from which a tepid wind of death blew.

The trucker got down from his cab, advancing towards the outskirts of the city-mirage with watery eyes and gaping mouth.

It wasn't like Roby, the old trucker, had described it so many years earlier.

No one who had died on the road, no architecture of sheet metal and cement.

At least, not for him.

For him, Uironda was flesh and torment. A colossal error — the final one — born of obsession, of the disintegration of that little he had managed to create in his existence.

It took him long minutes to be able to embrace and comprehend the vastness and complexity of the vision, to make out the individual parts of it.

From enormous, heinous acts come enormous, heinous hells.

First he took in the minor details, if that was the right term for thresholds and structures that were dozens of meters high: a nostril, a lip like a slimy snail, an ear. Then, stepping back, trying to observe the panorama in its entirety, like an explorer seeing an immense mountain chain for the first time, he had a fleeting view of the whole.

Buttocks and legs, bellies and ribs, forearms and hands turned into plains, plateaus, hills, mountains. Hairs like alien trees, wrinkles like streets, blood like rivers.

Everywhere, in the skin, destruction. Bare structures of tormented, lacerated epidermis, torn muscles, disarticulated joints. Immense wounds that had become doorways, gashes made into windows, bluish bruises like the mosaics of archaic, forgotten temples.

His Uironda.

Two colossal bodies entwined in a last embrace of blood, disbelief, and pain, a frozen anatomical city on the autopsy table of final understanding.

The bodies of a woman and a child.

Ermes screamed. That scream did not express fear or remorse. Simply astonishment, as every doubt left him, as he understood and remembered. He made out a hand the size of a cathedral raised towards the sky, manicured yellow-painted nails the size of whales. Pinkish hills of battered breasts, the dark portal of a navel.

Far off blazed what at first had seemed to him a surreal field of red-tinted grain. The stems waved in the hot wind, pungent with decay.

Hair so red that it called to mind a violent sunset.

The childish mouth open partway in a vain attempt to escape asphyxiation.

Simone.

Ermes wandered a long time in the territories of Uironda. He beheld the gigantic rosette of a neck without a head, separated from the body in a rage of senseless violence and thirst for vengeance.

Daniela. Oh, Daniela, I'm sorry.

The two windows of cerulean blue eyes in a face as large as Notre Dame.

He slipped into each of the city's orifices, under teeth archways and eyebrow columns; he passed through aisles of mucous membranes and earwax-encrusted caverns, his feet making squishy sounds in the ever-present crimson puddles.

He smelled the wounds and the cuts, where the knife had performed the martyrdom that no father and husband should ever carry out, he passed his trembling hands over the unusable tubes of the severed veins, stared crying at the buttresses of the vagina surmounted by the altar of the clitoris. He heard the death rattle of nerve endings damaged beyond repair.

When he was too tired to go on, Ermes Lenzi lay down under the shadow cast by Daniela's severed head, on a mattress of hair half covered in brain matter, contemplating the dark sky that was lit up by the blood of Uironda.

He lit the last remaining Camel. It smelled of smog and bodily fluids.

Simone's glassy eyes, immense like only a child's can be, studied him accusingly from the western extremity of the city-mirage that had revealed the truth to him.

My God, what did you do? My God my God my God . . .

His back sent him a lash of perverse pain.

The same pain experienced when he had crashed down on the rocks a few seconds after jumping off the viaduct.

The rotten wind ceased to blow.

The bloody fluorescence of Uironda dimmed like embers from a forgotten bonfire.

It wasn't long before Ermes Lenzi plunged into a dreamless sleep, the last Camel still clenched between his fingers.

And as his eyelids closed, as the motionless Uironda clung to him like an authoritarian and terrible mother, the trucker knew that the city, with its burden of hells and remorse, would be there waiting for him when he awoke.

Glistening, ruthless, dead.

For eternity.

The Carnival of the Stag Man

When the GPS hurled the stylized car into a grayish ocean of pixels, Omar slammed on the brakes and spat a loud 'Fuck!' The Ducato swerved and skidded before coming to a stop in the middle of the road. Putting his nose to the windshield, Omar took a look outside.

Darkness and silence. A heavy rain poured from the sky, forming liquid darts in the glare of the headlights. The tops of imposing beeches and maples swayed lazily in the distance, accepting the whims of the wind with indifference.

He didn't have the slightest idea where he was, nor how to get back on the main road.

'Watch out, GPS isn't worth a damn up in those hills. And there are more roads and lanes in the Volturno Valley than wrinkles in my scrotum,' his father had warned him a few hours earlier, with his typical classiness.

Omar had left home in late afternoon with plenty of time to spare, his GPS set to Castelnuovo al Volturno and a couple of glasses of Aglianico wine in him.

He couldn't be late for the carnival.

He hadn't been the least bit thrilled at the prospect of spending the whole night amid a cavalcade of idiots in masks. Parades, floats, and village festivals had lost all appeal for him centuries ago, when some screaming fatso in a gorilla suit had scared the crap out of him. That fucking monkey had haunted his childhood dreams for years.

But work was work. The managing editor of *L'Eco del Molise* had hinted that a nice piece on the Carnival of the Stag Man of Castelnuovo al Volturno might open new doors for him.

'One day, who knows, maybe editor-in-chief . . .' he'd said slyly, and Omar had let himself be suckered in like a rookie.

And now here he was. In the middle of nowhere. Up and down the hills with a GPS that wouldn't cooperate and only two Marlboros left in the pack.

The Carnival of the Stag Man was a nighttime parade, but if he kept dicking around in the mountains he'd miss it: his Swatch showed it was nine already.

He grabbed his phone, scrolled through his contacts, and called his friend Ivan 'Human Compass' Renzetti, who had gotten that nickname for his sense of direction. Asking for some tips – and hearing a familiar voice in that sea of shadows – sounded like a great idea. Then he saw that damned message glaring at him from the display: NO SIGNAL. Not even one bar.

'Shit!'

He lit his penultimate Marlboro and started the van again. He had to hurry. Get back to some spot recognized by those goddamned satellites whizzing around outside the atmosphere in their mysterious trajectories.

The vehicle rolled on into the night.

Twenty minutes later, along a mule track lined with pale shrubs and bramble bushes, a festering, mud-oozing wound in the soft flesh of the hill, the Ducato snorted, sputtered, jerked, and died.

'What the – ?'

Omar hadn't cried in years, but he felt a lump the size of a plum rising in his throat, bringing tears and snot along with it.

'No. Please,' he protested, turning the key.

Then he saw the fuel gauge pointing to empty and began punching the steering wheel until his fingers seemed on the verge of splitting open to show the bones underneath.

What the fuck do I do now? Huh? he thought, panic rising inside him.

He glanced at the GPS. The digital car was being tossed

around in a whirlwind of pixelated characters and nonexistent roads.

Oh God. Dad will never let me live this down.

He tried his phone again. Nothing. He cast a sad glance at the Marlboro packet, weighing whether to sacrifice the last cigarette. He decided not to.

'Better get a move on, cowboy,' he taunted himself, opening the door. He jumped down from the van and his feet sank into ten centimeters of slime. He stifled yet another curse and took a look around.

The headlights lit up an unpaved path that vanished into a cavern of trees, the black and starving mouth of a vegetal face. The hills pressed in on all sides, rustic giants encrusted with mud, rocks, and shrubbery.

He looked up at the sky. At least it had stopped raining. The clouds were starting to break up into lumpy bundles, allowing the starlight to illuminate the valley.

Omar switched off the headlights, grabbed the GPS, locked the Ducato, and turned on his heels, putting some distance between himself and the tunnel of trees. It gave him the creeps.

Get back on a paved road. Find a house. Find a phone. Find somebody —

He didn't have time to finish the thought. A sound in the distance

CRACKATUMP

made him turn around suddenly. In the uncertain light, he thought he could make out the outlines of two distant trees bending on the hill to his right. He looked closer, squinting. No, not bending, *toppling to the ground*.

CRACKATUMP

This time he saw it clearly with the help of a sliver of moon that had suddenly appeared in the sky. There were trees falling up there. Two. Three. Four.

Binoculars. There should be binoculars in the car.

He went back to the van and rummaged around in the glove compartment. He couldn't see anything. He switched on the overhead light. Then the headlights.

And then he spotted the human figure standing motionless in front of the windshield.

A human figure with only one arm.

Omar screamed.

Bucci was lying face down on his belly in a thicket of junipers. The thorns didn't bother him, nor did the icy rain drumming against his back.

The only thing that mattered was revenge. Eradication.

He reached towards the round mirror to stroke its surface, then made sure the welding goggles were still there, in the pocket of his filthy coat. They were.

He spat in the grass, held his breath, and listened. To try and catch a sound that would reveal the presence of the Beast. Hoping that this would be the time.

Nothing. The forest held its breath along with him.

He got to his feet and hid behind the trunk of a maple. He pulled a plastic bag from his inner coat pocket, slipped a hand inside, and grabbed a generous handful of animal dung, moss, rotten leaves, dead salamanders, mushrooms.

Forest smells.

Wild smells.

He rubbed the mush on his face, on his clothes, behind his ears, under his armpits. He had been doing it once a year for twenty years now; by now he was used to the stench. He managed to stifle the retching and not vomit on his feet. It was disgusting, but necessary.

He had to smother the stink of man. To keep the enemy's huge nostrils from catching a whiff of him. He had to catch it by surprise, it was the only way he could win. With cunning. Bucci knew it.

Twice he'd had contact with that ... *thing*. The first time when he was a boy, and he had lost an eye and his brother. The second as an adult, a hunter, and he'd almost gotten killed.

He had been waiting for it for twenty years. Twenty years during which he had spent the last Sunday of carnival crouching in damp caves, hidden beneath the roots of some centuries-old tree, lying in the underbrush. And the Beast hadn't shown up.

Gl'Cierv awoke according to his own cycles, after long periods of hibernation. But Bucci was an old man now. He was running out of time to settle the score.

He imagined the residents of Castelnuovo al Volturno, down in the village, dressed up as the Stag Man. At that very moment they would be tucked in their ridiculous costumes, laughing and dancing.

Fake fur and horns, witches with plastic noses, little kids in brown face paint.

But in their eyes, especially the old people's, shadows danced. Reflections of primal terrors.

A pantomime to exorcize the myth, tame it. A thousand-year-old ritual that had turned into buffoonery.

Laughing and dancing had always seemed pointless to Bucci. *Problems should be eliminated at the root*, he thought.

Leaning against the trunk, he was about to sit on the slimy ground when he heard the sound.

A vehicle.

'No, no, no!' he whispered to the darkness. Who the hell could have come all the way out there on a night like that one? Some tourist, no doubt, though it had never happened before. Arriving in that godforsaken part of the valley in the middle of the night was unlikely. And in that weather it was almost impossible. Unless they were very stupid. Or unlucky. Or both.

The beams from the two headlights pierced the darkness,

projecting oblong shadows of trees onto the ground.

'Go. Away,' Bucci pleaded. Then he heard the engine die with a choking sound. A car door opening. Stifled curses.

He hit the tree with his fist in a gesture of annoyance. If Gl'Cierv was out there, it would smell the poor sap. It would be aware there were humans in the woods. And his plan would be ruined.

What should he do?

He felt a rush of despair. He was tired. Twenty years of waiting, tears, searches, nightmares. Especially nightmares.

Suddenly he was struck by the certainty that he would die without the final showdown, that the creature that haunted the Volturno Valley would go on sleeping in its den dug out of the hills. That a life spent chasing his demon would end in a stalemate.

The headlights went out, plunging him into darkness again.

He would wait there, disheartened, waiting for morning to come, and not worry about the stranger, the night, the . . .

CRACKATUMP

Bucci jumped. Some trees had fallen.
Maybe it's a coincidence, the ground giving way because of the rain –

CRACKATUMP

No. It's here, he rejoiced mentally when he heard the sound again.

He put on the welding goggles, picked up the mirror, and left his hiding place, setting out at a run along the dirt road. He emerged from the cavern of vegetation the very same moment the headlights came back on, blinding him for an instant.

Bucci slipped in the mire. He swung his only arm to maintain his balance, running the risk of dropping the mirror, then stopped in front of the van, motionless as a statue.

The boy inside the Ducato screamed.

Omar barely had time to close the door before that cross between a tramp and a character from *Mad Max* came up to the vehicle and smashed the window with his fist.

'Help! Help!' he cried.

Bucci unlocked the door and threw it open.

'If you want to live, follow me.'

'Wh-what?' Omar stammered. 'D-don't hurt me, please.'

'I'm not here to hurt you – ' the old man began, and then suddenly went silent.

A deep, guttural sound reverberated through the woods, a sort of powerful gasp that echoed off the hills.

'I'm here to save your ass,' he finished, as Omar's eyes grew big at the sound of the noise.

'What was that?'

'There's no time to explain now. If you want to live, follow me!'

This guy is crazy, the young man thought.

Then the sound reached his ears again, even closer. Even more *pissed off*. He didn't know what it was, but it was . . . out of place. It elicited a long chill up his spine and an unpleasant contraction of his sphincter.

In the moonlight he saw other trees crashing down on the hill, vegetal dominoes collapsing in their direction.

He looked at the old man. He stank of shit and sweat. A gush of bile rose in his throat; he forced it down and spoke: 'I . . . got lost. What's going on here? And that mirror, what's that for? I was supposed to write an article on the Carnival of the Stag Man, then the GPS . . .'

Bucci's face lit up, splitting into a maze of wrinkles. 'You're in luck, boy. Maybe tonight you'll get to learn the origin of the carnival. The myth behind the masquerade. The only thing is – believe me – there's nothing human about that thing.'

Yes, he's crazy.

'I've got a hiding place close by. I'll explain everything.'

A warm puff of air swept through the forest, smelling of undergrowth and decomposed carcasses.

A gust of death.

Immediately after, the roar-scream-bellow-gasp-cry was repeated with renewed strength.

Omar jumped down from the van.

'Let's go.'

The old man led the way, crossing streams and rills slippery with moss, stopping every so often to catch his breath and sniff the air. He didn't say a word, but the whole way Omar had the clear sensation that something – something large plowing through the bushes with the breathing of an asthmatic – was following them.

Finally they reached a little alcove, dug out of a rocky wall centuries ago. Omar hesitated a moment before going inside.

What if this guy wants to rape me? Or kill me?

The animalistic cry that swept through the valley made his mind up for him.

Bucci concealed the opening with some shrubbery. Then he took the welding goggles off his forehead and handed them to the boy: 'Put these on. They'll protect you from ...' He finished his sentence by pointing distractedly at his left eye. Only then did Omar notice his eyeball was a shriveled, whitish prune in the socket.

'You owe me an explanation. I want it. Now.'

'Gl'Cierv. It lives in these woods, always has,' the man said, as if talking about something that was common knowledge.

'Gl'–what?'

'Gl'Cierv. The Beast Who Sleeps in the Hills. The monster at the origin of the Carnival of Castelnuovo al Volturno. It has reawakened.'

Omar burst out laughing. He was dreaming, of course, lying in the back of the van. Or else he had made it to the festival, overindulged on cheese and wine, and was now lost in an abstruse, drunken delirium.

'You laugh?' Bucci yelled, grabbing Omar's wrist and squeezing it hard. 'You think this is funny?'

'Let me go!'

Bucci released his prey; when he started to tell his story, his good eye seemed to be lost in another place, another time: 'The first time I saw it I was seven. I was here in the woods playing with my brother, the morning of carnival. It was hidden under the leaves, the son of a bitch, we had walked right on top of it, understand? It stood up, we fell over. My brother ... he ... couldn't get away. It tore him to pieces with its horns. And then it swallowed him.

'I looked for a moment into that creature's red eyes, and my eyeball exploded like a grape in a press. Hell was in those eyes. That's what the welding goggles are for. They protect you. For a bit, at least.'

'And the mirror?'

'To kill it. You've heard of Medusa?'

Omar shook his head. It was madness.

'I vowed revenge,' Bucci went on. 'I searched for it, I followed its traces for a long time, but that thing is good at hiding. It sleeps and wakes according to cycles that are beyond our comprehension. I was almost fifty when I met it the second time. Twenty years ago. This is the result,' he muttered, unbuttoning his coat and showing Omar the stump of his arm. It looked like a piece of gum that had been chewed, then spat out and left to dry in the sun.

'What is it?' Omar asked.

'I don't know. Nobody knows. But I've read a lot over the years. There's no question the Carnival of the Stag Man is the modern-day descendant of a ritual meant to appease the Beast. Anthropologists have tried interpreting it all kinds of ways, linking it to the myths of Dionysus, Faunus, Kernussos, the Wild Man of the Woods. What do I think? That beast is the specter of a vanished species. The hatred of a whole extinct race that has congealed into a creature that's monstrous, but real. Of flesh and blood.

'Thousands of years ago a species of giant deer, the Megaloceros, was widespread in Molise. Over six meters at the withers, and the antlers – the horns – eight, nine meters wide. Scholars are convinced that it went extinct as a result of our ancestors' relentless hunting. When it awakens, the Beast starts to roam through the woods, killing some poor wretch or making two young lovers disappear. To avenge its species and remind us that we are nothing. Nothing.'

The scream exploded about a hundred meters from the cave. Omar jumped.

'It'll smell you,' Bucci said with a smile.

'Wh-what?'

The old man took the bag of organic matter out of his coat.

'If you don't want to wind up in its belly, smear this stuff on you.'

'There's no way I'm –'

'Look. Look out there.'

Omar stuck his head out of the shelter. In the distance, along the steep ridge of a hill, four gnarled trees were moving.

When he noticed they were hairy, he realized they weren't trees.

They were legs, as big as oaks.

He smeared the filth on his face, puked in a corner of the cave, and fainted.

He awoke to the song of an owl. At first he didn't know where he was. Then he remembered everything. The old man, his story, that glimpse of a vision in the night.

He was alone. The welding goggles lay beside him. He put them on his head and cautiously left the cave.

No one.

'Hello?' he tried calling.

He began to follow a path that wound through the trees, feeling like an idiot. He'd let himself be taken in by a madman.

Yes, but those legs . . .

The power of suggestion, what else? He should be thankful that crackpot hadn't robbed, raped, butchered him.

He took his phone out of his filthy jeans. A signal. One bar, but a signal. He called his father. He answered on the third ring.

'Who is this?'

'Dad, listen – '

He was cut short when a figure burst from a thicket of ferns, screaming '*Gl' Cieeeeeeerv!*'

Then the old man crashed into him, dragging him to the ground. Instinctively, Omar lowered the lenses of the welding goggles over his eyes. He looked up.

The creature was advancing through the woods, mocking every known natural and anatomical law. Its antlers, twisted and leathery masses, blocked out the now cloudless sky. The head of the animal (*animal?*) was an offense to normality. Deer-like features, but caricatured, exaggerated. Enormous teeth riddled with holes, a misshapen snout that oozed fluorescent snot and, embedded in the skull, two eyes the size of soccer balls, two pupilless red sclerae from which a livid light emanated. Of a color that Omar had never seen before.

He blessed the welder's goggles, and knew that if he kept his gaze on the creature's any longer he would go mad.

He lowered his eyes, observing Gl'Cierv's body. The fur was torn in several places, allowing a glimpse of bones and entrails, but of something else too. Living things writhing in bubbling sewage. And eyes. Small yellow eyes. A deer's.

Old Bucci, soaked with sweat, held the mirror with his one hand. Omar, lying beside him after the tumble, gave him a distraught look as he spoke: 'It's . . . grown. Since the last time I saw it, it's grown!'

Bucci got up and went to meet the horror that reigned in those godforsaken woods. Holding the mirror in front of him like a shield, his eyelids tightly shut so he wouldn't lose his mind.

'Gl'Cierv! Bastard!'

The creature lowered its snout to ground level. When it saw its own reflection in the mirror Bucci was holding, it let out a gasp. Then it screamed, collapsing to its knees, making the valley quake, throwing up sodden earth and branches.

Omar felt something splitting inside his ears. There was a *crick* in his eardrums, then the pain exploded. He knew that if he survived his hearing would be damaged for life.

The Beast writhed. A disgusting milky serum began to flow from its eyes.

Suddenly Omar felt sorry for that enormous creature, struggling in desperate spasms as Bucci advanced with the mirror in front of him, spewing insults and curses. A man, a nonentity, was destroying a terrible, but extraordinary being.

An ancient one.

We're killing a god, part of his mind murmured. *We're killing a myth.*

As if in a trance, he picked up a large branch from the ground, then walked over to Bucci and hit him over the head with the improvised club.

The old man collapsed in a bed of leaves. Gl'Cierv let out a cry that Omar interpreted as a sigh of relief. Then it brought its snout close to the boy. Trembling, Omar closed his eyes, expecting the worst.

He felt something moist and foul-smelling, a huge rotten sponge, passing over his face.

Only when the creature started to move away did Omar realize the Beast had licked him.

As if to thank him.

He took the last Marlboro from the pack and put it in his mouth. He lit it and took a deep drag.

He watched Gl'Cierv staggering on its huge pointed hooves, wondering whether he had done the right thing.

And whether anyone would ever believe he had saved the specter of an extinct species.

Or maybe a god.

Queen of the Sewers

I t started one autumn morning. One of those mornings when the clouds hang low and still over Valdichiana like faded slabs of slate, staining the green of the hills with ash and haze.

The way it started was stupid, ridiculous.

The septic tank.

Jesus, it started with shit, and we were engulfed in it.

I was sitting in the kitchen sipping some black coffee, enjoying the warmth of the pellet stove and the view from the large arched window overlooking the northern foothills of the valley. I was waiting for Simona to get out of the bathroom. Not anxious, not in a hurry.

Balance. Everything was in perfect balance.

Business at our family's little shoe factory was on a roll. Two years of sacrifices, hard work, projects and investments, culminating in solid financial security and the fulfillment of our dream: restoring an old farmhouse in that charming corner of Tuscany.

'*One could not possibly find more beautiful fields; there is not a single spot in the terrain that is not worked to perfection in preparation for sowing.*' Goethe's words, taken from his *Italian Journey*, in which he describes Valdichiana as a flourishing, sunny, prosperous place.

For a while I thought so too.

We'd been enjoying our new nest for six months. We were

on cloud nine. And not only because of our prosperity, the house, the money.

'Almost finished!' echoed Simona's voice from the bathroom, muffled by toothpaste foam.

'Take your time, Simo. You want me to go with you?'

'No, thanks, I'll take my car so when I get off work I can stop in Arezzo. I want to do a little shopping. The doctor said it's important I move around. For my legs, the circulation, you know . . .'

I smiled. 'Okay, all right.'

A month earlier I had come home one Monday from the factory to find the table set with our good dishes. And my wife smiling as she opened a bottle of Chianti we had been saving for a special occasion. Her eyes shone with a mysterious light. I had understood right away, maybe precisely because of that light.

Moments like that are rare. They stand out in your memory, but at the same time there's an indistinct, surreal quality to them, as if they don't entirely belong there.

'Should we make a toast, Marco? Then I'll have to lay off wine for a while,' she had whispered, rubbing her belly. 'What do you say, *Daddy*?'

The sound of her footsteps in the hall brought me back to the present, wiping a silly smile from my face. I walked over to her and gave her a little kiss on the neck, savoring the scent of conditioner that lingered on her cherry-colored hair. She hugged me.

I held her tight, asking her, 'How are you today?'

'Mmm. Pretty good.' She had rings under her eyes. 'I didn't get much sleep last night, but the doctor says that's normal, especially at first. I had a weird dream, but I don't remember it . . .'

'Hey, hey, don't make me worry.' I took a step back, looking at her face.

'You're going to be a great father. It's nothing, don't worry.

I go to the gynecologist the day after tomorrow.' Then her expression suddenly changed, transforming into a mask somewhere between amused and disheartened. 'There is one thing . . . I think it's back again.'

'What do you mean?'

'The septic tank. There's that stench again, coming from the toilet and the sink. Stronger this time. Last night too, when I took a bath . . .'

'Are you serious? Fuck . . .'

'Hey, watch your language! Don't you know babies start learning while they're still in the womb?' She chuckled. 'Go and smell for yourself. It makes me sick to my stomach.'

I headed towards the bathroom with a defeated look, Simona following close behind me.

I caught a whiff of the unmistakable smell of rotten sewage as soon as I reached the doorway. A problem that had come up all too often since we had moved into the new house.

'You're right. Sweet Jesus, that stinks,' I blurted out, approaching the toilet with a disgusted grimace. The stench was intense, pungent, *different*.

'Could it be clogged?'

'I don't think so. It can't even be a month since we had someone here to clean it out. Did you flush anything strange down it? Tampons? Paper towels?'

'What are you talking about?' she replied emphatically. 'You've told me over and over again not to – '

'Okay, okay, I was just asking,' I snorted. 'I guess I'll have to go down and check the sewage level.'

Our farmhouse stood in an isolated area dotted with a few cottages, agricultural businesses, farms, and ranches. An old building dating back to the early 1700s, which we had restored to perfection, trying not to disturb the original structure and using trustworthy companies to do the work.

Because of their remote location, these buildings often aren't hooked up to the municipal sewer system. Like in our case.

The real estate agency had assured us that the septic tank, about ten feet deep, worked perfectly; all the same, we'd had it emptied and cleaned before we moved into the farmhouse on a permanent basis. But even during the first weeks we lived there a faint stench had begun to hover in the bathroom, floating through the hallway like a ghost until it reached the bedrooms, the living room, the kitchen. It didn't happen often, but it was a real pain in the ass, especially for Simona: pregnancy seemed to have heightened her sense of smell and sometimes she found the odor unbearable.

A second call to the plumbers seemed to have resolved the problem.

Until that morning.

'You remember what to do?' Simona asked. 'The guy from Mr. Flushy explained it all to you.'

I rolled my eyes, hugging and tickling her. 'Yes. I open the manhole, put the wooden rod in, and if the shit level goes over the notch it means the sewage is too high and the drain may be clogged . . . Mr. Flushy, were they really called that?'

'No, I was just kidding. And now I'd better go, I'm already late.'

We kissed, a long passionate kiss.

'All right, I'll call you later and let you know . . . Have a good day. I'll check it out, then I'm headed to work too.'

'Bye, baby.'

'Bye. Don't work too hard.'

I went back to the kitchen to finish my coffee. From the window I watched Simona going out into the courtyard, looking distractedly at the leaden sky.

It was cold in the garage.

Before going out I put on an old sweatshirt, grabbed the wooden rod to check the sewage level, and pressed the garage door opener.

Outside I was greeted by a damp fog that blurred the contours of the garden gate, the flowerpots, the wrought iron gazebo.

'This sucks,' I thought out loud. I didn't find the idea of breathing the stench of our excrement very appealing, especially at that hour.

I shivered as a violent blast of wind from the hills blew across the valley, making me squint. Soon the fog would clear, making way for a typical autumn day of gusty winds, leaves, and clouds.

The heavy manhole cover over the septic tank was just an indistinct circle, hard to make out in the intricate geometric design of the paving stones. I approached it grudgingly, while the bitter taste that sometimes comes with haze tingled at the back of my tongue.

The old cement slab covering the pit had a hinged metal lid, four inches on each side: the access to the inspection chamber. I lifted it with my foot.

I wasn't ready.

I doubled over almost at once, my hands on my knees.

Backing up, I held my breath.

The stench was unbearable.

When I was a child, Sammy, our family cat, disappeared. It was summer, a scorching August, moist like an infected wound. We looked for him for four days. My mother was desperate, she adored the little beast. The fourth day we found him. By following the smell.

Sammy was in the cellar, in the washing machine. He had slipped into the appliance through the opening in the back and had died there next to the motor, alone. My father said cats did that sometimes: when they felt the end was near, they went off to die somewhere, far away from everyone, trying not to disturb anyone, just like when they were alive.

Maybe Sammy hadn't wanted to cause a disturbance, but he hadn't succeeded: he had stunk up the cellar for at least two weeks.

The stench I smelled opening the inspection chamber – the stench of death – had something of the same quality but was definitely worse.

It lasted a few seconds. I retched several times. Then the odor was still just as intense and disgusting, but manageable.

I asked myself what we'd been eating the past few days, then with a silly giggle I pulled my sweatshirt over my nose and approached the pit, sticking the wooden rod in forcefully.

The end sank about eight inches into the opening, then met resistance. Something soft, like foam rubber or a trash bag full of rotting leaves. I pulled the rod out; it wasn't soaked with sewage, but with a thick, sticky substance that dripped onto the pavers, spreading that nauseating stench in the autumn air.

I hissed a curse. The tank was blocked then, and I wondered what could have built up inside to clog it like that. Judging from the small amount of free space in the inspection chamber, it must have created a massive stoppage. I was sure I hadn't put anything down the toilet or the other drains; it must have been Simona, even if she denied it. I imagined a bolus of Q-tips, tampons, cotton balls, all kinds of non-biodegradable materials united in one inextricable mass that had blocked the drain pipe. And yet the situation continued to bug me. I had told her many times: 'Only toilet paper down the toilet.'

And then there was that stench.

I went back to the garage to get the curved iron rod that I used to move the manhole cover. I would have to open it and check the extent of the damage, then put on rubber gloves and pull out the waste; the prospect of sticking my hands in there increased my nausea.

I fetched a face mask from the tool cupboard and put it on.

Outside the fog was starting to rise in coils, only to make way for the uniform grayness of the sky.

I inserted the curved end of the rod into the hook on the manhole cover and began to pull with a certain effort to move it aside. It was very heavy. The cement scraped against the pavers and somewhere far off a dog barked; then its cry turned into a terrified yelping.

When the passage was halfway open, the stench attacked my nostrils with renewed violence, despite the face mask.

Bending forward over the pit I made out a dark and shiny mass that I couldn't identify. It really looked like a bulging trash bag. I moved the cover all the way aside to allow the dim early morning light to filter underground and I looked again.

A movement.

A sound.

Waaah.

Another.

Waaah.

Like a lament, a call, a cry.

A baby's cry.

'No!'

Idle moments. Fragments of eternity. My brain unable to assimilate that sound, which had been described to me so many times when I was a boy.

I stayed there transfixed for a few seconds, empty, then a series of unprintable profanities issued from my lips. My voice, muffled by the mask and my fear, seemed to belong to someone else and made me waver. My heart pounding madly, I pushed the lid back in place with frantic movements.

'*Fuck fuck fuck!*'

My back was covered in a film of icy sweat.

I dropped the iron rod. Without thinking, I opened the garage door, got in the BMW X3, and started the engine. I backed out, stopping with the right rear wheel directly on top of the septic tank cover.

I didn't know if the weight of the manhole cover would be enough to hold back what I thought I had seen.

Then I went back inside and closed the door to the garage.

And double-locked all the others.

★

I couldn't say how long I wandered in a daze from room to room, telling myself that I must have heard and seen wrong, that I was mistaken.

Waaah.

Yet now the stench hovered in the rooms like an unclean, invisible presence, a phantom determined to prove my fears were well founded.

I had stopped smoking the day Simona told me she was pregnant. But now I was craving a cigarette.

When I managed to calm down, I called the shoe factory and told my secretary I wouldn't be in that day; I mentioned something about a fever, possibly the flu, then went to the living room and poured myself a generous helping of brandy. It was around nine-thirty a.m.

My cell phone rang, startling me; the glass almost fell out of my hand.

Simona. I answered, trying to hide the tremor in my voice.

'Hi, honey, how's it going? Are you already at work? I wanted to find out about the septic tank . . .'

'No, no, I'm at home, I'm not feeling too well. The tank . . . I haven't checked it yet,' I lied.

'Geez . . . Are you very sick? You seemed fine earlier . . .'

'It's nothing major, just a bit of a headache and a stuffy nose, but I think I'll stay home today. How are you?'

I walked over to the window facing the courtyard. Simona was saying that her day was going great.

Mine a bit less great.

I looked outside. A vise grip of terror seized my testicles; the SUV was moving slightly, like something was pressing on the manhole cover *from inside*, making the vehicle rock back and forth on its suspension.

'S-Simona . . . we'll talk later, okay? I'm gonna go lie down,' I managed to stammer into the phone. She said something I didn't catch; my eyes were fixed on the scene outside.

I hung up, ran to the bathroom, and threw up in the toilet.

I held my nose with my thumb and forefinger to fend off the smell.

And as I knelt there with my head hanging over the toilet, threads of gastric juices dripping from my lips, I thought I heard a sound slithering up the pipes, amplifying in the ceramic bowl as though it were a sound box.

Waaah.

Waaah.

Waaah.

I closed the bathroom door and fled to the kitchen.

I looked outside again.

The SUV wasn't moving.

The manhole cover was in its place.

I stared at the clock. Time had sped up; the hands were pointing almost to ten-thirty. Without even thinking about it, I called the plumbers. I don't know why. Maybe I just needed someone to disprove my fears. To confirm the words I kept repeating in my head.

You heard and saw wrong. It was foggy. You made a mistake. Stress. There's nothing down there.

I explained that something was wrong with the septic tank, that it must have gotten badly blocked, and yes, they had to come quickly.

I sprayed air freshener in every room; the sickly sweet aroma banished the miasma of sewage. I started to relax.

The fog was clearing. The sun filtered into the room, coloring the terracotta tiles. Two nightingales sat on an oak branch, warming their feathers and talking in their secret language. The day was blossoming and I began to laugh at my silly fears.

The shiny, quivering mass I had glimpsed in the septic tank? A bag of trash that had gotten stuck in there somehow.

The rocking SUV? The wind, there was no other explanation.

And that sound, like a baby's cry, desperate, distraught? Maybe air bubbles in the pipes that produced an imitation of wailing.

Then I considered that the plumbers would arrive soon and I would have to go down, show them what the problem was, maybe help . . .

The technician rang the doorbell a little before lunchtime while I was standing at the window sipping black coffee, keeping my eyes on the SUV.

Not moving.

Of course. The wind had gone down.

I opened the gate and met the man in the yard; he gave me a questioning look when I moved the BMW off the manhole cover.

'So, what's the problem?' he asked, wiping his hands on his filthy overalls.

'I don't know, but there's a terrible smell coming into the house . . .'

'Did you check the inspection chamber?'

'Yes, it looks like there's something stuck down there . . .'

'Did you open the cover?'

'No,' I lied again, swallowing hard. 'I thought it was better to call you, you know . . .'

'Yeah, yeah, okay . . .' the man interrupted me, annoyed. Then he got to work, fiddling with the iron bar to remove the cement slab. I started to walk over to help him, but held back.

'Be careful,' I warned him instinctively, stepping back.

This time his irritated expression turned to an amused scowl. 'Careful of what?'

I didn't answer. I stood there staring at him agape as he removed the cement cover, shaking his head with a half smile.

What if it jumps out? If it jumps out, what the fuck do we do? I pondered, kicking myself for my stupidity at the same moment the technician blurted out: '*Good God!*'

Here we go. It's there. He sees it too. It's there.

'Wh-what is it?' I managed to mutter, my mouth dry, my tongue tied.

The man ignored me and bent over on his knees, pinching

his nose, pointing a small flashlight into the darkness to see better. 'How did this end up down there?'

I took a couple of steps forward and looked down.

A large black cat. Dead. Like Sammy. Sammy who had gone off to die next to the washing machine motor. It was lying on the crusty surface of the waste, its mouth slightly open, the whites of its glassy eyes shining in the darkness.

'Well, of course it was clogged! These little beasts can slip in anywhere, but sometimes they can't get out again. He's sure a big one, but how the heck did he get in? Good God, I hate cats,' the technician prattled on as he got ready to remove the carcass.

The sunlight was beating down on my face and I realized I was smiling.

I sighed with relief, telling myself I'd been a jackass. I managed a business that provided a living for thirty families and I'd frightened myself over a bit of a smell, an SUV rocking on its suspension, and a dead cat?

Had it been that poor creature making those sounds? Probably. It didn't look like it had been dead long.

There was no trace of what I thought I had glimpsed down there a few hours earlier.

No trace of the Marroca.

Nothing abnormal, strange, monstrous.

All the same, in the back of my mind I went on thinking about the first wave of that stench, the cries, and the stories I was told when I was just a snot-nosed kid with skinned knees.

Most kids who grow up in the province of Arezzo have heard of the Marroca at least once. From a relative, a friend, an acquaintance.

The beast of cesspools, sewers, stagnant water.

The beast greedy for children's souls.

My big brother, Valter, had tormented me for years with that story. It was one of his favorite pastimes, cultivated with

QUEEN OF THE SEWERS 101

grim determination. In the darkness of our room he would indulge in detailed descriptions of the creature.

'You should see it, the Marroca. It lives in drains, wells, ditches, cesspools, and it can slither everywhere. It's a kind of black slug, covered in rough hairs, and it has a mouth like a suction cup. To suck up its prey. It catches small animals, swallows them, and digests them little by little while they're still alive. Can you imagine? *Digested alive!*'

And then I would beg him to stop, hiding my face in the blankets, but he would keep going: 'It eats poop, mice, but its favorite food is the souls of kids. Little kids, like you. And the Marroca cries, like a baby, always crying, like a newborn: *Waah! Waah!* It cries because it's always hungry. Do you hear it, Marco? Can you hear it? *Waaaaah!*'

Usually he would stop when I burst out crying or screamed for my mother.

Valter died in a car accident when he was barely twenty, and his descriptions of the Marroca are the clearest thing I have left of him.

I called Simona back around lunchtime, after forking over a hundred euros to the technician and watching him walk away hauling a black bag containing the cat's body.

She answered in a flat, monotone voice. 'Yes, Marco, I'm at lunch with some coworkers, but I'm not very hungry. I'm a little tired, I think I'll come straight home after work . . . How are you feeling?'

'Better. Definitely better. Don't overdo it. If you don't feel well, call me and I'll come get you, okay?'

'Okay, don't worry. So, what about the septic tank?'

I swallowed a couple of times before answering and decided not to mention the cat. 'The plumber came . . . anyway, yeah, the sewage level was a bit high, maybe all the rain the past few days . . . Nothing serious, he pumped out some of the filth, and even the smell is gone now . . .'

And it was true. The pungent stench that had hovered in the house most of the morning was gone, replaced by the exotic scent of some incense sticks I had lit a little earlier.

But I saw the dead cat once more in my mind's eye, encrusted with excrement, and I remembered my brother's words: 'It catches small animals. It swallows them and digests them alive . . .'

What if it was the Marroca who brought that cat down there? For a snack. To digest it alive, and I interrupted it, and . . .

'Marco, are you still there? Are you there?'

'Y-yes, sorry . . . I zoned out,' I said, as the thought faded away.

We chatted a little more, then said goodbye. 'I can't wait for you to get home,' I told her.

I microwaved some leftover tortelli from the night before and ate greedily, even though my stomach was still inside out. I washed the dishes, then stretched out on the couch to watch TV, slipping almost immediately into a slumber, lulled by the pointless chatter of an afternoon talk show.

I slept.

I dreamt.

Dark pipes sinking into a subsoil that was thick and yellowish like melted cheese, inside of which I crawled in search of an exit. The clear sense of being followed, hunted by a mindless, ravenous presence.

And the more I dragged myself on my elbows through the sewage, the narrower the pipes seemed to get, suffocating me, torturing me, squeezing my rib cage. I managed to turn on my back and lift my head slightly, just to catch a glimpse of the presence chasing me in the semi-darkness.

Valter. His face green and spongy like the body of a drowned corpse, his eyes about to roll out of their sockets. My dead brother advanced with his mouth gaping, becoming flatter, thinner in the sewers with the contortions of a monstrous tapeworm, close, ever closer . . .

Waah! Weee!
Waah! Weee!

I awoke with a start, knocking the remote to the floor, while the nightmare cry went on echoing in reality. I gasped.

Riiiing! Riiing!

The doorbell. I relaxed and strode over to the buzzer by the window, astonished at how long I had slept; afternoon was dying in a bloody sunset, while the first coils of fog were encircling the foot of the hills.

I pushed the receiver button. 'Who is it?'

'It's me, Marco!'

Simona.

'I forgot my keys!'

I opened the automatic gate and waited for her on the doorstep.

We hugged, but her grip was weak and her face exhausted.

'My body is changing. I'm a walking hormone storm, Marco. It's normal for me to feel like this.'

Simona, lying on the couch, was flipping through a magazine without reading it. She had left work early, crossing the shopping trip to Arezzo off her to-do list. Some dizziness, a general feeling of malaise.

I was busy at the stove, fixing dinner.

'Well, you shouldn't take this fatigue lightly. Stay at home tomorrow and rest,' I replied, peeling an onion. From the window over the sink I could see the valley submerged in darkness, the lights of several distant farmhouses shining like stars too low on the horizon.

'It's because I didn't sleep well last night,' she grumbled, dropping the magazine on the floor. 'This afternoon I remembered my dream. Weird stuff . . .'

'Like what?'

'I remember bits of it . . . I was in the kitchen, standing still in front of the window, naked, and I was holding my belly. I was looking down in the yard, but there was nothing but fog. Fog as thick as cream, impenetrable. And . . . in the dream I was thinking: *Thank God for the fog, that way I can't see the septic tank . . .*'

I felt the hairs on the back of my neck rise. 'And then?'

'And then nothing. I woke up and there was that stench coming from the bathroom. That's it. But it wasn't a nice dream. I wouldn't call it a nightmare, but it's had me on edge all day. That ever happen to you?'

'Sometimes.'

In the tunnels of my brain the Thing-Valter-Marroca let out a faint cry, which I stifled with a generous glass of wine.

That night as we ate dinner we discussed plans for the future – the baby's room, a new car, the pizza oven we wanted to install in the basement – not knowing that there wasn't any future.

We went to bed early, it had been an intense day for both of us. Simona cuddled up against my back, and her breathing lulled me to sleep like a mother's loving lullaby.

I didn't hear her get up and go into the bathroom.

But I heard her scream my name.

'Marco! Marcooooo!'

I struggled out of a heavy, restless sleep, a blade of light filtering from the hallway into the dark room. It took me a few moments to find the switch for the bedside lamp and fling my legs off the mattress, hurling myself towards the bathroom, running after my wife's voice.

She was sitting on the toilet, leaning forward, her hands pressed against her stomach. Her panties had slid down around her ankles. I thought stupidly that I had never seen her wear red underwear before, then realized that the satin fabric was soaked with blood.

I knelt down at her side on the frozen tiles, putting my hands on her knees. 'What's going on? Simo, what's happening?'

My voice came from a long way off, from somewhere above my head.

She raised her head to look at me: skin as white as paper, red eyelids, snot and tears, and above all those wide, frightened, bewildered eyes. 'Something's wrong,' she gasped. She pointed at her belly with a trembling finger. 'It hurts. Christ. Christ, it hurts.'

I ran my hand along her sweat-glistening forehead. She was ice cold. 'Okay, Simo, don't worry, I'll get my phone and call an ambulance, don't worry, baby . . .'

I tried to reassure her, but my voice quavered and I didn't know if my legs would make it all the way to the kitchen. I saw blood splatters on the toilet seat, thick, dark, sticky blood.

When I went to get up, Simona clung to my arm. 'Don't leave me. I'm scared. I'm scared!'

'It's going to be fine. Everything's going to be fine.'

I wriggled away gently, smacked a kiss on her hair, and rushed into the kitchen. I groped from the solid walnut table to the marble countertop by the sink, I looked on the window-sill, on the coffee table in front of the TV. Where had I put it? Where?

'Shit!' I cursed, spotting the phone between the couch cushions.

I had just dialed 911 when Simona called for me again. But this time her cries were so shrill and high-pitched that it sounded like her vocal cords were tearing.

The hairs on my arms stood up like pins.

She wasn't calling me. She was *begging* me. Then she started swearing in dialect, and that might have been what scared me most of all. I had never heard her use such expressions, ever.

Finally a tremendous *bleeaah* and the splash of vomit hitting the floor.

'I'm coming, Simo! I'm calling an ambulance! I'm coming, baby . . .'

As I ran to the bathroom I stubbed my little toe against the table leg, hard, and a dance of stars took my breath away and blurred my vision.

I limped to the bathroom doorway with my phone pressed to my ear.

I heard the operator's words, far away, as if through a wall.

Then I smelled it. The same as that morning at the septic tank, when I had lifted the cover of the inspection chamber.

I pressed a palm to my mouth, felt the stubble tickle my hand.

I fought the urge to vomit, the acidic taste of gastric juices rising in my throat.

Then the scene unfolding in the bathroom canceled out everything else, and sight was the only sense I had left.

Simona was on the floor, curled up under the sink, her arm shaking with uncontrollable spasms, pointing at the toilet. Her face was distorted by a scream, damp locks of hair clinging to her cheeks like wet rags. Vomit and blood stained the tiles, my wife's footprints stamped in that mess of bodily fluids.

I remember thinking: *If she opens her eyes any wider, they'll roll out of her head.*

I followed the direction of her delirious gaze.

Perched on the edge of the toilet, soft, as black as a brand-new tire, absurd, was the Marroca.

It wasn't how I had imagined it when Valter used to describe it to frighten me.

It was overwhelming, as overwhelming as the stench it gave off.

Lying there with the calmness of a dog in its kennel, rubbery, a leech/slug/worm out of a zoologist's wildest fantasies. It sat in a pose of strange complacency, like this was its right, like it was *fair*. Its two extremities, front and back, hung limply towards the floor, the one indistinguishable from the other. It might have been as large as a Labrador. Jesus Christ, it could have swallowed one whole. I wondered how the hell it had managed to come up through the drain, to leap out of the toilet in my house while Simona was sitting on it.

She was sitting on it!

The horror, the paralysis, gave way to a calm that astonished me. What I was looking at wasn't real, this wasn't happening to *me,* so I had all the time in the world to enjoy the show.

I saw it breathing, the lazy contractions of the center part of its body.

The small, flipper-like appendages covering its sides were pawing, endowed with a perverse autonomy. I guessed they were the creature's means of locomotion, how it pushed its way through the sludge, the sewage.

The streak of black fur on its back, a mane of shaggy hair.

And the pale outgrowth that suddenly stretched towards Simona from its front end, like an anteater's tongue, that started to slither and sniff the blood.

Blood.

Between my wife's thighs.

On her clothes.

On the floor.

Smeared on the wall.

The baby.

The Marroca.

The baby.

'What's happening there? What's happening?' someone was babbling from my Samsung.

Finally I resumed contact with reality. I muttered something at the operator, my wife's sick, Valdichiana, Strada dei Larici 14, help us.

What a stench.

Shock hampered my movements, but keeping my eyes fixed on the thing, I moved towards Simona, dropping the phone, launching myself beside her. When I got to her she had fainted and I thought that was good. Ideal.

Groping blindly, I managed to grab a heavy perfume bottle from over the sink. I hurled it furiously in the creature's direction: the bottle sank into the Marroca's side with a liquid gurgle.

The nightmare raised its head in our direction, spraying drops of foul-smelling drool on the mirror. Two small white dots, eyes washed out like those of an albino, peered into mine. With a sound much like a raspberry, the Marroca opened its mouth wide; I could make out nothing but a liquid and slimy darkness mottled with crimson hues.

Blood.

Then the queen of sewage took her leave with a farewell.

Waah!

Waah!

And before it slid into the toilet, like a filth-soaked sponge forced into a small container, it produced the sound that drove me to grab other bottles from the sink, hurling them towards the toilet, even when the beast had already vanished, reentering its underground world of feces, cockroaches, and darkness.

Daa-ddy! Daa-ddy!

The ambulance and squad car arrived twenty minutes later. The operator had heard the terrified screams and notified law enforcement.

Simona and I were still under the sink; she had fainted and I was in a state of extreme confusion. At the hospital they looked after my wife and tried to get me to talk, to help them understand what had happened. I don't remember what I said. I don't remember if I talked about the Marroca.

I emerged from that mental state several hours later. A doctor came to talk to me. She told me that miscarriages are more common than one might think and that the fetus can be *evacuated* – evacuated, that was the term she used – in simple cases of blood loss. In Simona's case the blood loss had been extensive. Excessive. But she was doing all right now. Physically, at least.

Oh, we could try again.

No problem.

Simona was strong.

The doctor rambled on while I sat there in a daze on the white bedsheets. She was concerned. She couldn't understand what had caused Simona's severe psychological distress, and, to a lesser extent, mine.

'What happened in that bathroom? Won't you tell us?'

I would have really liked to, if only she'd believe what I had to say.

I covered my face with my hands, letting out several sobs.

The woman looked at me with a perplexed air. She didn't find my response satisfactory, that much was clear.

I didn't care.

I just wanted to sleep.

I dreamed of unborn babies. Souls in limbo. Sentient stenches floating in the night. Cats and fetuses digested in a chilling darkness.

We never went back to our 'nest' in Valdichiana.

We moved to Arezzo, to the top floor of a nice apartment building downtown.

We underwent a number of couples' therapy sessions, and Simona managed to convince herself that what we had seen was the product of a trauma-induced *folie à deux*.

I had told her before about Valter, about the Marroca. The two of us had reworked and materialized that creature in the real world to explain away those terrible moments. An explanation that seemed to satisfy her, corroborated by large doses of psychiatric drugs.

A load of bullshit.

I didn't see things the same way, but I didn't feel like contradicting her. We tried to have another child. We tried hard, for months, to no avail. The doctors said there was nothing wrong. We just had to relax. It was all psychological, they thought.

Three years later Simona and I split up. She moved back in with her parents, I stayed in Arezzo on the top floor of a nice apartment building. Things weren't going well anymore. To tell the truth they hadn't gone well since that night. There was always a shadow. Black and stinking.

Now I get up, work, eat, watch a movie, read a book, sleep, start all over again, with few variations. The days are almost indistinguishable, and it's fine that way.

I feel guilty. I keep telling the empty rooms that I should have trusted my first impression that morning when I lifted the septic tank cover and heard the cry.

I decided not to believe it, and things turned out how they did.

Choices.

Forks in the road.

Mistakes.

They say time heals all wounds.

I say it depends on the wound.

If the wound gets infected, it just gets worse with time.

Every so often I hear from Simona. We never talk about what happened. She's getting by as well as possible. We've stayed on good terms.

Some nights, when I lie awake staring at the designs cast by the streetlights on the bedroom walls, I think I can hear the wailing of the Marocca, echoing up from the sewers through the building's pipes, in the basement, in the stairwell, faint vibrations that make the spiderwebs sway and the insects flee, until the wails manage to drag themselves out of the toilet, the bathroom sink, and the bidet.

Waah.

And then I get up and walk down the hall barefoot, so I don't make any noise.

Waah.

Air in the pipes, I tell myself, what else?

I lock the bathroom door, but I never have the courage to look inside. I remain there, my forehead leaning against the wood, my fingers on the doorknob.

Daa-ddy! Daa-ddy! someone seems to whisper from just beyond the door.

And then I go back to bed, pull the covers over my head and pray for the oblivion of sleep to come soon.

The Strait

My father was watching the sea from the window, the gray waves chasing each other faster and faster before crashing on the coast in a froth of white foam. It was impossible to distinguish the shadowy hues of the water from the ashen ceiling of the sky. As if sea and clouds had merged into a single, tormented entity.

Crumpled in a chair, my mother was crying silently, wiping her tears with the edge of her apron.

'Miché! Why doesn't he come back? Why isn't he back yet?'

My father didn't answer. His black eyes scanned a phantom horizon and I wondered what he was thinking. He was worrying at his right thumbnail, nibbling on it, the only gesture to betray his concern.

My mother repeated the question, her voice charged with anxiety. I had never seen her so worried. She was a strong woman, tempered by a life of waiting and sacrifice, the life of every woman who marries a fisherman. But this time it was her eldest son at the mercy of the rough waters.

'Miché ... You say the storm pushed them north, up that way, towards the Strait? My God, this waiting is giving me palpitations, I can't stand it anymore. Miché, it's one of those days, isn't it?'

'Mmm,' was Dad's response.

Sitting at the table, my nose in my homework, I watched the scene with a heavy heart. I was only ten years old, but I knew when the sea was bad.

Really bad.

And wicked.

I watched the breakers, the turmoil of the water feeding malevolent whirlpools, seagulls tossed about in the gusts like scraps of paper.

I wished the sun would come back.

My brother Antonino had set sail the day before from the little port of Villa San Giovanni along with his partner, Vituzzo. Then the south wind had risen.

Fishing was their life, just as it had been my father's. Until he broke his legs falling into the cargo hatch during an unfortunate outing. A force-seven sea, a miracle he got out alive. Since then he's kept busy doing small carpentry jobs and maintenance at the harbor.

I prayed for another miracle. Antonino and Vituzzo hadn't come back yet, they had been out for almost twenty-four hours. Not long enough to bring in the Coast Guard, and yet I knew that weather conditions like these would have spelled trouble even for sea dogs with more experience than my brother.

It was the dawn of the '70s, boats and navigation instruments weren't as reliable as the ones today. But I realized that it wasn't just the fury of the sea that was making my parents anxious. There was something else.

'Miché, are you going to answer me? It's one of those days, isn't it?'

My father sighed. 'Yes, Carmela. That is, I don't know ... It could be one of those days, yes. "When sea and sky become one, She emerges from her lair and the Other makes ready," that's what the old-timers used to say. The currents are pushing towards the Strait, but if the fishing was good maybe they didn't go out that far – '

'Two months ago Antonino saw the Fata Morgana!' my mother interrupted him. 'It's a bad omen!'

'The Fata Morgana is an optical illusion, Carmela. Nothing more.'

Dad had explained that strange phenomenon to me before.

On calm days, after a heavy rainfall, the water particles remain suspended in the air, creating a sort of natural magnifying lens, and the coasts of Sicily, observed from Calabria, appear much closer than they really are. Some fishermen believed that witnessing the Fata Morgana phenomenon was a harbinger of bad luck.

'Yes, but you believe in the story of the Strait!' Mom insisted. 'Don't you, yes or no?'

'I believe in what my father told me. And you know very well that my father was a man with both feet on the ground.' He chuckled, as if to break the tension. 'As far as it's possible for a fisherman to have his feet on the ground.'

He walked over to Mom, ran his hand through her hair. 'Carmé, if the sea calms a bit I'll take my boat and go find Antonino. If they're not back by tonight we'll notify the authorities. Everything will be fine.' He leaned down and gave her a kiss on the cheek. That gesture, a rare display of affection, surprised me. Mom and Dad were hard people who had grown up in a difficult place and time, a Calabria scourged by the war, poverty, and the Mafia.

I got up from my chair and went for a glass of water.

'Who emerges from her lair when the sea and sky become one? Who is the Other?' I asked.

They turned around to stare at me. I think that until that moment, gnawed by anxiety, they had hardly noticed my presence.

'Nobody, Giuseppe. They're just old fishermen's stories,' my father interrupted me, but I saw Mom covering her face with her hands. 'Now go to your room and keep quiet, your brother will be here soon. He's a clever boy.'

'Dad, the sea is really bad, huh? If you go out later to look for Antonino, can I come with you? To give you a hand.'

He looked back towards the sea. He was fifty years old, the skin on his face weathered from salt and squalls, but at that moment he looked like an old man, sad and worried. 'Not a chance. You stay here and keep your mom company. And anyway, nobody said I'm going out there. Only if the sea gets calmer and it's not too late.'

'But I could –'

'No arguments, Giusé. Go and finish your homework.'

'I already finished.'

'Well . . . Go upstairs, your mom and I have to talk.'

'Ugh,' I murmured, heading for the stairs.

I went upstairs to my room and flopped onto the bed. From the window I could watch the storm that was turning the sea into an unbridled beast, the heavy rainfall that was transforming the view into a uniform gray slab.

When sea and sky become one, She emerges from her lair and the Other makes ready.

The sirocco howled and ran over the foam, drawing bizarre shapes on the sand. I imagined it was the secret language of the wind, an ancient language, an alphabet that was incomprehensible to man.

I looked at the crucifix hanging above the headboard of my bed, then I knelt down, my elbows on the mattress, my hands clasped. 'Lord, I pray that Antonino is all right. Let him come back home. If you let him come back, I'll do anything you want and I'll go to Mass every Sunday.'

As if in response, the sky screamed. A powerful trail of thunder, like the roar of an avalanche.

A sound that wasn't enough to drown out my mother's hysterical cries from downstairs. 'No! No! Why don't you stop? St. John, help us, help my son!'

Around one in the afternoon the fury of the elements subsided. The wind had fallen.

I came out of my room, and as I went down the stairs I heard my parents arguing.

'Are you sure you want to go, Miché? Couldn't you ask someone to go with you?'

'There's no time, Carmela. The sea is calmer now. I'll push out northwards a few miles, then turn back. I know the area where they fish. Maybe they had engine trouble . . .'

Mom was silent a few moments. 'All right. Be careful,' she said finally.

'I'll go get ready.'

At that moment I should have been worried about my father, but instead I just felt really angry. Because I knew that no matter how much I insisted, he wouldn't let me go with him. Wouldn't let me give him a hand in looking for my brother. A refusal that hurt my childish pride.

As if in a dream, wondering what I was doing, I went back to my room and slipped on my raincoat.

I walked down the stairs softly, my legs quivering with excitement for what seemed the start of a great adventure. We would find Antonino, we would bring him home, and Villa San Giovanni would welcome us as heroes.

'Mom! I'm going to Mario's,' I lied. 'I left a notebook at his place last time. I'll be right back.'

She came to the front door with tired steps. She looked like a ghost, her eyes swollen from sobbing, and for a moment I felt a pang of guilt.

'All right. Don't be long. Dad's going out to look for Antonino.'

'Good luck, Dad,' I mumbled, noticing he had put Grandma's rosary around his neck.

He looked at me and smiled. 'Don't worry, Giuseppe. I'm sure your brother is fine.'

'I know.'

I said goodbye, then, without being seen, slipped out through the back door. The sky was gray; a fine drizzle was coming down. I started towards the marina at a run.

When I got there I spotted the *Siren*, Dad's small, salt-encrusted motorboat: a deck, a cabin, a rudder, and a small hold for storing fish.

Looking around, bundled up in my raincoat, I blessed the fact that there were no fishermen around to recognize me. Even though it was spring, it was cold. An abnormal temperature, unseasonable.

I considered the situation, the scolding I'd be in for, the opportunity to turn back; then, as a flock of seagulls darted along the surface of the water, filling the air with their discordant song, I jumped on deck and ducked into the hold, hiding in the dark under some tarps.

Once he found the deed was already done, it wasn't like Dad was going to throw me overboard.

I trembled. An image flashed through my mind: my mother at home alone, equal parts hopeful and hysterical.

Ten minutes later I heard the planks of the narrow wooden pier shaking beneath my father's heavy, limping gait.

I held my breath. He climbed aboard, messed with something on deck, then the motor roared to life. The boat pulled away from the dock, tossed by the waves, headed towards the unknowns of the open sea.

Though I was used to the smell of fish, the lingering stench in the cargo hold was nauseating. The reek of old, clotted blood. I held back a couple of impulses to vomit, maybe more because of the excitement than the stink.

I stayed hidden under the tarps, losing all sense of time, undecided what to do. I wanted to peek outside to see if we were already in open water. In one corner of the hold there was a little porthole. I slipped out of my hiding spot, praying that Dad wouldn't come down right at that moment.

A few seconds later I was holding on to the porthole's metal frame, my nose pressed to the glass. I noticed two things: we were already far from the port of Villa San Giovanni, and the wind had definitely started to pick up again – you could tell from the labored way the seagulls were flying.

I don't know exactly how far we were from the coast, but it

was strange watching the deserted beaches and the palm trees swaying in the wind while the *Siren* sped by, spurred on by the waves that raced towards the Strait. I knew that if there had been a porthole on the other side of the hold I would have been able to see Sicily, its proud and barren coasts that had seemed so close to my brother because of the Fata Morgana effect.

I was about to return to my hiding place, but a sound made me freeze: Dad's voice.

'Hail Mary, full of grace, the Lord is with thee ...'

He was saying the rosary.

I slipped under the tarps once more while I waited for the courage and the right moment to reveal my presence. Then, down there in the dark, with no company but the stench of the fish and the coughing sputter of the motor, I joined mentally in his prayer.

After a few minutes I drifted into a deep slumber.

I dreamed.

Dad and I were on the deck of the *Siren*, peering out at the sea. Every so often we would shout: 'Hey, Antonino! Vituzzo! Can you hear us?'

Suddenly two forms leapt from the water: it was my brother and his friend, naked, swimming like dolphins and following the boat, making acrobatic moves in the water a few yards from us.

As is often the case in the dream world, it seemed totally normal.

We waved at them happily, we had found them, they were alive, but then we noticed that their faces were swollen and nibbled by fish, the faces of drowned men left to steep for a long time in the water, and then we fled into the hold, unable to stop screaming and crying, and then other screams came from a far-off and indefinite place, echoing on the breakers, and I realized that place was the waking world.

The first thing I did when I woke up, ripped from the nightmare of screams, was kick myself for being stupid. How could I have let myself fall asleep down there?

There was no time for an answer. There was no time for anything. Just get out of the hold and get to Dad, who was yelling at the top of his lungs, an inarticulate flood of screams and prayers.

I'll remember those cries until the day I give up the ghost. Cries of dismay. Loss. Defeat.

Just like I'll remember the scene that met my eyes when I climbed the ladder and found myself outside again, in a lead-colored reality.

The engine was dead. Silence reigned. We were somewhere in the Strait of Messina, but every point of reference – the coasts of Calabria, those of Sicily – had vanished, swallowed up in a dense, milky fog that swayed over the sea, whirling in coils. Around the boat the water was dark and still like a stone slab, without a ripple. The black of the sea and the white of the haze created a disorienting, alien effect.

My father was at the bow, his calloused hands resting on the railing, continuing to call my brother's name.

'Dad? What's going on?'

He spun around, stared at me with a wide-open mouth, his cheeks wet with tears. He just stood there in that position, like a statue.

'Dad?'

He didn't move a muscle. I was terrified by the way he was acting. Because he was terrified too. I had never seen him cry before.

Fear feeds on fear, in a vicious circle.

I would have gladly welcomed a couple of slaps rather than see him in that state, confused and trembling. He was in shock.

I went closer, brushed his fingers with mine, then grabbed his muscular arm and shook it hard. He collapsed into a sitting position, covering his face with his hands, leaving me with a clear view.

About two yards off the bow of the *Siren* was my brother's boat, the *Queen*, cloaked in haze.

It was sinking.

Mesmerized, I watched the boat, reduced to a wreck, about to sink forever into the depths.

Whole portions of the ship had been ripped away. A section of the stern had broken off; there was nothing left to testify to its existence but a jumble of shredded planks and splinters. There was no trace of the engine. The cabin windows had exploded. The hull, its entire length covered in circular gashes of at least a foot and a half in diameter, resembled a slice of Swiss cheese.

I couldn't tear my eyes away from those holes that were taking in water, condemning the *Queen* to oblivion. They looked like *bites*. I can't think of a better word to describe them.

The way the planks had been mangled made me queasy.

Finally, unable to come up with a valid explanation for the disaster, I leaned over the railing and shifted my gaze to the deck. My young mind short-circuited.

In one corner, beside the twisted skeleton of the cabin, was what was left of Vituzzo. He was bare-chested, spattered in blood, his left arm chopped off at the elbow.

A shark, it was a shark, I thought, but I knew it wasn't possible.

My brother's partner was a doll ready for the dustbin. Broken. Unusable. That idea, pitiless and *irresolvable*, struck me like a punch to the gut, making me gasp.

Vituzzo no longer had a jaw. His tongue was sticking out of his mouth and touching his enormous Adam's apple, giving the corpse a mischievous, almost comical look. He looked like one of those masks representing Tibetan demons. His blind eyes studied the cloud-filled sky. The wind was blowing again, insistently.

Before he died Vituzzo had written something on the wall, using the only hand he had left. And using his blood like ink.

SHE

I remembered what Dad had said.

When sea and sky become one, She emerges from her lair and the Other makes ready.

Even today I don't know how I didn't lose my mind. The *Queen* was a miniature floating slaughterhouse. There was no trace of my brother.

'Antonino! Antonino!' I called, or thought I called.

The only response I got was a gust of wind that dissipated the mist around the boats. Then I heard a sort of sullen grumbling coming from my right, from the coast of Calabria. A low, continuous growl, then, unmistakable, the barking of several dogs. I turned around.

Something was moving towards us underwater at high speed, leaving a clearly visible trail of foam in its wake. First I thought of an abnormal motion of the sea, a caprice of the currents, then I noticed some bluish shapes coming to the surface, chasing each other like dolphins do when moving in large groups.

A bark, closer this time.

I ran to the cabin and grabbed the binoculars.

'Dad? What is it? What is it?'

He said nothing. With a movement that expressed an unspeakable weariness, he stood up.

I glued my eyes to the binoculars and pointed the lenses towards the wake.

And I could make out shapes in the mass that was approaching. They looked like muzzles, blue maws gaping in spasmodic and perverse expectation, eyes, heads covered in thick indigo fur, bobbing up and down at a frightful speed, coming straight for us.

They looked like dogs. Water dogs.

As they came closer, their disturbing bark blended with another sound, an attractive female voice. A song that made my hair stand on end and gave me the first erection of my life.

I told myself I was imagining it all. That Vituzzo and my

brother had been attacked by sharks. That the devastating sense of loss was making me hallucinate.

'I want to go home,' I murmured, bursting into tears.

I felt myself lifted up by two muscular arms. 'What are you doing here, damn it! What am I going to do with you, Giusé? We have to go!'

My father, returning to his senses, was shaking me a couple of inches from his face. He let me go, swearing, and cast a glance at the *Queen*. The boat was starting to tilt.

'Get below! Now!' he screamed.

The howls of the aquatic pack and the disturbing feminine warbling followed us into the hold, echoing in the silence of the afternoon like a curse.

Down there, in the semi-darkness, huddled in a corner, I watched my father and cried. I had realized that we would never see Antonino again and that the situation we were in was extremely dangerous.

An obscure, indecipherable danger.

Dad was fumbling with a crate. You could read determination in his movements, there was no longer any trace of the gibbering man I had seen on deck. Panting with the effort, he lifted the lid and pulled out a couple of cylindrical objects that looked like candles.

'D—Dad . . . Is Antonino dead? Like Vituzzo?'

A shadow passed over his face. He smiled, but it was a false, phony smile. 'No. We'll find him. He wasn't on the *Queen*. We'll find him,' he lied.

'And those things in the water . . . What kind of fish are they? Sharks?'

'No. I don't think so. Your grandfather used to talk about seeing something similar, a long time ago.'

'When sea and sky become one?'

'Right. When sea and sky become one. Stay calm. Everything will be fine.'

I realized that Dad knew a lot more than he was saying.

'What is that?' I asked, pointing at the two candles he was clutching in his hand.

'It's ... dynamite. We used to use it years ago. When our haul wasn't good, we'd try to catch a few extra fish with explosives. Now it's against the law. Well, it was then too.' He smiled. His gaze seemed to settle on another time. He slipped the sticks of dynamite and a lighter in a plastic bag. 'Come on, and do exactly what I tell you. And pray. We're going home.'

He put the rosary that had belonged to his mother around my neck and hugged me. He almost never did that. We stared at each other for a few moments, father and son, prey to unknown fears, then we rushed up on deck, turning our eyes towards Calabria.

'Don't look! Don't look!' Dad yelled.

But I couldn't help it. The spectacle offered to our eyes was chilling and hypnotic at the same time.

Fifty yards away from the boat the sea seethed with nightmare forms. Now I could make out more details of the things heading towards us. Details that revisit me in my dreams every night, thirty years later.

The water dogs. I counted seven of them, their snouts snarling, their blue fur crusty with salt deposits and algae, and yellowish fangs that opened and closed with metallic clacks, like bear traps. They had four enormous eyes on each side of their head. Black eyes, like a moray eel's, eyes whose sole function was to identify prey and tear it to pieces. Each of the beasts had a neck as thick as a tree trunk, shiny, slimy-looking.

Then, when I saw the throbbing suckers, the way their appendages knotted and twisted with sinuous movements, I realized they weren't necks. They were tentacles. Gigantic tentacles ending in dog faces.

The terror that had paralyzed us until that moment finally drove us to act.

'Help me!' Dad exclaimed, grabbing the cord to start the motor. 'We have to head for the coast!'

I joined him, while behind us the barking and growling of the beasts grew closer and closer. We pulled the cord together, hard. Once, twice, three times.

The motor refused to start. Finally, after one last vigorous tug, the boat set off.

But the dogs were right on top of us.

They were only a couple of yards from the *Siren* and the wreck of the *Queen*, which was now over halfway submerged. The seven creatures leapt out of the water in unison, arranging themselves in a sort of semicircle. Before our eyes, like in a vision, a woman emerged from the water, and I realized that we weren't dealing with multiple beings hunting us. There was only one.

The female figure was extremely beautiful. Completely bald, an angelic face, sultry lips, ample breasts; but just below the navel her olive skin changed into a thin and membranous epidermis, like a squid's, and from there the tentacles that acted as necks for the furious drooling mastiffs branched off.

The woman opened her mouth and screamed.

It wasn't a voice: it was the pitiless breath of the south wind. The affliction of a loneliness lost in the centuries. The eternal and unheard murmur of the tides.

From the coasts of Sicily someone – some*thing* – responded to the cry. A sound just as *alien*, abominable, impossible to describe in words.

'It's the Other,' my father whispered, as if in a trance. 'The one who swallows the seas.'

Then everything took on the speed and at the same time the slowness of a fever dream. Dad grabbed me, put my hand on the throttle lever of the outboard motor, looked at me, and said: 'Don't stop till you're on shore. Take care of your mother.'

He was crying again.

Then, with an agility born of desperation, he climbed over the railing of the *Siren* and threw himself into the waves. The water dogs made a dash for him. The woman disappeared among the waves, an enigmatic smile on her lips.

'Dad!' I shouted.

'Get out of here! Go! Go, for God's sake!' They were his parting words.

I steered the boat towards Calabria at full speed. I watched my father as he reached Antonino's boat with two powerful strokes. By now only part of the cabin was still above water. He climbed up, I saw him fiddling with something in his jacket pocket.

The plastic bag. The sticks of dynamite.

He managed to light one, holding it above his head. He let out a yell towards the sky. Even today I couldn't say whether it was a cry of defiance, anger, or frustration.

Then the beasts were upon him. They grabbed him in their jaws, shaking him. Dogs fighting for a bone.

The last thing I saw was the flash of the explosion. The water dogs stopping in amazement, yelping, frightened but unhurt, then launching into a banquet on the shredded remains of my father. My father who had sacrificed himself to give me time to escape.

I set the throttle to full power and slipped into the cabin to jam the rudder with a piece of rope. I took two steps on the bridge.

I went down in the hold like a robot, threw myself on the tarps.

Then a black wave submerged my brain.

All around, the sea sang its infinite song of secrets, deaths, and legends.

I fainted.

★   ★   ★

There's not much to add. My father, Antonino, and Vituzzo were never found. A fishing accident, that's what the authorities called it. No one believed my story. I was just a kid.

Mom almost went crazy with grief. So did I. But not only because of the grief.

Because of what I had seen.

Because I had understood that the legends of the sea, the dreadful stories the fishermen told in hushed tones as they reeled in their nets, sometimes hide unbearable truths.

Some nights I wake up screaming and I'm a ten-year-old boy on a beach again, next to my father's half-destroyed boat, surrounded by curious and worried faces.

'You say you found . . . You say you saw . . . *Her*?' a woman asks.

'Shhh. Quiet!' a man orders.

'Wh-where am I?' I ask.

'You're safe, son. Everything's fine. You're in the town of Scilla,' answers a voice, close and far away.

And it's a voice that conceals secrets.

A voice with the sound of the wind. And of the currents that stir beneath the surface of the Strait.

Black Hills of Torment

The glare from the filthy chandelier flutters in the glass of *amaro*, becoming the flight of a crazed moth. Things are what they are, not much we can do about it. At a certain point my hands start to shake.

The exhaustion, the thoughts.

The hills.

The roar of a car speeding down the street – there must still be gas – is reduced to the pernicious hiss of hospital equipment, muffled by the greasy carpet covering the walls and the voice of Wilma Goich.

'Somebody else decided to try?' the bartender, Eraldo, asks me. He's good at his job, can read his customers' minds and knows when to keep quiet, ask a question, or pour another drink.

Not tonight. It happens to the best of them. All I want is to sit here on my stool without having to make the enormous effort of connecting brain to tongue.

I sigh and look at him. Eyes tinged yellow in the light of the candles behind the bar. He's the only friend I have left. Not that I ever won any popularity contests.

There's nobody in the bar but me, him, and Wilma Goich singing 'Le colline sono in fiore'.

Barred windows, empty liquor bottles, and acid-green faux-Art Nouveau floral wallpaper – our set design.

Eraldo's white moustache is so filthy that it looks like a toothbrush that's been used to scrub grime from the grooves between tiles. Grooves like the wrinkles furrowing his neck, full of dirt, sweat, dead skin. In Orlasco, once home to 1,500 souls, now far fewer, hygiene is no longer in fashion. There are other things to worry about.

'I don't know.' I clear my throat because the toneless tone of my words makes me uncomfortable. 'I don't think anyone plans on trying again. After the priest, the already sparse ranks of volunteers have . . . thinned out.'

'Mmm. Have you thought about it? You said that maybe . . .' He breaks off, his eyes gleaming with expectation. Or maybe it's just the alcohol. 'I'd like to see my daughter again someday.'

From my shirt pocket I take out a cigarette rolled with dried grass and the last dregs of tea fished from a jar. I light it, it's like smoking pressed manure.

'I've been thinking about it for a year now, you know that. You ask me almost every night. Christ, I don't know,' I mutter, though really I've already made up my mind. I just don't want to talk about it.

'All right. Okay. Sorry, I didn't mean . . . More trouble? Violence, suicides?'

'Carmelo Pecce was the last one.'

The artisanal tincture that Eraldo passes off as a digestif disappears into my stomach. I put my hands on the dusty counter and get up, stifling a curse as my back cramps up.

The song vomited out by the universe – our little universe – finishes and starts up again. Since that day it hasn't stopped playing in every corner of the village, shot out in sticky decibels from an invisible cosmic jukebox. A constant, malevolent background, the soundtrack of the incomprehensible. An old and beloved Italian tune transformed into a sonic nightmare.

Not loud enough to keep you from having a conversation, but loud enough to make people snap, drive them to paranoia, to madness.

I've gotten used to it.

Le colline sono in fioreeeeee . . .

I rummage through my pockets and dump five euros in the

little terracotta tray with BAR ROMA written on it. Eraldo chuckles, grabs the cash, and makes it disappear in his pocket. It's a ritual; money doesn't matter one damn bit anymore. The bar is only open for me.

'See you.'

'Yeah. Take it easy.'

I go out dragging my feet, my shoes tolling a death knell on the floorboards of the entryway. I light another stinking cigarette and watch a beetle half the size of my fist crossing the little square, its chitinous shell reflecting a sky full of stars that have never seemed so badly arranged and far away.

The ring of sky we have left. I've given up looking at it in the hope of spotting the creamy wake of an airplane, a hang glider, the glassy, silent speck of a satellite.

Via Martiri della Libertà, the main street running through Orlasco, is dark and cold like the corridors of a morgue. I turn down it, blowing burnt steam from my sandpaper-dry lips.

The wind bombards my face in swirls of ice, carrying the lingering scent of grilled meat to my nostrils. Someone's making dinner.

Mice, judging from the smell.

I head towards home, trying not to look at them, to keep my eyes down, forcing myself, *Christ, look at the tips of your feet or up at the bell tower*, but I can't do it.

Hidden behind the houses of Orlasco, the slopes rise along the town's border like the walls of an amphitheater: a jagged and amorphous ring of nothing-black hills, blacker than a late night in January, blacker than a cellar, blacker than the blackest thing you can imagine. All around. The night sky battles them for supremacy of darkness, unsuccessfully.

The trails running through them are slightly lighter capillaries, limestone lanes, cuts in a huge necrotic organism.

The hills. They terrify, they oppress. They've crushed everything, what we were, what we could be. But it's impossible not to stop and behold them in their austere grandeur. Stare at them long enough and you start to see swarming shapes lurching their way across them, heavy light-blue masses hobbling on calcified appendages, abominations escaped from the nightmare of some cryptozoologist. But it's just my imagination, I tell myself.

I make it home.

I go inside and lie down on the bed, burying myself shivering under two comforters as heavy as sodden earth.

In the light from the cigarette butt squeezed between my lips I see the ear plugs on the nightstand. I decide not to put them in. I stub out the cigarette on the headboard.

I fall asleep to Wilma Goich warbling that a day is as long as a year, and that a year is so long it's like dying.

And tomorrow will be exactly a year since it all started. And it *has* been long.

Like dying, no doubt about it.

Luca Nordoroi. When he was born he didn't make a sound, didn't bother crying under the midwife's insistent slaps to announce his arrival in the world. He crossed his arms, wrinkled from amniotic fluid, as if he couldn't care less about the new world that greeted him.

At age four he could draw with some ability, and he would ask his father why that dead hedgehog they had found in the garden was dead, or why he sensed a presence all teeth and dust under the bed, or why he often dreamt of hills black like crows.

His father, weirded out and slightly worried, didn't know what to tell him most of the time.

Luca moved in a mental space that was entirely his own.

His parents were busy and important, owners of a lovely villa with a marble portico and emerald-green hedges in the residential part of Orlasco. People caught up in life, in the cogs of careers and success.

Their firstborn had come late, when they had already stopped hoping, when they had started to think it might be better if they didn't have one.

It happens.

Signor Nordoroi managed a popular, up-and-coming chain of bookstores called The Mad Hatter and was often away for work. Money, Mercedes, business trips, ladies' man, *bon viveur*, cocaine- and alcohol-fueled nights. The rare occasions he was in Orlasco he preferred to spend his free time at Bar Roma, sucking down spritzers and treating the other patrons to rounds of beer, rather than with his family.

Signora Nordoroi loved her husband very much, more than her scrawny son, more than anything else in the world, and couldn't stand his dalliances, the distance between them that was growing wider and wider and which since Luca's birth seemed to have become a crevasse.

After discovering yet another of her husband's trysts with an eighteen-year-old, she put 'Le colline sono in fiore' on the turntable and fixed herself a cocktail with vodka, ginger, and phenobarbital.

Luca was eight. He found his mother in an eternal sleep on the four-poster bed, a rosebud of pink foam on her lips. The turntable needle was crackling over the grooves in the vinyl.

Signor Nordoroi didn't seem too shaken by the tragedy. At the funeral he shed a few tears, then carried on with his life, lost in the triteness of affairs and fleeting pleasures. Babysitters came and went from the Orlasco villa.

In the long afternoons of fog and loneliness, Luca began to explore his world of light and shadow.

I look at the peak rising to the north as I slip out of the house into the still-life of the morning; it's not very tall, perhaps around a thousand meters of Bakelite shadow, but it's the tallest in the range and pointed like in a child's drawing. Yes, just like in a child's drawing.

It's cold. I linger in the yard by the dried-up rosemary bush. In the east the sun hasn't yet managed to make it over the hills. It will rise around ten and shine for about four hours without dispelling the eerie darkness of the hills, before it's swallowed by the walls rising to the west like a shimmering sugar cube in a cup of coffee.

We have become a town of shadows. A non-place.

I go back in the house, piddle around, talk to the walls, cry a little, go outside again and pass the gate whistling 'Simple Kind of Man' by Lynyrd Skynyrd. To hell with Wilma.

The backpack weighs me down, slowing my pace, but after all there's no hurry. It contains two cans of beans I had set aside, some bottles of water, a sweatshirt, pants, and several roasted mice. The pistol Eraldo gave me a month ago sticks out from my waistband. I keep it within reach of my hand. And my head.

Crossing Via Roma I glimpse the Church of the Holy Spirit, its wooden door torn off, the long pews overturned, the crucifix with the gaunt body of Jesus Christ wrapped in a shroud of cobwebs.

Father Beppe represented the final hope for a good chunk of the survivors. Especially the old people, trusting blindly in his god and his increasingly raving sermons, medieval discourses on sin, the devil, eternal damnation.

The priest's failure – I can still hear him screaming, *blaspheming* – was a tough blow for many.

I go on, casting nervous glances at the fields. The landscape changes, the colors fade.

Many trees are dead or dying. They wither, they droop; a fluid with the consistency of semen drips from the broken branches, but it's a jet-black liquid smelling of mold, dirty dishwashers, clogged drains. The grass has become a brittle, twice-baked, straw-yellow carpet. These phenomena become more obvious the closer you get to the foot of the hills. Even the orchards, the fruit and vegetable plants, have started to twist and curl into spirals with something extremely unpleasant about the way they flex in the wind, as if they wanted to capture the air blowing from the hills and the wan light, photosynthesizing them into toxic substances in an improbable botanical suicide.

That's why people don't eat vegetables anymore. That's why they started cooking mice when their pantries began to run bare.

'The hills are contaminating the town. Like an infection. It's like everything is rotting but also *alive in a different way*,' Eraldo told me one day as he showed me some ivy growing in his yard on the northern edge of Orlasco. The leaves were withered, almost dead, full of dark and gangrenous veins, and yet they moved slightly, with the vagueness of an optical effect, the undulation of a mirage, opening and closing like macabre vegetal hands. We pulled it up and burned it in a metal trash can; the dark and vaporous smoke rising from the bonfire, forming dense clouds above the reddish roof tiles, resembled a suffering face with pointed cheekbones, huge eyes, and a crushed head, so we extinguished it with buckets of water.

You can't get rid of gangrene in an arm by trimming the pinky nail.

Rumors circulate, gossip, stories nibbled like pencil stumps.

Stories of animals mutating, their bones twisting and exploding in bulbous masses of blackish corruption, rubbery growths and prolapses of muscles, collagen, tendons, and cartilage restructured in bizarre and terrifying anatomical modifications. I heard someone saw a cat with enormous jaws like a stag beetle's pissing a corrosive serum on the Punziano family's roof; the Izzia family's peacock vanished, disappearing from its pompous cage painted in Provençal style, though there are those who swear up and down that they have heard it flying over the apartment buildings and villas at night, squawking Wilma Goich's song in a tarry cry. Signora Martini asserts, making the sign of the cross, that the photos of the dead in the cemetery have been *altered* in a barely perceptible way, squinting eyes and sardonic grins, filaments of darkness in the deceased's nostrils in the snapshots, and that the burial dates have changed, pushed forward by decades, as if the corpses in the niches were not really corpses, as if we should expect to see them strolling nonchalantly and with placid aplomb through the square sipping a cocktail. There are even those who claim to have recognized the outline of a dead relative silhouetted in the twilight, gamboling on the crest of the hills in a ghostly shadow play, and those who are sure that nameless abominations are descending from the sooty mounds to take over the town. The braver ones bring up the tragic epilogue of Giorgio Magnaschi, the only one who *came back down*, but they are immediately silenced, because it's a story that many have tried to forget.

Carmelo Pecce, the person living closest to the slopes, which rise a few dozen meters from his farmhouse, set himself ablaze in his barn a few days ago. The reddish-orange, Dantesque flames of the pyre danced in the countryside all night, like a circle of hell vomited to the surface.

Another person who couldn't handle the nonsensical seclusion we're living in, some said, but others whispered that the farmer was turning into something *no longer human*, with the rib cage of a prehistoric beast, ears like coal-black explosions of mineralized concretions.

Rumors, gossip, fragments of stories. In a town of a thousand souls it's hard to tell hearsay from certainty, truth from fantasy, invention from reality.

It was hard enough before, let alone now.

It seems like all the birds have flown away, migrated to where spring and life are something more than a simple memory. I envy them, even if I can't be sure of their fate. Maybe they crashed into the peaks in an explosion of beaks and innards, maybe they never took flight and went off to die somewhere, all of them together, in an idyllic bird cemetery; but I like to imagine them free, held aloft by hollow bones and soft feathers, successfully flying behind the monstrous perimeter of hills that forms our cage.

Their song is gone, replaced by that neverending dirge. Three days ago Signora Petrini stuck a screwdriver through her eardrums so she wouldn't have to hear it anymore.

Le colline sono in fioreeeee . . .

But these hills aren't in bloom. They're dead structures, devoid of vegetation, cemeterial obelisks of darkness, indecipherable and impassible.

Luca Nordoroi started drawing the hills when he was about nine years old, shortly after his mother's death, and he didn't stop until the day he disappeared. At first he used a wide-tipped permanent marker, a Uniposca, running it over the sheets of paper forcefully because, as he confided to a classmate, he wanted 'a really black black'.

He inhaled more marker fumes than oxygen.

The town, overrun with gossips like any human community, began watching him out of the corner of its eye, hypothesizing that his mother's death had planted a seed in his already complex and introverted personality.

When he walked down the street, his nose in his notebook, focused on sketching the church or the long rows of poplars, his tongue between his lips in a grimace of extreme concentration, the Orlasco gossips would whisper and smirk, thinking how lucky they were that Nordoroi the Freak wasn't their kid.

They blamed the father, the insensitive bastard who left the boy to himself more than was healthy for a child of that age. Or at least that was their opinion.

'He should take him to a psychiatrist,' they would chatter outside the school, leaning against their SUVs, tapping their foreheads with their flawless fake nails.

Luca kept his distance from everyone. He simply preferred to mind his own business. He took no part in church activities, summer camps, ball games, he didn't share his peers' competitive vision of the world.

He read. He brooded. He put his mother's old 45 on the turntable and devoted himself to the hills.

Long walks in the Orlascan countryside, lost in thoughts of

mysterious universes and polar dawns, of shadows and forgotten secrets, of worlds and cultures upended by miscommunication and misunderstandings.

He grazed on his own artistic self-teaching, on his own fantasy.

Social interaction wasn't a priority for him. What interested him were the dark hills that had popped up from who knows what recess in his mind.

Those surreal artworks were a concentrate of unease in black and white, the bichromatic visions of a different soul; Nordoroi drew his town, Orlasco (it was recognizable from several elements – the bell tower, Via Martiri della Libertà, the square) and, warped to the point that their tops met to form an arch, the peat-colored mountains. The subject of each picture was the same, with simple variations of perspective or landscape. A glimpse of the playground across from the kindergarten, slides, swings, and sycamores swollen with pollen. The town hall and the old trail that passed near the schools before plunging into the fields. Bar Roma tucked beneath the looming bulk of the Diamante Apartments. Public housing. Aerial drawings of Orlasco like an old map, crossroads of streets and two-dimensional houses clustered in a modern slum.

Over everything, always present, the hills.

It was an activity that absorbed him.

Obsessed him.

He grew up in the bleak self-satisfaction of his art, in the ebony shadow of the hills.

His years of adolescence and high school (an ordinary and rather gloomy technical institute at which he enrolled at the insistence of his father, who didn't approve of his artistic tendencies) were not easy.

He wasn't friendly, he didn't speak unless spoken to, he wasn't very handsome. A bit too thin, on the verge of being stunted. Hair a little too dark. With those tragically huge eyes, like an insect's.

Kids are nasty little beasts, predators that move in packs to isolate the weakest.

Hyenas.

They tortured him.

Nordoroi the scrawny, the depressed, the crazy, the nutcase, the mute, the goddamned-artist-of-this-fucking-crap.

The one obsessed with the hills.

As calm as an undertow, Luca responded to the teasing and abuse in the only way he found logical and comforting: he drew. And that only enraged his persecutors more.

In tenth grade a classmate took one of his sketches from under his desk, hid it, and during the break tore it up in front of the whole class, spraying saliva as she giggled, climbing onto the teacher's desk to show the class her work of destruction.

The quiet, inoffensive, and weird Luca Nordoroi got up from the tubular plywood chair, went up to her without saying a word, knocked her off her improvised stage and, amid the terrified cries of his classmates, stuck the point of a compass in the soft pulp of her right eye.

Sixteen times.

I pass Signor and Signora Biolatti's house and think about how they were found, cozied up together in the bathtub surrounded by rose petals, their wrists and ankles slashed open, marinating in the water and their own blood in a final crimson embrace.

They were the first to try to escape that way, putting an end to their lives. Later there were others, and the number of suicides grows with each passing month. I've considered it too. We all have.

I feel the looks. From behind the windows of an apartment building, from the half-open garage door, from the gaps in a boarded-up doorway.

Looks of hate, contempt, hope, uncertainty.

And I feel the hills. When I look up suddenly from the trash-strewn sidewalk they seem to pulsate like an organ pumping poison, a lung that inhales fear and exhales despair, hallucinations, madness.

The contrast between the clear sky and the foul blackness of the barrier is unsettling; from a distance the hills look two-dimensional, so cold and detached and dark that I wouldn't be surprised to see a satellite or an asteroid whizzing around within their contours. They have a color, if you can call it that, reminiscent of the cosmic void, the dark space between strands of galaxies, an *absence*.

Unbearable. It's unbearable to think about the implications of their birth, the silent sedimentation of unknown material in the course of a single night.

One year ago Orlasco woke to the sound of Wilma Goich's voice dancing eerily through the streets, creeping into apartments at that hour that is no longer night and not yet dawn, Bergman's Hour of the Wolf, when so many people are born and die, when sleep is deepest and nightmares most vivid.

People took to the streets, bleary-eyed and in nightgowns as if they had been awoken from their sleep by an earthquake; they emerged from their homes to pinpoint the source of the sound, and when they saw the hills clearer than the night sky, many thought they were dreaming.

Some of them still do.

'It'll end sooner or later. It's like one of those weird dreams that seem to last forever, a nesting-doll nightmare that starts over again every time you wake up, but it'll end sooner or later,' they say.

They had popped up out of nowhere, like a dreadful news story interrupting a banal afternoon talk show, a fence around the world we used to know.

I heard the song, the screams, the police sirens, I rushed outside. I remember the trembling, the wide-open eyes, the tears, a city councilman pinching his cheeks in a vain attempt to wake up, the excited conversations, as we gathered in Orlasco's little town square, the center of our newborn crepuscular horizon.

'What the hell are they?'

'Can you make that stop, please? Can someone turn that goddamned song off, PLEASE? It's driving me crazy, *can some-one please stop it!*'

'It's a dream, it has to be.'

'Let's call the Carabinieri, yes, the Carabinieri, right away!'

Very soon we discovered that cell phones, landlines, internet didn't work. The means of communication were reduced to bits of useless plastic, vestiges of a vanished civilization.

No news on the television, nothing at all, except for a disheartening snowy static.

Only the radios worked. And they still work now – even though the electricity went out months ago – tuned to a single station that continually broadcasts a single song.

Le colline sono in fioreeeee . . .

Cut off. Trapped *inside*.

Those with a good memory, who had lived in Orlasco long enough, thought of Luca Nordoroi and his compulsive art form – it was hard not to – but nobody mentioned his name, including me. He had left a year ago and no one knew what had become of him.

I stood there with my mouth gaping and a face that must have been a mixture of wonder, confusion, and terror, Eraldo's hand on my shoulder as he went on reciting his rosary: 'It's unbelievable, truly unbelievable. Mother Mary, it's just unbelievable.'

Some families went back inside their houses before we managed to overcome the devastating initial shock, as if within their home's four walls it was possible, *preferable*, to shut out the mystery, cancel the unknown.

But there was no way of shutting Wilma Goich up: her voice seemed to ring out from the town's every atom.

Adriano Nicolodi, the local police chief, climbed into his Fiat Stilo and muttered something to the frightened townspeople through the open window along the lines of: 'It has to be a prank, I'll go check it out. Wait for me here.'

He set off down Via Martiri della Libertà with tires screeching and headed south, towards Garzigliana, the next town over. In that direction the hills didn't seem as high, almost a low plateau of black basalt. The golden brushstrokes of dawn tinged the peaks with a livid, pink color, accentuating their massive shape, a gigantic iron upside down on the plains.

We followed the Stilo's tail lights until it vanished around a curve in a cloud of bluish exhaust fumes.

The car was found the following day, the driver's side door open, a trail of footprints ending at the slightly inclined base of the hills, near a path just over half a meter wide that led upwards at an angle.

Since then no one has been able to trace Adriano Nicolodi, like almost all those who have tried to climb the hills, to make it to the other side.

The girl, through some freak chance, didn't lose her eye. It might have been better if she had, since it was left atrophied and squinting, a wilted prune supported by a damaged optic nerve, her vision limited to a few diopters. Her parents filed charges, won the case, and Luca was suspended for two weeks, thus guaranteeing he would be held back at the end of the year and exponentially increasing his reputation as a psycho.

Signor Nordoroi was forced to take the boy to a psychologist. He went ballistic. He had other things to worry about. He was obliged to return early from a pleasure-seeking weekend at the Pré Saint Didier spa to clean up the mess caused by his son, who sat in his bedroom drawing as if having almost gouged out his classmate's eye were no big deal.

Luca was his own flesh and blood, but he hardly knew him.

The doctor rattled off the usual things: teenage depression, apathy, anhedonia, bursts of anger, it will pass, give the boy these drops three times a day, you need to be there for him, it's a difficult phase, losing his mother, that'll be 125 euros for the session, do you want a receipt?

Luca went back to school. His grades were worse than mediocre – only the two weekly hours of Art and Design seemed to shake him from his torpor – and at the end of the year, when he flunked, it was obvious that getting his diploma wasn't high on his to-do list.

He devoted more and more time to art, neglecting everything else. From a technical point of view he made considerable leaps forward, astonishing given the self-taught nature of his artistic journey. He experimented, painting with excellent results on paper, canvas, wood panels, fabric: any surface at all was a suitable home for the hills. He abandoned markers in favor of brushes, charcoal pencils, watercolors. One single color. And he started to title his works.

BLACK HILLS OF TORMENT

Always the same title for every picture, as if every drawing were part of *another larger design* that only he could see.

Although he obviously had talent, the paintings he hung in his bedroom exuded an aura of extraordinary *wrongness*; looking at them too long caused a subtle unease, a powerful detachment from commonly accepted notions of good taste, even if the subjects were in no way obscene, provocative, or frightening.

They were dark hills looming over Orlasco, nothing more.

But the quality of the traced lines, the brushstrokes of thick paint, pressed in layers upon layers onto the white canvas, the way the tiny houses seemed to retreat in search of a hiding place before the sinuous curves of the hills, would have had trouble finding favor with gallery owners or art aficionados.

One summer night Luca declared to his father in a faint voice that he planned to quit school and devote himself to painting. He was eighteen years old.

Signor Nordoroi had just gotten back from a dinner with the higher-ups at his company and had learned that the much-desired joint venture with a major publishing group, which he had championed with the board in exchange for gifts and generous bribes, didn't have a majority of the votes and wasn't written in The Mad Hatter's immediate future.

He had drunk quite a lot to ease his disappointment, drown it, and snorted cocaine to fuel the anger pulsating at the base of his skull. He was wasted, high, pissed off, and afraid his schemes would come to light and get him fired, which was in fact what happened a few weeks later.

He came home to find Luca in the living room with his proposal to become a future sponger, a canvas-smearer, his overly large eyes drooping under lids as thin as butterfly wings, and the 45 of Wilma Goich spinning on the turntable in a swirl of vinyl.

'Well, Dad, what do you think?' he asked in his high-pitched and toneless little voice, the metallic squawk of a robot. 'Can I?'

Well, Dad, what do you think? Can I?

Signor Nordoroi's vision went blurry for a moment. Then he took out his altered mental state on his son. He slapped him and knocked him onto the couch with a kick in the ass, then ran into his bedroom-studio, punching the easels and tearing up hills.

'Is this what you want to do with your life? Go on being the nothing that you are?' he roared, foaming at the mouth as he attacked a large panel depicting Orlasco as seen from the window of his mother's little library upstairs.

Luca reacted the same way he had with his classmate.

He jumped on his father's back, his fingers scratching to tear out his eyes, his teeth bared like an animal's, his face contorted by a superhuman rage. He tried to bite off his nose. The two struggled in a whirlwind of paper and ink and black paint until they collapsed on the floor like trash bags full of rotting leaves and remained there, drained, dead, soulless.

Signor Nordoroi got up from the floor, his eyes black and bleeding, cast a look at Luca, then went upstairs to his room and collapsed on his bed in exhaustion.

He cried.

He showed up distraught at Bar Roma the next day, telling Eraldo that after an ugly fight his son had left in the night, taking his drawings and his mother's 45 with him.

He notified the authorities, who didn't try very hard to find him. Luca was of age and the strained relationship with his father spoke volumes: voluntary departure.

Orlasco quickly forgot about one of its shyest and strangest residents. Until the following year, when the hills appeared.

I stop in front of Eraldo's house, at the dark walnut door. I'm sure he's asleep, that after saying goodbye to me last night he had wound up guzzling his homemade liqueur and dragging himself home from the bar, his chubby legs hardly able to keep him upright.

I raise my fist to knock, stop in mid-air. There's no point in bothering him, waking him up. I'd like to talk to him one last time, tell him what really happened, have him come with me to the foot of the hills, but what would be the point?

I have to do it alone.

Eraldo has already gone above and beyond. He hasn't gotten anything from me, not even a hint of the truth; he's given me companionship and drinks for months. And a gun. I feel it pressing against my protruding pelvic bone, the scuffed-up Beretta that in all likelihood I'll have to use in a few hours. Not to defend myself. To avoid the torment the others have suffered.

I bend down, pick up a chunk of brick from the path and use it to write a word in front of the bartender's door: THANKS.

As I head towards the main street I recall the question he asked me months earlier, while we were sharing a cigarette.

'If Luca were still in Orlasco we could question him, don't you think? About *his* hills.'

'Yes. If he were still here in Orlasco, yes. But he left. He's on the other side,' I responded.

It was the first and last time we spoke about him.

I quicken my pace. It doesn't take long to reach them. As I make my way through the mutilated countryside and enter the shadow zone of the hills, I feel something like resignation warming my heart. But resignation isn't enough to ease my fear, nor my guilty conscience.

I keep my eyes fixed on the wall that rises before me, a wedge of coal dropped in the fields by a cruel god.

I'm close. No one has tried climbing this side. I chose this part because it was the furthest point from my house.

In a field off to my right I seem to see voluminous eyeballs floating between the poplars like skeins of yellowish pollen, hundreds of pupils fixed on my progress, but when I stop to look at the grove more closely all I see are dead branches and the carcass of a wild boar, its four legs pointed to the sky, overly long legs, like a spider, or an elephant by Dalì.

I'm well aware that I don't have much hope of reaching the top of the black mountain I've decided to challenge. And even if I reached the summit, a possibility that seems unlikely in light of recent events, who says I'll be able to climb to the other side? Who says there *is* another side and not just an immense, terrible, cold expanse of black hills covering the continents, the oceans, the planet?

Orlasco could be the last remaining inhabited place, encircled by a boundless expanse of nothingness. Or maybe it was wiped from the map along with all of us, dragged into another dimension we know nothing about.

I stop at the foot of the barrier, near an irrigation canal bubbling with blackish liquid. I think I can make out the vague reflection of a pale claw beneath the water's surface.

I've been followed. Men and women peer at me from a distance, their hands pressed to their chests. They're nothing but outlines shrouded in a blurry purplish-gray mist. I have the impression that one of them is waving at me or giving me a sign of encouragement, but I don't return it.

I turn around, sit down on the embankment. I've saved one last Marlboro. I smoke it slowly, telling myself I'll be free soon, one way or another.

Our isolation from the rest of the world began to make itself felt after a few weeks. It's unbelievable how quickly food runs out when you're cut off from the supply we take for granted. Trash piles up in yards and houses, poisoning the air. The electricity and gas went out the second week, just like that, from one moment to the next, as if someone had turned off the tap. Speaking of taps, fortunately we still have water, even if it has a strange, sickly-sweet taste.

People don't help each other. They didn't before, why should they now? Everybody only thinks about themselves; in the nightmarish dimension that greets us every time we wake up there is no room for understanding, solidarity, mutual support. Isolation, mistrust, violence, doubt, malice. That's all Orlasco was able to create to deal with the horror.

For a while I wondered when people would start killing each other over canned food. For a blanket. For a mouse or a dog. Or simply for the fun of it, to break up the monotony of always identical days.

Then the senseless looting and vandalism started, and just three months ago Signor Cappellaro killed his wife with a meat tenderizer, then hammered away at the corpse until every bone was broken and threw it in the front yard. A carcass staring at the ring of empty sky with dead eyes and blood-swollen lumps on its forehead.

No one did anything. Asked why.

And Signor Cappellaro staggered around picking flowers and talking to himself and singing along with Wilma Goich, but he always forgot the words even if he had already heard the song thousands of times, and nobody dared to stop him or tell him to bury his wife's decomposing corpse, now nothing but a clump of tissue and bits of bone, a tired scarecrow collapsed in the grass.

Authorities, police, laws, work: concepts that no longer have any place in Orlasco.

And yet in the wake of the hills' appearance and the police chief's disappearance, the town tried to regroup, to use logic to deal with a problem that had nothing logical about it.

The townspeople gathered in the middle school gym shortly after the police chief's car was found. From the large windows you could make out the menacing outline of the hills, like a wave of tar.

When the hysteria had died down, people started reeling off hypotheses and possible solutions to deal with the 'crisis'.

'If you ask me, it's an experiment. Military stuff. If so, we're screwed.'

'Martians. It was Martians.'

'And that song? Why doesn't it stop playing? Huh?'

'Hidden speakers. A prank.'

'I say we should wait. By now people in the nearby towns will have noticed the hills. They'll send someone to help us. Helicopters, the army. Right?'

'It's that Nordoroi kid's fault. You all remember his drawings, don't you?'

Mayor Andreoli was the only one to voice what was gnawing foremost at his mind. Silence fell, the residents exchanged terrified glances. Many turned to look at me.

'He's right,' someone muttered.

'The "painter",' the word spat out in a tone of scorn and contempt, 'went off a year ago. What does it mean?'

'It's like . . . it's like we've been plunged into his world, into his disgusting, depressing paintings . . .'

'And you? What do you say?' a woman with tousled hair asked me, her expression wild-eyed, full of uncertainty, disdain, anxiety, her wrinkly mouth seeming to want to gobble me up.

'I don't know. I really don't know. I'm sorry,' I answered, stepping back. It was true. I felt shaken, my senses dulled, unable to think. Only in the months that followed did I come up with my own hypothesis: sometimes evil and indifference are paid back to us with interest, in ways so vile that they can hardly be guessed at and never understood.

'Whatever they are, we have to climb them and see what's on the other side. They're not very high. No big deal,' said a boy with a muscular neck, stepping forward with his arms around the shoulders of two of his friends. Young, strong, handsome, with the self-confidence and physique of those who don't settle for second place. I knew all three of them. 'We'll get ready and set off in an hour, by the Bertoretti farmhouse. Okay? In one hour. I'm sure there's a logical explanation for all . . . all this.'

Dozens and dozens of heads nodded in a sign of assent. 'Good, yes, such good boys,' an old woman muttered.

Then the crowd dispersed and everyone took refuge in their own houses. So did I. Behind the windows of the houses I glimpsed shadows of heads, the frantic dance of limbs engaged in quarrels or explanations, eyes pointed toward the barrier that defied certainty. Children cried, women screamed, Wilma Goich lamented.

An hour later a large group of us assembled at the meeting point, where the three boys were waiting for us with backpacks and North Face sweatshirts. It was the first time I had been so close to the hills. Their darkness was dizzying. I imagined it was the only color seen by the blind, by those whose eyes had been put out with red-hot firebrands in centuries past.

'All right, wish the expedition good luck,' the biggest of the teenagers said as he put in his earbuds to drown out 'Le colline sono in fiore'.

The three of them gave themselves a pep talk, then they turned to the business at hand and were no longer so arrogant and sure of themselves. Now they seemed small, scared, trembling like little kids having to jump off a high dive for the first time. But now they had volunteered.

'You don't have to do this if you don't – ' I tried to suggest.

'Good luck, boys,' the mayor interrupted me, giving me a glare as sharp as a dagger.

As if they'd received an order, the youths gave a thumbs up and began climbing the hill in single file along one of the many little paths leading to the unknown.

We watched them in silence with bated breath, our heads bent back like worshippers beneath a pulpit. They advanced in slow motion, with sticky and uncoordinated movements, looking around apprehensively in all directions. Every so often one of the three looked back and we saw the pink circle of his face in that black mass.

They proceeded until they became nothing but slightly lighter dots on the sloping ebony plane; by then they were about two hundred meters in altitude below the top, a lumpy hump reminiscent of a fist with gnarled knuckles raised to challenge the sky.

'They'll make it. I'm sure,' a girl panted, her voice cracking with emotion.

One by one, snowflakes melting on the asphalt, they disappeared into the blackness, as if they had gone around a bend in that absurd material or had descended into a gully that we couldn't see from where we stood.

A moment of suspense.

Then the screams exploded in the desolate landscape, mixing with Wilma Goich's song to create a grotesque effect.

Hard to describe them. They were like a howl, the agonizing wail of someone tortured to death. Three oral cavities united in a single chorus of suffering. The mangled voices rolled down from the hills, swooping down upon us in an avalanche of pain, an anathema. From time to time the discordant shrieks changed into something like words, pleading prayers, but even the most articulate vocalizations remained unintelligible, a new language celebrating defeat and the incinerated loneliness of the hills.

The mother of one of the boys collapsed to her knees and began tearing out her hair. A man dragged her away. Father Beppe recited an Ave Maria with half-closed eyes, like a martyr. Pino Zagaria, Orlasco's hairdresser, started babbling that the hills were moving, devouring and regurgitating themselves with lazy undulations, a sight that reminded him of 'back when we used to get fucked up on psychedelics'.

'We have to ... go and see what's happening. Help them,' one boy ventured, but no one moved a muscle and we avoided looking at one another, shaken to our core by what was happening on the hills (*what was happening?*) and our own cowardice.

It was awful. It went on for hours. We huddled in a silent circle and I remember wondering how it was possible to scream for so long without the uvula or vocal chords tearing, without the brain deciding to allow itself a blackout.

Finally the shrieks died away, little by little, a wind dropping to make way for quiet, and out of the corner of my eye I saw Eraldo's arm raised to point at the hills.

'Look. Look!'

Around the spot where the three volunteers had vanished a patch of color reappeared that began crawling downwards, moving in a zigzag pattern with the random trajectories of a pinball. One of the boys from what would later become known as 'the shitty first expedition'.

It was obvious from the way he was advancing that the climbing attempt had not ended well. He tumbled several times on his personal Way of the Cross, taking fifteen minutes or more to get back to his feet each time.

'Come on! You can do it!' the crowd began to encourage him.

We waited. No one went to meet him.

Enrico Mauceri, a retiree who dabbled in birdwatching, ran

home and returned with binoculars; I'll never forget how the expression on his face changed when he spotted the boy.

Nor the expressions of my fellow townspeople at the sight of Giorgio Magnaschi, who finally crawled to the foot of the mountain, to the point of departure that also became his final point of arrival.

He was naked. Transformed.

The majority of those present fled sobbing, a couple of women fainted.

Giorgio Magnaschi wanted us to help him: it was clear from how he stretched his arms towards the crowd (what was left of his arms) and from how his mouth tried to pronounce the word HELP (what was left of his mouth), but no one wanted to touch him, fearful of contracting a fatal malady. After Giorgio, many tried to flee, including Father Beppe, but no one ever returned.

He was the only one, and there have been days when I've wondered why.

It was as though entire portions of his body – hands, fore-arms, half his face, genital organs, most of the torso – had been turned *inside out*. With the indifference reserved for old socks, wool gloves ready to be thrown away.

The muscle bundles exposed, the labyrinthine highways of capillaries perfectly visible, clusters of organs and lymph nodes hanging like juicy, ripe fruit, the pulsating lump of a kidney, the wet berries of the testicles, gray cerebral prolapses, and that eye whirling around *backward*, staring at panoramas we couldn't see.

Clumps of black material foamed where the contortions and rotations had occurred, and that was what seemed to give an appearance of locomotion and mobility.

'Oh God. Oh God.'

I took a step back and stumbled, repressing a sour rush of vomit, dozens of eyes fixed on my retreat, dozens of legs back-ing away with mine.

The last thing I saw before I turned around and started to

run towards my house was the boy who had once been Giorgio Magnaschi toppling over on his back in a fountain of bodily fluids, lifting his twisted limbs towards the marbled dusk.

Wilma Goich sang and sang and sang, and as I fled I felt the urge to laugh and laugh and laugh, but I bit my tongue and the inside of my cheek until tears formed.

I knew that if I started I wouldn't be able to stop.

My joints crack as I pull myself up and climb over the irrigation canal with an awkward leap. I let out a cry like a wounded beast, lean forward and spit on the ground. I smoked a piece of filter and there's a taste in my mouth like burnt plastic bags, like tires set ablaze.

Now the crowd of people behind me has gotten closer; someone saw me making my way through the streets of Orlasco with my backpack on my shoulder, and word must have gotten around quickly.

The town is small, people talk.

I realize how gaunt and hollow their faces have gotten, from bad nutrition, isolation, and the madness of being imprisoned for a year inside a circle. Their eyes liquid abysses that no longer shine. And yet I can feel the expectation, the tension that binds us.

A little girl with a swollen belly clings to her mother's torn skirt; with her free hand she holds a bit of flabby meat that she nibbles as if it were a delicious sweet pastry, a cream donut. I don't want to know what animal it came from.

I don't want to know anything anymore.

Many of them are confident I can do it, or at least break the spell of the black hills of torment.

'So you finally decided to do it?' asks a man, keeping his distance. He staggers. Looks like the survivor of a death camp. I don't recognize him.

'Looks that way . . .' I reply, and my words are the echo of a thought ricocheting in the morning stillness.

'It's about time.'

'Right.'

'Good luck, Nordoroi.'

Pulling the collar of my jacket up to shield my neck, I turn around. The gray grass stops at the point where the hills begin. They seem to be stuck in the lowlands, the earth around them scarred with crossroads of cracks.

I caress the pistol once more, inhale deeply, and take a step. The journey begins. I make an effort not to turn around in search of the meager comfort of a human presence, my lips sing a song: 'Le colline sono in fioreeeeee . . .'

I ascend in long strides along the path of seething darkness, my forehead covered in sweat that runs down my face, gets in my eyes. Black sweat, as thick as ink, paint. As I advance I'm gradually submerged in darkness. I feel it forcing its way into every orifice, through the pores of my skin, into my lungs, alive, cold, conscious. It's like being locked in a dark closet, huddled under a thick blanket smelling of dust and old junk.

I can no longer see anything, but the path is clear.

In the limbo of pitch I relive the fatal evening, Luca attacking me, his mouth drooling and his eyes empty, me pushing and hitting and insulting him, him falling between the easels and banging his temple on the turntable cabinet, the *crack!* of his skull, the sound of a coconut, I see his corpse in a pool of paint surrounded by a corolla of paintings, sketches, hills.

I continue my climb in the realm of shadows, a hot wind disarranges my features, singes my hair, and baptizes me with ashes.

I think about my son buried in the courtyard with his drawings and the single by Wilma Goich, next to the rosemary bush.

I stop.

In the dark something stretches its bones and with a smile of icy fangs invites me to follow it.

The Last Box

How do you do it? How the hell do you manage to fit inside such a small box without breaking your back?

I've been asked that question so many times.

You see, it's a matter of training every day since I was a kid, combined with a peculiar physical predisposition. Apparently people like me have ligaments that are unusually long, more flexible than the average person's.

You might say that I live in a perpetually stretched state. That I'm constantly practicing how to disappear.

An illusionist of the flesh.

In the morning I get up and go through my stretching exercises. Then I rehearse my numbers for the performance until late afternoon, allowing myself only a short break for a frugal, hamster-sized lunch.

My numbers are difficult ones; my organs shift in my rib cage, my backbone bends like a reed, I slip my head under one knee and then the other, keeping my balance with my hands. Finally I scrunch up on the floor like a dying spider, and when I'm limber enough, my muscles warmed up, my joints greased, I can finally get in the box.

The most complicated number, the one that makes the little kids scream and the young ladies wrinkle their noses: my half-naked body closes in on itself, following abstruse angles and geometries, squeezing into a cube a little bigger than a shoebox.

That's roughly what my days are like. Marked by discipline, fatigue, and sadness. When we don't perform I go to bed early, lying in the rundown camper listening to the sounds from the

Bertacca Circus. The subdued snorting of the horses, the fakir's blaring television, the clowns' mournful laughter, the panting of wild beasts deprived of their liberty.

And I think. Try to find new contortions and new ways to bend. To occupy spaces inaccessible to most. To make myself smaller and smaller and smaller.

I think about the interstices and the last box, about the spectators who laugh and clap but whisper 'monster' when they see my hairless, limber body, whose thinness borders on emaciation.

And above all I think about my parents.

My mother, a trapeze artist, whose beautiful, radiant face I can barely recall.

My father, a snake-man like me, driven mad by grief, consumed by loss. One of the best contortionists in the world, without a doubt. I learned the secrets of the craft from him.

My father knew many secrets.

He told me all of them, except for one.

The circus where I was born and raised was a small one. Always on the brink of bankruptcy. I remember the holes in the big top, the starving lions whose ribs you could count, the cannonball lady's obscene, drunken screaming.

There was nothing romantic about that life. Up and down the boot-shaped peninsula, stopping in nameless provincial towns where permit costs were low and the circus manager knew he could at least sell enough tickets to cover expenses.

We passed through foggy landscapes and sunlit roads in a slow caravan of campers, trucks, and trailers; we trudged through regions and seasons to meet yet another audience of dull-eyed yokels in search of cheap thrills, exposed flesh, and cut-rate exoticism.

Every morning, if we weren't traveling, my parents would practice.

Mom on the trapeze, pirouetting in mid-air like a feather,

defying gravity and the sixty feet that separated her from the safety net. Alone. She had no partner aside from those two iron bars supported on four ropes. And the safety net.

Dad outside, in the square or the field where we pitched the big top, curving his body into insane positions that would have meant dislocations (or worse) for most human beings. And I, only a child, trained along with him. Contortionism is also a matter of genetics. Of the distance between vertebrae, the flexibility of collagen. I had taken after him.

'You're going to be good. Very good. Maybe better than your dad,' he would often tell me, smiling as I imitated his positions. 'We'll do our first show together before long.'

Mom would join us after she had finished twirling under the red and yellow apse of the big top, squeezed into a gold-sequined outfit, her legs muscular and shapely, her eyes big with love and adrenaline, and she would stop to exercise with us.

I said earlier that there was nothing romantic about our lives. That's untrue, a statement dictated by years of loneliness and regret, by the dark shadows of depression that have crept into my adult mind.

We were the romantic part. Our family. My mother and father, young, in love, beautiful, the circus's main attraction, the only two artists able to elicit a standing ovation from the spectators, half asleep from their work in the fields, from their abusive drinking, from the tedious and repetitive way their strings were pulled by the wretched puppeteer that is provincial life.

Us.

I don't know how my parents wound up working at such a shabby circus, but the other performers were all of the opinion that they would soon be noticed by some major showman who would help them make the leap to better things. They deserved to perform in a great show. The Togni Circus, the Orfei, the Balzelli, or maybe abroad, in France, under a huge and shiny pavilion where the pay was guaranteed and life was easier.

They never got the chance.

There were shadows on the horizon, a plague infesting the future with a seething, wormy rot, a blackness that not even the lights of the most glorious circus in the world could penetrate.

Winter. It was an ashen and skeletal day that greeted our arrival in Orlasco, a rosary of houses and potato fields beading towards the Alps, twenty miles from Turin. In the sky, vapors of fog sketched a perfect backdrop for the crows gliding over the frost-encrusted fields in search of food.

I was only seven, but I can still distinctly remember the architecture of the village and the far-off mountains. As well as the feeling that our caravan was entering hostile territory, a ghost town. A mantle of abandonment and anguish seemed to weigh on the main street, a strip of asphalt lined with decaying buildings and sad poplars.

'Nice place,' my mother observed, her eyes squinting to peer through the waves of mist beyond the camper's windshield.

'Nice place indeed,' Dad echoed her. 'But it's not going to be like this forever. I can feel it, we just have to hang in there.'

But dreams of glory lead nowhere, even in the best of cases. In the worst, they lead to disaster, like what happened to my family. There's no such thing as glory. One day even the greatest conductor, the best writer, will vanish from memory, from the chronicles, from history, because sooner or later the chronicles and history will disappear too and only the void that follows us will remain. Within that void, always at our heels, there are axioms in motion that we can't understand. And which sometimes, if we're unlucky enough, can haunt our earthly path. I realized this later, as I cried for the caresses I would never receive again, while my father, insane from suffering, would lock himself in the camper, continuing his crazy contortions.

We made our way slowly through the soft stillness of

Orlasco, a funeral procession in search of the burial site, all the way to the center of town. We were met by some townspeople, some children.

The circus exists, *lives*, for children. But in that place even they seemed little more than haze, the sketch of something in progress that would never fully take shape.

Hurrying through the administrative small talk, the ringmaster returned to the square, shouting orders at us with the ugly expression of someone who has realized that business is not going to be good. The tapeworms of bankruptcy had been eating at him for a while. A few years later he would commit suicide by sprinkling goat's blood on himself and walking naked into the tiger cage.

We rushed to set up the big top under a fat city councilman's straw-colored and suspicious eye, shrouded in a damp cold that seemed to seep through our clothes, our bones, our marrow.

Our performance was scheduled for the following evening.

I'll never know how the news made its way through the trailers and sideshows the next morning. But word started to jump from mouth to mouth, lighting the fire of hope in our eyes. There were quite a few of us who longed for something better for the years to come.

'The manager of the Balzelli circus is supposed to be here tonight, looking for new talent!'

'They're on tour in Turin. Maybe Madame Balzelli herself will come too, the divine Madame Balzelli!'

'They might sign one of us . . .'

Although none of this could be verified, my parents exploded with joy, for illusions often have a greater power than truth.

All eyes were on them. Envious eyes, for the most part. They were the likeliest candidates. Definitely not the cannonball lady, as irritating as a mosquito, nor the sword swallower who had injured his palate a few weeks earlier, nor the crackhead lion tamer, the squalid clowns, the thuggish strong man.

As if fleeing a hailstorm, all the circus performers retreated to their mobile dwellings, including us. It was time to work out a strategy, refine our tricks, make changes to the performance, in case the manager or Madame Balzelli made an appearance.

There was determination in my father's eyes. He took me in his arms and ruffled my hair, and I can still smell his scent of aftershave, coffee, sweat, and tobacco. 'Tonight you'll perform with me. You'll do the exercises I taught you, you'll bend into the Frog Boy. The audience will love it. You want to?'

It was what I had been longing for. I almost burst into tears of happiness. I quivered.

My first performance.

A moment later I saw it in my mother's eyes: she was already there among the circus elite, conquering the world, in a future of high-tech campers, spotlights, big cities, and deafening applause.

'Tonight I'll perform without a net,' she announced. 'Like the great trapeze artists. Without a net.'

Dad shook his head in fear but did nothing to dissuade her.

In a greasy fog, thick as lard, the first spectators began to materialize in the streets of Orlasco around nine o'clock that night. Little more than distorted outlines, queuing at the box office to buy a ticket that would give them a break in their routine for a couple of hours. They entered the big top in silence, their mouths open wide and eyes looking upwards, as if they were entering an awe-inspiring cathedral or disembarking on an alien planet.

Children laughed and shouted.

The ringmaster shouted his 'Come one, come all!' towards the still-undecided townspeople at the edge of the square.

We artists followed the pantomime from behind the scenes, anxiously wondering whether some representative of the Balzelli circus would settle down in the uncomfortable plastic seats or if we'd gotten excited over nothing.

Despite the cold, dismal night, the big top was nearly full. The villagers munched on peanut brittle and cotton candy, rumbling with anticipation under the spotlights that reduced their faces to featureless blobs.

And when we were about to give up on our dreams of glory, five minutes before the start of the show, a loud 'Oooh' rose from the crowd, and we saw the ringmaster give an obsequious bow, guiding a small procession towards the best seats.

It was her. The divine Madame Balzelli, accompanied by two no-neck henchmen, bulls with dim-witted faces.

I had often heard about her.

Even as a child I wondered the reason for that nickname. *Divine*. There was nothing divine about the woman. Very tall, thin as a willow, wrapped in a golden tunic marked with strange arabesques, she looked like an Egyptian mummy. An enormous turban covered her egg-shaped head, competing in size with the aquiline nose that dominated the center of her wizened face, in which the sly and very black eyes of a predator gleamed.

There were cackles, shouts, and applause as Madame Balzelli made her way through the audience and settled into one of the frontmost seats with the movements of an eel, eyeing our battered big top with a mixture of amusement and disgust.

Then the lights went out.

The ringmaster, a misshapen pupil in the eye of the spotlight, made his little introductory speech.

Backstage the performers held their breath, their eyes fixed on Madame Balzelli.

'We're starting,' someone rasped.

Mom, Dad, and I hugged.

And the show began.

Everyone gave their all, everyone performed to the best of their ability.

In the air there was a smell of revenge, redemption.

The Divine Balzelli followed our adventures with an impassive look, huddling in conversation every so often with her henchmen.

The minutes flew by.

When the ringmaster introduced our number, mine and Dad's, I experienced a moment of extreme terror, followed by a flash of excitement.

My first show, and in the presence of Madame Balzelli!

'Everything will be fine,' Dad said.

'You'll both be great,' Mom said with a laugh. 'I love you. Show that old witch a thing or two.'

A kiss on the cheek, and the next moment we were out there, in front of about two hundred people, distorting our bodies for glory and because it was all we knew how to do.

It didn't go well. It went *brilliantly*.

Synchronicity, elegance, virtuosity, harmony. The audience let out cries at each of our feats, as our choreographies grew increasingly daring and complex.

I transformed myself into the Frog Boy, dislocating my shoulders and legs in such an unnatural way that it forced a shout of surprise from the crowd.

At the end, my father and I squeezed together into a box twenty-eight inches on each side, knotted around each other like two snakes. As we extricated ourselves from our monstrous and harmonic embrace and emerged from the box, we realized our number had been a success. That maybe our dreams would come true.

Everyone was on their feet clapping.

Even Madame Balzelli.

Mad with joy, I whirled around to meet my mother's eyes.

I didn't find them.

She had already climbed up, to a world that was only hers, a universe where life depended on two trapezes dangling lazily over the mere mortals below.

★

The drum roll. Mom sixty feet above the ground, hundreds of eyes turned towards her, a goddess in silver sequins suspended above our heads. The lights low, the lights low.

She performed alone, as I've already told you, she always had. She didn't trust anybody but herself, that's what she always said . . .

Platform, trapeze, trapeze, platform. Perfect moves, practiced thousands of times, wrapping and twisting her body like a mermaid of the air, then grasping the bar forcefully, escaping the fall.

Some nights, when I close my eyes, I still seem to see her white, sinuous body twirling in the dark, surrounded in a fluorescence emanating from her strength, her love.

I didn't realize then the danger of a performance without safeguards. She was my mother. Nothing could go wrong.

Dad was smiling and staring at her, but in his face I read an enormous fear. That was the moment when I realized how much he loved her. I wanted to love someone like that when I grew up, I thought.

Silence after the roar of the drums. Lungs paralyzed from holding in breath.

And then it started.

Without a net. Nothing beneath her but emptiness, sand, the clowns' melted grease paint, and remnants of horse manure.

Increasingly difficult maneuvers.

Madame Balzelli was mesmerized, her beaky nose stretching upwards, her tiny eyes shining with amazement. When the show was over she would go and talk with the ringmaster, would cough up a good sum of money and take us away from there, away from mediocrity, yes.

My mother had never made a mistake. She wouldn't make one this time either. And as a matter of fact she didn't. She fired up the crowd with a triple back flip, landed lightly on the platform, a goldfinch, and we knew the performance was over, and the lights came on, and it was a triumph.

But Mom wasn't finished with her number yet. Why she decided to keep going, to attempt one last risky and reckless feat, remains a mystery to me. Maybe she wanted to push herself to the limit, assure a future for herself in Madame Balzelli's circus. Maybe it was just plain vanity. Or maybe, I sometimes tell myself, she had crossed the line that divides bitter reality from happy ending.

She silenced the enraptured crowd with a brusque hand gesture, then made another hand signal to the technicians to dim the lights.

And she jumped again.

I heard my father moan, 'She's going to do the reverse pike! No! Why . . . ?' and I squeezed his arm tighter.

A slow-motion tragedy.

Mom swung with force, glued to the trapeze, muscles and nerves tensed to the utmost, then finally let go of the bar. The second trapeze didn't swing in sync with her angle of descent. She tried to grab it, but it was too far away. A matter of a couple of inches.

She came down like a hunk of lead, screaming.

I still hear that scream, followed by the rumble of shock from the spectators, and then a thud.

Thump.

A block of wood, a sack of potatoes, an inanimate object.

Dad hurtled towards the crumpled bundle in the sand, all sequins and bodily fluids, and although someone tried to hold me back I managed to wriggle away and follow him.

Mom no longer looked like a goddess.

The fall, accelerated by the spin of her leap, had been catastrophic. Her graceful body was completely altered; her neck and spine were twisted at a freakish angle, her face planted in the sand, which was turning black with blood, her legs disarticulated like a puppet's. Two lines of tears and mascara flowed from her dead eyes, the irises turned towards the bridge of her nose in a tragicomic squint. Subjected to a cruel game of levers, her leotard and the skin on her belly were torn, opening into a red and yellow eye of entrails.

The spine broken at an acute angle.

My mother, in death, had become a work of modern art celebrating the fallibility of the material of which Man is made.

I saw the clowns crying, the strong man vomiting, a distraught Madame Balzelli fleeing for the exit. The locals, torn between alarm and morbid curiosity, circled like a human Ouroboros around the circumference of the rink.

Before they dragged me away from the horror of the scene in a state of shock, I looked at my father.

He was studying my mother's back as though trying to understand, to comprehend the new and abstruse angles and perspectives of cartilage, bones, muscles. His eyes were bulging out of his head.

For a fraction of a second he turned towards me. He was someone else. I almost didn't recognize him.

I've never seen an expression like that since, thank heavens.

The expression of someone who has understood that even gods can die.

We stayed in the shabby circus.

Dad went crazy.

I think from guilt: blinded perhaps by the chance of success, he hadn't done anything to force my mother to perform with safety measures in place. The final image of her we would carry with us would be nightmarish, terrible.

I understood that he wanted to be left alone, and so I kept my distance, praying every night that he could process his grief and somehow we could be a family again, him and me.

He closed himself off in a pain made up of silence, obsession, and training. It was like I no longer existed, as if the passing of the woman he loved had erased me as well.

We stopped practicing together, but at night we would perform our show in tandem at the circus, which since the accident had fallen into disarray.

Every day, every night, he did nothing but train, shut inside the trailer's little bedroom, wallpapered with photos of my mother, of their life together. He wouldn't let me inside for any reason. He would practice up to eighteen hours a day, and his diet became a nightmare of seeds, apples, and self-pity. Already as thin as a rail, he lost another ten kilos. His face seemed to change, becoming closer and closer to that of a repulsive human snake.

I practiced alone outside, with him always shut up in the damned trailer, cold as stone, his eyes empty, not even a tear.

I was little and couldn't understand everything. But when about three months had passed since Mom's death, by which time I had become a ghost too, I made a decision: I would spy on him through the keyhole.

What was he doing in there, without any sound filtering under the door? Why didn't he want me with him, why did he forbid me to be near him?

It was an evening in late spring when my eye approached the keyhole. It took me a few moments to spot my father, whose body an anorexic model would have envied. He stood lazily doing warm-up exercises. Nothing else. Routine movements for a professional contortionist. He went on for at least an hour, with me there the whole time holding my breath. Then, for another hour, he carried out increasingly daring maneuvers, several of which I had never seen him do before and which caused even me to groan in amazement. I had to cover my mouth to avoid giving myself away.

After some cool-down exercises, I watched him head towards the center of the room, where there was a very small box, around fourteen inches on each side. He sat down beside it and began the most absurd and harrowing contortion I had ever seen. And yet I had seen it before.

I couldn't believe my eyes. I would have liked to gouge them out, but I couldn't look away.

He was imitating my mother's death pose.

His spine at an acute angle. His legs twisted behind his back, his head on the floor, turned at an angle not contemplated by a living body, on his face a dreadful and yet ecstatic mask that *looked beyond*, or perhaps *into the great beyond,* whatever that means.

It wasn't possible. It wasn't possible for him to bend like that without breaking his neck, without his bones, muscles, tendons, and ligaments snapping apart.

It was a caricature of human anatomy, of medical science, even of contortionism.

Anyone would have died in such a position.

Finally – and I heard his joints creak, his tendons *whistle* – he reassumed a 'normal' position, and with a fluid, reptilian movement, he slipped into that tiny box. An incredible feat, but it was nothing compared to what he had done before.

I stifled a cry, moved away from the door, left the trailer and ran through the fields, into swampy, mosquito-infested poplar groves, freaked out and wondering what I had just witnessed. When I got back to the circus two hours later, my father was still locked in his room.

I promised myself I would never peep through the keyhole again, not for any reason.

I never asked him why he did it, and above all how he had managed it.

Was it pain, love, my mother's death, that had allowed him to do it? And doing it, did he feel closer to her, did he *go to her*?

I think so, but . . . who can say?

I can only tell you that my father never recovered . . . How can you survive the death of the greatest love of your life? You can't. But for a brief period he was the best contortionist in the world.

He pushed the limits further and further every day, even during his performances. One night he caused a couple of audience members to faint when he squeezed into a box nine inches on each side. It sounds impossible, I know. And yet he did it. I didn't dare imagine what he got up to in the semi-darkness of his room, half starved, more and more withered, obsessed, *elastic*.

'It's not even fucking contortionism anymore.' One night I heard these words seep from the ringmaster's trailer. 'Never seen anything like it. It's magic. *Witchcraft*. Since his wife died he hasn't been in his right mind anymore. But he's my best artist, the circus is still standing thanks to him . . .'

In an atmosphere of constant anguish, the heaviness which precedes those events that trace a boundary line in life, an entire year of mourning, performances, and wanderings passed.

The anniversary of my mother's death arrived. We were in the vicinity of Idrasca, not too far from Orlasco, another one of those places nobody ever goes – not even by accident – unless they were born there. The big top was pitched, the show scheduled for that evening.

Morning. Dad came out of his room and made me breakfast. He hadn't done that in a long time. I thought it was a good sign and hugged him, and he returned my embrace, whispering, 'I'm sorry. I'm so sorry.'

We ate in silence, father and son sitting at a small table in a dilapidated trailer, the dirty windows turning the sunlight the color of an egg yolk.

He drank an entire pot of coffee by himself, smoked a cigarette without looking at me, and I knew he was thinking about Mom. He never thought of anything but her. Neither did I, for that matter.

Finally he stood up, put out his cigarette, and headed for his bedroom. 'I'm going to practice my routine. Be good. I love you.'

The door closed, I heard the click of the lock.

I waited and waited and waited, never walking away.

Late that night, worried, I knocked softly. 'Everything all right, Dad?'

No response but silence.

The keyhole. Inside, darkness.

I knocked harder, then I shouted, I cried, and still there was nothing but silence. Someone heard me. A bunch of people came running.

The strong man knocked down the door. We turned on the light. There was no one in the room. The little window was latched from inside. While everyone was calling my father's name, I noticed something in the middle of the room.

A tiny cardboard box, an inch and a half on each side. With trembling hands I picked it up, looked inside.

Empty.

A faint aroma of coffee, aftershave, sweat, and tobacco reached my nostrils.

No one ever saw him again.

Many years have passed. I've performed in many circuses, visited thousands of places, and I've been working for years now at the Bertacca. I've never stopped practicing, pushing myself a little further every day.

Extreme training, smaller and smaller boxes, even during performances.

Like Dad.

During the shows I often watch the trapeze artists and lose myself in my memories.

But I can't get distracted.

I have to go on, keep bending my body, disassembling my flesh, discovering new levers and new spaces to reach my parents.

I think I'm making good progress. And maybe there will come a tomorrow when I too manage to get inside the last, smallest box. An inch and a half on each side. It's only a question of perseverance, physical predisposition, pain, and love.

There's something magical and terrible about pain and love. They can open doors that are sometimes better left closed. But I'll do everything I can to open them and explore that emptiness that follows us and grants us no respite.

Like Dogs

I take the bus to Turin.
Once a month. Or twice.

I go there for the lights. The archways. The voices. To get away from the country, the darkness, the farm, the manure basin, the strange bushes that sprout from the ground, the sounds that echo in the belly of the earth . . . And from the bad memories. Although the memories are always there. I could go all the way to the North Pole, but they would still be there.

I also go there for the homeless. And to get hold of books.

I sit under the shelter in my worn-out overalls, waiting for the bus that goes from Orlasco to the city. Sometimes there are kids with stylish haircuts and backpacks on their shoulders waiting too.

'What is he wearing? And look how fat he is!'

'Does he ever wash those filthy overalls?'

'Look at those glasses, they're like Coke bottles!'

And so on. I don't pay any attention. With everything I've been through . . . well, their insults are caresses. I just shrug and wait for the bus to come. Sometimes I think about Dog and smile.

Dog was my only friend.

He still is.

United by despair. Brothers in loneliness.

And when two wretched souls meet, reality can take some twists and turns.

Terrible, surprising, unimaginable.

This story will take some twists and turns too. It won't be a linear narrative. It will be a mule track full of curves, hairpin bends, and wrong turns. Isn't life the same way?

I hope you'll come along for the ride.

My name is Danilo Marosso.

An only child.

Class of 1986.

When I was born Dad was forty, Mom thirty-eight. Not exactly spring chickens.

And I grew up on the family farm on the outskirts of Orlasco, a little village of one thousand souls located six kilometers from Pinerolo, twenty-eight from Turin, at the foot of the Alps.

I still live here.

A corner of Piedmont untouched by modern life. Everything is just like it was thirty years ago: the gravel road leading to the farm, the skeletal poplars standing guard over piles of steaming manure, the darkness that swallows up the irrigation ditches on moonless nights, the horizon broken up by the ruined remnants of old houses along the railroad tracks.

It's comforting and at the same time awful how some things don't change, always staying the same. In some places time doesn't pass, just like in some people's minds. The two things are related, I think, and there's nothing anyone can do about it. It's just how it is, and that's all there is to it.

My parents 'worked the land', as they say in these parts. Farmers and ranchers. They had acres and acres of land (mostly for growing corn and poplar trees) and ninety hogs, crammed into a sty whose stench spread throughout our house and for a radius of miles, sometimes all the way to the center of town. That might be why we weren't looked on too fondly in Orlasco. Besides the fact that my father was a violent drunk and my mother the granddaughter of a woman who had killed herself at age 90 by drinking a liter of lye because she was convinced a witch had put a hex on her and eyeballs were popping up in her stomach . . . but that's another story.

Anyway.

The pigs' piss and shit flowed into an enormous cement basin in the middle of the yard, forming a disgusting sludge (we called it *sughet*) of a ghastly color. A horrible brown, covered in frothy yellowish bubbles. The color of excrement, of refuse, of a manure too acidic to be used for fertilizer.

Now the basin is empty because the hogs are gone, but sometimes as I walk across the yard at dusk I can still smell the stink of it. The stench is in my head, I know that, just like I know that it will be there until I breathe my final breath.

Memory can hold on to smells, and a lot of other things.

Memory can be a curse.

Mornings I went to school, where I had no friends and everyone made fun of me because I was fat and smelled like manure. Hygiene wasn't a priority on the farm.

Afternoons I helped my father in the fields and with the livestock. It wasn't my choice to help him. I had to. I would have rather stayed in my room reading poetry or flipping through Mom's magazines and making up fantasy stories, imaginary adventures of cops and robbers, of travels and wonders, of distant lands where beautiful princesses conquer the forces of darkness.

But that wasn't possible.

We had to 'work the land', break our backs, hoard up money to buy more hogs, more tractors, more poplars.

I had always liked poetry, ever since the first grade. Rodari. And later Buzzati and Ungaretti. And Leopardi: 'Bitter and tedious life is, nothing more; and the world is mud'.

But my favorite is Dickinson. There's something so poignant about her verse (and her life, reclusive, solitary) that I'm moved just thinking about it . . .

I've written some too. I don't know where this penchant of mine came from, but it was one of the few things I had any interest in. I started when I was about eight. With little compositions in which I described life in the country. They weren't happy verses. Stuff like:

The sow's cry
Scares the flies
The poplars
Grow crooked
From the dry earth.

I never let anyone read them. No one would have read them anyway. They would have said: 'Can you believe it, that idiot Danilo Marosso has gotten it into his head that he's a poet!' Although that's not entirely accurate; one of my poems, the best one I think, someone did read, and . . . But I'm getting off track again. We're getting there, we're getting there. I warned you it wouldn't be a simple path.

Sorry.

As I was saying.

My parents: if school hadn't been mandatory, if I'd been born thirty years earlier, they would have dedicated my whole life to laboring like a peasant. Shovels, tractors, and feed. Sows, wells, and plows.

Mom was a quiet, submissive creature locked in a constant battle with the stove, the oven, the chickens, the turkeys, the vegetable garden. She never stuck up for me. If she had tried, Dad's terrible wrath would have fallen on her as well. She was more afraid of him than anything else. Everyone was afraid of him. Even the animals. *Especially* the animals.

He had always beaten me. Ever since I was a little kid. Everyone is born with the seed of hatred; if your life is hard and exhausting and if you don't root out that seed, well . . . it'll grow into a poisonous, parasitic plant, consuming you and feeding you at the same time. Dad tended to his seed for years. It was easy for him: just like invasive plants, evil doesn't need much care. All you have to do is leave it alone and it'll grow strong and luxuriant.

He beat me because I'd been born and maybe because I reminded him of what he hated most – himself. Another Marosso. A bloodline of peasants enervated by the earth, by wine, by the hard, dry sod of the Pinerolese lowlands.

He kicked me and punched me because I existed.

Just like Dog.

Every day my father said that Dog and I were alike. Useless. Stupid. I don't think it was true (I like to read and fantasize and put my thoughts down on paper, which you already know because you're reading this, and the dog responded to commands), but when you hear it constantly and take so many beatings and thrashings . . . well, maybe you can't help becoming a little bit stupid.

When his hands got the itch, which was almost always, it was best to keep a safe distance. Hide.

But in the end he would find you.

He would always find you.

In front of the Louis Vuitton display windows in Via Roma homeless people lie on beds of cardboard and rags, bundles that at first glance don't even seem human, but rather creatures of cardboard and rags. It's funny. There's them sleeping in a cocoon of plastic bags and newspapers, the Christmas lights, the young people strolling through the city's wealthy corridor, and middle-aged couples deformed by Botox who stop in front of the stores to ponder the purchase of a seven-hundred euro handbag, and then there's me, leaning against one of the archway columns and watching them with a beer in my hand, in old clothes and short of breath from the strain of hauling my weight around.

I think we're all pretty sorry cases.

Aren't we?

We're these things that struggle to survive and find refuge from the darkness that looms over our heads, always, even on days of blinding sun, even when we're walking beneath the glow of the holiday lights in the glittering avenues of Turin.

In the end we're all alone like dogs, even if dogs are better than us.

They aren't bad, unless we make them bad.

They don't know they're going to die.

In normal families, the dog becomes part of the pack.

But ours wasn't a normal family.

And the dog was just a dog. In fact, his name was Dog. A large mutt, ugly and gnarled, his tail thin and mangy . . . But I have to back up a bit.

Dad brought him home when he was little more than a puppy; I was ten. I don't know where he got him. In all likelihood from one of his drinking buddies (I can't call them 'friends', because he wasn't the type to make friends) or from some outlying farm.

I remember we were in the kitchen when he pulled him out of his jacket, a puffy brown ball, scared and shivering. Medium-length fur. Floppy ears. A tail ending in a corolla of fluff. Sad eyes. Judging from the size of his head and paws he was going to get nice and big, I thought.

I instinctively reached out a hand to pet him – was I finally going to have a playmate, a friend? – and like a whip came the backhand slap in my face that made my nose bleed.

'Don't touch him!' thundered my father, pulling the little animal away. An alcoholic miasma gushed from his mouth along with the words. 'He's gonna be a guard dog! If we start pampering him, he'll turn into a pansy. He's gotta keep watch. Now he's going outside, that way he'll start figuring out how things are in this house. We'll call him . . . Dog! That's a good name. Just right for a dog.'

I looked for Mom's eyes, but all I found was a curved back, a head bent over needle and thread. The kitchen stank of wood smoke and milk burnt on the stove and ineradicable loneliness.

I went to the bathroom and rinsed my face. In the mirror my nose and lip were swelling into a caramelized bruise.

After dinner, when my father gave me a kick in the pants and sent me out to check the hogs, Dog was already chained up between the entrance gate and the barn. In the half-light of an aseptic moon, his little eyes gleaming white like glass lenses, he looked like a ghost, the pale specter of a living creature.

He was looking at me, staring at me, and I'll never forget the sound that came from his coffee-colored muzzle: a throaty howl, poignant, the sob of one who realizes that things have taken a bad turn and won't get any better, definitely won't get any better. I wondered how many slaps or pinches the drunken ogre had already given him.

He wagged his bizarre feather duster of a tail a little, just barely, to get my attention, to seek comfort, just as I would have liked to be comforted by him.

'I can't,' I whimpered in the autumn evening, an evening of wind and dust. 'I can't.'

If I went near him, I'd wind up hurting somewhere besides my nose.

I whimpered again and ran towards the pigsty, in the odor of the sows and manure, thinking of some lines from a poem they had made us read in school the week before:

> *A dog without a head,*
> *poor beast.*
> *No one knows*
> *how he barks.*

I cried until I was heaving, and as I crossed the yard on the way back to the house I didn't even glance at Dog and his chain.

From that day on, for twenty years, I never once saw him loose from those few iron links.

He broke free from his yoke one cold and rainy May morning.

When he bit my father.
When he died.
The first time.

As I stroll along Via Po, passing by all the happy couples walking arm in arm, I think about how we all have chains. Some longer than others. But almost all of us have them, even if we don't think so.

Maybe some vagabonds don't have them. The ones who live in the most squalid parts of the city, in alleys in rundown neighborhoods where the soundtrack is the vulgar voices of dealers and whores; the ones who have gone crazy, wrecks with nothing left to lose but their life, which they'd be glad to lose, obviously, just look at them, only they don't have the courage or strength to commit the ultimate act, so they do it in installments instead, wasting away from cold and alcohol, a little at a time; the ones who watch me from the photos on flyers hung up along the city streets, distorted faces with capital letters written over them:

ATTILIO LOFFREDO – HOMELESS – MISSING –
Last seen Feb. 16 at Porta Nuova station, wearing black jacket,
white sneakers . . .

And so on, and so on.

They're the real ghosts, invisible people able to lead lonely lives with no present or future.

I have a roof over my head – the only thing my parents left me, besides a small inheritance – but in some ways I'm like them.

I pass unseen, even though I'm quite fat.

A specter.

A shadow lost in the foggy limbo that stretches between the countryside and the city.

A child of fear and loneliness and human indifference.

Sometimes I exchange a few words with these derelicts, hand them some cash, examine them under their torn hoodies, their filthy, greasy beards. They torment me, those sad eyes of theirs. They remind me of Dog's, crushed and empty and crazy, my father's, my mother's in her final days, mine studying myself from the other side of the mirror . . .

If it weren't for Dog, I would have killed myself by now. Maybe by sticking my head in the oven like Sylvia Plath.

But I endure.

Because I'm a curious guy, and just like you, I want to know how this story – or should I say poem? – is going to end.

If it ever ends.

After Dog showed up, I have to admit I felt less alone. I empathized with that forlorn quadruped. And as ridiculous as it might sound, I think he felt empathy for me.

He became a good guard dog. Whenever a stranger approached the gate he would bark and growl until he foamed at the mouth, yanking his chain with a tenacious animal hatred. He loathed the postman, who would ride his bicycle around town on his days off, constantly whistling a silly little tune. Whenever Dog saw him he would pull so hard that I was afraid the chain's post would come out of the ground; the mailman seemed to enjoy provoking him and would whistle louder as he passed our gate. Dad, spitting on the ground, maintained that one day he'd shoot the bastard with the rifle he used for hunting wild boars.

Every time my father passed by Dog he would give him a kick. To toughen him up, he said. Don't want him turning into a queer dog. The same went for me, more or less. I was luckier, however. Mornings I went to school, and however much the other kids bullied me, it was still better than being at home.

I had a little bedroom, plenty of decent food. And an empty space inside that I tried to fill by stuffing myself. I got fatter, day after day after day.

Not Dog.

Whether it was the infamous August sun or the excruciating February cold, he was always there, a skeleton in the heat waves, a bag of bones in the swirling snow, destined to get nothing but scraps and hunks of stale bread.

We would watch each other from a distance. He would move his funny little tail whenever he saw me. But not too much.

We grew up together. He on his chain, I on mine. He turned into a large-sized dog, all ribs and sharp teeth and scars, I into an obese and nearsighted boy who dragged himself through middle school in silence, with little talent in any subject except Italian.

They stuck me with a special needs teacher. Because I was odd, quiet, and had trouble learning, especially in science class. But I don't think I actually had a learning disability. It's just that numbers didn't interest me; science couldn't break through the shell of fear and hostility that had formed around me. Why apply myself at something I wasn't interested in? I had no use for numbers. I knew how to count the sows in the pigsty, that was enough for me.

'He has a slight disability,' they said. What was the point in contradicting them? To prove what? What could other people possibly know about what someone has inside them, their interior world, and why let them in if you're doing just fine on your own?

'Poetry seems to be the only thing capable of moving him,' they said, and it was true. The verses would sink into my head like a red-hot needle into butter. I imagined my brain with the letters embedded in its slimy curves, the punctuation marks floating between the dura mater and the cranium. A really beautiful image, I think.

The special needs teacher, Mirella, was a middle-aged woman with a good, kind face, who tried to encourage my passion: she gave me a lot of books, which I hid under my mattress: if Dad had found them, they would have met an ugly end.

Books were for queers, of course. In our house you wouldn't find anything but handbooks on agricultural machinery and crop growing.

At the beginning of seventh grade, Mirella died in a car accident and was replaced by a teacher whose only concern was doing what the school system expected of him. That was my first real encounter with the Black Lady: Mirella didn't show up at school one morning, and she never returned. Gone. In the wreckage. No more books, no more of the affection I wasn't getting at home.

I felt lonelier than ever, depressed, and at the end of the year they held me back. When my father saw my report card I defended myself, saying I'd gotten an A in Italian: he whipped my ass so hard with his belt that I still have the marks even now. Then he threw the bowl of minestrone he was eating in my mother's face, claiming that roadkill would have tasted better. Finally he went up to my room and returned to the kitchen with the books I had hidden for months under the mattress.

'You think I don't know you stay up all night reading this crap?' he spat in my face. 'That's why you're getting bad grades in every other subject, you little bastard! Because you don't sleep, you just think about poetry, books! We work the land here, Danilo. There's no time for bullshit here, goddamnit. You've gotta hurry up and finish school, there's the farm to take care of!'

Like in a slow-motion nightmare, I saw him walk towards the stove.

Open it.

The light from the dancing flames made him look like a demon, a drunken satyr that even the woods of poplars and beeches around Orlasco had rejected, chasing him off towards civilization.

'No, not the books, please,' I begged.

And a moment later the volumes I had so jealously saved – *Nursery Rhymes All Year Round*, *Pinocchio*, *The Bears' Famous*

Invasion of Sicily, *Barnabo of the Mountains*, and many others —
became nothing but smoke, ash, and cinders.

It was like dying.

Another of my countless little deaths.

Then, as if nothing had happened, Dad said: 'I'm going to
the shop for a popsicle.'

As he walked across the yard he had time to vent his cruelty
on Dog too. I heard the hisses and pops of the ash-wood stick. I
heard the poor beast howl and cry, and the rattling of the chain
links as he tried to dodge the blows.

My mother picked up the broken dish, her face covered in
minestrone and sadness. 'Patience is a virtue . . .' she muttered,
and I understood that she wanted to cry but was all out of tears.

That was when I decided I was going to kill him.

Sooner or later I would kill him with my own hands.

I dragged myself to my room, realizing that I too had no
more tears left to cry.

At night I couldn't sleep because of the pain. And I don't
mean from the belt lashes. I stood at the window until dawn
watching the dog, Dog, crouched in the summer downpour
falling over the plains like a juggernaut of water and lightning.

Ribs and mange and ragged tail and malnutrition and
wounds left by the sharpened ash stick.

He stared at me, trembling.

Whimpering.

But it wasn't a cry of pain. It was the sound of terror that had
turned into madness. It was a sound I had never heard before,
which seemed to reverberate in the earth and the countryside
and the darkest part of my brain.

I could feel his mad gaze fixed on me, even if I could hardly
make out his outline in the torrent of water pissing down from
the sky.

I could tell that he wanted to kill him too. And I promised
him it would happen. He would suffer. For every slap, insult,
kick, humiliation.

The next moment, as if my mind and body no longer belonged to me, I watched myself take a pencil from the desk and start dashing off verses, grinding my teeth in the darkness of the bedroom:

> *There are chains of nails and iron,*
> *and others, invisible, that torment,*
> *my eyes search for you*
> *while the wind shakes with your whimpers.*

> *Cast aside, stray dogs,*
> *soaking wet hounds*
> *in the driving rain,*
> *we dream our separate ways*
> *in the violence*
> *of the storm.*

At daybreak, when it had stopped raining and a pale sun dispersed the mist hanging over the yard, I was still at the window.

Dog was still watching me. His tongue, purple and swollen, hung from his muzzle like a rotten sausage. He had steeped and brooded in hatred with me all night long. He wagged his tail slightly, pissed on the pole holding the chain, and let out a soundless howl towards the sun.

As if he loathed it.

As if he belonged to darkness, and darkness belonged to him.

I remembered with dismay that school was over.

Summer break.

It meant three months trapped in the prison of the farmhouse, toiling, suffering, and trying to survive.

It was a hot summer, the hottest of my life. Spent mostly cutting down poplars, which had to dry in the woodshed so they could be sold to a joinery in Pinerolo in the winter.

If you've never spent a summer in the Pinerolese lowlands

(and why would you?) you can't understand the extent of the heat that blankets it from June to August. A scorching curtain that manifests with a humidity rate of over ninety percent, a deadly pall, the 'tuf,' as the farmers call it, almost an onomatopoeic sound to describe the sluggish feeling caused by that microclimate.

We sawed the trees, loaded the pieces on the cart, and sweated; even the ogre was drained of energy, a husk dangling in the countryside, uttering insults to Christ and the summer.

It didn't even cross his mind to let Dog off the chain, to build him a shelter from the slow heatwave that was singeing the plains. I thought he would die, that he would dissolve into a puddle of blood and fur. I would see him stick his head in his water bowl in search of relief. When I dared to suggest keeping him in the shade, the response was as simple as it was terrifying: 'If he croaks, I'll put you on the chain to keep watch. Hurry up, get a move on!'

Even the corn died from the heat. The stalks we had planted were thin and yellow; no matter how much we irrigated the rows, it never seemed to be enough water to turn them green again.

What a boiling-hot summer, the hottest I can ever remember ... But I remember it in particular because it was the summer when the ogre taught me how to operate the combine harvester.

'If anything happens to me, you'll have to know how to drive the Beast,' he explained to me one morning in mid-July, as he ate his breakfast of cheap wine and fried eggs. That's what he called it, the Beast, and every time he said it I couldn't help thinking that the only beast around there was him. Not Barba Bertu's cows, not our hogs, not Dog, not the harvester. Him. 'You're a big boy now. That is ... you're a dumbass, but you've got to know how to drive the Beast. I'm getting old ...'

It wasn't easy. But it wasn't that difficult either. When every mistake you make earns you a calloused slap, you learn quickly.

And I'd already known how to run the tractor for a couple of years: I drove it with the trailer in tow, following the Beast, which shot the shucked corn into it.

Combines are monsters of metal and pistons and belts and gears. They have a mowing head in the front that you might call the mouth: teeth-like blades that detach the stems from the cobs and ingest the latter, pushing them towards the stomach, the threshing drum and the concave. Two spinning drums which, using friction, separate the kernels from the ears and eject them onto the trailer through the expulsion duct, the intestine.

It was a nice feeling, driving that juggernaut through the fields. Every so often I would dream of showing up at school astride the combine and running over the bullies who made fun of me because I was fat, the teachers who didn't understand me.

In September, when the heat subsided, I did my first threshing. In the course of just three days, running up and down the rows atop the Beast, making it digest the ears and defecate kernels. My father followed me the whole time on the tractor, a satisfied grin on his face.

When the work was finished, while I was putting the equipment back in the shed, he handed me some cash. He was smiling.

'Bravo, good job,' he said, giving me a pat on the back that almost collapsed my lungs.

It was the only time I felt even vaguely that I was his son.

With no small difficulty I finished my mandatory schooling and became a full-time prisoner. Of the country, of the farm, of depression.

The years rolled slowly on, punctuated by work and the seasons. Living in the country, the seasons aren't an abstract concept, they're real and vivid and you feel them in your flesh, because they control life and death, and you're a participant in this death and rebirth, death and rebirth, and you know that one day you too will die but won't be reborn.

Nature, which gives us struggles and gives us life, a serpent of poplars and wheat and tomatoes and sows and calves, a mammoth snake of meat and vegetables and mud and manure and men, forever devouring its own tail, to feed itself and feed you, one day it'll spit you out of its eternal coils, and that's that.

Think about it too much and you'll go out of your mind. But you can't help thinking about it, because in the country death is always there. *It's the irrigation canal that dries up, the crop that withers, the calf born dead*, as the poet Montale might have put it . . .

Mom got sick. I was twenty-two when she started to complain of pain in her face, under her left eye. At the hospital they did a CAT scan and found a tumor in the lining of her cheek. A carcinoma. They operated, but the cancer grew back, despite the chemo, the treatments, the prayers. It was an incorrigible bastard that refused to die.

Her hair fell out and her face swelled and started to develop a calcified growth, like a tuber, a horrible purplish tuber of crazed skin and tissue. She was made of strong stuff and kept going for quite a while, almost nine years. Unfortunately for her.

After her diagnosis Dad got worse, if it was possible for him to be any worse. Dog and I were the scapegoats he vented his frustrations on.

Dog was still on his chain. Aged, to be sure. You would shrivel up too if you were left to the mercy of the serpent of the seasons for years on end, imprisoned by a few meters of iron.

I was no longer prohibited from petting him, being close to him. He had become what he had been raised and beaten for: a living burglar alarm. And the ogre had other things to worry about: cancer, wine, the corn, which no longer brought in much money. The kicks were less frequent, but when they came, they always hurt.

At night, when silence fell over the farm, sometimes I would sit at my desk putting my poems to paper, stashing them after-

ward in a special hidden compartment I'd made in a drawer
because . . . well, you understand why.

I wrote one for Mom. It went like this:

> *Inside your face,*
> *corrupt galaxies*
> *in recalcitrant*
> *universes.*

> *Bald, you dance*
> *your chemotherapy waltz*
> *on the snow-white*
> *sheets of sacrifice*

> *Aseptic, surgical dance which,*
> *like an abandoned railroad track,*
> *never ends.*

And every night around three a.m. I would go downstairs
to get some food from the kitchen and take it outside to Dog,
the poor mutt: he would eat it straight from my hands, licking
my fingers. I would stay a while petting him, looking into his
eyes, which in the starlight had something human about them,
all too human, and almost every time I would recite the poem
that I had dedicated to him, that *I'd dedicated to myself*, repeating
it like a prayer: 'There are chains of nails and iron . . . cast aside,
stray dogs . . . we dream our separate ways . . .'

Then I would go to bed, and before I fell asleep I would think
about the next day's chores, about Mom's face transformed by
an unrelenting horror, and about the promise I had made to my
four-legged friend.

I hadn't forgotten.

Turin is a lovely city. I started going there once I was all on
my own. To take my mind off things.

They say it's a magical city.

I've read a lot of books on the subject. Some buildings are constructed according to certain laws, capable of absorbing the Universe's positive energy. And then there are other 'dark' places, where the terrible things you see on the news happen, or where the Devil has left his mark. And these good and bad energies have been at war since Turin was nothing more than an agglomeration of huts, and wizards and witches worshipped wooden idols on the banks of the Po.

I don't know if it's true.

What I do know for certain is that the countryside is magical. And terrible.

I've lived there my whole life and can guarantee it. How many stories I had heard from the farmers, from my parents and elderly aunts, before getting the proof myself!

Tales of ghosts, sorceresses, and horrible beasts that wallow in the irrigation canals, eyewitness accounts of age-old rituals to bring rain and bountiful harvests, legends of the *meisnur*, ancient healers able to get rid of illnesses and tumors with a simple touch of their hand, and tales of calves born with two heads on the coldest day of the year, of subterranean tunnels dug in ages long past, of votive pillars dedicated to snake-headed saints, of rocks with indecipherable engravings depicting pools of water with curative properties, of plots of land where they buried unbaptized newborns, who returned to life for a few moments, just long enough to receive the holy sacrament and escape Limbo . . .

I could go on for hours telling you those kinds of stories . . . but I'm telling you mine, and it's a story that still has to come to an end.

A story that's scary as hell.

Trim the poplars, feed the hogs, work the combine, shovel the snow, irrigate the corn rows, take advantage of the night-time to seek refuge in my little universe of poetry.

Never saying a word, never fighting back.

There were no significant changes in my sad existence until 2016.

I was thirty years old.

Dog was twenty.

I wouldn't have bet a cent on his living so long, no way. You should have seen him: he looked like one of those specters from popular folklore, a lost soul destined to haunt farmhouses and barns, waiting for redemption, for one of the living to right a wrong he had suffered to give him his well-deserved eternal rest.

You could count his ribs, and his eyes had become covered in cataracts; the skin of his nose was always chapped, and he'd lost a good part of his fur to mange and the bad weather; nevertheless, he hadn't stopped wagging his tail as soon as he noticed my presence, nor licking my hands every time I offered him a bread crust or a bone. The chain was still there, still the same, rusty and shameful, and had dug a groove around his neck. It must have looked ridiculous, the sight of us together: Dog a skeleton and me a big, chunky boy well on my way to a massive coronary.

Dad's face had gone purple from all the wine, and he persisted in his favorite activities: getting drunk, farming, kicking Dog in the ass, and making our lives a living hell.

As I already mentioned, my mother held on, but that winter the illness got the upper hand and overran her body, confining her to bed most of the time; I brought food and medicine to her in bed, I gave her painkillers, managing not to look at her face, covered in the cancerous lumps that by then had devoured half her head and a good part of her soul. She watched me with her right eye, which the carcinoma hadn't yet taken, and mumbled that I was a good son, and I responded that she was a good mom, even if it wasn't true.

One morning in January the pain became unbearable, and I gave her a double dose of morphine; I realized it was the last vial, so I grabbed the doctor's prescription and mounted my bike to ride to the pharmacy.

Tied to his chain, Dog started to wag his tail with an unusual frenzy, directing an agitated cry towards me like a shrill, malignant laugh. I lingered a few seconds to pet him and let him lick my fingers, then I rode out of the yard, pumping the pedals, my belly dangling over my groin. As I made my way along Via Portasa, the narrow strip of asphalt that connects the outlying areas with the village proper, I thought about how Mom couldn't make it much longer.

I didn't often go to downtown Orlasco; usually it was my father who ran the errands, but that day he had been drunk since the night before, so it fell to me.

Downtown (a square, a bar, some shops, and two rows of parallel archways) buzzed with activity, despite the damp cold and the mist that crept into the marrow of your bones: it was market day.

And as I made my way slowly on my bicycle, the voices of the village gossips followed me like poisoned darts.

'Marosso's son, my God, look at the belly on him!'

'Eh, it's not easy growing up with a dad who's a drunk. And his mother . . . she's being eaten alive by tumors.'

'Danilo Marosso . . . he talks all funny, like a six-year-old kid.'

'All those beatings knocked the sense out of him.'

'He used to go to school with my daughter. He had a special needs teacher, he's half retarded . . .'

And so on.

When I reached the pharmacy my cheeks were lined with tears, and not because of the cold. It wasn't the first time the sharp tongues of the village gossips stabbed me with their mixture of pity and derision, but that morning . . . I don't know, it cut deeper.

I hated them.

I cursed them.

I wasn't to blame.

My father was to blame.

For their jokes, for their bullying sons, for this backward environment, for the countryside, for the isolation.

By their standards I was different, a mistake.

But I was also their product.

Their legacy.

I went in the shop, bought the morphine, and went back out into the cold. As I was closing the glass door I saw the flyer, next to the ads for pharmaceutical products.

A faded photocopy, stuck to the glass with scotch tape.

That flyer changed everything, set in motion the final chapters of this story.

It said:

THE ORLASCO LIBRARY
ANNOUNCES THE SECOND NATIONAL
VALENTINE'S DAY POETRY CONTEST
Poems about Love
Send two copies of each entry (max. 2) to the following address:
Orlasco Library, Via Roma 205, Turin 10060
Deadline February 14!
The top three will be contacted by registered mail by March 20

A local contest, the kind they do in small towns to build a sense of community, promote a little culture.

I don't know how long I stood there gawping at the notice, memorizing it. Too long, apparently, since the pharmacist pushed the door open a crack and asked me with a perplexed look: 'Everything all right, son?'

There was pity in his eyes.

And I'd had enough of pity.

I mounted my bike without answering him and let myself be swallowed up in the mist.

The roofs looked like a dog's teeth, bared to challenge the sky.

It was the busiest and most exciting night of my life.

When the old drunk collapsed on the couch and Mom stopped hollering, sinking into her opioid oblivion, I opened the secret compartment in my drawer and reread all my poems, jotted on scraps of paper, Post-its, and sheets of newspaper over the span of two decades. There weren't many, and I couldn't be an impartial judge, but for me some of them meant something, had a nice ring to them.

I had decided that afternoon after feeding the hogs: I would enter the library's poetry contest.

Why not?

Maybe they would like my verses . . . maybe they would see I wasn't stupid, the village idiot, poor Danilo Marosso . . .

There was just one problem: the entries had to be about love, and I had never known love, nor had I ever written about it.

I pondered and pondered . . .

The only two living beings I had interacted with who had aroused in me something akin to that feeling had been Dog and Mirella, my sixth-grade special needs teacher.

I went to fish out the verses I had dashed off for my chained-up friend. The ones I recited to him on moonless nights, written the night when Dad had thrashed me with his belt and Dog with his stick. The night when he'd hurled his bowl of soup in Mom's face.

The night when I had sworn I would kill him.

Yes, they were verses of hatred and despair that I could turn into a love poem. Don't those things go hand in hand? Hate, love, despair, death, madness . . .

It took me a couple of hours to find the right rhythm, the proper words, lulled by my mother's sickly snoring and the rattling chain of the four-legged beast pacing in circles around the pole that had been the only fixed point in his life.

Finally, satisfied, I copied the poem onto two clean sheets of paper, in my awful handwriting, and gave it a title:

LIKE DOGS

There are days when you don't love me,
moments when you don't notice.
I search for you with my eyes
and your hair moves the wind.

Cast aside, stray dogs,
soaking wet hounds
in the pouring rain,
let us explore deserted cities
in the snow-white clouds
of our old age.

At the bottom I jotted down my personal details and home address, filled with a wearying sense of discouragement and insecurity. Would the jury of teachers and librarians from Orlasco laugh at my composition? Would it give them another reason to make fun of me?

Who cares, I told myself. *Who cares.*

I went over to the desk, folded the poems, and slipped them into two white envelopes; I heard Dog bark and I walked to the window. He was watching me. All tremors and tongue and old age.

I licked the glue on the envelope. It was bitter.

Then I sneaked out, got my bike, and went to mail the poems.

I certainly didn't think I would win. For me, the important thing was to participate. To show them I existed.

And that with poetry, in some way, I had fought against hell.

Mom's health got worse, and the competition faded into the background.

She screamed.

She was always screaming.

Her head was like a rotten pumpkin.

And as if the screams weren't enough, there was Dad's shout-ing on top of it, barking out orders to me and railing against the Creator who had sent this pestilence into our home.

Every so often I checked the mailbox, never finding any-thing there but bills and feed catalogs; as the days went by, part of me started to fantasize, to hope, that one morning the mail-man would deliver a registered letter from the library.

The more I read 'Like Dogs', the more I liked it.

Yes, maybe the judges would too . . .

One night I dreamt of my teacher Mirella wrapped in her burial shroud, perched atop a poplar tree like some mysterious bird of rags and cemetery dirt: she told me I had written some very beautiful lines, and that soon the whole town would know I wasn't a halfwit, but a boy who'd had an unfortunate life and who had a knack for poetry and something to say.

February ended, then came March; spring arrived and with it milder temperatures and a warm wind that made the boars squeal restlessly and made Dog – who was more and more with-ered, disoriented, and haggard – howl. Every day I thought it would be his last. I thought the same about my mother.

At the beginning of April I stopped checking the mail, unable to conceal from myself my disappointment, my shame. Had I really let myself be lulled the past few weeks into the idea that I could win the competition, or even have a place on the podium? I, Danilo Marosso, the stupid farmer who had grown up covered in the stench of manure, the son of a troglodyte, capable of nothing better than steering the combine?

So they were right.

They had won.

On Easter night I had a sort of nervous breakdown. My room went all pink, then black, as an unbearable weight pressed against my chest; when I came to, I was sitting in front of the kitchen stove: my poems were blazing in the fire, being consumed forever. I burned them all, except 'Like Dogs', which I slipped into my wallet between the banknotes. A prayer card to remind me forever of my failure.

I stopped writing.

In early May Mom got out of bed: she was an agonizing sight, an anomaly of lumps and abscesses, but she said she felt better. I think the carcinoma had decided to grant her a bit of a reprieve before mounting the final attack.

And finally we come to the ninth of May. The fateful day.

Since the previous evening an icy wind, unusual for the season, had begun to blow from the Alps over the plain. It rained all morning and the temperature plummeted.

It happens sometimes in the Pinerolese lowlands. Spring retreats for a few days, as if wanting to remind us that the seasons of blossoms and harvests won't last long, that frost and mist will return to torment the area because it's their right.

Moisture had crept into the house's thick stone walls, and as I descended the stairs in the grayness of the cloudy dawn that was filtering inside, I shivered. I found Mom in the kitchen on the couch, wrapped in a torn shawl; through the French doors I spotted my father in the yard, swathed in an absurd yellow raincoat, focused on sharpening the blade of a spade. Dog was watching him with empty eyes from a short distance away.

The stove had gone out.

'We'd better light this, it's cold,' I said to my mother, kneeling before the stove. She answered with an affirmative gurgle through the swelling that had overtaken the roof of her mouth.

We kept the things necessary for lighting the fire – matches, twigs, waste paper – in a bucket beside the stove. I grabbed a crumpled sheet of newspaper and some twigs, then something at the bottom of the bucket caught my attention.

A yellow envelope.

The kind they use for registered letters.

It had been opened, then torn in two.

I felt a sharp pain at the base of my neck, and then black and purple lightning danced before my eyes, like the night when I had burned all my poems to ash.

With hands like dough I picked up the envelope and the sheet it contained.

It was addressed to me.

Then I saw the sender.

Orlasco Library.

And putting the two torn halves together, I read the contents of the letter.

Dear Mr. Danilo Marosso,

The library of the City of Orlasco is pleased to inform you that your composition LIKE DOGS *has been awarded first place in the national Valentine's Day poetry competition, from among more than one hundred entries received from all across Italy.*

The awards ceremony will be held at the Enrico Bedolis multipurpose hall on April 4. Trusting in your attendance, we repeat our congratulations and send you our best regards.

The Awards Jury

I read it once, twice, three, six, twelve times, grinding my teeth, trembling from my head to my bowels, unable to rise from my kneeling posture by the stove.

I bit my fist.

Mom's cancer-riddled voice came to me from an infinite distance: 'What's happening, Danilo? What's wrong?'

I opened my mouth a couple of times, but all that came out was the cry of a dying sparrow. Then I managed to get to my feet and focused my eyes on him.

It was him.

Him, wrapped in his grotesque yellow raincoat, a spade in one hand and a black hole where his heart should be.

All right, I thought. *That's it.*

On impulse, I grabbed the fireplace poker and went out into the rain, waving the letter.

'Why?' I shouted, rending the sky. 'Why didn't you tell me? Why, why, why?'

I went up to him. Only a few steps separated us. He didn't lose his composure. He stared at me, his eyes dulled by wine.

'Tell you what?'

Behind me I could hear Dog barking with the little bit of breath he had left in his worn-out lungs, tugging at the chain like he was possessed.

'The letter! From the library! Good God, you read it and you threw . . . I knew it! I won!'

The ogre smiled.

It was a fiendish smile.

Sick.

Diseased.

He spoke with all the calm in the world. He stank of the stables and wine. 'You're a farmer, Danilo. Not a poet. And there's your mother to take care of. You're good at driving the combine. Forget about the poetry. Forget about it. Forg –'

I didn't let him finish. I raised my arm and the poker came down.

But maybe because I was blinded by rage, or possibly off balance, all I did was give him a glancing blow on the shoulder, ripping his raincoat a little.

He never stopped smiling.

Not even when he fought back, hitting me in the face with the handle of his spade, throwing me into the mud of the farm-yard with my front teeth smashed.

Behind me, Dog barked and growled and the chain sounded *clang cling, cling clang*.

The world was blotted out by my tormentor's ruddy face, as I spat blood and bits of teeth.

'You've gotta be a farmer, Danilo. Not a poet. How about a cold bath to clear your head, eh?'

He kicked me in my side with his safety boots, knocking the wind out of me and cracking my ribs, and an instant later he grabbed me by the neck of my T-shirt.

Even though he was over seventy, he was still strong as a bull.

He began dragging me across the yard with one hand, holding the spade with the other, and almost at once I understood what he planned to do.

Ten meters away.

He was going to throw me in the tub we used to collect the *sughet*.

Five meters.

Hog piss and shit.

Four.

The stink would never come off me, never.

Two.

'No, no,' I begged.

And in the silence that had fallen all around, as if the countryside were holding its breath and taking in the scene, there echoed a harsh, metallic *crack*.

With my face in the mud and my lip split open, I raised my head a little and smiled; for the first time since he'd set foot on the farm, he was free.

After twenty years, he was finally free.

And he was running.

Limping.

Pitiful.

Lopsided.

Because he was old (they say each dog year is like seven human years), because his muscles had atrophied from his limited range of movement, because he had received so many beatings that even the Almighty must have lost count, because he had more scars than teeth.

Dog had broken the chain. By dint of pulling and suffering and crushing his vertebrae, finally he had done it.

His eyes were no longer glassy and tired.

They were completely black, the blackness of caves.

In his eye sockets abysses swirled.

And he was headed straight for his tormentor.

Who turned to challenge him.

'Oh, look who it is!'

He made as if to kick him, and my mangy friend shot forward, biting his shin. Oh, he got him good, really good, and he squeezed with all the strength he had, you'd better believe it.

He bit and he stared at me with those black gorges. Without letting go of his hold on the leg that had kicked him for two decades.

He looked happy.

'Filthy bastard!' Dad's cry echoed off the walls of the farmhouse. He released his hold on me and wrapped his hand around the handle of the spade. The tool made a half arc behind his back, then the freshly sharpened blade landed with a mushy sound on Dog's neck.

It severed his head almost cleanly.

As I shouted and cried and held my ribs, I watched the wretched body collapse to the ground as if in slow motion, the head still attached to the body by a strip of mangy fur, the blood gushing from the severed white tube of the carotid artery.

His poor arthritic paws continued to move for a while in a post-mortem reflex, kicking up water and pebbles. As if Dog wanted to go on running, now that the damn chain no longer held him back.

Now that he was free.

A dog without a head, poor beast, no one knows how he barks, I thought.

Then I got another kick in the chest and lost consciousness.

I didn't end up in the *sughet*. Thanks to my four-legged pal's intervention.

When I came to and found myself lying next to the basin,

the odor of pig feces in my nostrils, Dog's body was no longer in the yard. The rain had washed away the blood. There wasn't so much as a trace of the ogre. I figured he had gone to bury Dog in one of our fields.

I was empty. I was nothing anymore.

I limped back into the house; my mother, a monster at the window, was crying.

She had witnessed the spectacle.

I hadn't seen her shed a tear in years.

I would have liked to hug her, but I couldn't. I dragged myself upstairs to get in the shower.

He came back after dinner, stinking drunk, his leg clumsily bandaged. I had put Mom to bed half an hour earlier and was lying on the mattress, floating in a bubble of cocoon-like, liquid well-being.

He appeared in my bedroom doorway, unsteady on his legs, asking me as if nothing had happened: 'How is she?'

'She's dying.'

'You gave her the morphine?'

'Of course.' I didn't tell him I'd injected a vial of it into myself as well. That's why I was feeling good. I was calm. *Soft*. 'Where did you bury him?'

'In the poplar grove, over by the Martini place.'

'It should've been you who got cancer,' I replied. Or maybe I only thought it.

I heard him stagger down the steps and slip into the wine cellar.

I was ripped from my oblivion by Mom's cries.

I dragged myself out of bed, my knees trembling, my mouth and chest bandaged in bonds of pain. Now that the effects of the morphine and sleep had worn off, the blows I'd received were claiming their due. My broken incisors scraped against my tongue.

Hunched over and dazed, I made my way through the semi-darkness of the hallway to my parents' bedroom, where he was snoring between the covers like a beached whale; Mom's screams were coming from downstairs.

And they were different.

Not caused by the metastasis, by the illness. They were the product of fear.

I hurled myself down the stairs as fast as my aching body would carry me and found her at the window, her mouth open wide and a continuous, frightening groan coming from it as she pointed one finger outside towards the yard.

She had suffered from hallucinations before, caused by the medicines and the tumorous ganglia that had by then reached her nervous system. In a few steps I was by her side, comforting her.

I followed the direction of her finger and looked outside.

In the distance, beyond the collection basin for the *sughet*, I thought I glimpsed something sticking out from behind one of the supporting columns of the pigsty.

A tuft of fur.

A brown tail, bald and funny-looking, moving slightly in the drizzle coming down from the sky.

It was a matter of a few moments, only a few moments, then it disappeared behind the gray mass of the pigsty. I wondered if I'd gone crazy because of the blows, or if I was still wandering lost in a morphine-chiseled dream.

I rubbed my eyelids.

The yard was empty.

No movement.

Only desolation.

And yet . . .

Why was Mom screaming like that?

I grabbed her by her shoulders and asked her what she had seen.

'Dead . . .' she murmured through the tumors. 'Dead.' Then

she slid over to the sofa and sat down, holding her swollen head in her hands.

I clung to the windowsill, watching the drenched farmyard for an infinite length of time, telling myself that I mustn't succumb to the lure of the madness that had been creeping through my wretched family for generations, until I heard steps behind me.

Dad.

'What are you looking at? Why is your mom screaming like that? Did you feed the hogs? Get a move on, I'll take care of the chickens.'

I didn't turn around. I still saw that tuft of tortured fur popping out from the outline of the building where the pigs wallowed in their own shit. I heard the ogre say something, I watched him go out into the rain holding a bucket of feed, headed towards the chicken coop.

He was whistling.

When he went into the shed, the whistle turned to a scream.

Unprintable swear words.

And in his voice I caught a note I had never heard before: fear.

Before I had time to think what might be happening, I had caught up with him in the doorway of the chicken coop.

You should know by now that I'm not the fussy type. In my life I've helped sows give birth, I've slaughtered and skinned dozens and dozens of rabbits, drowned kittens . . . but when I stuck my head in the shed and saw my father running his hands through his hair and the state of the walls, well, I doubled over, overcome with a fit of retching.

The chicken coop looked like a slaughterhouse. The smell of blood and excrement and death was stupefying, throbbing in the air like a wall of heat and humidity.

'Jesus Christ, Jesus Christ, Jesus Christ,' my father kept on repeating, with no end in sight.

It was like the hens had exploded, like they'd been mangled

by an uncontrollable fury. Forty-five hens had been reduced to feathers, splintered bones, and guts coating the ceiling, walls, and floor. Some, I don't know by what miracle, were still alive, a eulogy of mutilation. They stared at us with their stupid yellow eyes, on the verge of their demise, emitting pitiful cries from broken beaks.

'What happened?' I managed to mutter. 'Weasels?'

But we both knew that no weasel, not even a whole platoon of weasels, for heaven's sake, no animal we knew of could have carried out that kind of massacre. And then, in that riot of offal and red and multicolored feathers, I caught a glimpse of tufts of fur.

Brown, of course.

The color of café au lait, to be precise.

My father turned to glare at me and I thought someone must have switched his eyes for glass marbles. He loved those hens. And he made a tidy sum from the sale of their eggs. His wine-stained lips were quivering. He swallowed hard, producing a sort of liquid gurgle, then backed out, hunched in the rain.

I felt a shiver of pleasure. He was terrified; for the first time in my life I sensed shock in him, powerlessness.

'Clean up all this crap,' he ordered.

And I cleaned up that crap, with a smile on my lips and a thousand questions pecking in the farmyard of my brain like hungry chickens.

It's hard to describe the months that followed.

Several days after the chicken massacre strange things started to happen, stranger and stranger, and day by day the impression grew in me that everyday life was cracking, that it would never be the same again because it had become unhinged by illogical events, absurd implications.

At first we started to find curls of dog shit scattered around the yard. They were usually concentrated around Dog's chain post.

Stamped in the ground, well-defined paw prints began to infest the farmyard. They went around the pigsty, the *sughet* basin; when we tried to follow them, to figure out if some stray mutt was slipping through gaps in the fence, we couldn't trace a precise path, an access point. It was like the beast had fallen from the sky. Dad closed the holes in the fence with crude patches of barbed wire, but from that point on, our property was never free of dog shit and paw prints.

Some nights I began to hear yelping in the distance, a yelping I knew well, more like an infant's cry than an animal's. It echoed across the fields, through the poplar groves, then slid under the rickety doors and windows, plunging me into insomnia.

My mother wore out her vocal chords claiming that the farm was cursed and that we should burn it down. Dad looked at her with eyes clouded with terror, maintaining that the cancer had taken the place of her brain.

One night I got up around two to take a piss and as I stood at the toilet I heard a metallic sound coming from outside, making its way through my ear drums, overpowering my father's pig-like snoring.

Clang clang clang.

Cling, clang, clang.

I ran to the window with my pants still down, opened it, and squinted to peer out into the darkness of the farmyard. I didn't see anything, only the vague outlines of the pole and the chain, which had remained there since the day when Dog went to a better world. I wondered if he'd really gone to a better world. Or if for some dark reason he had remained trapped in our yard, on our land. In our torment.

The next morning my father uprooted the pole and got rid of the broken chain. Every day he looked more worried, more tired.

I enjoyed it.

We got word that the Orlasco postman, returning home on his bicycle at the end of his work day, had been attacked by a silent dog that had gotten him from behind, tearing off a good portion of one calf as though it were a juicy veal steak.

Something was hovering at the edge of our lives, a presence that reeked of dog kennels, wet fur, and pain.

We all sensed it.

Even my mother. Especially my mother. Maybe because she was already more there than here, I told myself.

Dad spent more and more time in the wine cellar. He stopped harassing, beating, and ridiculing me. I knew that he was doing his share of thinking too. I knew that he had also heard that otherworldly barking, coming from the very atoms of that earth which feeds us and exhausts us. He became taciturn, listless, he aged fifteen years in the course of a few weeks, became what he had always been: shadow, ghost, semblance, *excretion*. But every time he looked in my eyes I could see the same evil light shining behind his pupils that had always been there.

I meandered through the dandelion-studded fields, my soul tormented between terror and expectation.

Neither I nor Dad ever found the courage to go and check whether Dog's body was still in the ditch among the poplars, nor was it something we ever talked about openly.

But we both knew, yes, in some dark well of our consciousness we knew.

In some way, vague and yet awful, Dog had come back.

You're wondering if I have an explanation for what was happening.

Oh, I have one all right . . .

The countryside is *magical*.

And terrible.

That's all you need to know.

Mom quitted her abhorrent mortal remains in June and on her deathbed she hissed that Dog was the devil of the fields. I closed her eyelids, feeling envious.

Nobody came to her funeral except me, her husband, the priest, and the coffin bearers from the funeral home.

When we left the church, as we headed to the cemetery, I thought I could make out Dog's angular, waggling form outlined against the horizon, out where the fields meet the sharp tooth of Monte Viso, and I thought maybe that beast was an anomaly, something like the tumor that had taken away the woman who had given me life: an incorrigible bastard that refused to die.

September came, the harvest time. The corn was flourishing and very green; it seemed to whisper in the wind.

I took the combine out from the shed and we got to work, Dad pulling the trailer with the tractor, following me with a large bottle of wine squeezed between his thighs. Now that he was harmless I hated him even more.

The final day of threshing, as I maneuvered the Beast through the last two acres of corn, I glimpsed a dark shadow following us between the rows, a four-legged scarecrow of brown fur and dried blood, and I knew that the moment had come.

It was easy.

For me, not for the ogre.

I stopped the machine abruptly, pressing hard on the brake, and interrupted the rotation of the mowing head.

'What's going on? Why'd you stop?' Dad yelled from the tractor, stopping for his own part a few yards ahead.

'It wasn't me,' I answered, and in my groin I felt something that might have been an erection or an urge to urinate. 'It got stuck somehow. Maybe a rock got caught in the gears, why don't you check . . .'

'I can't believe it. Fucking hell.'

He dismounted from the machine, swaying, and stopped in front of the Beast, looking between the blades of the mower with an unconscious frown, leaning his calloused hands on the frame of the header.

'There's nothing here, son of a bitch . . .'

Son of a bitch.

His last words on earth. Besides the screams. Ironic, isn't it?

I put it in first gear, activated the combine's teeth, its starving belly of pistons and grinders, and stepped on the accelerator.

My father fell backwards and the gears caught him instantly by his pants, sucking him in.

I've never heard a human being produce so many decibels.

And the sound of the bones!

I set the rotating drums at their minimum speed so he would suffer longer, so the torture would last as long as possible.

In the rearview mirror I watched the ejection chute become tinged with vibrant colors, with flesh, offal, gray matter, and shredded clothing, while the man to whom I owed my life – *big deal!* – was scattered all around in a gritty pulp, among the rows of corn he had spent a lifetime caring for.

I leaned over to vomit outside the combine's cab, my eyes misty with tears, and at the edge of my vision I could make out Dog's crippled form emerging from the corn in great leaps to nibble at the meaty sauce that had once been my father. A few moments later he disappeared between the cornstalks: I figured he was finally going off somewhere to die.

Then, collapsing over the wheel, I giggled and cried until I fainted.

I explained that it had been an accident. I don't remember what story I made up. There was an investigation, of course. They asked me a ton of questions and in the end they believed me. After all, I was nothing but a slightly dim-witted farmer who had lost his father in a terrible way, something that should never happen to anybody, not to anybody.

From that day on, I never saw Dog's crooked form again.

But I've felt it, I feel it.

A few months after Dad's tragic demise, I was awakened by a tremendous sound, a rumble that seemed to exude from all over, booming in my head. I immediately thought of an earth-quake and ran down the stairs in a flash. Once I was in the yard the sound changed into a growl that came from the country-side, from the poplars, from the corn.

From underground.

I knew whose growl it was.

I started to wander through the tracts of land under the full moon, heading towards the spot where I thought the rumbling was coming from.

Half an hour later I found myself in the poplar grove where he had buried Dog, and in the bluish light that fell between the trunks I saw tufts of fur sticking out of the ground like freakish shrubs, thick and brown and shiny and soft, and I lay down in the middle of them, and I slept in that soft mantle until dawn, and below me, below all of Orlasco, I could sense giant bones creaking and tissue regenerating and a four-legged animal's maniacal eyes throbbing gigantic and blind in the chthonic darkness, waiting to come back and observe the starry sky swirling over the fields and the farms and the world, and I heard the snapping of teeth, the Tartarean knell of an unsatisfied appetite . . .

Yeah.

The land is becoming like a dog's coat. A mangy, starving dog, maddened by pain, hatred, and its chain.

Dog is still hungry.

I know it, I feel it, he talks to me every twilight: in dreams and in the earth, with his low bark that makes the fields tremble and the potato beetles flee.

He's not hungry for dry bread, chicken bones, or turkey heads anymore.

It's an older hunger.

Ancient.

Once you've tasted some dishes, you can't do without them, they say.

That's why, sometimes, I convince a homeless person from

Turin to follow me, to get on the last bus of the night with me, all the way to Orlasco. I pick one who looks like Dad, I offer him money, a drink, and once he sits down in the kitchen it's easy to get him drunk out of his senses, or stun him with one of the leftover vials of morphine.

Then I transport him with the wheelbarrow to Dog's poplar grove, sink a knife into his neck like Dad used to do with the sows, and bury him where the ground is soft, between the tufts of fur springing from the clods, so that my four-legged friend can be nourished, grow, get stronger, and one fine day emerge from his underground oblivion in all his dark splendor, returning to frolic on the plains after shaking off the crickets, soil, and grubs, colossal and unstoppable, with no more chains to hold him back.

To devour the kids who make fun of me at the bus stop, to rend the flesh of Orlasco, to sink his teeth into its residents and into its memory, and finally into me.

In the meantime, I've started writing poetry again.

All in all, I'm not doing so bad.

Pupils

Once upon a time there was a lord of dust.
    One of many.

The lord of dust had always lived in Idrasca, since before the town existed or had a name, long before human beings rose up out of the primordial ooze to build the seed of the settlement on a strip of land reclaimed with difficulty from a swampy, unhealthy terrain.

The lord of dust was a specter of the lost future, a genius loci generated by an inevitable drift.

He witnessed the passing of centuries and the birth of Idrasca, watched men build the ball bearing factory and the thermal power plant where they burned pallets filthy with oil, saw the buildings, villas, and elementary school spring up. He decided to settle down in the latter, to haunt it: inside it was where the children grew and learned, creatures who were like him and yet at the same time different, ghosts of the future still unaware of the nostalgia for the times to come.

One gray winter day he took over the school's book storeroom, an underground warehouse of unconsulted knowledge and dust, a cozy and overlooked place, ideal for spending some of the time that remained of his existence, a time that approached eternity and yet was not eternity.

But the lord of dust began to feel lonely.

Every so often he emerged from his refuge, crawling unseen, little more than shadow and blur in the school's hallways, and spied on the children, feeling a pang in his heart of mites and refuse. Those little creatures, just sketches really, aroused pain and torment in him: their unawareness terrified him, their light-heartedness provoked envy.

He decided to open their eyes, to make them become like him, to share what he knew, to fight his loneliness — and what better way than with a story, a fairy tale? Children loved them. He would write a fairy tale (and fairy tales, as everyone knows, are terrible) to teach them about what awaited them: dust, desire, global warming, lethargy, violence, wars, pollution, mass suicide, widespread slaughter, the birth of bloodthirsty apocalyptic cults, pandemics, the destruction of Creation. He would show them the Black Antarctic, the Chronicles of the End, the Mysteries of the Anthropocene, the Catabasis on Earth, the Maelström of the Removed, the Essence of the Necromilieu.

So he made his lair in the storeroom, found an old unused ledger and turned his appendages into fingers of pen and ink, beginning to compose his own story. It took him a long time to compile, illustrate, and finish the volume. Years. It wasn't a volume like any other. In its sentences and images there were magical formulas and spells to manipulate Time, Matter, and Space, to make eyeballs grow that would look within and peer into the frightening container of the future, explore it.

And when the book was ready, he invited the children into his dark manor of paper and oblivion; he summoned them down there one by one when they left class to use the restroom, or during recess when the teachers were distracted and the janitors were dozing in their broom closets, and like an attentive teacher he instructed them, reading the cruelest and most important story that had ever been written.

To open their eyes.

The children listened to the tale in mute fascination.

And their eyes were born and opened.

And they saw.

Sofia Ratti had never heard her daughter scream like that, not even when her husband – now her ex – accidentally ran her over while backing the van into the driveway when the girl was only a little over a year old, crushing her leg and disabling her for life.

The shouts had woken her abruptly from an erotic dream in which a lumberjack was taking her from behind on a black sand beach caressed by the crimson waves of a sea where jets of foam shot up from the blowholes of absurd, three-headed whales.

When she reached her daughter's bedroom, the sounds coming from the girl – a mixture of sobs and muffled words – seemed so anomalous and out of place that she wondered if she was still dreaming.

She threw open the door; the carpet enveloped her numb feet, cold from the frozen tiles in the hallway.

Beatrice was sitting on the mattress, her porcelain-white face illuminated by the bedside Tigger lamp, her eyelids tightly shut, her mouth gaping in a *scream-groan-cry*.

She had turned eight the week before, but she was naked, her unripe caterpillar body twitching in the sheets, her crippled leg resting on a pillow, and she was masturbating. As if she'd noticed her mother's presence in the room, she slowly raised her eyelids and stared at her. She let out an idiotic laugh and finally croaked, 'I'm full of eyes. I'm full of eyeballs *inside*, Mommy.'

Then with a curse she collapsed on the pillow.

Sofia Ratti took half a step, mumbled her daughter's name, tried to grab the door jamb and saw only blackness.

When she came to a few minutes later, she was in a heap at the foot of the bed; Beatrice was asleep like nothing had happened, dressed in her pajamas, one hand resting carelessly on her cheek, a relaxed expression on her face.

Was it a dream? Did you really faint? Are you turning into a sleep-walker?

She wondered if she should wake her up, ask her questions; frightened and confused, she decided they would talk about it in the morning.

If there was really anything to talk about.

She went back to her room and lay awake until dawn.

'Are the biscuits good, Bea?'
'Yes, Mommy. Goodgoodgood!'
'Finish your breakfast, okay?'
'Okayyy.'

'Beatrice . . . Listen . . . Last night . . . Did you maybe have a bad dream last night?'

'Mmm . . . No, why?'

'Nothing . . . Nothing, dear.'

The sky was thickening with clouds. Slow, lenticular clouds rolling low over the countryside, dampening its contours in an ashy gray, packing together to form a nuclear mushroom with the promise of rain.

Holding her daughter's hand in front of the elementary school gate, waiting for the eight o'clock bell whose strident tones would signal the start of classes, Sofia Ratti observed the other parents waiting to entrust their own children to the educational system.

Was it just her imagination or did they seem tired, sleepier than usual, frightened, with ugly, purplish bags under their eyes? Did she look like that too? And why did Carla Bandini, whose son Daniele Crisaldi was a classmate of Beatrice's, always smiling and sleek in her custom-made pantsuits, appear so slovenly and taciturn, in a tracksuit and with disheveled hair? And Dario Desseri, so self-confident and good-looking, why were his lips crusty with nighttime drool and why was he standing so far away from his son and biting his nails?

Oh, it was hard being a parent, exhausting. Everything revolved around those little human beings in the making. Feeding them, putting them to bed, waking them up, washing them, loving them, taking them to school, to soccer practice, to swim meets, teaching them right from wrong, bringing them up to face adulthood and the uncertainty of the future . . .

She caught the scent of imminent rain in the air and shivered; she let go of Beatrice, who was chattering away with a classmate, and hugged herself tight. The atmosphere was different that morning. A nervousness that traveled through the adults' bleary gazes, a silence interrupted every so often by fits of coughing, by whispered words, by the secret language of a cluster of crows roosting on an electrical wire, by the irrigation canals and distant poplars in the countryside that spoke in an ancient language.

I'm full of eyes. I'm full of eyeballs inside, Mommy.

However hard she tried to tuck last night's events away in some corner of her mind, she was unable to think of anything else.

She couldn't explain it.

It had been a sleepwalking nightmare brought on by the stress of the past few months, yes ... She had to cling to that hypothesis, make it a certainty, because the alternative was chilling. Besides, she had been sleeping badly and suffering from anxiety for weeks, right?

She thought about calling Mario, the man she had loved and with whom she had conceived Bea, *the man who had crippled Bea*, to tell him what had happened, seek comfort from him; then she told herself he'd think she was crazy, would tell her to get a good shrink, that the divorce was getting to her.

She felt *hideously* alone.

Mario was no longer the person she had married. Hadn't been for a long time.

He was going out with another woman, he had changed.

Everything changes.

The world changes.

People change.

Just like kids, children.

Everything changes.

And ends.

Her dark thoughts were interrupted by the bell announcing the start of class; the ringing, at first muffled, grew into an irritating wail that lashed the sky when a chubby janitor opened the school gate, greeting the children with an enthusiasm that Sofia found excessive, affected.

The crows took flight, silent.

The poplars trembled in the wind, whispering.

On the horizon, the colossal ball bearing factory, with its

thermal power station, erupted a pillar of white smoke into the sky that tickled the bellies of the clouds.

She patted Bea gently on the head and followed her with her eyes as she limped to join the little stream of students who were invading the lobby.

Before Sofia headed back to where her car was parked a short distance away, her daughter turned around and blew her a kiss with her little hand. Sofia thought she saw a smile stamped on her face that she had never seen there before, a smirk in the flickering glow of a broken neon sign.

The grin of a rabid dog.

She didn't return the greeting.

It was Carla Bandini who came up to her, touching her arm with a gentleness Sofia wouldn't have expected from her. She had always considered her a chic, snooty woman, lost in a frenzy of cosmetics, business dinners, and her career; even though Beatrice and Daniele were in the same third-grade class the two mothers had rarely interacted.

The tracksuit and disheveled hair gave her an aura of normality. Without makeup her skin looked white and squishy, the underside of a carp. She took a long drag from a cigarette thinner than a toothpick, her hand trembling.

'Hi,' she said, looking wild-eyed at the leaden sky weighing on the roofs. 'How's it going? Nasty day, huh?'

'Hi, I'm all right, thanks. Yeah, crap weather.' Sofia wondered why this woman, who had always looked down on her, was suddenly speaking to her using the oldest pretext in the book, the weather. Looking at her now from close up, she looked like an old woman. 'I'd better get going, it's about to start raining.'

'Your daughter, how is she doing?' The question was fired off point-blank, and for a moment she found herself again in the little bedroom, in the greasy light of the Tigger lamp, watched by an army of stuffed animals.

I'm full of eyeballs.

A number of parents still lingered in front of the austere, almost brutalist, little school. Talking. *Huddling.* They seemed relieved now that they had abandoned their children to the teachers. But why didn't they leave, go for a coffee, go to work, to their daily errands? On their faces Sofia read a disturbance, she saw wrinkles like little cracks, allowing discomfort, dismay, even *fear* to seep through.

Wasn't it fear she was feeling too, the clear sensation that something wasn't right?

The smoke from Carla's scrawny cigarette pervaded her nostrils.

'Fine, Beatrice is fine,' she stammered, on the defensive. Trying to smile. 'And Daniele?'

The scene that followed was surreal. All of a sudden Carla crumpled, as if the question had brought to the surface a torment held back for days. Her already sagging features were marred by sobbing, then by a tearless crying. She threw the butt to the ground and stomped on it furiously. It was obvious she had something she needed to get off her chest. Maybe she didn't have any 'mom' friends to talk to.

Embarrassed, Sofia found herself putting a hand on Carla's arm. 'Hey, what's wrong?'

'Oh, it's weird right now, so weird . . .' the woman sniveled. 'Daniele . . . I don't know what's going on with him, I'm worried, really worried. I'm going to have to take him to a doctor.'

'Is he not well? I hope it's nothing serious . . .'

'He hasn't been sleeping well. For . . . for a few days now he's been doing and saying strange things. I don't understand it.'

Sofia Ratti felt cold. And not because of the gust of wind sweeping through the town, stirring up leaves and dust, making the crowd of parents squint. Her hand tightened around Carla's elbow. 'What do you mean?'

'Oh . . . nightmares, bad ones; he wets the bed, and in the

morning he doesn't remember anything. I'm afraid he's sleep-walking. He always sleeps with our cat; last night we heard him screaming and when we ran into his room . . . well, we found him sitting on the floor and . . . he was saying things that didn't make any sense and holding the cat by its neck and squeezing it hard, like he wanted to strang— Oh God, I don't know why I'm telling you all this.'

'What was he saying?'

'Something about . . . about eyes, eyeballs. I don't really remember. Why do you ask?'

Sofia opened and closed her mouth a couple of times, then the words flowed out in a quick, liberating whisper, as a frozen hand touched her between her shoulder blades. 'Bea had . . . had a nightmare last night too. She said something about eyeballs too. And this morning . . . everything's normal, like nothing happened.'

'Are you kidding me?' Carla looked dazed, incredulous.

'No. And she also acted in a . . . bizarre way.' She didn't dwell on what she'd seen her daughter doing, but she felt her cheeks flush. 'I thought I'd imagined it all, that it was a nightmare.'

And then it happened. The father of Edoardo Repetti, a second grader, who had overheard a couple of sentences, jumped into the conversation.

His son had walked in his sleep and squirted tempera paint into the living-room aquarium, killing a little school of rare tropical fish.

Giada Mereu's mother joined the discussion, telling how she had found the girl standing on her mattress holding a box cutter to her throat.

Then it was Monica Massini's turn to explain how she had found her twins at the computer in the middle of the night watching a video of terrorist beheadings in Iraq.

And still more: Simona Conserti had gotten hold of a bottle of alcohol and tried to set fire to her mother's bonsai trees, Edoardo Martinelli had destroyed the models of classic cars expertly assembled by his father, Luisa Amadeo had terrorized the canaries, Giacomo Favero had dry-humped the enormous teddy bear he always slept with.

In the span of a few minutes, the parents of Idrasca's elementary school children gathered in the concrete forecourt of the school, united by the inexplicable behavior of their offspring, a nocturnal aberration that had led them to commit bizarre, rash, obscene, dangerous, disturbing acts, of which they remembered nothing in the morning.

Acts accompanied by a few bizarre words.

I'm full of eyes, mommy.

I'm full of eyeballs inside, daddy.

Sofia Ratti gazed at the sky, at the heavy clouds, at Carla's expressionless face, at the other parents, feeling nothing but an immense, boundless void, a void in which harbingers of bad times darted by.

'There must be an explanation,' someone muttered.

'Yes, there must be an explanation, we have to understand,' whispered someone else.

They kept on talking until the rain came, then the adults opened their umbrellas and said goodbye, their backs bowed and their heads full of questions, promising they would speak soon, keep each other informed; they patted each other on the back, exchanging tired smiles, maintaining that everything would be all right again soon, they were worrying too much, for God's sake, but what a strange coincidence, that business with the eyeballs, how strange, eh, but you know kids, they tell each other all kinds of things when we're not around to watch them . . .

'Everything will be fine, it's all under control,' they said, and they kept on repeating it in their heads as they made their way to their houses, work, the post office, the supermarket, the bank.

They didn't notice the crows chasing each other over the roof of the school in abstruse trajectories, their bony wings hissing in the wet wind, vultures hovering over the carcasses of dark days.

'How was school today, Beatrice?'

'Fine.'

'What did you do?'

'Nothing.'

'What's that supposed to mean, nothing?'

'Nothing special, Mom. The usual.'

As she set the table, Sofia Ratti thought about the exchange she had just had with her daughter. Lots of kids say 'nothing' when you ask them what they did today, right?

Right, but what do they really get up to when they're not gravitating in the orbit of adults, when they're with each other, when they're shut up in their bedrooms, alone? And what do they dream at night, what do they imagine for the future? What don't they tell us about their inner worlds?

She put some plates on the table, grabbed her cell phone, ordered two pizzas from La Sfiziosa in Pinerolo, and made herself comfortable on the couch with a magazine, flipping through it without reading it. The day was coming to an end. Bea was sitting at the walnut table in the living room doing her homework. Every so often Sofia raised her eyes to observe her, trying not to let her tension show.

She was the same girl she had always been. Keen, attentive, polite. Or at least that's how she seemed. She raised her head from the workbook and gave her mother a smile, bright and serene, then started singing some cartoon theme song between half-closed lips, absorbed in her math homework.

At 7:20 the doorbell rang. The delivery man, wet from the rain which had gotten more intense over the course of the day, handed her the pizzas and smiled at the tip.

When Sofia had opened the boxes, flooding the kitchen with the strong smell of wood oven and mushrooms, her daughter announced from her seat: 'I'm not really hungry, Mom.'

'Why's that? You told me earlier you were dying for pizza
... Are you feeling all right?'

'Yes ... it's just that I'm not hungry. I feel full. Like I already
ate.'

'You don't even want to try a slice?'

'Not now. Maybe later.'

Sofia ate half the pizza despite herself, while Beatrice followed her movements with an enigmatic expression as she fiddled with the utensils. She asked her several times if she wanted
something else, maybe milk and cookies – really, she had to try
and get some food down – but each time the response was a
peremptory 'I'm not hungry.'

All through dinner she was harassed by the idea that her
daughter was on the verge of confiding in her, revealing a
secret. She didn't take her eyes off her.

'You're sure you're all right?'

'Yes, I'm fine.'

'I'll finish eating and we'll watch a DVD before we hit the
sack?'

'Okay!'

They snuggled up on the couch around nine, wrapped in
a blue blanket, the rain drumming on the windows while the
credits of *The Sword in the Stone* rolled on the television screen.
It was one of Beatrice's favorite cartoons, an old Disney classic
that wound up in the DVD player at least once a week, to the
point where Sofia had now learned the dialogue and songs by
heart.

Arthur had just tumbled into Merlin's bizarre hovel when
Sofia noticed that her daughter, who was resting against her
knees, had started breathing heavily. Sofia leaned over her and
saw her eyelids closed, her half-open mouth emitting a slight
snore. Her hand brushed against the crippled leg, a reminder
of that terrible accident so many years earlier, and just like
always she couldn't help wondering: would she have a happy
life, would she find someone to love her, would she have chil-

dren? Questions that no one, not even she, her mother, could answer.

She picked her up gently and carried her to her room. The Tigger lamp cast a dull orange tint across the bedroom, illuminating the stuffed animals and knick-knacks with a dusky light.

She prayed for a quiet night. She prayed that the events that had so disturbed her and the other parents were just an absurd coincidence, an ambiguous and isolated quirk in the monotonous passing of everyday life, brought about by who knows what influence.

A warm bath and then I'm off to bed too, I'm beat . . .

She unloaded Beatrice's weight onto the mattress and lingered for a long time, studying her sleeping face; what panoramas were her eyes looking on behind her eyelids? Would she have a restful sleep or would nocturnal fears come to pay her a visit? And Idrasca's other children: would their acts of the previous night be played out again?

She leaned over to tuck her in, and just then her daughter's eyes shot open.

'Mommy, will you read me a story?'

She sat down on the bed beside her daughter's warm body. They had never read her bedtime stories, neither she nor Mario, not even when she was younger. They weren't that type of people. She didn't understand. 'A story? But you were sleeping, baby, try to rest . . .'

Bea's smile changed to a coarse yawn of mucous membranes and small rows of teeth. A hand slipped out of the covers to touch her mother's. The Tigger lamp flickered for several seconds, as if from an electrical glitch, and the shadows of toys became a gang of devils chasing each other in a magic lantern. 'Mommy, I want you to read me a story . . . like the lord of dust does . . .'

She imagined her daughter must be half asleep, babbling words that didn't mean anything, but she couldn't repress a shudder, the goosebumps forming on her arms. Outside the rain had turned to a downpour that was making the sheet metal gutters shriek. 'The lord of dust?' she repeated in a whisper. 'Who is that?'

Beatrice drew herself up into a sitting position in bed, rubbing her eyes. No, not sleepy: she was lucid, wide awake. She yawned again, then gave an explanation that didn't explain anything: 'The lord of dust who lives in the book storage room at school. The one who reads us the book about eyeballs . . .'

Again. Again that story.

She thought back to the faces of the mothers and fathers, devoured by rain and worries in front of the elementary school . . .

I'm full of eyeballs inside, Mommy . . .

A slight dizziness, as she realized that sadness and worry were giving way to frustration and anger. What the hell was this latest development? Couldn't there be just one calm moment? Why did her daughter have to speak in riddles, good God, didn't she have enough problems already, between her ex-husband, her daughter's leg, work, anxiety attacks, the goddamn everyday bullshit?

She took her daughter's face in her hands as the thunder roared over the rooftops, sending metallic vibrations through the houses of Idrasca. 'Beatrice, either you tell me what this story is about the eyeballs or I'm going to get angry, okay? You have to tell mommy everything . . .'

The girl retreated between the covers, away from her mother's worried embrace, curling up against the headboard.

Then, with the vehemence of a series of sneezes, the retching started. Violent, riotous. She doubled over, holding her stomach, hunched over. From the depths of her stomach came the wet, greasy sound of a cauldron full of meat being stirred vigorously.

'Baby, what is it? Are you sick? Do you need to throw up?'

'My stomach hurts, Mommy,' Bea complained, threads of drool dripping from her mouth.

Sofia grabbed her under her armpits. She was burning hot. And she felt extremely heavy, a tiny creature made of lead; as she dragged her to the bathroom she heard her vertebrae crack. She set her down in front of the toilet bowl, supporting her forehead with one hand, giving her gentle pats on the back with the other.

'Go on, baby, let it out and then you'll feel better, everything will be fine. What did you eat for lunch today? Go on . . .'

And Beatrice let it out.

The retching turned to a violent regurgitation of half-digested food and gastric juices, dark and greenish, whose trails stained the ceramic.

And she kept on.

For a long time.

It seemed as though she would never stop, to the point where Sofia, stunned and terrified, wondered how a body so small could contain so much stuff, so much *filth*.

Beatrice was shaking, her head in the toilet bowl, letting out sharp, plaintive gurgles, arching her spine with her little hands clenching the toilet seat.

The stench was unbearable. Mixed with the acidic stink of the vomit she picked up some wrong notes, odors that didn't seem to come from a human being but from a chemical factory, from a smog-polluted street, something that stank of burnt wood, phosphates, putrid water, wet cement, brackish pools, gas. Of decomposition. For some strange reason, images flashed through her mind like a slide projector: cities in decay, metropolises overrun with stagnant waters, and then boundless expanses of land brutalized by drought, polluting clouds, cataclysms. She barely kept from vomiting.

'There you go, baby, it's almost over, good girl . . .'

When the girl collapsed in her arms, exhausted, pale and sweaty, she must have been vomiting nonstop for at least three minutes. Sofia took her in her arms, wiped her mouth as best she could with a wet towel and carried her back to bed. Now she seemed as light as a feather.

'I feel a lot better, Mommy. But I'm so sleepy . . .'

She wrapped her in the comforter, whispering words of comfort as she weighed whether to call a doctor or give her some Pepto-Bismol, then smacked a kiss on her cheek.

'I'll be right back, honey. Don't worry, I'm just going to get the thermometer.'

On the way from the bedroom to the bathroom, passing by the window that looked out on the building's interior courtyard, she thought she heard a scream. A woman's, torn and distant, coming from another apartment in the building, muffled by layers of bricks, pipes, electrical cables, plaster. Someone having a fight, maybe, although the cry seemed the result of terror, a nightmare, a repugnant sight.

She threw open the medicine cabinet to grab the thermometer; then, retracing her steps, she reached over the toilet: she hadn't flushed it yet. A moment before her fingers met the drain lever, her gaze stopped at the contents of the bowl.

In the broth of gastric juices and mush of food, something was moving, *simmering*. At first she attributed the movement to the defective flushing mechanism, which sometimes got blocked, letting a thin stream of water run.

Then she bent closer to take a better look, and the barrier of fragile certainties behind which she had moved during her forty-two years of life shattered, revealing a view dominated by madness.

Eyes.

Little sclerae, the size of small buttons, thousands of semi-transparent grayish eyes, like fish eggs, streaked with purplish veins, perfectly round like marbles, rolling around and swimming and throbbing in the toilet bowl in a viscid and mucous orgy, a myriad of alien eyeballs fixed on her in a disembodied musing.

Oh, she felt them, those monstrous little eyes, the eyes of some abyssal fish, felt that they had sensed her presence, that they were staring at her, studying her carefully from the bottom of a suburban apartment toilet, burrowing inside her, filled with a keen and shared intelligence, gleaming with annihilating awareness, and Sofia Ratti took in the full ridiculousness and absurdity of the situation when her mind informed her that it had been Bea, that it had been her daughter, who had produced this riddle of minuscule eyeballs.

I'm full of eyeballs inside, Mommy.

She had to draw on forces she didn't know she possessed in order not to go crazy, *to take her eyes off the eyes.*

She didn't want to see them anymore. She didn't want to see them anymore.

Terrified, she groped for the drain lever and let herself collapse on the tile floor between the washing machine and the bidet, holding her face in her hands.

Empty and trembling.

Wondering if she was losing her mind, if she had already lost it.

Beatrice appeared in the doorway suddenly, with the abruptness of an apparition, a limping specter on a crushed limb painted with scars. She was in her underwear.

'I looked inside myself, Mommy ... And now that *they're* out, we've seen *ahead.* Why did you bring me into the world? Why did you have me?' she uttered, before crumpling onto the hard floor like a puppet whose strings have been cut.

Sofia Ratti started to scream her daughter's name.

And in the houses of Idrasca, in the apartments, in the mansions and bungalows, the parents of the elementary school pupils were screaming along with her, wondering what would become of their children, of their well-ordered lives.

The little eyes, constantly watching and judging, once expelled from the bodies of Idrasca's children, were captured by the whirlpools of water in the toilets, the waterfalls of the sinks, the drains of the bathtubs, and left the houses, falling into ducts and pipes, floating in black and white waters, settling in septic tanks. Others remained for some time in the

basins, on the floor, between the blankets where they had been ejected.
Very soon they dissolved, vanished; but somehow they still existed.

Always vigilant, always alert.

Seers.

They passed through sewers and subterranean bowels, seeped through
floors and plastic buckets, slithered through walls and houses, until they
reached the soil, observant, observant, they moved into the realms of
scraps, waste, and human by-products, and they reached the pestiferous
rivers, seas, and oceans, and the lowest layers of the soil, down, down,
to contemplate and evaluate, and others floated in the air, up, up, to the
upper layers of the atmosphere, beyond the mantle of hydrocarbons, little
aerostatic balloons of veins and retinas and crystalline lenses.

They were invisible, a nothing held together by nothing, but they
were capable of beholding the future hell, the Black Antarctic.

They still existed, they had always existed, just like the lord of dust
who had summoned them.

They proliferated, prolific.

Most of the children's parents loaded their kids in the car
and drove like mad to Giovanni Agnelli Hospital in Pinerolo.
Almost all of them had seen the eyes birthed from the blood
of their blood. Some, the more distracted, the more fortunate,
hadn't witnessed that monstrous manifestation – or hadn't
withstood it, pretending not to see, their short-circuited minds
focused solely on saving themselves through the process of
repression.

After the vomiting, which had struck every elementary
school pupil without exception, all at about the same time, a
heavy sleepiness came over them, a profound torpor not unlike
catalepsy.

Sofia Ratti entered the Pinerolo emergency room at 10:30
p.m. holding Beatrice tightly in her arms, went to the check-in
window babbling about vomit and eyeballs, and experienced a
mixture of relief and dismay when she found herself in a waiting room filled with other townspeople hugging their kids,

inert and comatose, like useless puppets. She knew almost all of them. Carla Bandini was there too, slumped over a green plastic chair with Daniele in her lap snoring like a bellows.

'What's going on? What's happening?' she asked, addressing the small crowd gathered in the room. Worried looks and stammered responses. Then she waylaid a bearded doctor who was darting down the hall towards a dark little room, grabbing his white coat to stop him. 'She's sick. My daughter is sick.'

'She's not the only one, ma'am. Wait here, please.' The doctor looked as though drained by an unprecedented fatigue, as if he hadn't slept for days. 'We'll examine her as soon as we can.'

'What's happening?'

'That's what we're trying to find out.'

'Eyes. My daughter threw up fucking eyes!' Sofia barked, and she was echoed by the parents behind her.

'My son did too!' 'So did my daughter!'

The doctor looked at them as if they had just escaped from a mental institution. 'You've already told us about the eyes. We're looking into it.'

Then he backed away and disappeared without another word, amid the protests and anguished groans of the parents of Idrasca.

While the children were being seen, the parents talked about what had happened. Some of them pinched their cheeks and arms, hard, to make sure they weren't living in some alternate, nightmarish Piedmont. Crowded in the squalid little pea-green hospital waiting room, they discussed at length what for them would always be 'the night of the eyes' or 'the night of the eyeballs'.

A few things were clear, even if in reality there was nothing clear, normal, rational about the whole business –

– the previous night, the children of Idrasca had displayed alarming behavior and babbled about *eyes inside*;

– they had alluded in various ways to a 'lord of dust who

lives in the storage room at school and reads us the eyeball book', and shortly afterwards they had felt sick;

– they had regurgitated, for a long time, a paste of an unusual odor ('artificial, like gasoline,' Carla Bandini described it), and in the vomit the adults had discovered the impossible: eyes, a lot of them, grayish, moving, watchful, *alive*;

– the little eyeballs had dissolved shortly after coming to light. Not all the children had vomited into the toilet like Beatrice. Many had spewed all over their blankets or the ground, or had filled buckets and basins. The parents had watched the spectacle in horror, only to see the sclerae liquefy, disappear, turn to nothing. Dario Desseri had scooped up some of the little eyes and sealed them in a glass jar with the idea of bringing them to the hospital for examination, but by the time he left his house there was nothing in the jar but empty space.

– after clearing their stomachs, the children had asked strange questions ('*Why did you give me life?*' '*What did I do wrong to have to endure all of this?*' '*What's the point of living and growing up in a world like this?*') and then collapsed like empty husks, prey to a catatonia from which they had not yet recovered.

The adults, after considering every aspect of the situation, waited and waited and waited. Some of them cried, others shouted outbursts at the nurses, hungry for answers.

Sofia Ratti tried to get hold of her ex-husband, but his phone was off; she imagined him in bed with his new girlfriend and hated him, and then she thought of Bea in the hands of the doctors, her leg crushed by the van's tire, and she bit her knuckles, wondering whether they had done the right thing in bringing her into the world, if it hadn't all been a mistake.

At the end of the night, after blood tests, CAT scans, EKGs, X-rays, and assorted tests, the doctors of Giovanni Agnelli Hospital, joined by several prominent pediatricians from Turin, stared at each other, shaking their heads, continuing to analyze the collected data without understanding.

There was nothing wrong with the children: their little bodies showed no abnormalities, their hearts beat in the proper way, their blood wasn't contaminated with any foreign substance that could explain that deep and extraordinary collective sleep.

Psychologists were called in, sleep luminaries contacted, and a special ward was set up in the hospital for them (forty-two children total, all between six and eleven years of age), to try to understand the origin and progress of the syndrome.

The parents were listened to at length: they told about worrying behaviors, strange conversations, the lord of dust, and the eyes, especially the little eyes. Obviously, none of the doctors believed their story.

How could they?

The news leaked out, somewhat toned down and distorted, and *L'Eco del Chisone* and *La Stampa* devoted short articles to it, in which reference was made to an unspecified malady, a bizarre flu-like virus that had struck every pupil at a small provincial school.

And finally, two days after 'the night of the eyeballs', the children awoke, stretching and smiling, rested: they seemed normal and healthy and said they didn't remember anything. They were bombarded with questions, but their answers were always the same: 'I fell asleep and woke up here.'

They stayed at the hospital a few more days, were subjected to further tests, sessions with therapists were organized.

Everything in order.

All they wanted was to go back home, to school, to their little bedrooms stuffed full of toys.

The doctors put forward several hypotheses – more as a way of keeping the unknown from creeping its way into the safe garden of the medical profession than out of a real belief in their own claims – mass hysteria, a mental change caused by the inhalation of fumes from the enormous burner at the thermal power plant, a nasty case of food poisoning at the school cafeteria.

And yet there was no objective evidence for any of these theories, none of which ever solidified into certainty or a valid explanation. Of course the parents were happy their children were better, but they were haunted by the nagging thought of what they had seen – thought they had seen – and experienced and terrified at the possibility that something similar, or worse, might still come to pass.

What were those eyes, grayish and disgusting? Would they come back? Had they really seen them? And the lord of dust: a shared childhood fantasy, or a real event mascarading as a children's fantasy? And if they were asked again, how would they answer those terrible questions to which their children had subjected them before being rushed to the hospital: *Why did you bring us into the world? Why did you do this to us?*

Besides the doubts, there was the embarrassment of talking about the night of the eyes, the frustration of not being believed.

The teachers, informed by the students' parents, went down to the school's book storeroom. Obviously they found nothing except volumes that no one would ever read again, along with junk, remnants of old masonry work, and piles of dust.

Especially dust.

They were strange, fearful days.

Then, one by one, the children were discharged: there was nothing more the doctors could do for them.

And finally their parents brought them home.

Along with the torment they had begotten.

Now that the children had heard the fairy tale and seen the world with new eyes, from a new perspective, they had become like him.

The lord of dust rejoiced in their new consciousness, in their false laughs echoing through the halls, the gym, the playground. They had seen, and knowing that they knew was enough to make him feel less alone; it was enough to let him face the semi-eternity that awaited him.

The lord of dust, however, hadn't taken the adults into account. By freeing their children's eyes, opening them wide to look on crumbling futures, he had upset the established order, let loose uncertainties and fears, torn away the thick veil of routine and banality concealing cliffs that look out on oblivion.

He had allowed madness and truth to seep into the small community of Idrasca, and madness and truth have always caused fear, since the dawn of time.

Everywhere.

The lord of dust didn't know it yet, but soon he would be alone once again, without a story to read and tell.

The crows continued to perform strange dances in the air over the roof of the school building.

At night the furnace of the thermal power plant shone with a sinister glow beneath the worm-eaten sclera of the moon.

The irrigation canals dragged freshwater shrimp along their path, mutated into aberrations by illegal discharges of toxic wastewater.

The children went back to school and behaved like they always had. They slept for eight hours straight, went to class, played, took part in after-school sports.

They returned to the hospital at regular intervals for physical and psychological check-ups.

They were fine.

But they had changed.

They had *looked. Within and ahead.*

They had surveyed new landscapes in those two days of semi-coma and absence spent in the hospital.

Panoramas of the future.

Crumbled mountains. Scarlet skies furrowed by pitch-colored, poisonous cirrocumulus clouds. Major urban areas scourged by poverty, overpopulation, violence. Human migration marked by madness and cannibalism. Factories that dumped noxious ashes into rivers, fish gasping for breath in contaminated springs. Crazed oceans and deserts creeping towards the settlements of civilization. The absence of inhibitions, a return to the caves, to a primitive hunger, to mating without love, rape. The cracking of humanity, a prelude to extinction.

Every so often, the pupils would evade their teachers' supervision and descend to the storage room to hear the tremendous fairy tale again which they had already learned by heart, a fable of cataclysms and collapses that would become reality for their and future generations.

Yes, by now they knew the tale, but they sneaked into the basement to keep the lord of dust company and to hear his rasping voice in that realm where dream, reality, and future merge.

For the adults, the real trouble started after 'the night of the eyeballs': they began to spot little eyes everywhere. Eyes staring at them accusingly from the most unthinkable places: down sink drains, nestled in car hubcaps, hidden in the back of nightstand drawers between handkerchiefs and condoms, stuck in the corners of rooms in disgusting, flaccid clusters, floating in mid-air at the edge of their vision, clinging in gluey masses in closets, in the warm belly of their beds, darting along the wires of light fixtures like obscene bulbous centipedes, lazing about in workplace photocopiers, wedged in cracks and crevices and notches in the walls.

They seemed to be making fun of them. They were eyeballs without a facial structure and thus lacking any means of expression, and yet they seemed to stare at them with derision, with a sardonic irony that gave them the sense of being nullities, helpless children at the mercy of a gang of sadistic and merciless bullies.

The visions only lasted a fraction of a second, but they were enough to destabilize rational thought; the time of a blink of an eye, of a startled cry, of reaching out a hand in disgust to verify its solidity, its *realness*, and the small globes vanished just like they appeared, the pupils dilating or contracting due to variations of light, withdrawing into the dust that had spawned them, leaving the adults dumbfounded, doubting their own mental faculties.

Some of them got themselves checked out: stress, nothing but the stress related to their children's inexplicable ordeal, or minor visual disturbances due to age, the doctors suggested, but sleeping pills and anti-anxiety medications didn't get rid of those hallucinations that were chipping away at the bastions of reason.

Many of them resorted to psychologists, but the more the doctors of the mind dug around in their patients' emotional, cognitive, and social processes, the more they fumbled in the dark, unable to furnish a response to the question of the eyes, which might go for days without revealing themselves only to make an appearance at the most inopportune moment.

Three days after her daughter's discharge from the hospital, while she was eating in a restaurant with Beatrice and her ex-husband Mario, like a family, like the old days, Sofia Ratti noticed out of the corner of her eye a repulsive lump on the dessert cart, between cups of pannacotta and trays of bunet.

She stared: masses of pupils planted in little sclerae were fixed on her, accusatory, flaccid, greasy. Mocking her. She stood up and took a step back, knocking over her chair, while Beatrice studied her with an empty expression, her scrawny, crippled leg dangling a couple of inches from the floor.

When the woman turned to look at the dessert cart, the little eyes had vanished.

But they didn't vanish from her mind.

They planted themselves there and multiplied all through the night and in the days that followed, and they showed up again in the drum of the washing machine, in the bidet, in the cookie tin.

Sofia Ratti – and many other adults in Idrasca along with her – came to the verge of a nervous breakdown. They felt they no longer had full control of the mental processes which had guided them until a few weeks earlier. They discussed the situation amongst themselves, of course, but furtively, like thieves, as if they had contracted an illness to be kept secret from the community, and just when they had reached the limit of desperation, the eyeballs withdrew for several weeks. And then, just when it seemed that things were going better, that reality was returning to the way it had always been, they appeared again out of nowhere to spy on them, in a perverse circle that fed a sort of hallucinatory parasitosis, nights gnawed by nightmares and irredeemable thoughts.

No one believed what they said.

It was only a matter of time before one of them committed some desperate act.

Before tragedy struck.

Carla Bandini, a woman who had built her life around her managerial career, her model family, and rationality, cracked under the weight of the events she had been witness to. Since that goddamn night when she had caught Daniele trying to strangle the cat, she hadn't been the same. And since her son came home from the hospital, the intrusions of the eyes into her everyday life had become an unremitting torment, throwing off the coordinates she used to orient herself in the world.

Something inside her broke for good one afternoon during a meeting with an industrialist from a Danish automotive firm to close an important contract, when she glimpsed the sparkle of a sclera inside the man's mouth and nostrils while he continued talking about 'joint ventures' and 'data analysis' like everything was normal. She snapped and insulted and spat on him, accusing him of being 'another fucking vehicle for those fucking eyes'.

She was fired on the spot from the company to which she had devoted the past fifteen years of her life.

On her way home, the explosion of rage she'd had at the office gave way to a glacial calmness.

To a decision brought on by madness.

It was Daniele who spawned those little gray eyes that had ruined her life.

Her son had destroyed her career.

She knew what her next move should be.

At 4:30 p.m. she was waiting for Daniele at the entrance to the Idrasca elementary school, shut up in her SUV, after fixing her makeup and drinking a large glass of vodka.

She spotted a tangle of eyes pointed at her from the black mouth of a drainpipe, but she didn't pay much attention to it. Soon, she hoped, she wouldn't have to worry about it anymore.

Later, several parents who had seen her that day, including Sofia Ratti, told the authorities they had seen her smoking a toothpick-thin cigarette out the driver's side window, watching the school. She seemed calm, maybe a little preoccupied.

And indeed Carla Bandini had a lot on her mind.

She greeted the boy with a smile as he got in the car and asked him how his day had been, what he had done.

'Nothing,' Daniele answered.

'And the eyes, the lord of dust, what do you have to tell me about them?'

'What are you talking about, Mom? I don't know what you mean,' the boy answered, and his mother knew he was lying.

She drove him to a remote poplar wood in the country, near the old Idrasca train station, a massive building abandoned since the eighties and covered in brambles, and smashed his head and face in with her heavy work laptop, aiming especially at his eyes.

Then she attached a rubber tube to her tailpipe, slipped it in through the window out of which she had smoked her last cigarette a few minutes earlier, first closing off every air passage with large quantities of duct tape, started the ignition of her €60,000 SUV, snuggled up with Daniele's corpse in the back seat and let the exhaust fumes do the rest.

She took deep lungfuls of oxygen thinned by carbon monoxide.

As she suffocated, she prayed there was no hereafter, and

if there had to be, she prayed there would be no curious eyes waiting for her there.

The news of the tragedy bounced off the tongues of Idrasca's gossips with the nimbleness of a young gymnast.

From phone to phone, from WhatsApp to WhatsApp, by around 10:15 p.m. the whole town knew about the macabre discovery a farmer had made when returning home after a day in the fields. One of the most extreme acts imaginable: a mother killing her son, then taking her own life.

Sofia Ratti heard the news from an old friend, a former traffic warden from Orlasco, the little village bordering Idrasca. The woman knew one detail that hadn't yet leaked out: a piece of paper had been found in Carla Bandini's pocket with these few words:

They're everywhere, staring at me. If they won't go away, then we will.

Sic transit gloria mundi.

It was this detail, along with a couple of eyes that had stared at her from the edge of the kitchen sink before bursting like soap bubbles, which drove Sofia to make a decision. In a flash, she remembered Carla's face when they were in front of the school two months ago, a face cracked with worry. Since then, things had plunged in a downward spiral into the twilight zone.

She couldn't stand there wringing her hands, enduring the attacks of the eyeballs, or she would meet the same end as Carla. Or worse.

She had to act.

To understand.

After drying her tears, she went to Beatrice in the bathroom; her daughter was washing in the tub. For several moments she stood there looking at her pale body, her crumpled leg, and the constellations of little eyes floating in the white of the bubble bath; then she sat on the toilet seat and said, 'I have some awful news, baby.'

Bea beat her to it. 'Daniele's dead and his mom too. I know. Everybody dies sooner or later, right?'

She didn't answer. Trying to control her trembling, she waited for her daughter to finish bathing, dried her hair, and put her to bed. She watched her fall asleep, gave her a kiss on the forehead, and went back to the kitchen. She sipped a glass of wine as she waited for midnight, then fetched a flashlight and slipped out of the apartment, shivering in the hazy Idrasca night.

She had to go to where the whole story started.

She had to check for herself whether there was anything besides rubbish in the book depository.

She went down the street almost at a run, the thermal power plant glowing in the fog, a feeble lighthouse in a stormy sea.

Thousands of eyeballs followed her route, cryptically.

The lord of dust was leafing through the magical book when he heard the underground warehouse's door creak in the darkness of the school.

The bouncing of the flashlight beam down the stairs caught him by surprise, blinding his dusty eyes, forcing him to retreat behind a pile of boxes full of musty files.

Who could it be at that hour? Who was making their way through the dark belly of the Idrasca elementary school?

The sound of footsteps ticked on the marble steps and from his hiding place he spied on the disheveled woman who was slowly descending the stairs.

What was she doing there?

An intruder.

An intruder who smelled like a child he knew well, one of the most attentive and captivated by the tale of the End, that little limping girl who always struggled to reach him in the basement.

Beatrice.

Beatrice's mother.

What did she want?

This is no place for one who does not know the nostalgia of

the future, who has not seen the Black Antarctic, *the lord of dust thought.*

The woman wandered around the basement for a long time, running her fingers along the spines of educational books ready to be pulped, poking around in the archives, sniffing out the surroundings.

She was careful and determined. She was not afraid. She wanted a return to normalcy, for her daughter and the town, but especially for the adults. The restoration of the status quo.

She wanted an end to the haunting of the eyes.

At 4:48 a.m. she laid her hand on the strange book that the lord of dust had written with his own essence and knowledge, with hard work and dedication.

Getting into the school through a window left open in the gym locker room and finding the storage room was easier than she had expected.

She went down the stairs, holding the flashlight in front of her with both hands. Like it was a weapon, a sword.

The book depository was vast and forgotten. Down there, besides the musty smell of a place that has been closed up and rarely visited, besides the scent of moldy books, she detected a stench that she recognized: the odor of chemical waste and gasoline that had emanated from her daughter's vomit the night of the eyeballs, the odor of stale, wet dust, the stink of rotten fish, and carcasses, and factory waste and discharges, and of the refuse and death that were products of progress.

She sensed that the origin of the fainting fit and the confusion of the past few months was in that place.

She explored.

She dug through piles of papers and ledgers, rummaged among ancient newspapers and primers on which purplish humps of fungus grew, sneezed in the accumulations of dust mites as she moved notebooks from students who by now must be old, disillusioned human beings at the end of the line, or even dead, ghosts.

And all this time, the impression that someone was watching her from many angles didn't leave her for a moment.

It wasn't the little eyes, no.

It was another scowl. New, but just as ancient.

She wasn't alone in the bowels of the school.

The sensation grew stronger when her hands met the water-damaged, spongy cover of an old accounting book, one of those tomes with blank pages that people used to fill with numbers and earnings and losses before the advent of the personal computer.

Underground, Sofia Ratti sensed a bending in the air, a sudden atmospheric change, as if someone were about to materialize out of the sticky darkness. Or some*thing*.

Instead of fleeing, as common sense and her trembling knees advised, she held on tight to her fear.

Fear can help us fight, she thought, perceiving the shapes of little eyes studying her from the darkness.

And she opened the volume, lighting it up with her flashlight to immerse herself in those pages of collapses, apocalypses, and eyeballs.

It wasn't a printed book. It was handwritten, in a calligraphy that was antiquated and modern at the same time, a hand that had no precedents; it was if the characters changed imperceptibly, devouring themselves in Art Nouveau flourishes, then in old typographic engravings, and again in a river of iridescent ink, and in decorations, and in dark smudges: looking at the frontispiece, she visualized a room full of scribes enveloped in twilight, intent on the creation of a New Bible, a manual of wonders for a new creed.

And when her gaze fell on the penned title on the back side of the cover, and on the floral frame around it, a sort of plant with tiny eyes for flowers, she let out a groan.

PUPILS (FABLE OF THE END)

She leafed through the pages quickly, skimming: the text sometimes assumed a confusing spiral layout, and she shuddered at the phantasmagoric illustrations accompanying it, which were of an impressive quality, almost three-dimensional, images of a suburban town, of continents black with smoke and war, of children haunted by eyes, of incandescent arctic expanses where nude figures danced to the soundtrack of mankind's end.

She turned to the first page of the volume and started to read, trying to ignore the conviction that someone was reading along with her.

It began thus:

'Once upon a time there was a lord of dust, one of many.

'The lord of dust had always lived in Idrasca, since before the town existed or had a name, long before human beings rose up . . .'

At first Sofia Ratti thought it the continuation of a vicious nightmare, then a joke, finally the work of a madman up-to-date on the recent anomalies in Idrasca, the handiwork of an obsessive who had wound up down there through who knew what intricate paths, for who knew what reasons.

She went on reading, mouthing the phrases, hypnotized, and journeyed on narrow bridges of ice, looking down into the ravines of the Black Antarctic, and wandered in the poplar woods where lonely drunken farmers hang themselves. Only with the arrival of the first rays of dawn, when she finished reading, when her mind processed the final words of the tale (*'And they lived happily ever after . . .'*) did she manage to lift her gaze from the pages.

Her eyes felt heavy, encrusted with grit, and in the flickering milky incandescence filtering from the plains into the store-room through a skylight, she saw him.

The lord of dust was in front of her, staring right at her.

A mishmash of eyes, ganglions of dust, and disorder, held together by bonds of darkness and the contradictions of progress. A shape with vaguely anthropomorphic contours from which stretched pulsating and translucent curls of filth, a silhouette that flickered like a badly tuned television showing future panoramas of necrosis and disease, of pollution and civil wars, of nuclearization, of electrified towers in which the powerful consummated their latest orgies to keep the claws of entropic death at bay.

He spoke with a mouth full of sawdust and bedbugs, his breath fetid with the centuries that had passed and those yet to come, and at the sound of his voice Sofia felt a few drops of urine leak out to wet her panties.

One simple question: '*What do you want?*'

Instinctively she raised *Pupils* and clutched it to her chest like a shield. She opened her mouth, but all that came out was an astonished gasp. She was frozen to the spot and thought she would die, or go mad, if she went on looking at that creature. She shut the portcullis of her eyes, seeking the courage to formulate a response.

'*What do you want?*' the lord of dust insisted. '*What do you want?*'

Sofia swallowed hard. Then found the strength to answer. 'Who are you?'

'*You know who I am. And one does not respond to a question with another question . . . What do you want?*'

'I want you to get rid of the eyes. Those fucking eyes,' the woman rasped. 'I want you to leave us alone.'

'*I can do that. I can get rid of the eyes. But I want something in exchange.*'

'What?'

'*You know that too, don't you? You've read the fairy tale, you know how this story ends . . .*'

Sofia Ratti dropped the book and scratched her head, racked with confusion. Images of acid storms, of children perishing from hunger and thirst, of highways swept away by abnormal weather events, crossed her brain in a hallucinatory parade, but try as she might, she couldn't remember how the story ended, only the words that any fairy tale ends with.

And they lived happily ever after . . .

'No,' she stammered. 'I don't know how the story ends.'

'That's what's wrong with you humans. You don't remember the past, or even the future. Oooh, I'll free you from the eyes, certainly, without asking for much in return: only the chance to stay here, in the school. With the children. And you must not speak to anyone of our meeting. Deal?'

A stunted protuberance that might have been a hand extended from the lord of dust's silhouette. Sofia stretched out hers, hesitantly, and squeezed that insubstantial appendage, a sponge of old junk and faded memories. 'Deal,' she whispered, sealing the agreement, while rays of sunlight invaded the storeroom and the lord of dust disintegrated into billions of particles swirling in the blades of light intensified by the skylight.

Sofia was alone down there again.

When she left the school, a warm sun was shining low over the deserted streets. She got home shortly before the alarm went off. Beatrice was asleep; in the courtyard sparrows perched on the fir trees and chirped.

While she made coffee, a couple of little eyes rolled out of the microwave onto the kitchen floor, observing her for an instant before vanishing in a vaporous puff.

She hoped they wouldn't come back.

That the lord of dust would keep his promise.

The lord of dust kept his promises.

He always had, he always would.

He waited for Idrasca to fall asleep, for the moon and night to rise and conquer the town, then he left the storage room and the school, reshaping his hands into a long magic whistle, a tapered flute with the power to call the eyes back like faithful little dogs.

Reaching the market square, he brought the instrument to his mouth, beginning to modulate a heartrending melody.

The little eyes wriggled out of the cracks where they were resting, rolled through the empty streets, along the rural dirt roads, down from the sky and from the drainpipes, and in an orderly stream they began to follow the lord of dust, who, dancing, pirouetting, and performing acrobatics and cartwheels, had begun to head towards the gigantic ball bearing factory.

The parade proceeded through the fields, under the poplars, along the irrigation canals, to the accompaniment of the sound of the magical instrument.

Arriving in the vicinity of the thermal power plant, the lord of dust blew harder, tightening his dry lips around the rounded end of the hand-flute, and the sound that echoed through the sterile nocturnal countryside was the oldest and sweetest that had ever traveled through those regions.

The eyes, as if obeying a peremptory command, threw themselves into the boiler room, one at a time, without hesitation, squeezing into the furnace that burned inside, into the purifying fire of pallets and oil and carpentry scraps.

They screamed as they burned, screamed from the gaping mouth of their pupils, and their cry was a cry of triumph. They had done the job for which they had been summoned and their end was only a beginning.

The lord of dust returned to the depository and leafed through Pupils, *waiting for morning to come and for the children to start their lessons.*

Carla and Daniele Bandini's funeral coincided, ironically, with a return to normalcy. That day, none of the parents gathered at the cemetery saw the eyes. Nor the day after, or the day after that, and so on and so on.

With the echo of the tragedy that had struck Idrasca having faded away, the night of the eyeballs having slipped backwards into time, the appearances of the eyes having ceased, the town enjoyed a period of calm and prosperity.

Spring arrived with its fair and carnival rides and the green of the poplars. The factory was working at full capacity, guaranteeing income for local activities, and the fog that had besieged the lowlands in the cold months was little more than a memory. The children were serene, and therefore so were the parents.

Only every now and then did they think back on the terrifying period of the little eyes, but they didn't talk about it
anymore, as if a single reference to those fateful days might
summon them, make them materialize.

However there was one parent, in a way the architect of this
happy time, who found herself unable to enjoy the restoration of the status quo. Sofia Ratti had nightmares. She lived
in obsession and doubt. It wasn't enough that the eyeballs had
disappeared, it didn't suffice that Beatrice seemed the happiest
girl in the world and her grades at school were outstanding.

In the book storage room at the elementary school she had
seen something that should not exist.

The lord of dust, a strange book, *Pupils*, whose plot she
couldn't remember, only glimpses of illustrations that returned
in tormenting flashes to visit her in her dreams.

And she had bartered the community's mental sanity, sealing a wicked pact, permitting that creature to haunt the school,
to be near their children.

She couldn't accept it. What would he do in the future, the
lord of dust? Would he stay well-behaved in his lair, would he
respect his promise, or would he once again torment the children and parents with his terrible sleight of hand?

Every thought, every action, every awakening, led her to
that decaying basement of dust and made her tremble with fear.
The future was cloaked in the unknown, and she sometimes
dreamed of the lord of dust in the role of a fearsome puppeteer,
a colossal gray figure whose silhouette was cast over the town,
spiderwebs dangling from his fingers like threads with which
he manipulated the fates of Idrasca and the world.

A terrible summer arrived, the hottest ever recorded in Piedmont; the schools closed for summer vacation, and while the
TV news talked of global warming and an inevitable collapse
if humanity didn't change course, and of a contagious illness
similar to SARS that was affecting several regions in China,
Sofia Ratti decided she had no choice: to ensure a stable future

for herself, her daughter, and the town, she had to take one last step. She had to break her promise and wipe the lord of dust from the face of the earth. Or at least try.

Coming home from work one night in June, she stopped at a service station and filled a can with ten liters of gasoline.

It was the crackling that woke him.

The lord of dust was lying down resting on a shelf full of old textbooks when he heard the noise; it was an evil, popping sound, the same sound the little eyes had made when they threw themselves in the furnace at the factory's boiler room, burning and screaming from their pupils.

It was coming from the floor above, from the classrooms, the gym.

The lord of dust staggered out of the storeroom on weak, trembling legs, and as soon as he threw open the door leading to the main hallway he was hit by the wave of heat.

The school was burning.

His home was burning.

Whirlwinds of flame ran through the building, devouring the curtains, the desks, the chalkboards, the notebooks, the memories.

The lord of dust howled and howled his powerlessness, running through the classrooms and the bathrooms and the burning hallways as the fire spread everywhere with the speed of a deadly epidemic.

Underneath the smell of fire and gasoline he detected the scent of Beatrice's mother, and he cursed her.

And his curses became anathemas when he returned to the storeroom and found it enveloped in a shroud of embers, fed by the tons of dry paper hidden inside it. The den that had sheltered him, where he had taught the children about the future, was going up in flames.

Pupils burned among the cinders and will-o'-the-wisps of old school books. He tried to save the fable of the End, stretching his protuberances into the bonfire to safeguard the work to which he had devoted years, but incandescent tongues lashed out to singe his essence, forcing him to retreat. To flee from the basement.

A loud creaking announced the imminent collapse of the roof. Rubble and fiery confetti hit him, tearing off strips of his grayish body; the windowpanes exploded from the heat, hurling a storm of splinters at him, puncturing him like shotgun pellets through a sheet of newspaper.

The lord of dust crawled out of the elementary school that had given him refuge for a long time, leaving behind a trail of sparks and insults, and his tears were black with smoke and revenge. He lurched into the countryside, scorched, spitting charred mites, until he found shelter in a crumbling farmhouse, cool with shadows and ivy.

He felt as though disinherited, he felt lost, and in the lump of filth that was his heart throbbed pain and rage.

The pact was broken.

He lowered his head to his chest and died, awaiting his regeneration.

Sirens of fire trucks screamed in the distance like heralds of the Apocalypse.

The children's parents lingered in front of the school, but the school was no more, replaced by a cemetery of smoking rubble, encrusted with the foam from the firefighters' tanker trucks. Flashing lights lashed the summer morning like lightning in a thunderstorm. There was nothing left to save in the smoke-blackened debris. The knowledge, the laughter, and the memories that those walls had housed for decades furled up into the air in a pale cloud of ash and fog.

The adults didn't say a word, wondering what had happened, how the fire could have broken out, where their children would go to school when September came around, trembling at the thought that this event might be the prelude to a new period of mystery and terror.

In the back of the little crowd, Sofia Ratti was the only parent with a smug grin. She prayed that under the charred bricks, under the tons of tile and plaster, was lying the carcass of that foul being who had made Beatrice vomit eyes, the creature who had destabilized her peaceful small-town life.

It had to be, of course.

Fire purified, it always had.

Ashes to ashes, dust to dust.

She felt she had won, had given a solid future to her family, to the community of which she was part. She would sleep soundly, she would no longer traverse the terrifying oneiric glaciers of the Black Antarctic, and Beatrice would never again turn down a pizza from La Sfiziosa.

She looked at the carcass of the school and told herself that the children of Idrasca would have their classes in a temporary location while they waited for the school to be rebuilt.

Everything would be right with the world.

Everything *will* be all right, her mind growled, doing away with the conditional, and her smile grew even wider.

The crows flew low.

It was only just past dawn, but the summer was already hotter than ever.

The lord of dust got better. Little by little, in the cool darkness of the ruined farmhouse. And as he recovered and his frame gained a new covering of dust and mites, his rancor grew. He thought of the school and Pupils, annihilated by the flames, destroyed by the fear of facing a new understanding, a new era.

He slept and dreamed of vengeance.

Soon he would be reborn from the ashes of the future like a phoenix, to take back what was his and settle the score with an unkept promise.

In September.

In September Idrasca would experience the coldest and most disturbing ravines of the Black Antarctic.

It was the night before the start of the new school year.

Although it was summer, the storms that had beaten down on Idrasca over the course of the day had caused temperatures to plummet into an early autumn.

Eating pizza and drinking Coke, Sofia Ratti and her daughter Beatrice watched the disturbing images unfold on the kitchen television.

Huge wildfires were running up and down the Australian continent, consuming millions of acres of forest and countless animal lives, pushing towards the inhabited areas, discharging fumes and ashes into the atmosphere and the marine ecosystems.

An iceberg measuring more than two hundred square miles had detached from the Pine Island glacier in Antarctica, drifting in a fleet of fragments and causing a chain of micro-tsunamis.

A hurricane of a size never before recorded was tormenting India and Bangladesh, claiming thousands of victims and resulting in damage for billions.

The strange illness born in China seemed to be getting more aggressive, mysterious, and contagious, venturing outside the national borders. The World Health Organization feared an epidemic of global proportions, an unprecedented health catastrophe.

In a remote province of Madagascar dozens of people belonging to a solar cult had taken their lives in a violent mass suicide.

Sofia Ratti clawed at the remote and switched off the television in a fit of annoyance, interrupting the shots of factory farming in which terror-stricken cows jostled one another as they tried to flee the men who were loading them onto a truck bound for the slaughterhouse.

'Why did you turn it off?' asked the girl.

'Too much bad news,' her mother explained.

The news program's disheartening outlook had left her with a sticky, unpleasant feeling. 'Let's talk a bit, OK?'

'Mm-hmm.'

'So, are you glad to be going back to school tomorrow?'

'A little bit . . .'

'Only a little bit? Why's that?'

'Because the school burned down, Mom.'

'Right, okay . . .' A moment of hesitation, of awkward emptiness. 'But you'll have your classes in the classrooms at the chapel, Bea.'

'It's not the same thing.'

'The teachers are the same.'

'Yes, but . . .'

'What?'

'Nothing, Mommy. Nothing. Can I have some more Coke?'

'Sure.'

The lord of dust kept his promises.

He always had, he always would. Unlike people.

He waited for Idrasca to fall asleep, for the moon and night to rise and conquer the town, and he left the farmhouse where he had licked his wounds, reforming his hands into a long magic flute, a tapered flute with the power to attract the children like faithful dogs.

He played the sweet song of revenge, the ballad of the Black Antarctic.

And the elementary school children of Idrasca awoke to follow him.

The children of Idrasca went to bed early.

The calendar said it was still summer, but for them it was over. The next day they would go back to school. At the chapel. Before they fell asleep they cried, wondering if they would find their friend the lord of dust waiting for them in some unused room in the old parochial building, or if the fire that had destroyed the school had also annihilated the strange creature with his strange book.

They slept.

And they dreamt, the elementary school children.

They dreamt of a fire that burned for eternity, erasing everything. A pyre to lose and abandon yourself in, a devouring supernova in which to find an answer to a question that was simple and yet tremendously difficult: *Why did you bring us into this world?*

Then, in the small hours of the night, a melody started to echo through the streets of the town and the countryside, slipping into dreams and houses, awakening the children, pulling their sleep-weakened bodies from their beds.

A melody that was a call.

They left the little rooms and the toys they had had fun with for years, and with quiet steps so they would not be heard by their parents, they slipped out of their apartments and houses to walk towards that hypnotic music that beckoned them with the promise of a new sleep, deeper, serene, permanent.

Their eyes were white as they walked in a silent procession through the streets of Idrasca and then along an unpaved secondary road that led to the boiler room at the factory, cutting their bare feet on the rocks as they went. Swaying through the night in a somnambulistic parade, they followed the lord of dust, who led the column, dancing like a jester, flooding their eardrums and the sky with the indescribable and bewitching melody coming from his finger-whistle.

All the children kept pace.

All but one.

Beatrice, with her atrophied leg, couldn't keep up with her classmates, who proceeded at the heels of the dusty piper, their self-styled master and executioner.

Bea shouted and cried for them to wait for her, but they all thought only of themselves; everyone was concentrating on the music echoing from a dead future.

She stayed behind while the other children scaled the factory's fence like gigantic anthropomorphic spiders and left the September night to sneak into the bright cauldron of the boiler room through a side door.

Beatrice stopped with her hands gripping the metal fence that enclosed the factory, her eyes misty with tears. She yelled. She begged someone to come get her, help her. She would never manage to climb over and join her friends and the lord of dust. She screamed with all her might, but no one came to her aid.

She saw the throng of children disappear into the boiler room, dancing and pirouetting; the screams came a few moments later. Sharp and petulant, shrieks of ecstasy, pain, understanding, and dissolution.

And the burners hurled blackish flames skyward as the children of Idrasca threw themselves into the red-hot furnace, one after the other, to reunite with the little eyes, guided by the symphony of the creature of dust which was now the very sound of Armageddon.

Bea understood, and shrieked with them, shrieked until the flute music stopped, finally collapsing in the grass like an empty garbage bag, dreaming of the Black Antarctic.

The lord of dust stopped playing, and so he was able to hear her and go to her; he lifted her in his arms and caressed her forehead, then he sucked the eyes out of her face with a sloppy aspiration of his mite lips and assimilated the little girl's eyeballs into his dusty body: they would be useful to him in the future.

He laid Beatrice down gently in the dried bed of an irrigation ditch, so she could continue to sleep, to dream, and so that her mother would be able to find her the next day; then he returned to the farmhouse, to sleep and enjoy his own work.

When he awoke he would begin rewriting a new version of *Pupils*.

Sofia Ratti and the other parents awoke terrified in their beds shortly before dawn, glimpses of nightmares of black glaciers stuck behind their eyelids, the seed of a melody planted in their eardrums, and discovered that their children were gone from their rooms; they looked for them, first in their houses, garages, bathrooms, and then outside in the yards, the streets, the fields, the poplar groves, but there was no trace of the children, and they never learned what became of them.

Only the lord of dust knew.

The children were with him.

They were home.

Beatrice was the only one found, lying in an irrigation ditch, crumpled up on her crippled leg. Nothing was left of the little girl but a shell, a mindless and motionless container. Someone had taken her eyes, without leaving any other damage or wounds. But they hadn't taken away her power of speech.

Her mother, Sofia Ratti, went mad from remorse: she committed suicide by setting herself ablaze in an open field near a dilapidated farmhouse overrun by ivy, weeds, and shadows. An ancient farmhouse cluttered with dust.

Beatrice was confided to the care of a nursing home and she lived a long time, very long; she passed away in a hospital many years later, as the foundations of the world were beginning to wobble at the prospect of a new world conflict triggered by a lack of drinking water. She never answered the questions she was asked. She never said what had become of the other children of Idrasca. Until her final day, blind and paralyzed, she continued to repeat a few simple words, the same ones she had whispered to her mother when she was found eyeless in the ditch near the factory.

The words that close every fairy tale, and which are truth and lie at the same time:

'And they lived happily ever after, and they lived happily ever after, and they lived happily ever after, *andtheylivedhappilyeverafter.*'

A Different Darkness

There is such peace in helplessness.
Kathe Koja, *The Cipher*

The apartment smelled of neglect.

And despair.

And mystery.

The windows, filthy with dust and fly droppings, transformed the sunlight into a gray patina that stuck to the walls and ceilings and furniture like a mold capable of infesting the very fabric of reality.

An oppressive atmosphere in the place, a memory of the lives lived there, a memory with the stench of a sink full of dirty dishes.

Of tears and insomnia.

Of absence.

Captain Ernesto Gange sniffed the air, his stomach doing backflips. He staggered through the living room, letting his gaze fall on objects and furnishings, even the most insignificant, in a vain effort to splice together the film of the Balduzzis' life. The detectives buzzed around, rummaging in closets, collecting evidence. He wished he could tell them to be quiet, to go away, to leave him alone so he could ponder why people sometimes get lost and the odds of bringing them back are infinitesimal.

He slipped a cigarette between his lips but didn't light it, since it wasn't his home and he couldn't say whether it was still anybody's home, then stopped to look at a wall covered in photos.

A man.

A woman.

A little girl.

Smiles. Sunsets. Everyday life. Vacations. Slices of life, snapshots like you'd find in millions of other apartments.

He went closer to study the faces, the bodies frozen by the camera in eternal embraces, and he felt a rift open above his head; for a brief moment he had the sensation of being pulled out of his own body. Out of the apartment, out of the building, up, into the sky, observing the blue curves of the Earth, praying to find the answer to one simple question.

Where are you? Where did you go?

He turned away from the photos – *oh, looking at Luna's face hurts so much* – and, turning towards the hallway that split the apartment in two, headed for what looked like a storage room. In the doorway one of his men stood scratching his head in bewilderment, as if he didn't know what the heck he was doing there; Gange pushed him out of the way and peeked inside.

He had seen every color in his thirty years on the force; those colors often took on a nuance of degradation, of pain, of violence, but he was surprised to feel a wave of nausea when he saw the altogether innocuous contents of the little studio.

Inside, the predominant color was black.

Like a moth drawn to a flame he entered, stepping carefully, a traveler leaving behind the well-trodden paths to venture into unexplored territory.

'What the fuck . . .' someone mumbled behind him, and again he wished for silence, a chance to get his thoughts in order.

There were paintings everywhere. On canvases, sheets of paper, scraps of fabric. Dozens and dozens of them. Scattered across the floor, hanging on the walls, propped against easels and boxes. An enormous canvas, possibly an old sheet, hung from the ceiling: a dark nipple swelling with poisonous serum.

They weren't the kind of paintings one would expect to find in a middle-class suburban home.

The pictures didn't depict death, pornography, indecency, graphic scenes that might provoke disgust; they were abstract, focused on a single subject, and it was clear they represented an obsession, a disease, the product of a mind derailed from the tracks of normality.

Looking at their hypnotic hopelessness, his intention not to smoke went by the wayside.

It took him a few seconds to light the Zippo: sweat, fingers like play-dough.

He pulled on the cigarette angrily.

He wanted the Marlboro to make him dizzy.

For the nicotine to disperse the lump of anguish in his throat that was scurrying around like a fat cockroach in the vicinity of his Adam's apple.

He wanted to get out of that nightmarish little art gallery.

And he went out.

Into the hall.

Into the drab light filtered by filth and fly shit.

Anything was better than Eleonora Balduzzi's studio. He thought about that woman, about the first time he had met her at the police station, and about the indecent way she had shrunk in the weeks that followed.

Air. Air. Stuffy air.

A voice called to him from the bedroom. Hesitantly.

'Captain . . . could you come here for a sec?'

He could. Even though an itch in the back of his throat hinted to him that he'd better not. That something was waiting for him in that room that he'd never get free of.

Sheets piled up at the foot of the queen-sized bed like the cocoon of some monster. Semi-darkness that reminded him of the hospice room where his mother died, flailing with her withered legs and with her eyes. A sickly-sweet smell, musty, of sweat mixed with more sweat.

Pino Bertea, one of his most efficient officers, was sitting on the mattress waiting for him. He shot him a look saturated with sleepless nights and the dark thoughts of a middle-aged cop.

'I think that's for you, Captain,' he said in a drawling voice, pointing at the nightstand on the left side of the bed and switching on the Ikea bedside lamp.

'What is it?'

'An envelope. Your name's on it.'

Gange knelt down – *crack!* creaked his kneecaps, reminding him that old age wasn't far off, even if retirement still was – and examined the package. A bulging white envelope, legal size, on which a nervous hand had traced in block letters:

CAPTAIN GANGE

There was also a Samsung cell phone lying on the nightstand, and he wondered if, in its belly of chips and silicon, the answer was hidden to the enigma that stalked him like a starving dog. He took off his cap and dropped it on the bed, then turned back to his colleague: 'Mind leaving me alone for a minute, Pino? Make sure the boys in there don't miss anything . . .'

'Sure. You all right?'

'I'm tired. Exhausted.'

'I understand. There's better days ahead, Captain.'

'Right . . . better days.'

Bertea left the room and Gange remained in the shabby cone of light from the shabby Ikea lamp, tempted to collapse on the bed and surrender to sleep. Instead he slipped on a pair of latex gloves, took the envelope between his thumb and index finger, and opened it.

Sheets of paper.

Dozens of sheets of paper blackened with a cramped, spiky handwriting, filled with notes and erasures.

Where are you? Where did you go?

Only when he began to read did he notice the cigarette burning down between his lips, making specters of smoke dance in that room which had once hosted life; he felt like a nocturnal insect in the darkness, desperately seeking the artificial light of a streetlamp.

∞

If you're reading these words, it means we're gone. You know a lot of the story, of course. But only the part ON THE SURFACE.

I'm not sure why I decided to leave my account to you after I finished writing it.

It's all very chaotic.

But is there anything that's not chaotic, flawed, out of balance?

Light. Darkness.

Love. Hate.

Hope. Despair.

Joy. Sadness.

There's never a balance.

Never.

Thank you for what you did for us.

It's like it's pulsating.

Like it's promising something.

It's black, *but it shines*.

It can't be worse than here.

It can't be.

In hindsight we always manage to find glaring errors in our actions. Wrong turns at the crossroads of existence.

The ability to blame yourself is one of the misfortunes of being human.

Everything can change in an instant.

A second too late, a minute too early, can change the course of our lives in unimaginable ways. Turning the days before that fateful moment into a hazy vision. Into a path that no longer belongs to us.

It's a platitude, I know, a simple concept, but . . .

It's a concept on which religions should be founded. Cathedrals built.

There should be signs in the streets to remind us, every time we step foot outside our homes wearing our armor of fragile certainties.

For me it was a brief chat with a friend I hadn't seen in a long time, in an ordinary small-town supermarket.

For me it was the end of the dream I had built up over thirty-five years on this planet and the beginning of a murky nightmare I still haven't woken up from.

This is the story of the last two years of my life.

A story I never wanted to tell.

But sometimes *telling* is all we have left, before the long goodbye.

I go down to the basement of the building a couple of times a day, move the pallet covering the manhole, and sit in front of it.

I stay there for hours, staring down into the reflecting gloom of that darkness.

The time goes by quickly as I watch its stirring.

Sometimes it's as if I find comfort in it. Other times I'm overcome by a nameless panic, and I think about my wife up in the apartment, shut up in her room, fading away, and I wonder what will become of her, of us. And of the world.

I've lost everything, that's why death doesn't frighten me. Life stopped frightening me long ago.

But I'm terrified of the things *in between*, the bulwarks of uncertainty.

It was three days before Christmas.

I was standing at the bedroom window, and I didn't want anything in my life to be any different.

Overnight the sky had deposited a thin layer of snow on the streets, which the frigid dawn temperatures had frozen into a shimmering crust. The roofs white, the sky an aluminum sheet, all external sounds muffled . . . Back then I used to love how a snowfall could dull the soundtrack of the real world: that muffling seemed to give the hours a feeling of intimacy, especially when I was inside the apartment's four walls with my family. Now I can't bear that icy stillness. It terrifies me, opens scenes in my mind of a world in ruins, shrouded in a new ice age where the cities that once belonged to us are now overrun by wild animals and shadows of monsters, rapists, murderers.

Well, our feelings can change, depending on events and the weight of memories: another truism to which we don't give enough importance.

From the living room I heard the sound of Luna laughing as she sat on the couch watching cartoons. I finished getting dressed and went to my wife in the little studio set up in the guest room.

She was very beautiful.

It was the last time I saw her looking so lovely.

She was painting an enchanted forest where a silly creature, something halfway between a bear and a rabbit, was frolicking around.

'Cute . . . what is it?' I asked, kissing the top of her head. Her auburn hair smelled good.

'It's Frisky, the prankster of the woods. How many times do I have to tell you?'

'Oh, right, Frisky, I forgot . . .' I hugged her and squeezed her breasts gently, brushing my lips along her neck. 'I'll show you frisky . . .'

She burst out laughing. 'Stop that. You're breaking my concentration!'

'That was just what I was going for, you know?' I said, making a disappointed face. 'All right, I'll stop . . . So, should I go and get the groceries? You're not coming?'

She turned to look at me. She had a drop of black paint on the tip of her nose. 'Do you mind? I have to hand in this painting by the day after tomorrow and I'm a little behind. You'd be doing me a *huge* favor . . .'

'No problem, Ele.'

'You're a sweetheart, Diego. I left the list in the kitchen for you.'

'I'll be expecting a reward,' I whispered, sticking out my tongue and reaching for her thighs.

'Cut it out! Is that all you think about?'

'Yes.'

'I know.' She got up from the stool and gave me a wet, voluptuous kiss. I felt the blood rushing towards my groin. 'Take Luna too so she can get a little fresh air.'

'Sure.'

'I love you.' She never said those three simple words again.

'You too. So much.'

'And remember the smoked salmon.'

'Aye-aye.'

'It's going to be a great Christmas.'

'You can say that again.'

We had a full schedule: dinners with friends and relatives, several days in the mountains for New Year's, the search for a bigger apartment; my work as a project manager had taken off and money wasn't a problem. Eleonora was doing well too: her illustrations for children had attracted the notice of a well-known publishing company with which she had signed a major contract.

We had big dreams.

We were happy.

And then there was Luna.

Our sunshine.

Our daughter.

Carrot-red hair, her face dotted with freckles, two big eyes that would have melted Bluebeard's heart, and a heck of a temper. Just like her mother. Next year she'd be starting elementary school.

A bright girl, so full of life. That's what people always say, right?

I went to the living room and stopped in the doorway for a few moments to watch her. 'Come on, Lù, put on your coat, you're coming with me to the grocery store.'

She was sprawled out on the couch with her eyes glued to some silly cartoon. 'I don't want to, Daddy. Can't I stay with Mommy?'

'No, Lù, Mommy has to work. We're going grocery shopping so she can have a little peace and quiet.'

'But Daddddyyy, cartoons are on!'

I snorted, somewhere between annoyance and bewilderment. She used to love going to the supermarket, she had never made a fuss before. She always found some excuse to get me to buy her a present, usually a Kinder egg or some candy. 'No tantrums, Lù.'

'Ugh.'

'Daddy'll buy you a Kinder egg. And bring your gloves so when we come back we can make a snowman in the yard.'

'I want to stay with Mommy.'

It took a lot of prodding to get her to stand up from the couch and put on her electric blue jacket. In the end she gave in, not without a certain reluctance. I thought maybe she was coming down with the flu or something.

'Bye, Ele,' I yelled from the entryway.

'Bye, Mommy!' Luna echoed me.

'Bye, be good, you two. And don't forget the salmon!'

'I hate salmon. And I want to stay home with Mommy, ugh!'

We went down the stairs of the old apartment building hand in hand, and she went on sulking until I fastened her into her car seat; I said something goofy and only then did she melt into one of her mischievous little smiles.

I've turned my daughter's behavior that morning over in my mind so many times.

I've punched myself in the head, torn out my hair in front of the mirror, cried until my eyes burst, telling myself that if I had just left her at home our life would have proceeded along a totally different set of coordinates.

I couldn't have known.

I couldn't.

But I regret it every day.

I shouldn't have insisted, I keep telling myself. And then I wonder if certain mechanisms can't be stopped once they've been put in motion. If that terrible thing we call *destiny* really exists, a puppeteer who makes all our choices futile. If what happened to us, what *is* happening to us, is real. And if the decision we made, the final one, will reveal the truth to me, or whether it will be nothing more than the cause of our annihilation, our permanent dissolution.

Either way, it's fine.

It's fine.

Eleonora is in the bedroom, in bed. Has been for weeks now. She's almost always asleep. She makes a strange sound when she snores, as if there's something blocking her airways, like she has soaking wet sponges stuck in her lungs, even though, to be honest, I don't see how she still has a respiratory system. Sometimes she paints. She no longer cares about anything, and we both agree that seeing a doctor wouldn't do any good. Besides, it would reveal our secret. We don't want that. The only thing that matters to us is facing it.

Every so often I visit her. I sit on the mattress and we chat a little, but I'm careful not to touch her. Where there's still something left to touch.

We rarely talk about Luna. More often we talk about the manhole in the cellar, about what it contains or what we think it contains, even if we don't have any answers.

She says she doesn't feel any pain, and I think that's true. Actually, I think she even feels well, that what's happening to her is in some way comforting. Which doesn't make it any less horrible to look at.

The only consolation is that it won't go on much longer.

Soon we'll have to say our goodbyes.

We're going away.

She wants to go first. She feels ready, she says.

I am too.

I'll throw her down.

Then I'll follow.

The Carrefour supermarket is about a fifteen-minute drive from our apartment, located in an industrial area surrounded by a wood of scraggly poplars. We were halfway there when Luna, a little bundle wrapped in a scarf and hood in the back seat, started singing.

'Jingle Bells.'

She didn't know the words, so what issued from her lips was something like: '*Jinglsh bell, jinglsh bell, shalalalalabell!*'

I joined in with her chant and we laughed till we cried. It had started snowing again, a dry, powdery snow that swooped down from the sky, wrapping itself into spirals in the gusts; there was something reassuring about the *chaf chaf* of the wind-shield wipers, which barely kept up with sweeping it away.

I parked in the supermarket's underground garage a few minutes later, and we launched ourselves into the pre-holiday crowd, bright with garlands and Christmas lights. My daughter's cheeks were red, her eyes shining with excitement, and she seemed to have shaken off her morning grouchiness. She wouldn't stop running up and down the aisles; when I suggested she sit in the shopping cart so she wouldn't tire herself out too much, she gave me a serious, adult look and told me, 'No, I'm a big girl now.'

I bent down and gave her a kiss on the cheek. I smelled the

scent of her skin and vanilla, like always. Thanks to her favorite shampoo, which she called her 'shampooey'.

'Right, you're getting big. So are you going to give me a hand with the groceries?'

We went crazy with our purchases, even buying things that weren't on Eleonora's list. Luna stopped to talk with an elderly woman and said something funny to her; the old lady burst into a hearty laugh, and I thought about how at Christmastime some people went totally nuts while others were a little more serene than usual, a little nicer, and I reflected that the world needed more smiles like that woman's.

It was almost noon when Luna reminded me not to forget the smoked salmon, and as we headed towards the refrigerated seafood case she asked if she could go get a Kinder egg in the candy section, by the checkout stands.

'Okay, sure. I'll wait here, go fast.'

'Thank you, Daddy!'

I won't try to justify myself. But I'm not – I wasn't – a careless father. I never would have left her alone if I couldn't keep an eye on her. The registers were only a few meters from where I was standing, and I watched Luna make her way between people and shopping carts to reach her beloved eggs. I saw her reach out her hand to pick one, and then I got a slap on the back that knocked the wind out of me.

'Hey, asshole!'

I turned around aghast and found myself face to face with features that had changed but which I knew well.

'You ugly fuck!' I replied, with the comradely finesse that's typical with close friends.

Gualtiero Ferretti had been one of my best partners in crime during my high school and college years, until our ways separated because . . . Well, you know how these things go . . . You grow up, there's work, family, you follow different paths . . .

I was truly happy to see him again, and all the crazy shit we had done together flashed through my mind, a slideshow from another time, a time when we were young and carefree.

'Gualtiè! But didn't you move to Venice? What are you doing here? How long has it been?'

We hugged, then started to chat. I don't think I was distracted for more than two minutes, two goddamned minutes. Because one of the first questions he asked me was: 'And your wife, your daughter, how are they doing?'

'Great, fantastic! Luna's right over there,' I responded, pointing towards the checkout lanes.

But Luna *was no longer there*.

I felt a spasm in my guts, a rush of cold creeping up to the base of my neck. I think every parent in every supermarket in the world has experienced a similar feeling. You lose sight of your child for a few seconds, you shit your pants, then find them a few moments later picking their nose in the toy aisle or nibbling on a package of Pringles.

'Sorry, Gualtiero, she was there just a second ago, she must have wandered off. I'll be right back, okay?' I explained, then headed briskly towards the spot where I had seen her last.

I heard my friend saying, 'Okay, I'll wait for you here,' but his voice was light years away.

I looked all around the Kinder egg display. She wasn't there.

I forced myself to stay calm. *She must be behind that shelf, chatting with some old lady*, I told myself, trying to downplay it.

'Luna? Luna honey, where are you?' I called, peering down the aisles in search of an electric blue jacket, my throat raspy like sandpaper.

Five minutes later I was running through the toy section, calling my daughter's name loudly and asking everyone I met, 'Have you seen a little girl, red hair, blue jacket?'

Several customers tried to help, and as I stumbled past the pickles and canned tuna, a horrible slideshow was playing in my head.

Gualtiero caught up with me, his face flushed. 'Did you find her?'

'No. She was right by the checkout stands a minute ago. Fuck!'

'Calm down, Diego, she has to be around here somewhere . . . What was she wearing? I'll keep looking for her. You go to customer service and have them make an announcement.'

'Blue jacket. Red hair,' I murmured, and my voice seemed to have taken on a disturbing, metallic tone.

After that, my memories become confused. I had a sort of emotional short circuit, as if I could see myself from the outside, like I had turned into someone watching a film.

I remember I thought about Eleonora, how if I didn't find Luna she'd kill me with her own hands.

I heard the speakers thundering between the lights and Christmas trees: '*Crrr . . . Luna's father is waiting for her at the customer service counter, by the Kinder eggs. Luna, your father is waiting for you by the Kinder eggs . . . Crrr . . .*'

And as the minutes passed, a sort of electric panic pervaded the supermarket, infecting the other customers.

Someone yammered, 'A girl is lost, they're looking for her.'

My vision blurry, I plunged into the Christmas decorations department. A couple of people turned to stare at me in shock as I screamed, 'All right, Luna, that's enough now, come on out!'

And then I saw it, on the floor.

A Kinder egg.

I don't know if it was my daughter's, but it was certainly a bizarre coincidence, and at that moment I felt faint. I picked it up and slipped it into my coat pocket, then went back to squawking around the Carrefour.

Some security guards arrived, they asked me some questions, we looked for her everywhere, everywhere, in the parking garage, outside, in the storerooms, behind the butcher's counter, in the bathrooms.

Half an hour later we still hadn't found her. I was dizzy from anxiety and adrenaline; I went on running with Gualtiero at my heels, and these ridiculous words kept echoing in my brain: *Remember the smoked salmon. You have to remember the smoked salmon.*

I think it was my brain's defense mechanism to keep me anchored to reality, to keep me from going haywire and collapsing on the floor in a nervous breakdown.

We called the police.

An hour later, my Samsung rang. Eleonora. I considered declining the call, flinging the smartphone as far away as possible.

What could I say to her? What?

I answered.

I don't know what I said, but at a certain point she interrupted me, sobbing. Of that I'm certain. She listened in silence, then made a horrible noise, an animalistic groan, and that cry was like an omen thundering in my marrow with a heartbreaking echo, confirming that *things will never be the same again, Diego, never again.*

Eleonora croaked into the phone: 'I'll be right there. She must be hiding somewhere, you know how Luna is . . .'

After my wife's arrival – I'll never forget her eyes when they fixed on mine, bright with tears, but at the same time inquisitorial – the search went on for a period of time I'm unable to quantify. Then two friendly police officers invited us to follow them to the station.

Ele finally flipped out. She didn't want to leave. She wanted to stay there, to find her daughter. The three of us had to drag her to get her in the car. A grotesque scene amid the swirl of holiday sights and sounds. As we left the supermarket the radio was playing 'Jingle Bells', and I prayed to a god I hadn't turned to in a long time, begging for all of this to have a happy ending.

At the police station we were greeted by Captain Ernesto Gange. I told him what had happened. He explained that the first forty-eight hours are crucial in finding a missing child. He also said that, given the suddenness of her disappearance, we had to consider the possibility of kidnapping. My wife again emitted that throaty cry and this time it was no longer an omen but the crash of the universe collapsing on top of me.

Kidnapping. Kidnapping. Three syllables that rang out like a death knell. Who could have taken our little girl? Why?

They bombarded us with questions. Did we have any enemies, family disputes, problems at work? I didn't understand. Or I didn't want to understand.

As we speak, several patrols are combing the area around the store, we have our best men on it, they told us.

We'll find her, they told us.

Late that afternoon, as the snow fell and fell and fell, they let us go home.

The final image of that day is branded in my memory: Eleonora and I, in the dead of night, sitting on the couch where a few hours earlier Luna was watching cartoons, both of us crying as we stared at the Kinder egg and our cell phones, praying that someone would call and tell us they had found her.

Unfortunately that's not what happened.

At night, while I lie stretched out in bed, I have the impression it's calling to us.

No, no.

It's not an impression.

It's calling . . .

There are six stories between us and the basement, but in the darkest hours of night, just before dawn, the town wrapped in a treacherous silence, it's like the building becomes an organic, viscous structure murmuring Christmas songs or unprintable obscenities and trickling down towards the basement, unraveling and swirling in a nosedive to reach that one point, the underground drain of our existences.

Eleonora is able to sleep. Sometimes I watch her in the orange glow of the alarm clock radio, but I can't let my gaze linger on her for more than a few seconds. And then I remember the nights we made love, when I would spend fifteen minutes or more watching her sleep and thinking she was a miracle, then slip down the hall and check to make sure Luna was sleeping soundly in her little bed, in the small bedroom with the Winnie the Pooh wallpaper.

Our daughter's room is inhabited by her absence now. We left it as it was: toys scattered on the floor, stuffed animals on the desk, the bed unmade and her rumpled pajamas hanging on the chair.

Sometimes I still go in there on my way to the bathroom or the kitchen in the middle of the night, but I never stay there long.

A few seconds.

It scares me.

The bed is empty, the shadows are hunchbacked in the light from the streetlamps filtering in from outside, and the Winnie the Pooh characters look like deformed, malevolent creatures, madmen that limp through alleys late at night to infect decent people with their insanity, carrying away their innocent children to do unspeakable things to them.

We were on a rollercoaster, a ride without half measures: either it would hurtle us towards heights of shimmering hope or else plunge us into tunnels of dark despair.

For the first week, the police investigation proceeded at a frantic pace.

The surveillance videos were reviewed; unfortunately there was no trace of Luna in any of the footage, and the cameras didn't cover the entire perimeter of the supermarket.

Several witnesses were interviewed, among them my friend Gualtiero, as well as a woman who remembered a little girl in a blue jacket in the company of a gangly man, well dressed, 'odd'. It turned out not to be much of a lead, whether because of the advanced age of the lady (who maintained that the girl's hair was black) or else because the world is full of blue jackets and odd people.

But I dreamed about him, *the gangly man*, the night of Christmas. I was at Carrefour, trying to catch up to him as he carried Luna off; his back was to me, dressed in a coal-black suit, and I was yelling something at him, but as is often the case in dreams, I was powerless. I stumbled with every step, I kept falling to the ground, and he and my daughter vanished into the crowd, while the echo of 'Jingle Bells' turned into a disturbing melody playing from a rusty music box.

The police K-9 unit combed the poplar grove around the industrial area; divers searched a small private pond in the terrible possibility that our daughter had left the supermarket and fallen in.

They didn't find anything.

Eleonora and I tried to make ourselves useful. To keep ourselves busy. So we wouldn't go crazy. She was dazed by the shock, plunged into a world whose only emotions were apathy or a disturbing hyperactivity. She was prescribed some drops to calm her nerves, and we saw a psychotherapist.

On December 26th we printed some flyers and plastered the streets of our town and the neighboring towns with them; we appeared on a TV show dedicated to finding missing persons, we aired a call for help on the major networks.

And Luna's story became a nationwide case.

The little red-headed angel.

The news reporters' trucks would park outside our apartment building. Absurd. It was all absurd. The tabloids indulged in crazy conjectures; one went so far as to suggest that I had something to do with her disappearance. I sued them.

We hardly slept, barely ate, drove around aimlessly for hours in the hope of spotting a flash of electric blue in the snow-covered streets. We waited for good news. One night we went to church to pray. We hadn't done that in years.

New Year's Eve arrived. We spent it crying, sitting on the bed in Luna's room, looking at photos of her.

When the clock struck midnight, as the sky erupted with fireworks, I hugged Eleonora and told her, 'We have to be strong.' She pulled away and fixed her resentful, tear-swollen eyes on me. She was no longer herself at that moment. Or maybe she had never been *so much herself* as at that moment.

'How could you let her out of your sight? How the fuck could you lose her?' she hissed, then let out a cry of frustration and ran towards the bathroom.

I didn't try to stop her.

I heard her crying and smashing perfume bottles.

I stayed there, sitting on our daughter's little bed, frozen, looking outside.

Fireworks exploded over the rooftops to welcome the new year, red like flowers of blood on a lake of tar.

A few days before the Epiphany, Captain Gange summoned us to the station. His face was drawn and tired (you were a wreck, eh, Captain?), with an ashen complexion and deep purple rings under his eyes, as if the Luna case was draining away his energy. When we sat down at his desk, I noticed his hands were trembling.

We hoped he had important news. Instead he cleared his throat, started fiddling with a pen, and said: 'It's a complicated case. We don't really have much to go on. I know this is a tough time for you both, but I need to ask you whether you can think of anything else that might help us.'

I freaked out. The anxiety that had been gnawing at my insides for two weeks exploded; I thought I was dealing with idiots, that because of them we would never find our little girl. I banged my fists on the table, and I don't remember precisely what words came out of my mouth. It was a real scene. It was a mistake, one of many. Eleonora, sitting beside me, sobbed into her handkerchief.

Ernesto Gange is a good man and didn't lose his cool. He waited for me to vent, to get it all out. Or at least some of it. Then he went on.

'Signor Balduzzi, I'm putting myself in your shoes and . . . I'm trying to understand what you're going through, I'm trying. I have children too. We're doing everything we can, I assure you. My men are working around the clock. I'm only asking you . . . if anything comes to mind, anything at all that could help us, don't hesitate to let us know. We have no witnesses, no video footage, nothing solid to go on. In the next few days we'll try to get things moving a little with a televised press conference. We'll say we're hot on the kidnappers' trail. Maybe they'll slip up.'

I covered my face in my hands, exhausted. 'All right. Okay. I . . . I'm sorry for . . . for earlier. So . . . you're convinced that Luna was kidnapped?'

'If your daughter had gone off on her own, we would have found her almost immediately,' he replied tersely.

'Find her, please. You have to find her . . .' whined Eleonora. 'Bring her back home.'

'That's my greatest wish, too, ma'am. I haven't been sleeping at night, you know?' the captain said. 'I'll do everything in my power, and more. I promise you.'

He looked me in the eyes and I knew it was true.

But it didn't change anything.

Is what I've written legible?
Does it matter?
No.
Maybe.
No.

The fake announcement didn't do a damn thing.

More days passed. Then weeks. In the end, months. It's hard to explain the anxiety, the minutes that turned into centuries, the questions that continuously tormented us, needles stabbing into our brains.

Is she all right? Is she still alive? Where is she? Did they hurt her?

Every now and then the investigators got a tip, followed a new lead, inevitably going nowhere.

A gypsy caravan. Organ trafficking. Pedophilia.

We slid down into a pit where the light of hope became more and more feeble and distant as time went on.

Hard work and sacrifice had gotten me where I wanted to be: financial security, nice house, perfect family, brilliant career; but now none of it meant anything anymore. Chaos had stormed into our lives, leaving us bewildered and terrified. I no longer felt I was in control of my own existence. I was moved by invisible strings manipulated by a demiurge with a sick sense of humor, a puppet at the mercy of events I was unprepared to face.

Powerless.

Was it really like that? Oh, yes, it was. A crumbling castle strewn with traps and snares, with trapdoors that swallowed up kids, and with monsters ready to devour the rational, the flow of quiet and settled lives.

I fantasized about investigating it myself, becoming a sort of private detective who would solve the case of his own daughter's disappearance, like you see on TV shows. But when I tried to gather information and ideas to start my personal investigation, I found myself in Captain Gange's shoes: *We really don't have much to go on . . .*

Media interest in Luna's case started to wane. Her disappearance became a blurb in the back pages of the newspaper, the flyers with her smiling face faded in the weather; the TV news likened her to Denise Pipitone, Angela Celentano, other girls who had vanished and never been found.

Despair turned into obsession. Paranoid obsession. I read hundreds of articles on missing persons, on the aftermath left by such experiences, and the numbers were monstrous, inconceivable.

Every year eight million children disappear worldwide. Two hundred and seventy thousand in Europe. Taken by a parent, runaways, kidnapped, or murdered and hidden in unmarked graves, never to be found. In Italy fifteen kids vanish every month and only twenty percent of these make it back home.

How is it possible to live on such a planet? How can one even imagine not giving in to entropy when such possibilities exist?

In my head, Luna became an ambiguous figure. On the one hand she was still our daughter, *our sunshine*, on the other she had become a sort of goddess of the nonsensical. The emblem of everything that should not happen.

But can happen.

Until true horror caressed us with its cadaverous fingers, we had no idea of its reality.

But it's always there, chuckling and dancing over our heads.

It operates autonomously, it doesn't need our consciousness and thoughts to exist.

Horror is real, it *is*.

And sometimes it decides to knock on our door. It slips in stealthily, whether we invite it in or not, then it starts screaming and wrecking our home.

We were fumbling in the dark, all of us. Me, Eleonora, Captain Gange, our friends, our families, Luna's little kindergarten classmates, the whole world.

And as impossible as it seems even writing it, the worst, the dazzling splendor of a different darkness, was yet to come.

When does a person really disappear? When they die? When there's no one left who remembers them? When they're torn away from their loved ones, from their identity? Or when the void left in those who knew them becomes too deep ever to be filled?

These are questions I often ask myself. Sometimes I tell myself that some part of us will always remain, a flicker of what we were, of the energy that allowed us to love, move, think.

Other times I tell myself it's not like that; that ultimately we've all vanished already. Like when you look at the stars knowing that many of the ones you see no longer exist; they've been dead for thousands of years. You're looking at the past, but at the same time the future. It's the same with human beings. It's a sinister thing. I look at myself in the mirror and I glimpse traces of the child I was, but at the same time I know that the image reflected one day *will not be*. There will be nothing left. We're an infinitesimal flash in the history of this meat grinder we call the Universe, and soon the memory will fade even of the lives and ideas we consider unassailable, eternal: Catholicism, Jesus Christ, Darwin, Julius Caesar, Plato, God, Love . . . Some star will go *poof*, and everything will be wiped out by its gravitational collapse. We'll be digested by the great cosmic mechanism.

The end of history, of civilization, of human consciousness, of the millennia we spent struggling to rise out of the mud.

All that remains will be dust, gas, and disassembled matter.

Maybe not even that.

Maybe there will be nothing left but a black hole, an absence capable of devouring light, something beyond the scope of our imagination.

Something like the darkness that lives down in our basement.

When tragedy strikes, time can take strange paths. Oh, how old my wife and I got! We've always been in good shape, healthy diet, mountains and outdoor activities whenever possible.

We withered.

We became recluses, sequestered in prisons of pain.

Eleonora's shiny red hair, so like Luna's, sagged into a stringy mass. Mine grew streaked with white. Worry lines dug deep furrows in our skin.

I can't say we gave up, that would be awful, but . . . well, we sensed a black shadow, a cancer eating away at our hope. Captain Gange's phone calls grew more and more infrequent, just like the reportings of possible sightings.

We didn't want to admit it, but eight months after her disappearance, I'm convinced that my wife and I were experiencing the same feelings. A parent lives on feelings, and I had the clear sense that Luna *was no more*. She was gone, however much I might tell myself the contrary, however much I might try to hold on tooth and nail to a positive attitude.

I carried a tremendous burden in my stomach, a martyrdom of the spirit, and that weight grew every time I met Eleonora's eyes.

Mother.

A mother understands certain things.

A mother knows them, period.

Our marriage fell apart. The cracks that had undermined it spread like a spiderweb and reduced it to rubble. Two shadows had slipped into the conjugal nest, the shadows of blame and a guilty conscience. She no longer looked me in the eyes; every time I hugged her, every time I *touched* her, I felt her body tense, become a bundle of nerves. I knew the question she had yelled in my face on New Year's Eve — *how the fuck could you lose her?* was still nagging at her, and that a corner of her heart would always hold me responsible. And was she totally wrong? Oh no. I hadn't been capable of protecting the dearest thing I had in the world. I hadn't been able to defend Luna from the indifferent jaws of darkness, defend my family from the madness of the world.

My guilt made me short of breath. Even getting out of bed was hard, let alone arguing, fighting: I never had the courage to face the problem head-on because deep down I agreed with her, and I thought her resentment was justified.

We moped around the apartment, barely exchanging a word, two strangers who had once loved each other but no longer remembered why. We would go to bed in the semi-darkness of the bedroom and fall asleep without saying goodnight. Sex became a memory, a blur of caresses and pleasures belonging to another life.

Pain can unite, pain can divide. In our case, it built a wall that was impossible to knock down.

I could have tried harder, that's for sure. Maybe if I had tried to stitch the shreds of our relationship back together, that thing in the basement would never have manifested . . . who can say?

But I wasn't strong enough.

God help me, I wasn't strong enough.

One night I awoke with a start, bathed in sweat, convinced I had heard scuffling steps in the hall, and Luna was standing in the bedroom doorway, lit up by the blades of light from the town filtering through the shutters.

She was staring at me, but her eyes were no longer there. Or rather, they were there, but they had become completely black, as if the pupils had expanded and overrun them with a color that wasn't a color, but an *absence*.

An absence of love.

She looked like the depictions of aliens you see on those stupid late-night 'unsolved mysteries' shows, *the Greys*, they're called, little creatures with enormous black eyes who *are among us* and who abduct us to study and subjugate us.

She was wearing the electric blue jacket, filthy with dirt and leaves, and her little hands were clutching the Kinder egg, holding it level with her heart. Her mouth was little more than a horizontal line, her livid lips slightly curled in a horrible palsy, a grimace of accusation and disillusion.

'Lù, baby . . . what are you doing here? You're back?' I asked, but she didn't answer. Without taking her enormous eyes off mine, she cracked the egg in two with a mechanical movement of her hands, producing a sound of shattered lives, the noise dogs make when crunching on a chicken bone, and from the Kinder egg a surprise of darkness began to pour out, a substance halfway between liquid and gas, darker than the darkest night, which took over the room little by little, pinning me to the bed, crawling in through my nostrils, mouth, navel, anus, preventing me from letting out a scream that was a thousand screams, the cries of newborns vomited from the womb, of vanished children, of their parents, and of the emptiness that divides us . . .

I didn't wake up. That hazy darkness swallowed my consciousness, and when I awoke the next morning I remembered nothing, I only noticed an unusual taste stuck in the back of my throat, a bitter taste, of gastric juices and rotten chestnuts.

I slipped into the kitchen and waited for the burbling of the moka pot, then crept into the living room with the little cup in my hands, letting myself fall onto the couch. The egg was still on the table where I had left it. I had promised myself I would open it the day when I got to hug her again.

But I didn't wait.

I unwrapped it on the spur of the moment and split the two milk chocolate halves.

It was empty.

No surprise inside, no plastic yellow container.

A production defect, I thought, and the previous night's nightmare came back to me, striking me like a slap in the face.

A dream of empty eyes.

And gaseous darkness.

And detachment.

But was it really just a dream, nothing more?

Six floors down, in a filthy manhole, was the darkness already looking forward to its feast?

Eleonora took up painting again. Every morning after breakfast she would drag herself to her little studio. And close the door. She had never done that before. Some days I didn't see her again until dinner.

'I don't want to be disturbed,' she insisted before barricading herself inside. 'I *need* to be alone.'

Sometimes I would hear her crying, shouting. I preferred those explosions of anger and frustration to the stagnant silence that reigned in the apartment.

Sometimes she would emerge from her kingdom of paint-brushes and torment to indulge in a brief pilgrimage to the liquor cabinet.

I went back to the office after ten months. Only then did I realize how a tragedy changes the perception other people have of us. My co-workers were kind, my boss was understanding, but their supportive words and gestures couldn't hide what their looks, their whispers, their uneasy faces expressed when I walked into the conference room.

I had become a strange, rare beast. A creature you feel sorry for but keep your distance from, because it's suffering from an incurable illness that might be contagious, the plague of the unknown, whose buboes ravage the spirits of normal people.

They kept a safe distance. They no longer involved me in decision-making processes, and my opinion carried less weight than before. They talked to me about business plans and group objectives, but their faces said: '*Oh fuck, I don't want to end up like you, I don't want anything to happen to me that's even remotely comparable to what happened to you, God forbid . . .*'

It was like that away from work too.

Things began to settle down, as far as that was possible. We rarely heard from friends and family; they seldom called, they forgot to invite us to parties or assumed we wouldn't come, and I sensed the barricades of an unwanted quarantine being built up around me and my wife.

The world was making a void around us.

Caterpillars.

We had become caterpillars plodding along on the leaf of life, changed from butterflies to crawling creatures through a perverse process of regression.

I had a hard time picturing Luna's face; more and more often I found myself rummaging through boxes of old photos to remember her features, our life together.

One day before the tragic anniversary, coming home from work, I found Eleonora sitting at the kitchen table with her gaze lost on an inscrutable horizon and a bottle of Amaro del Capo in her lap. She was so thin . . . so lifeless.

She was no longer the woman I had married.

She belched.

I don't think she even realized it.

A dissonant, bewildered, bilious regurgitation.

A soft, organic sound that echoed in immense underground caverns of the spirit.

She took her eyes off that universe that was entirely hers, to which I didn't have access, and fixed them on mine. They were yellowish, the sclerae of sick cattle.

I guessed what she was going to say before she started to speak.

'Diego, I . . . I'm going to my mom's for a while. I'll pack some things in a suitcase tomorrow and move in with her for a few weeks. Being here isn't good for me. Being here is . . .'

She burst into tears. I went over to her and put an arm around her shoulders.

A bundle of nerves.

'All right,' I said. And then I added, 'I'm sorry.'

'So am I,' she mumbled. She smelled of alcohol and sweat.

I don't know how long we stayed like that, not saying anything, hugging, but with a crevasse between us.

I knew that once she went out the door she would never come back.

But in the end she didn't leave.

The next morning she went down to the basement and discovered the incomprehensible.

The day was neverending.

We were approaching Christmas, again, and it had snowed, again.

The second Christmas without Luna.

A year had passed.

The weight of memories, of the terrible minutes at the supermarket, crushed me under a blanket of anxiety.

On the way to work I was seized with a panic attack and had to stop the car on the side of the road to catch my breath, while black tentacles sharpened themselves at the edges of the windshield, threatening to take control.

I got little or nothing done at the office. I kept on wondering if Eleonora would wait to say goodbye or if I'd come home to a cold, empty apartment, and for the first time in my life I considered the possibility of putting an end to it all.

It was an option. And that day it didn't seem like such a bad one; there was comfort in the idea of *stopping*. Maybe it was the only way of finding out what had happened to my daughter.

I would park in the garage, close the heavy metal door, connect a rubber tube to the exhaust pipe, *et voilà, les jeux sont faits*. And who knows, maybe after the carbon monoxide had put an end to my functioning, I would change into pure spirit, an all-seeing ghost able to answer the terrible questions, finding peace at last. Or maybe I'd slide into oblivion, and so long.

That afternoon Captain Gange called me. I hadn't heard from him in a couple of weeks. Every time his name appeared on the phone's screen my heart skipped a beat. New clues? Had they found her? Dead or alive?

'How are you doing, Signor Balduzzi?' His voice was hoarse, frayed.

'We're getting by,' I lied. Sometimes getting by isn't possible. Sometimes all you can do is stay in limbo. 'Any news?'

'No, unfortunately not,' I heard him sigh. 'But we're not giving up. We're not giving up. I wish I could give you answers for . . . well, for Christmas.'

'I know. Thanks.'

'Your wife?'

'She's holding up,' I lied again. 'She's started doing a little work again.'

'Good. Good. You have to try to return to a semblance of normality, as much as possible.'

We chatted a little more. I don't remember what about (do you remember, Gange?) Empty words. I talked, but I was thinking about 'Jingle Bells', about smoked salmon, Kinder eggs, the aisles of a stupid suburban grocery store that had swallowed up a five-year-old girl.

The end-of-shift bell sounded at 5:15 p.m., and it felt like geological eras had passed since I set foot in the office that morning.

I drove on autopilot.

I parked behind the Carrefour and cried.

Finally I went home.

I didn't park in the garage.

When I opened the apartment door, Eleonora was waiting for me in the hallway.

She was wearing a rumpled tracksuit, carrying a flashlight in her hand and staring at me with an unreadable expression that I had never seen before, not even a year earlier at the police station.

'What ... what's going on?' Suddenly I realized her face terrified me. 'I thought ... you'd already be gone.'

'No,' she croaked. Then she swallowed hard, her eyes bulging from their sockets, fixed on the landing behind me. 'Diego, I ... think I'm losing my mind. I ... I *found* something. You have to come down to the basement and see.'

The cellars of our apartment building are cement guts connected to the various building stairways (six in total) by a rusty metal gate. Warm, full of moisture leaks, and basically unusable.

In the '60s, the insightful engineers who had planned the building hadn't taken into account a spring that passed through the area, an underground stream that in the decades to come would pour condensation into the basement, making it wet and unwholesome, like a cave.

The building's owner, given the exorbitant costs, refused to proceed with the remediation of the space, but to keep the tenants happy he gave them favorable rates on garage rental. At every residents' meeting someone would bring it up, proposing waterproofing projects or building crawl spaces, but since we moved into the apartment, a couple of years before Luna was born, the only workers who had been down there had been from a pest control company. Cockroaches, spiders, convoluted moldy growths, and mice had found a natural habitat in the building's sweaty and seldom-visited belly.

Our cellar was at the end of a narrow, cobweb-infested corridor, near one of the stairwells; it was one of the better ones in the building, maybe because it was far from the underground canal, maybe because it was ventilated by a little skylight that looked onto the inner courtyard.

We had converted it into a storage area and rarely used it: a place for old clothes, junk, boxes, our cathode-ray tube TV, camping gear, and various amenities we could do without in our everyday lives.

And then there were Luna's things. Especially Luna's things. The crib, the stroller, the toys she'd gotten bored with, boxes full of bibs and onesies, the Mattel play kitchen . . . and a jewelry box with little gold necklaces and tacky medallions given to her at her baptism, which we had decided to hide in one of the stroller's pockets.

We had wrapped all these objects in plastic sheeting and stacked them in a corner, between a metal shelving unit and the back wall, on top of an old pallet that was already there when we moved in.

I hadn't been down there in months.

That evening, as we went down the stairs and along the gloomy corridor that was barely lit by a dusty bulb, Eleonora followed me like a puppy, digging her nails into my arm. Worried by her distraught appearance, I asked her several times: 'What is it?', but the only response I got was: 'You have to see for yourself. I . . . I can't explain it. I don't even know . . . if it's real.'

As I turned the key in the lock I imagined an enormous dead rat, some bizarre explosion of mold, even a suitcase full of banknotes forgotten down there by a previous tenant, and I let a grin slip.

I imagined a number of things, but nothing that could justify my wife's anxiety.

Nothing that could prepare me for such a mystery, for something that should not exist, for a manifestation that forces me to wonder every day if I've been plunged into a vicious nightmare or if I'm the victim of a terrible joke orchestrated by the demons of delirium, of absence.

We went inside.

Eleonora had left the light on; a fluorescent bulb flickered, causing the objects to exude faint, quivering shadows.

In the cellar chaos reigned.

Clothes, torn plastic sheeting, and sheets of newspaper covered the ground. Overturned boxes. A rusty old bike lying on its handlebars, its seat next to the shelves full of empty cans and bottles. Some of Luna's stuffed animals studied me from the top of the colossal old Philips television with dull plastic eyes.

I turned towards Eleonora. 'What's with all this mess? What happened?'

She bit her thumbnail, staring at the corner where the pallet was; I cast a look behind me, noticing that all our daughter's things had been moved.

Then she tried to explain.

Disconnected phrases. I was afraid she really had gone crazy. She didn't move her eyes from that spot while she spoke.

They were glowing.

'You remember the gold pendant my mother gave Luna for her baptism?'

Yes, I remembered it. A gaudy thing that not even a mafia boss would wear.

'This morning I woke up and started packing my things to leave and . . . when I was in Luna's room it came to mind. You remember what my mother said when she gave it to us?'

No, I didn't remember.

' "It will bring her good luck. Don't lose it." So it occurred to me that I had to find the pendant no matter what, and I came down to look for it, but the more I looked, the more . . . I didn't remember where the little jewelry box was, I was down here opening packages and boxes for an hour and . . . I about had a nervous breakdown and . . . I'm sorry.'

I sighed. 'Christ, Ele, you could have called me . . . the jewelry box is in the pocket of the stroller.'

'I know, I know, in the end I remembered . . .' She tore her eyes away from the pallet and looked at me for a few seconds with an unhinged smirk, her teeth bared. 'But that's not . . .'

'What the fuck's going on, Ele? You're really starting to worry me. Tell me!' My angry voice echoed through the cellars, becoming lost in the shadows.

'I found the jewelry case, and it slipped out of my hands and fell between the planks of that pallet and . . . went under it. But it didn't make a sound. It just went down . . .'

'Down where?'

'I don't know. Into the darkness.' She started to tremble, hugging her elbows, her teeth chattering like castanets.

Yes, she's lost her mind, I thought. *She couldn't take it. I have to get her upstairs.*

'Ele, try to calm down.'

'Look,' she interrupted me. Almost screaming. 'Look. Lift up the pallet. Be careful.'

'Ele, let's go back up, please . . .'

'Look!' she barked.

I ran a hand over my face, digging into my cheeks with my fingers, telling myself that if I indulged her, maybe she'd stop babbling nonsense. The beginnings of a headache pulsated at the base of my nose, stretching towards my temples, and I couldn't wait to take a shower, eat dinner, and hit the sack.

I took a deep breath and swallowed a curse as I walked towards the pallet and picked it up, leaning it against the wall.

A manhole.

That's what was under the wooden top.

A manhole.

Round, about half a meter in diameter, covered only with a wide-mesh metal screen of the sort used for chicken coops. It had to be a sump, most likely installed to drain the water in the event the basement got flooded in a violent storm. Or maybe an inspection shaft for the sewers, unused for decades.

'So the jewelry box fell down there?' I asked, leaning over the opening, then stopping with my head stretched forward; I didn't understand just then what the problem was, why Eleonora was coming unhinged over a stupid box full of almost worthless jewelry when we had plenty of other problems, but the more I looked down, the more I noticed something abnormal. Like I couldn't focus on what I was seeing; in the recesses of my mind something creaked. My eyes perceived an anomaly, but my brain couldn't take it in.

I didn't feel uneasiness or fear, but staring down into the darkness of those sixty centimeters in diameter sinking underground, I felt a dull, yet familiar sensation tickling my unconscious. A sort of call, ancient and alluring, eternal and terrible, that made me feel tiny.

I saw myself young and athletic, on a reckless expedition with two friends to climb Monte Viso, the highest peak of the Cottian Alps. I was eighteen then and thought I was invincible, immortal. But during the final stretch of the climb we found ourselves tackling a rather exposed passage that we had to cross with our backs to the valley, glued to a schist rock wall, overlooking a gully filled with rubble and plants crushed by winter avalanches. Five or six hundred meters straight down, ending in a bed of detritus vomited from the mountain in its thousands of years of life. One mistake would mean the end of everything. For the first time in my young life, clinging to that wall like a spider, all tendons and muscles, I had felt in my flesh and my spirit all the weight of my fragility and littleness. And at the same time I had felt the allure of the end, what the French call *l'appel du vide*, the call of the void, a sort of force that inexplicably attracts us toward the abyss, tickling us with soft, warm fingers, and that summer morning, for a fraction of a second, I was driven to wonder: '*What if I let go? If I let myself fall from this seemingly endless cliff, what would I feel?*'

In front of that manhole, in the untidy cellar of an ordinary apartment building in a small provincial town like thousands of others, I experienced something similar.

Only much more intense.

I crouched down, squinting to see better; the epileptic fluorescent light managed to drip into the pit for a couple of meters, illuminating lime and soaking-wet brickwork; after that, darkness took over.

But the darkness was too dense, too pronounced, and that was the incongruity, a shade of darkness I had never experienced, not even when, years after the triumphant trip to the summit of Monte Viso, I had slipped into a cavern of the Marguareis massif and, arriving in a narrow womb of limestone, I had switched off my headlamp.

A darkness that burned your retinas, like when you look at the sun too long and bizarre filaments start to dance in your field of vision; I could use a thousand different adjectives to describe it, but none of them would be able to give a vague semblance of it.

It was every adjective, and none.

It was oily, indifferent, filthy, hypnotic. Dense, deep, reassuring, vile, starving, liquid, hot, unclean.

And it was bright.

Oh, so bright.

It was an oxymoron.

I tried to say something.

I remained kneeling, I don't know how long, peering into the vile darkness, using my hand as a visor to shield my eyes from its murky reflection, trying to reason.

It wasn't until my wife put her hand on my shoulder that I came to with a start and moved away from the opening. It felt like I had been there for hours.

'Diego . . .' she mumbled, looking at me as if waiting for an explanation, some truth I could pull out of my pocket like a handkerchief. 'You see it too?'

'I . . . yes . . . I don't understand. What in God's name is it?'

'I have no idea. No idea whatsoever. But I thought I was going crazy.' She turned on the flashlight she was holding and pointed its beam downward. The pit swallowed it and canceled it out, like a wall of vantablack.

'Then we're both going crazy,' I stammered, and I saw her take a few steps back and grab a chunk of cement that had crumbled from a waterlogged wall.

'Look.' She reached out her hand and dropped the chunk in the well. Then she started to count out loud. 'One, two, three, four . . .'

I watched the fragment of wall plummet for a couple of seconds before it was swallowed up by the black, Eleonora's fatigue-splintered voice thundering in my head.

'Five, six, seven . . .'

She counted to ninety.

No thud or splash came from the pit.

No sound at all.

I stood frozen to the spot, dumbfounded.

'It's not possible,' I squeaked. 'Fuck, it doesn't make sense.'

Filled with a bleak euphoria, I removed the wire mesh and tried again.

With a coin, a glass bottle, two rusty pans.

No thud, no splash, no clang.

No echo.

The objects plunged into the pit, but it was like they never reached the bottom. My stomach churned, and the excessive amount of coffee I had drunk at the office came back up my esophagus in an acidic gush.

Absurdly, I thought of an old Eddie Murphy film, *The Golden Child*, the part where the actor crosses a crevasse by balancing on tree stumps so he can recover the sacred dagger of Ajanti, and finally discovers that the dark abyss stretching beneath his feet is bottomless. 'There's no ground here!' a dejected Eddie Murphy concludes, teetering. 'There's no . . .'

I felt dazed, but more than anything I felt *excited*. And even though part of me screamed loudly that I should put the pallet back, get out of the basement and never return, I didn't listen to it.

I stood there dazed, looking for Eleonora's face. She continued to make the flashlight beam roam in the unfathomable, her face deformed by her amazement.

'There has to be an explanation, Ele,' I reasoned. 'There must be.'

'There's not always an explanation for everything, Diego,' she replied icily. Tears began to well in her eyes. 'And that's not all . . .' she added. Now she was crying.

'What do you mean?'

'Go closer . . . put your face close to the hole. As close as you can. Close your eyes.'

'Why?'

'Do it. Do it for me, please . . . I have to . . . I have to know if you smell it too.'

Once more I obeyed. My mind shrouded in fog, I grabbed a sheet of plastic and stretched out on it face down, my face a few centimeters from the pit's opening. Strands of gray cobwebs clinging to the bricks swayed slightly as if moved by a weak underground breeze coming from who knows where. I shut my eyelids tight, because Eleonora had told me to, because I wasn't sure I wanted my gaze to linger on the shimmering darkness again.

I held my breath; a light gust of air rose from the opening. A lukewarm breath that ruffled a lock of hair hanging down over my forehead.

A lukewarm breath that for several seconds, only a few seconds, brought with it a sweet and spicy scent.

A scent I knew well.

I felt the hair stand up on my arms and the back of my neck, I saw Luna again, sitting in the back seat of the car singing 'Jingle Bells', and I saw myself inside the Carrefour giving her a kiss, and . . .

I burst into tears, holding on to the edge of the manhole.

Tears of frustration, joy, sadness. Opening my eyes, I watched them plunge like falling stars in the light from the flashlight and crash into the blinding and leaden nothingness that stretched beneath the building's foundation.

Eleonora grabbed me under the armpits and pulled me back; I put up a weak resistance, fell on my butt, she hugged me, then took my face in her hands.

'You smelled it?'

I let out a sob, swallowing tears and mucus. 'What the hell is going on? What the hell does it mean?'

It lingered in my nostrils still, a balm and a poison, that scent I knew so well.

Vanilla.

Vanilla shampoo.

Her shampooey.

It was almost ten when we went back up to the apartment, barely able to stand, stunned at how time had passed so quickly, unable to remember exactly what we had done during those hours down in the cellar.

It was like pieces were missing.

Shock, adrenaline, I thought.

We had talked, of course; about darkness and the pit, whose depth we hadn't been able to determine using our limited means: objects, chunks of cement, and coins; about possibly notifying someone, the superintendent, the university, CERN; about the idea of both of us seeing a shrink; about the scent of vanilla.

But I didn't have a clear recollection of the words we had exchanged or the actions we had taken, like my memories were all mixed together in a whirlpool that was being sucked down, down, towards . . .

Oh, *that* I remembered well.

That different darkness.

We slid under the covers without saying a word, and despite our fatigue, despite the absurdity of what we had just been through, I was shocked to realize one simple fact: I felt good. It was a feeling of relief, like an immense weight had been taken off my shoulders. It was the same for Eleonora: she fell asleep almost immediately, peacefully, and almost at once she began to mumble in her sleep. More than once I heard her call our daughter's name with a gentleness that made my heart ache.

It didn't take me long to drift into sleep. The church bells were sounding midnight when, in the region between sleep and waking, I realized that the Christmas holidays would start the following day.

I dreamed of gigantic halls and underground passages, monstrous nocturnal expanses where I ran at breakneck speed or plunged without finding a reference point, a foothold, but behind the anxiety caused by these immense spaces there throbbed the comfort arising from the awareness that that bewilderment, that fear of trudging through a labyrinth for eternity, wouldn't last forever. Sooner or later the warm and vanilla-scented embrace of oblivion would arrive. Sooner or later I would hit the bottom.

The next morning Eleonora cooked me breakfast. How long had it been since that had happened?

There was no need for words; when we had finished our coffee we changed clothes and went back to the cellar.

We just wanted to know if it had all been a hallucination, a shared delusion, a brief incursion of the uncanny into our world, like in that old TV show introduced by a well-dressed man with a cigarette between his fingers.

But under the pallet nothing had changed.

The sunbeams that filtered through the skylight in parallel splinters seemed to curve towards the manhole, as if pulled by an enormous force.

During the holidays, Eleonora and I became like two explorers totally addicted to their discovery. Every foray into the basement assumed the features of a descent into an ancient temple, pregnant with mysteries and wonders. We went down there two or three times a day; we might spend a few minutes there, or else whole hours might pass in the decay of the cellar. I don't think it was up to us.

I would pick up the pallet and we'd sit at the edge of the manhole and stay there, staring at the lazy and luminous ripples of darkness.

We wore sunglasses to protect us from the glare of the darkness, but we quickly realized that looking at it with protection, a filter, wasn't the same thing. *It didn't offer the same satisfaction*, even if I'm not sure I can explain to you what sort of fulfillment it was . . . It was a shiver at the base of your skull, an incomparable wave of well-being that lasted only a few moments, stimulated by the gust coming from the bowels of the pit, which, when it chose to, brought the scent of Luna to our olfactory receptors, the scent of vanilla shampoo. I might compare it to the climax of an orgasm or the high from ecstasy, which I had only tried once in my life, one crazy night at a club in Sestriere.

'Diego?' whispered Eleonora when it happened, leaning over the hole and sniffing, her eyes half closed in an expression of rapture. 'Her scent, her shampooey, do you smell it?'

We continued to plumb the pit's depth, throwing in various objects. At first things of little value, jars, coins, empty beer bottles. No sound ever rose from those depths.

Until one afternoon I grabbed one of Luna's old dolls from the shelf, one of those heavy plastic ones that close their eyes when you put them to bed, and dropped it down. Eleonora gave me an approving smile. The toy knocked against a wall of the shaft, then plunged downward and disappeared.

We counted.

We did every time.

Like always, no thud or splash came by way of answer.

But something else did answer.

We had just gotten to ninety-nine when a blast of air rose from the darkness that made the glass of the skylight shake, followed by a distant sound, so faint that I thought it was only in my head, nothing more than a projection of my wishes.

Then I saw my wife's face, one hand pressed to her mouth, and I knew that she had heard it too.

It sounded like laughter.

The laughter of a five-year-old girl.

'Lù, honey, are you there?' I called.

'Luna?' Eleonora ventured, stretched over the opening.

The darkness didn't breathe.

But we saw it quiver, and to us it seemed alive, reassuring like a lost presence that sooner or later would return.

One of those nights, after hours of kneeling before the hole, my hand and Eleonora's met; we ended up naked, fucking on the pallet amid the old stuffed animals and dust, a perfunctory, animalistic fuck, which ended with the most powerful orgasm of my life. During the few minutes of intercourse it was like being watched and mocked by that act that I had almost forgotten.

There was no love in that friction of flesh and mucous membranes. Only sparks of life trying to counteract the collapse of the walls of our miniature world.

It was the last time I was inside her.

My holidays vanished, swallowed by a thick, dark haze, through which I could make out only the glimmer of the darkness that had revealed itself to us. On the 2nd of January I had to go back to work.

I envied Eleonora, who could go down to the basement and enjoy the comfort of the darkness whenever she pleased. Before I left the house, I begged her to be careful, not to tell anyone what we had discovered.

'Don't worry . . .' she said. 'I'll take care of it.'

And I knew she would. Just like I knew that in only a few days we had become addicted to the hole and its secrets. I got my confirmation when I pulled away from the apartment in my car and halfway to the office I started sweating and shaking like a drug addict. It took all my willpower to keep on driving to the plant.

My colleagues asked me if I was all right, if I shouldn't maybe stay home a bit longer. Looking at myself in the bathroom mirror I understood why: I was pale, eyes red as if from bad sunstroke, emaciated. Had we eaten anything the past few days? I didn't remember, nor did I care.

Midway through the morning I called Eleonora; she didn't answer. I figured she was down in the basement.

I stared at the monitor for hours, unable to work, my mind busy with a single thought; but after a hurried lunch in the company cafeteria it was like a clearing had opened in the storm passing through my brain: I had to try to understand, to analyze what was happening.

I found myself wandering around on the Internet, looking for information on an experience that had no explanation.

When I typed 'bottomless pit', Google gave me hundreds of results; I spent the afternoon reading, lost among bizarre articles on urban legends, biblical narratives, and two-bit conspiracy theories.

In the Book of Revelation, one passage made reference to an endless chasm:

'The fifth angel sounded his trumpet, and I saw a star fall from heaven to the earth, and the key to the bottomless pit was given to him. And when he opened it, there arose a smoke from the pit, like the smoke of a great furnace, which darkened the sun and the air.'

An article I found on an American site specializing in urban legends talked about 'Mel's hole'; in 1997 a nighttime radio show, Coast to Coast, had gotten a call from one Mel Waters, a farmer from Ellensburg, Washington, who claimed to have discovered a strange, gaping hole on a piece of land he owned. According to the account of this man, who had tried to fathom the pit using fishing line and a weight, the abyss was infinite and had some connection to disturbing alien activity in the area. The farmer said he had conducted numerous experiments and had even lowered a live lamb into it; when he activated the winch and pulled the animal up, he had found himself looking at a tortured and bloody creature, its organs exposed, 'turned inside out like a glove and scorched', but, incredibly, still alive.

The article's editor characterized the question of Mel's hole as 'a modern rural myth'. The story had caught the attention of the American media and UFO and occult enthusiasts, to the point where expeditions were organized to locate the mysterious hole, all of which proved fruitless.

Clicking from link to link, I ran into the unsettling legend of the Kola Hole, nicknamed the Devil's Hole. The site was unearthed during a Russian geological expedition begun in the Kola Peninsula in the 1970s, aimed at using drilling to study the geochemistry and geophysics of the deepest layers of the Earth's crust; eyewitness accounts from several members of the scientific group were reported, in particular that of the project leader Dimitri Azzacov, who vanished into thin air sometime in the mid-eighties. Azzacov told of the incredible progress they made in their underground drilling and how once they had reached a depth of twelve thousand meters the drill had started to spin in the air.

An underground cavity.

Using a water-cooled device, survey instruments were lowered into the abyss, including an ultrasensitive microphone. Down there the temperature fluctuated between 1000 and 1200 degrees Celsius, but it was what the microphone picked up that drove the team of scientists to seal the hole and flee the peninsula: screams.

A multitude of screams, shrill and frightening, noises that flowed into cries and sobs, as if a desperate and tormented human crowd were stirring in the belly of the earth.

I read in a daze, barely aware of the presence of my colleagues in the open-plan office, sometimes grinning at the articles that struck me as downright bullshit; then, behind my tired eyelids, images of the manhole would flash, and I told myself that those articles, deep down (*ha ha!*), must have some truth to them. I wondered for the umpteenth time whether I was locked in a psych ward, loaded up on drugs and wearing a shit-filled diaper, and a moment later I found myself again working out hypotheses and questions.

Had the hole in the basement been *produced* when they were digging the foundation of the apartment building? Did anybody else know about it, or was it only my wife and I who could see it? Was it an objective reality, independent from us, which was worming its way into our pain for who knew what reasons, or was it nothing but the manifestation of an absence, of an unimaginable torment that had been able to make itself felt in the soft underbelly of our shattered inner world? How many unexplainable pits existed, hidden from the eyes of the many, in the basements or overgrown back yards of people whose lives had been taken over by their suffering, leaving only the black, hungry void of a crippling personal apocalypse?

The majority of sites inclined to flights of fancy and disposed towards a supernatural interpretation of the phenomenon arrived at the same conclusion: the bottomless pits were gateways to alternate dimensions, located in regions not belonging to our space-time, or, more simply, entrances to a place we've been taught to fear since childhood: Hell, repository of all suffering, the crucible of torments in which our souls are called to expiate earthly misdeeds.

But at the same time it was all nonsense, absurd, as demonstrated by an article from the Italian Committee for the Investigation of Pseudoscientific Claims, which examined their physical plausibility. The text's author, an esteemed professor of geophysics, concluded his piece thus: 'The existence of a bottomless pit, or anyway of such a depth that the echo of an object dropped inside it cannot be heard, is physically and geologically impossible: it would collapse in on itself from the tremendous pressure and heat exerted by the layers of the earth's crust.'

When my shift was over, I practically ran out of the building and rushed onto the freeway, oppressed by a suffocating sense of urgency. It was almost dark. Tongues of darkness licked the roof tiles and the chimneys, smearing them with night. Before going home I stopped at a home improvement warehouse to buy several 100-meter spools of twine and a lead weight.

After I parked the car I rushed to the basement. The fluorescent lights were off, and when I opened the door I thought Eleonora must be in the apartment.

I was wrong.

I glimpsed her outline in the semi-darkness as I stood there with one hand on the light switch, and a shiver ran up my spine. There was no reaction from her when I turned on the light. She was kneeling in front of the manhole, her back to me, her head bowed, a pillar of salt.

'Ele . . .' I called to her, going closer. Her face made me retreat a couple of steps. Her gaping mouth, her greenish hue, a thread of drool running down her chin: her eyes were glued on the darkness. She rolled her eyes back, turning them into white marbles, and the conjunctiva shone a bright, infected red.

From deep in her throat, a low, watery wheezing.

Gggggbrrrhhhhh . . .

I leaned over the pit, and the darkness seemed even more shadowy and alluring than ever; dazed, for a moment I considered just sitting down and doing nothing but peer into the bright nothingness. I *wanted* to. Only the cry vomited from my wife's vocal chords kept me from doing it, allowed me to look away with a tremendous effort. I felt the void behind me writhing, calling me, and diffusing the scent of vanilla shampoo through the cellar; but behind that smell, this time, there was a different note, a pungent sweetness, the stench of rotten carcasses decomposing in a forest, of spoiled food, of irrigation canals filled with sewage from rural slaughterhouses. For the first time since I lifted the pallet, I sensed a mysterious and irresistible force bent on destruction.

Gggggbrrraahhhhhh . . .

'Ele!'

I grabbed her shoulders, and the rigidity of her body (I thought of the rigidity of the dead, of rigor mortis) filled me with such disgust that I felt relieved when her muscles relaxed. It took five minutes of slapping her face and massaging her embalmed arms before she recovered and her cheeks took on a healthy color. She looked at me like I was a stranger, started to shake. I realized she had pissed herself.

'Diego . . . What's happening?'

'You tell me, Ele . . .'

'I . . . I just wanted to take a look.' She chuckled, raising one hand to touch my chin. She acted like she was high. 'It's so beautiful down there . . . So . . . *peaceful* . . .'

'How . . . how long have you been down here?'

'I . . . a few minutes, I came down half an hour after you left for work . . . speaking of which, what are you doing home already?'

'Jesus Christ.'

I picked her up off the ground and she seemed so light, a bag of bones. I managed to carry her to the apartment and put her to bed; she was in an odd state of torpor, alternating with moments of malaise and whining, like someone who's just woken up with a colossal hangover. As I tucked her in, she grabbed my arm and squeezed it hard.

'I'm so tired. She talked to me, you know?'

'Who, Ele?'

'Luna. From the shaft. She told me she's fine, that if we want to, we can all be together again as a family . . .'

I didn't respond. I stroked her cheek, then went to the bathroom, got the sleeping drops and prepared a large dose for her. She drank it from the glass without a fuss. I sat on the edge of the bed, watching her as she fell asleep, and just before she closed her eyes I thought they had turned black even where they should have been white.

'Eleonora, you shouldn't . . . You shouldn't go down there anymore . . . We shouldn't . . . There's something . . . Look what it's done to you. Look . . .'

She didn't hear me, she was already snoring. I kissed her forehead and grabbed my cell phone, a little bottle of Vicks Vaporub, and some cotton balls, then tiptoed out of the apartment like a thief.

It seemed like the stairs had multiplied and would never bring me where I wanted to go, through some absurd optical illusion in the building's architecture that I couldn't see in its entirety, like in a drawing by Escher.

But in the end I made it.

'Just the two of us,' I murmured in the doorway, looking at the wooden pallet, the fluorescent light seeming to fade to a gray bubble near the manhole's grinning mouth.

Then I closed the door behind me and got to work.

Until that afternoon we had limited ourselves to throwing

objects into the abyss, devastated believers before a St. Patrick's Well that was unable to fulfill their wishes.

My perambulations online, and, I assume, the time away from the cellar, from the building, had oiled the gears in my brain. Mindful of the story of Mel Waters and his mysterious pit, lost somewhere in the fields of Washington, I had decided to conduct four 'experiments', at the same time ordering myself to stay in the cellar as little as possible, not to give in to the allurements coming from the chasm.

Outside the cellar door I smeared a massive dose of Vaporub above my upper lip and around my nostrils, like coroners do to shield themselves from the odors of decomposition. And I stuffed two wads of cotton deep into my ears. I knew that if I smelled the scent of 'shampooey' or heard a voice I thought I recognized, I would remain there, in thrall to its spell.

It took me some time to tie together the ends of the twine I had bought at the hardware store; when I finished, I found myself with a single cord around six hundred meters long, to which I attached the lead weight. I put on a pair of welder's goggles to protect myself from the glare of the darkness, then, holding the line tightly in my hands, I began slowly lowering it. It was a crude method, but, as I had predicted, I was able to unroll the entire length of the twine without it slackening between my fingers. If there was a bottom, it had to be deeper than six hundred meters, which was absurd, impossible.

I pulled the probe back up and examined it; it appeared to be covered in a thin layer of *frost*, and when I held it in my hands it was so frozen that it almost stuck to my palm. I attached the flashlight in its place, securing it to the string with a couple of tight knots; then I turned it on and started to lower it, observing its descent, the smell of menthol seeping into my nostrils and making my eyes water. The powerful beam of light wavered, was reduced to a bright dot after a couple of meters, reminding me of a submarine lost in dizzying abyssal depths.

It disappeared.

Once again I let the twine unwind all the way, then I pulled it back up. The flashlight was out, the bulb's filament disintegrated.

For the third experiment, I repeated the procedure, lowering my Samsung smartphone into the pit with the camera on. As the thread ran through my hands I fantasized about what the phone would record, what scenes its digital eye would view: only shadow and darkness, or would it bring back images? Mad souls, wailing in an eternal cycle of torment? Alternate dimensions peopled with unspeakable creatures, so alien that our limited brains can't even conceive of them?

My questions went unanswered: when the phone returned to the surface it was dead, and no matter what I tried it gave no signs of life, as if the battery had run all the way down or the motherboard was shot.

The pit didn't want to be studied. Every one of my attempts to explore it was mocked, thwarted. Yet again I wondered if that darkness possessed a sort of *sentience*, and I told myself yes, even if I couldn't have said where that conviction came from.

I stepped away from the hole and grabbed two small jars from the shelf; as I left the cellar, with my back to the pit, I felt a sort of malevolent call, an *aura*, and the impression of being watched by hungry eyes.

I closed the metal door, gasping in the unhealthy air of the dimly lit passage, and quickly headed towards the open space under the staircase leading to the basement.

The kingdom of cobwebs.

That's how it had been christened by Eleonora, who had been terrified of arachnids since an unpleasant encounter with one as a child; every time she passed that part of the basement she kept a safe distance from the shadowy corner chosen by the spiders as their favorite lair.

They were fat, grayish bastards, spotted with white, architects of thick, convoluted webs that dangled in banners just below the railings, over which they swayed like expert trapeze artists.

Years earlier I had caught a little boy from our building, Renzo Natale, in the act as he trapped one of the beasts in a jar using a method that was as simple as it was brilliant: he held the container under the spider and used a lighter to burn the web around it in a circular pattern; when the circle closed, the animal and the fragment of burnt web, separated from the main structure, toppled into the jar for the obscure prepubescent purposes of Renzo and his little friends.

Following the same procedure, I caught one in a jar. Then I knocked a second one to the ground with a rolled-up newspaper and stepped on it with sufficient force to kill it, but without reducing its body to mush; the corpse, its legs curled in a final desperate act of self-defense, wound up in the other jar.

Then I went back in.

I was thinking.

I was thinking about Mel Waters's lamb, reemerging from underground transformed into a mishmash of minced meat, turned inside out like a glove, and I wondered what the poor creature had seen. It didn't really matter to me whether it was an urban legend or whether that story, rattled off on some overseas radio program, had some truth to it.

I had my own personal abyss, and I was determined to fathom it. To know it.

I tied the jar with the living spider to the string and let it plunge into the darkness. 'Bon voyage, my friend.'

The jar seemed to remain suspended for a moment at the point where the fluorescent light met the darkness, then it vanished. Letting the twine run between my palms, I tried to put myself in the arachnid's place.

Did it feel fear?

Were its segmented eyes looking on the incomprehensible, was its body undergoing a horrid mutation like Mel's sheep?

After I had let the probe go all the way, I don't know how long I let it dangle there, nor how long I spent pulling it back up. And when the jar re-emerged in the dampened glow of the cellar and returned to my hands, cold like marble, I couldn't repress a feeling of horror at the simplicity of what I saw.

The spider had vanished.

It was simply no longer inside the jar, sucked away, erased from reality.

Overcoming my nausea, I lowered the dead spider into the pit.

The same thing happened.

As if the darkness didn't distinguish between life and death, but confined itself to digesting organic matter, canceling it. However terrible it was, the physical side of the question was what bothered me least . . . what happened to the spider's intellect, its faculties, the energy that animated it?

And the dead spider? *Was it alive in some other place?*

I thought about Luna, about the nightmare where she was standing at the foot of our bed with ebony eyes while a waterfall of black spilled out of the Kinder egg, impossible to overcome except by waking up.

Through the welding goggles I let my gaze wander in the hole. The void seemed to reshape itself into anatomical forms and faces and mouths, but how can an absence form itself into a shape, I wondered?

I threw the pallet down over it and put the heavy old television on top, then left, double-locking the door behind me.

At that moment I promised myself I would never go down there again, and that I would do everything in my power to keep Eleonora far away from the illogicality that had decided to manifest in our cellar.

Whatever it might be.

It wasn't easy to stick to my resolution, to resist. Above all, it was hard to convince Eleonora to take my side, to persuade her that the pit, no matter how it might try to lure us, represented an aberration that could destroy the little (*very little*) bit of good that was left in our lives.

I told her about the pitiful state in which I'd found her the night before.

About the probe, the cell phone, the spiders.

Luna is not down there, I told her.

Maybe a semblance, a monstrous and toxic manifestation of her absence, which we have to stay far away from if we don't want to end up like the spiders.

Dissolved, erased. Or who knows what else.

The day after my experiments, she tried four times to leave the apartment and go down to the cellar. Each time I dragged her back, like a desperate mother trying to keep her heroin-addicted son from going out to buy another dose.

And several times I was on the verge of giving into the call too ... was it coming from the manhole, or from a compromised part of my psyche?

L'appel du vide.

I took the Samsung to a service center, where they told me several circuits appeared to be oxidized, irreparably damaged, then I went back to the hardware store and bought a latch and a massive padlock, which I fastened to the outside of the cellar door; while I was messing with the tools, I thought I heard a low and distressing cry spreading inside, a lament *born from and nourished by* an endless loneliness.

My work finished, I left the building and threw the padlock keys in a garbage bin.

I asked for two weeks off work.

I stayed by my wife's side.

As the days passed, she seemed better, even if every now and then she would just sit staring vacantly at the walls, her thoughts captivated by something I didn't dare ask about.

I brought her to a vacation farm in the Langhe, far from the apartment, far from the town that had taken away our daughter. It went pretty well, and that weekend we decided to move. Deep down we already wanted to, and now we had a thousand more reasons.

We tried to make love but couldn't. And yet I sensed faint glimmers flickering in the darkness, after such a long time.

Sometimes I thought about the hole (often, more often than I would have liked), wondering if it was still there or if it had all been a dream, and it took all my strength not to yield to the temptation of *checking*.

It went well, yes, for a few weeks.

Captain Gange called several times and expressed his sympathy, reassured us that the search for Luna would go on uninterrupted.

My wife resumed painting with renewed vigor, I returned to the office. In the afternoons we made the rounds of real estate agencies, looking for a new apartment.

About a month had passed since I closed up the cellar door when I passed Folchini on the stairs, a quiet old man who lived on the top floor. A gruff sort of guy, about as likable as a cold sore.

'Hey there, Balduzzi,' he stopped me. I think it was the first time he had ever spoken to me. 'Did you hear what happened to Signora Izzia?'

'No, why?' I replied, perplexed. 'The lady on the ground floor, right?'

'That's her . . .' He tapped a gnarled index finger against his temple, looking at me with his yellow eyes buried in purplish bags of capillaries. 'She went off her rocker. They took her away in an ambulance a few hours ago. A 72-hour psychiatric hold. Her husband found her in the basement hallway, crying like a madwoman . . .'

A flush of heat went up my neck and I wished the old man would stop talking. But he kept going.

'I saw her when they were loading her on the stretcher. You should have seen the face she was making! And screams that

would pierce your eardrums. Stuff that didn't make any sense
... Sometimes the mind just goes off the rails, all of a sudden.
Terrible ...'

'What ... what was she saying?' I heard myself mutter.

'Spiders ... She said she saw two spiders as big as St. Bernards
at the end of the corridor, very black, not really spiders but shadows of spiders, she said, that swayed on half-meter-long legs,
like they were dancing. She said they were too black, like stains
... The mind can play some pretty mean tricks sometimes, huh?
I've been meaning to ask you ... why'd you put that padlock on
your cellar door? Are you feeling all right, Balduzzi?'

Without answering, I ran back to the apartment and closed
the door behind me, hyperventilating.

What did it mean? So the darkness could emerge from down
below, form itself into other shapes? Maybe come looking for
us?

Eleonora, busy ironing in the living room, looked me up and
down with an enigmatic expression. 'What's going on?'

'We have to get out of here as soon as possible.'

And we tried.

But you can't run away from your nightmares, or yourself.

In the weeks that followed, strange voices started chasing
each other through the apartment building, growing ever more
sinister.

Voices of shadows sticking anomalously to the walls of the
garage, stories of strange glimmers in the elevator shafts, of
pets vanishing into thin air, of doormats moving on their own,
of children's laughter vomited out of gas meters, of crazed fluorescent bulbs that emitted black light, erasing entire portions
of hallways and staircases for several moments at a time.

The building's tenants screamed in their sleep.

Nightmares, panic attacks, domestic violence.

Several times I was tempted to go down to the cellar, remove
the padlock, enter, pick up the pallet, check whether the void

was still there, if it had changed, with its hypnotic, magmatic throbbing, its scent of shampooey . . .

I managed to resist.

Eleonora too.

We focused on our work and apartment hunting; we found one that seemed to fit the bill in a quiet town not far away and made a purchase offer.

We would leave. Fuck it. Somebody else could worry about finding out what was down there, lift the Veil, if there was really a veil to lift.

Disaster struck one rainy morning, the little town overwhelmed by a low, foul-looking sky, a slate tombstone. That afternoon we were supposed to stop by the real estate agent's office to meet with the property owner and come to an agreement over the price.

I was at the office and around eleven I realized I'd forgotten some important work papers at home that I needed for an afternoon meeting with the design office. I explained the mix-up to my boss and left the plant, the sky looking like it was mourning all the misfortunes of the world.

Passing the Carrefour, I thought about how once we moved to the new place we wouldn't have to take this street anymore, wouldn't have to lay eyes on the store that triggered such painful memories.

I ran the few meters separating me from the front door through a frozen drizzle. I went up the stairs two at a time, entered the apartment, and called Eleonora.

She didn't answer.

I thought she must be in her studio.

'I forgot some paperwork, Ele. You want to have a quick coffee together before I go back to work?'

Nothing.

'Ele?'

I knocked lightly on the door, but there was no answer. I opened it.

It was as if an evil presence latched onto my back.

The studio, where once upon a time wood gnomes and fairy tale creatures had frolicked, had been turned into a modern-day shrine dedicated to the Abyss.

The canvases were scattered all over the floor, placed on easels and old boxes; when Eleonora had run out of those, she had continued her delirious work on sheets of paper and rags. One of our bedsheets hung from the ceiling, filthy with black and black and black. Dozens of little pictures, like obscene votive offerings, had been hung on the wall with nails and strips of brown packing tape.

On the easel in the middle of the room reigned a very large painting, and as I looked at its imagery I told myself it was of meager quality, nothing compared with my wife's usual technique, but somehow it hit me in the stomach, in my very core, with the impact of a violent blow.

I wondered when she had painted them. In the span of a few hours, seized with a fit of artistic madness? Or over the course of weeks, her mind dwelling on the gloom of the imponderable?

No more enchanted forests, no bucolic pseudo-fantasy scenes to gladden happy babies' first years of life.

Only brushstrokes on top of brushstrokes, thick like molasses, an attempt to represent the different darkness through a vague circular structure, spiraling towards a center that had been left untouched in the white of the cloth or paper.

Looking at those paintings was like being attacked, violated.

Then, in one corner of the room, I noticed the climbing gear we used when we were younger piled on the floor by the cupboard where we had stored it away years ago.

Several carabiners, some ropes.

'No!' I yelled, rushing out of the apartment and down the stairs. 'Ele!'

I felt my legs give way beneath me when I found myself in front of the wide-open storage-room door, padlock and latch pried off.

The first thing I saw inside was the television, moved off the pallet and turned over on its side, then the nylon cord tied to one of the heavy metal shelving units. It was stretched diagonally across the storeroom, vibrating a little, ending up inside the pit at an angle of about thirty degrees.

Weak with shock, I staggered to the opening and lay down on my stomach, looking down into the brick bowels.

Tied to a double rope, crudely wrapped in a harness that went around her waist and buttocks, Eleonora was descending towards the darkness. She barely fit in the shaft. I told myself I had arrived in the nick of time, but no, that's not true. It's not the right expression.

I watched her working the descender, I heard the hissing noises from the friction of the ropes, I saw her descending, little by little, little by little.

Now her feet were dangling only a few centimeters from the charcoal blackness. The manhole vomited whiffs of vanilla and rotten meat. I grabbed the rope with both hands to stop her from descending any further.

'Ele, don't do it, please, come back, *pleasepleaseplease* . . .' I panted, realizing I didn't have enough strength left in my arm muscles to pull her out. She looked up: in the scant light that the fluorescent bulbs managed to diffuse inside the shaft, in the pale oval of her face, her eyes looked black.

Completely black.

An exultant grin corroded her features.

'Leave me alone, Diego. I have to see. Before we leave, I have to know what's down there, goddammit. If *she's* down there . . .'

She operated the descender again and slid into the darkness. Up to her ankles. And then she screamed. It was an inhuman scream, intense and very brief, immediately stifled by a low gasp. Then she switched off, her senses left her; she dangled in the void like a corpse on the gallows, knocking lightly against the wet bricks. I don't know what energy powered my body, but I pulled and pulled that fucking rope, stripping the flesh from my hands, I tugged and yanked until I managed to get her out, and puffing like a bellows I lay her down on the dusty floor.

When I leaned over her, panting, and my gaze slid to her legs, I noticed an error in her anatomical structure. I thought it was a trick of the light, a bizarre optical illusion. I moved to get a better look; I saw. It was no optical illusion. I screamed or thought I did, overwhelmed by a wave of panic.

Eleonora's feet, up to the ankles, were gone.

Vanished.

Dissolved.

As if someone had run an enormous eraser over them and deleted the atoms.

I thought about the spiders, the missing children, the legends of bottomless pits eating away at the flesh of the Earth.

I pulled her jeans up her calves to see better, and I was able to examine the inside of her legs. I could see *inside her legs*, understand?

There was no blood, or anyway the blood wasn't spurting, as if she had become a plastic anatomical model in cross-section, the kind you sometimes see in a doctor's office, only a circle of flesh, muscles, and broken capillaries; a bright red steak in whose center the severed bones of the tibia and fibula stood out, along with their marrow, yellow, bright, succulent.

The various layers of the epidermis.

The lumpy deposits of fat.

The cross-section throbbed, pregnant with life and cells and blood matter.

I wondered where her feet had ended up. Or had they ended up anywhere?

I threw up in a corner, then crawled to the edge of the hole.

Why? What the fuck do you want? Why?

No more scent of shampoo. Only the stench of huge mistakes, a guilty conscience, and a putrid cellar.

The darkness laughed, squirmed, swallowed its meal.

At that moment I realized there was nowhere we could go but there, into the seething void that yearned for us. I sat there staring at it for hours, until Eleonora came to, looked at her feet, or rather at the nothing that had once been her feet, and said simply: 'Strange.'

I had to laugh.

She crawled over to me on the stumps that weren't stumps. I asked her if she was in pain and she said no, she'd experienced worse.

She smiled.

Then she laid her head on my knees and we were spectators of the darkness's hypnotic excretions, never so honeyed and splendid as that night.

At dawn I carried Eleonora up in my arms, cradling her gently. A feather. A mummy. That was the last time she went down to the cellar. She no longer needed to. The inhabitant (?) of the manhole (*the manhole?*) had become a part of her, and day after day, a millimeter at a time, it was gaining the upper hand, erasing her.

The black, translucent edges encircling her ankles started to crawl upwards, deleting the underlying organic matter; in the span of two weeks they reached her knees, then they slowed as they approached her thighs, but there was little doubt that the process was irreversible. And monstrous.

I quit work and we barricaded ourselves in the apartment. Fascinated and disgusted, I spent the days watching in real time as the body of what had been the woman of my life was erased: the flesh quivered, severed arteries and veins and organs pumped blood without spilling a drop, the pulp of the marrow bubbled in the white cradle of the bones, collagen, mucous membranes, and tendons showed off their repertoire of flexibility, and Eleonora alternated between moments of what I considered a sort of mystic ecstasy and lucid intervals in which we discussed her condition, the pit, and what we should do.

Me?

I started going down to the cellar again, sitting in front of the pit. It was the only thing to be done, the only action that seemed – and seems – to make any sense.

And meanwhile the nothingness went on consuming her. A millimeter at a time, with the inevitable progress of an incurable illness.

Eleonora painted as long as she had hands. Dead vortexes of blackness, screaming faces of darkness collapsing towards a central lump of immaculate white.

Pustules and buboes of darkness.

I brought canvases and brushes to her in bed, and she would work for hours, almost without looking at what she was doing, as if an invisible hand were guiding hers.

We made the fateful decision one evening as the wind and leaves and dust ticked against the shutters; by then the darkness had erased her legs and had started to eat away at her genitals. I could see the bulbous beads of her ovaries, filaments of flab and moist membranes, some indefinite masses I imagined were the fallopian tubes, the pink canal of the vagina.

Her eyes would stare at the ceiling, opaque like frosted glass. One night she took my hand, and I had to make an enormous effort not to pull it away; still without looking at me, she spoke, her vocal cords transforming the words into a liquid and terrible sound, as of rats wallowing in slimy sewers.

'We have to go down. Together.'

'Yes,' I said simply, as if it were the most normal thing in the world. 'When?'

'Before it takes all of me. When I'm just a head.'

'Okay . . . Are you scared?'

'Not anymore.'

'Me either.'

Then Eleonora fell asleep and I went down to the cellar to pray.

We've decided to do it the day after tomorrow.

It will be two years since Luna disappeared.

Anniversaries should be celebrated, even the worst ones.

Besides, I don't think Eleonora can hold out much longer.

She's going away. All that's left of her is her head, one shoulder, and part of her neck.

We've done all we can to understand it, without coming to any conclusion. Assuming there's anything to understand.

We've explored the abyss, we've looked into it, in some way *worshipped* it, but it's barely given us a glance.

A charitable glance, at first, which soon changed into the scowl of a mad and nefarious god.

It was strange watching her lungs, the mazelike networks of her bronchial tubes, and then her heart, atria and ventricles cross-sectioned, *thump thump thump*, and the hemming of darkness around her torso at the height of her breasts, and the arteries dissolved, and the yellow tube of the trachea that took in air, distributing it to the nothingness below.

Why does everything vanish?

Where does it end up?

We're powerless. And the powerlessness is somehow reassuring, peaceful.

Now that the moment is approaching, I'm no longer thinking clearly, I realize that, but I'm at peace.

I dreamed of Luna again. She was walking among her mother's paintings, along endless corridors of paintings of vortexes and pits and shafts, and this time her eyes were white and she was smiling.

I look in the mirror, but I don't see myself. Or rather, I see myself distorted, bulbous, a photograph badly developed using expired chemicals. I'm vanishing too.

It feels like the apartment building is a gigantic cadaver. An enormous corpse, and we're the parasites. The mealworms of the building's floury foundation.

Cobwebs like connective tissue in the cellar.

I open my eyelids in front of the manhole and the more I look at it, the more I seem to see a veil of light beyond the macerating pockets of darkness.

Like when you stare at the sun through closed eyes.

Has it always been there?

I only want to know what happened.

Sometimes I spit in it, and I imagine my saliva unraveling, disappearing, dissolving in the darkness like fragments of a comet in the atmosphere. Sometimes, the manhole sends up whiffs of smoked salmon, Kinder eggs, and melted snow on the roadside.

Supermarkets at Christmas.

Tar.

We'll travel light.

Naked like larvae.

Will we wind up with the spiders? With Luna? Will we return to haunt the building like faded apparitions, a simulacrum of what we were?

They say there's no darkness without light, nor light without darkness.

I hope so.

I really hope so.

Ah, the shampooey.

'Jinglsh bell, jinglsh bell, shalalalalabell!'

I've decided to leave these pages for Captain Gange.

In a few minutes we'll go down.

I put Eleonora in a Carrefour bag.

She's just a head without a chin.

I see her tongue and her upper palate *from below*.

She screams. I don't know how she does it without vocal chords. She curses, says we have to get moving.

She's right.

I can't wait.

We're going.

We're going into the different darkness.

Goodbye . . .

Or maybe, see you later.

∞

The apartment smelled of neglect.

And despair.

And mystery.

One hand on his thigh, the other holding the pages, Gange sat for several seconds without moving, looking at the white of the paper below the black border of the final words traced by Diego Balduzzi.

He felt empty.

No, not empty, *full*, saturated with the flow of words that had the bitter aftertaste of madness.

Where are you?

As hard as he tried to find sense in what he had just read, his reflections led him towards a single solution: Balduzzi had gone out of his mind. There was no other conclusion to be drawn from that narrative, which read like a bad ripoff of a second-rate horror novel.

A thousand hypotheses began chasing each other through the captain's mind: murder-suicide, double suicide, a flight abroad, even involvement in Luna's disappearance for who knows what reasons . . .

He couldn't think clearly.

He had to get out of there, go back to headquarters, rest . . .

He was putting the delusional manuscript back in its envelope when he heard a vibration.

Bzzzzzzz.

Shrill, insistent.

He looked at the Samsung smartphone on the nightstand.

Is . . . is that the one Balduzzi said he had?

He barely had time to finish formulating the question: the phone display flickered in a burst of pixels, then it was like all the light of the sun was concentrated in the little screen.

White light, enormously white, blinding, awful, flaring up in the bedroom in an inconceivably powerful flash.

It lasted a few moments, during which he put a hand over his eyes, gritting his teeth from fear and disbelief at the horror perceived by his retinal tissues: through his fingers, before the phone died forever, he could make out moving shapes in the immeasurable whiteness vomited from the Samsung.

Three black shapes, human, two taller and one small, holding hands as they went off into the distance towards an invisible horizon, sinking into the snowy whiteness of an untouched, spotless canvas of light.

The envelope fell from his hands, slid across the floor, and settled under the nightstand. He looked at his own trembling hands, the walls, the blankets piled at the foot of the bed, he heard the voices of his colleagues rummaging around in the apartment, he sniffed the musty air, touched the softness of the memory foam mattress, and wondered if what he had just seen was real or a hallucinatory flash caused by stress and fatigue.

The phone was dead.

No white, only the twilight of a bedroom in which particles of dust spun like planets in a decaying cosmos.

Crack! His kneecaps greeted him as he got up from the bed, and like a ghost he slipped to the apartment door, opened it.

He had only taken two steps onto the landing when a voice rang out behind him.

Pino Bertea.

'Anything interesting in that envelope?'

He didn't turn around. The hunched shoulders of a lost and tired old man in front of a construction site. 'No, Pino, nothing . . .'

'Got it . . . Captain, where were you heading? Are you sure you're feeling all right? We've got a bit more to do here still . . .'

'I just need to check something. I'll be right back, don't worry.'

A cigarette between his teeth, he started to climb down the stairs, holding on to the handrail, his hunchbacked shadow following close behind him like a weary soul.

He went down and down and down, it was like he would never reach the bottom. But finally he did, and his shadow was overwhelmed by other shadows, of cobwebs and staircases, recesses and cavities.

'Where are you?' he asked the underground shadows, covered in mold and damp patches. 'Where did you go?'

A gust of warm air passed through the cellar.

It smelled of vanilla and absence, and it promised peace.

Ernesto Gange entered the dark passage in search of a manhole and three fading shapes, faceless forms in the white of a different darkness.

Luigi Musolino was born in 1982 in the province of Turin, where he lives and works. A specialist in Italian folklore, he is the author of several collections of tales of weird fiction, horror, and rural Gothic. His first novel, *Eredità di carne* [*Legacy of Flesh*], was published by Acheron Books in 2019 and his novella *Pupille* [*Pupils*] was published by Zona42 in 2021. He has translated into Italian works by Brian Keene, Lisa Mannetti, Michael Laimo, and the autobiographical writings of H. P. Lovecraft. His most recent publication in Italian, *Un buio diverso – Voci dai Necromileus* [*A Different Darkness – Voices from the Necromilieus*], is published by Edizioni Hypnos, one of the most important Italian publishers of speculative fiction. His work has also been published in the U.S., Canada, Ireland, and South Africa. (Author portrait copyright © by David Fragale.)

CPSIA information can be obtained
at www.ICGtesting.com
Printed in the USA
LVHW041748270123
738095LV00003B/117